THE STAR TREK
THE NEXT GENERATION
COMPANION

THE STAR TREK

THE NEXT GENERATION™

COMPANION

by LARRY NEMECEK

POCKET BOOKS

New York   London   Toronto   Sydney   Tokyo   Singapore

26787198

An *Original* Publication of POCKET BOOKS

POCKET BOOKS, a division of Simon & Schuster Inc.
1230 Avenue of the Americas, New York, NY 10020

This book is published by Pocket Books, a division of Simon & Schuster Inc., under exclusive license from Paramount Pictures.

ISBN: 0-671-79460-4

First Pocket Books trade paperback printing November 1992

10 9 8 7 6 5 4 3

POCKET and colophon are registered trademarks of Simon & Schuster Inc.

Printed in the U.S.A.

This book is lovingly dedicated:

To the memory of the man who dreamed he could fill us with wonder again,
Eugene Wesley Roddenberry;

To those involved at every turn in making sure that dream stays alive;

and

To those who most helped me achieve *this* dream by sacrificing a
large part of our first year together:
my own Janet and Andrew, Sarah and Nathan.

"Fate protects fools, little children, and ships named
Enterprise."

—Riker, "Contagion"

Acknowledgments

A reference book this complex has come together from so many sources and so many roots that dozens of people had a hand in it. For starters, thanks go out to Geoffrey Mandel, wherever you are, for letting a kid from Oklahoma know he could add to the hunt for *Star Trek* background way back in the late 1970s, when everything was so much simpler—until the best-laid plans fell through; to my mom and dad, who helped get the Macintosh hardware that made my return to Trek research a reality; and to all those fans at home and around the world whose feedback was so appreciated on my yearly self-produced *TNG* concordances.

A special thank-you also goes to those on the home front: Mike and Tamara Hodge, for the long-distance and last-minute missing credits cut by the local TNG affiliate; Mark Alfred, for more of the same; and, at the ol' *Norman Transcript*, to my boss Jane Bryant for understanding about my "other job," co-workers Ed Montgomery for the baseball trivia, Charles Stookey for my start with Macs, Jan Burton for support "above and beyond," and Karen Dorrell for trivia, tapes, and too many details to even remember.

I also wish to thank my agent, Sherry Robb, and my Pocket Books editor, Dave Stern, as well as those who will use this work and take the time, I hope, to forward any suggestions or corrections, and the like.

At the source, of course, are those connected with ST:TNG and Paramount Pictures past and present who toil long hours behind those studio walls. From the *past*: Eric A. Stillwell, trying to keep up with all my day-to-day questions of the ongoing series; Richard Arnold, spending countless hours by phone helping check the minutiae of Trek stories during the *TNG* concordance years; Ed Milkis, recalling his TNG efforts on very short notice; and Bob Justman, graciously sharing more of his personal memos and recollections from TNG's formative stage than I ever expected.

And my gratitude to those at 5555 Melrose Avenue *today* who cared so much and provided invaluable help: Carla Mason and Paula Block in Paramount Licensing; Junie Lowry-Johnson's casting office and J. R. Gonzalez; Matt Timothy in Paramount Research; the assistants who "hold the fort": Heidi Julian, Terri Martinez, Kim Fitzgerald, Lolita Fatjo, Kristine Fernandes, and Maggie Allen; Guy Vardeman; and Michael Okuda, Rick Sternbach, Rob Legato, Brannon Braga, Jeri Taylor, and of course, Michael Piller and Rick Berman.

Finally, to all those on TNG's creative team whom time and circumstances prevented me from talking with personally: thanks for sharing your thoughts and memories in previous interviews—and I look forward to the day we *can* meet.

Contents

Introduction

It would be an understatement to say that long-time Trekfans were wary when plans for a new *Star Trek* series were first announced. Even as episodes of *Star Trek: The Next Generation* (TNG) began airing, debates raged in many circles, egged on by the mainstream press, as to how there could ever be a new Trek without Kirk & Co., much less without William Shatner & Co. I was personally thrilled to see the mythos back in weekly production in any form as long as the right people were in charge, but the situation raised a different question in my own mind: which was the bigger challenge—competing with a legend twenty years later, or creating, selling, and maintaining an unappreciated classic in the first place?

That question led to an overall look at the differences in our world at the time each Trek series was born. There were the contrasting "big picture" political and sociological implications of the 1960s and 1980s, to be sure, but the most immediate differences were on the living room level: VCRs in most every U.S. household in the 1980s, fax machines, home computers and bulletin board services, cable television and syndicated programming, and of course an army of fans already in place, fed by two decades of familiarity with the earlier series.

Could the original series have been born in a similar test tube of almost impossibly high expectations? While classic *Star Trek* didn't come with a pedigree and, in fact, suffered through two pilots before finally being sold to a network, it shared many traits with its offspring: a grueling first-season in-house shakedown, hours of backbreaking work by its creator and staff, fre-netic last-minute rewrites, and shooting on a tight budget.

(By the way, those who have only come into the *Star Trek* fold since the debut of TNG and have not yet discovered its forebear are missing out. Besides an entirely new world of people and adventures, those early shows are the key to an appreciation of the dozens of loving tips of the hat among the background details laid in by TNG's creators.)

Though the new kid on the block has actually been around for only five years now—six since development first got under way—the world is moving fast, and it's not too early for a book like this, since the show has picked up more fans as it has "lived long and prospered."

Still, this *Companion* is not meant to be an exhaustive work on all facets of TNG's production history, the past credits of its stars and creators, and the greater implications of every story. It can't be; it's simply too soon for that, although writers are hard at work now, and more in-depth coverage will surely follow. Neither is this work a tabloid tell-all on the clash of egos and personalities that inevitably occurs when so much is expected of a mere television series.

What we do have here is a handy guide to the first five seasons of the new *Star Trek* show, as well as a brief look back at TNG's evolution that I hope will add to your enjoyment of the series.

This book was a labor of love. Enjoy!

LARRY NEMECEK
Norman, Oklahoma
July 1, 1992

REBIRTH

Could lightning strike twice? The

bombshell announcement that posed that question and simultaneously ended fifteen years of rumors was delivered officially by Mel Harris, then president of Paramount Television Group, during a studio press conference on Friday, October 10, 1986, in Los Angeles.

"Twenty years ago, the genius of one man brought to television a program that has transcended the medium," Harris said. "We are enormously pleased that that man, Gene Roddenberry, is going to do it again. Just as public demand kept the original series on the air, this new series is also a result of grass roots support for Gene and his vision."

The new series would come to be called *Star Trek: The Next Generation*. The syndicated hour-long drama with an all-new cast would be introduced in a two-hour pilot movie in September 1987, and that would be followed by twenty-four one-hour episodes budgeted at one million dollars each, with Roddenberry as executive producer.

The regular cast (*opposite*), sans Worf (Michael Dorn), on the planet "Hell" set.

"Wait a minute," fans said. "An all-new cast? New actors playing the old familiar roles of Kirk, Spock, and McCoy?" That issue had been hotly debated among both fans and studio executives whenever talk of a new *Star Trek* came up.

No, Harris said, this new series would be set "a century after Kirk and Spock." Harris mentioned that the earlier heroes had trekked "two hundred years into the future." That remark, of course, revealed the uncertainty of the evolving TNG time frame as well as the confusion that still reigned over the exact era of the earlier series—a mystery that was finally solved once and for all in the movie *Star Trek IV: The Voyage Home:* the original series took place in the late twenty-third century.

As if to repeat Paramount's emphasis on who would be in charge, a studio spokesperson reassured the press that day that the new series would adhere to Gene Roddenberry's "vision, credibility, and approach." It might have been enough to say that "the Great Bird of the Galaxy"—a nickname given to Roddenberry by original series producer Robert H. "Bob" Justman—had come home to roost.

Even so, it was something of a miracle that Roddenberry even considered coming back to the weekly grind of churning out a quality series, especially in light of the bumps and bruises of budget battles and network hassles in the 1960s and the fact that the original show's syndicated success in the 1970s yielded few financial or professional rewards.

"It was a hard time for me," Roddenberry recalled later, speaking of the seventies. "I was perceived as the guy who had made the show that was an expensive flop, and I couldn't get work. Thank God college kids discovered the show, because I made enough money lecturing to pay the mortgage."[1]

Roddenberry came close to doing a remake of the Kirk-era series with *Star Trek II,* but that project was abandoned in 1977 after the landmark SF movie *Star Wars* premiered. The short-lived series idea gave way to plans for a splashy big-budget theatrical release, but Roddenberry relinquished direct control of the films after *Star Trek: The Motion Picture* drew the disdain of critics and many fans alike—the result of a host of problems he often had no control over. Then, in 1986, there was a reunion party for the twentieth anniversary of *Star Trek,* and the emotions that were rekindled in some of the original production staff gathered there really got the ball rolling once and for all on a new Trek television series. Earlier that spring, Roddenberry had turned down the concepts for a remake that were pitched by studio executives flushed with optimism over the hit they knew they had with *Star Trek IV*—until they unexpectedly agreed with his claim that the only one who could do *Star Trek* right was Roddenberry himself.

"I said absolutely not, no way," he recalled. "The first show took too much out of me. I didn't see my family for two years.

"It was only when the Paramount people agreed with me and said a sequel was probably impossible anyway that my interest was piqued."[2]

Why a *new* series? Local stations had bombarded Paramount with requests for new episodes, studio executives said at the time of the initial announcement. More bluntly, an all-new cast and setting would provide fresh, less costly, and longer-lived actors to take advantage of the never-ending appeal of the Trek phenomenon—and that phenomenon was already quite obvious to a studio with one eye on the steady *Star Trek* profits and the other on the mounting ages and salaries of the original cast and their limited availability.

Roddenberry, too, knew a weekly series with the original players was impractical, but he couldn't see recasting the roles—a point on which most fans agreed with him—and so the decision was made to set the new series sometime in the more distant future and to create a whole new set of characters.

"I don't think we need a retread crew with people playing the same kinds of roles," Roddenberry said then. "I'm not at all sure we'll have a retread Vulcan. I would hate to think our imagination is so slender that there aren't other possibilities to think about."

A year later, after the debut of the new series, he seemed even more certain about that decision. "How can you get the best writers and the best directors and tell them to do a retread?" he said.

"To get the kind of energy and enthusiasm we needed, you have to have new characters and a new series." Still, he acknowledged later, such a path in light of the original show's popularity had constituted "a considerable risk."

The embryonic series had a handle on characters and format, but would there again be bitter ongoing duels with network accountants and censors? For Roddenberry, it was just as well that all four networks, including the fledgling Fox, eventually turned down the new series. All had been intrigued, but none would commit itself to a full twenty-six-hour first season, an unchanging time slot, and an intense promotional campaign. "Nobody was going to give it the same kind of attention and care that we could give it," Mel Harris said later, calling Paramount's Trek franchise "one of our family jewels."

"I'm happy we're not on the network," Gene Roddenberry said. "It's one more level of censorship and so on that I don't have to deal with. I'm still bruised from some of those 1966 battles!"

Bob Justman, who had begun with Roddenberry on the original pilot for *Star Trek* in 1964 as first assistant director and wound up as associate producer by series' end, recalled some of those battles while reflecting on why he and others from the old show would take up the banner once again.

"When I left *Star Trek* in 1968 it was a disaster," Justman said. "It was a failure as far as the network was concerned, and the industry. . . . So

I had a need to return to prove that the show did have value and was successful and that you can go home again and prove to the people who doubted you that there was value there all along, that this was a worthwhile—if you'll pardon the pun—enterprise."[3]

So the motivation and the assurances and the basic blueprint were in place. Now all Roddenberry and Company—whoever they were to be—needed was the other 98 percent of the series. They had to tackle the fine points of twenty-fourth-century characters and technology updates, as well as the twentieth-century dilemmas surrounding budgeting, special effects, organizing a crew, and topping a classic. Those were the issues that had to be faced as Roddenberry, armed for once with complete studio backing, began assembling a team and organizing his ideas for the first TNG writers' guide—the series "bible."

In the beginning, the new series didn't even have a name. In an October 24 memo, Justman suggested forty-four series titles. *Star Trek: The Next Generation* was not on the list, although a couple came close: "The New Generation" and "The Second Generation." The first-draft series bible of November 26 carried the ST:TNG moniker, but another Justman memo, dated December 15, suggested nineteen more possible titles. Earlier, on October 31, he had even suggested just keeping the title *Star Trek* and letting the obvious differences between the two shows clear up any confusion.

Creation in Flux

As good as the original *Star Trek* had been, even the most devout fan had to admit it was far from perfect in both execution and concept. Even as Roddenberry faced the challenge of making *The Next Generation* click, he was aware that few creators ever got a chance to improve on their earlier successes. The problems of time, budget,

and censorship might have disappeared, but how could he improve the series itself?

David Gerrold, writer of the classic Trek episode "The Trouble with Tribbles," pointed out many of the original Trek's problems in his book *The World of Star Trek*. For one, there was the folly of beaming a starship captain right into the middle of an unknown, possibly dangerous situation week after week. Not only did it make the drama too easy, it simply wasn't very practical—or prudent. Then there was the duration of the ship's mission and its impact on crew members of both sexes. How did humans, single and married, deal with such a career? Still another plot device overused for jeopardy's sake was the failure of technology on a recurring basis, including the good old transporter. Why would anyone want to use devices with such a high failure rate?

Roddenberry and his team also had to deal with the "simple" problem of updating the starship, the technology, and the crew. How much of the old series' familiarity had to be retained to make it *Star Trek*? And how many changes had to be made, especially with a new set of character relationships, to make TNG stand alone?

To sound out his ideas, Roddenberry first gathered around him a small circle of people he knew he could depend on, those who had helped spark the triumph of the original Trek. That group included Roddenberry's former co-producer, Bob Justman, as well as Eddie Milkis, a onetime Trek associate producer who had gone on to produce hit series like *Happy Days* and *Laverne and Shirley* and numerous films. David Gerrold was also on Roddenberry's team. The new think tank hit the ground running, screening SF films like *Blade Runner* and *Aliens* and meeting for daily brainstorming lunches at the Paramount commissary.

Memos began flying back and forth between the two small offices TNG then occupied in Building L on the Paramount lot. On October 17, 1986, alone—barely a week after the new series was announced—Justman proposed three concepts: a so-called Noah's Ark premise that involved crew members bringing their families along; the use of an android as a regular character, and an idea that would grow into the holodeck concept. The next day he was summarizing the group's suggestions for developing new hostile or friendly alien races while also surmounting Roddenberry's aversion to retreads by suggesting a Klingon marine as a regular character. On October 20 he wondered if his android character might provide a Spock-like mystique for the new series.

From those early brainstorming sessions came a few ideas that, in hindsight, might be labeled as clinkers: on October 18 Justman suggested a female science officer in the mold of Sean Young, possibly part Vulcan and Spock's great-great-granddaughter, or a recent Academy grad who is Kirk's great-great-granddaughter.

"It was a very homogenous kind of thing," Milkis said of the creative mix at work. He recalled that it was Justman who always kept and filed the memos. "We all had input and built off the ideas of each other. Nobody really takes particular credit for anything."

"Gene was very wise," Justman said. "He would listen to people—[some] that he trusted and some that he didn't know—but he would make up his own mind about everything. And if he liked something, then he'd make use of it, and if he didn't he'd throw it away. But Gene had definite ideas; he always had definite ideas!"

After weeks of listening—and working with Gerrold on the text—Gene Roddenberry emerged on November 26, 1986, with a twenty-two-page writers' bible that described and explained the characters, sets, and terminology and laid down the format the series would follow.

Actually, some of the flaws in the old series, made obvious to fans and critics alike by fifteen years of returns, were to have been corrected in the abortive 1970s series *Star Trek II*. That show, for example, was to have fought the old captain-in-danger weakness by having First Officer Will Decker lead most landing parties while Kirk stayed aboard the ship. This idea was eventually used in TNG. In fact, in a November 8, 1986, memo, Justman proposed that this Starfleet directive be credited to Jean-Luc Picard, who recommended it when he was first officer of *Stargazer* after his captain was killed in a tragic beam-down.

Roddenberry was also adamant in his insistence that the new series would not rely on failed technology as a plot device week after week. "Although this creates some additional difficulty in maneuvering our people into danger," he wrote in the infant writers' guide, "story believability demands that our twenty-fifth-century technology be at least as capable as our twentieth-century technology in this area—perhaps not such a difficulty if one realizes that twenty-fifth-century villains are no doubt capable of technological countermeasures."

His mention of the twenty-fifth century, by the way, was no mistake. At this stage the new show *was* set in that time frame.

The starship in the new series was first designated as NCC-1701-7, but the generational notation was later changed to a letter, following the pattern established in the recently released feature film *Star Trek IV*. The new ship was made the eighth *Enterprise*, NCC-1701-G.

One sign of the changes that had occurred between Kirk's era and Picard's was on page 1 of the new writers' bible, where it was stated that 19 percent of the Milky Way galaxy had been charted in this new century, compared to only 4 percent in Kirk's time.

But, more important, GR had always insisted that *people* be at the heart of any Trek yarn, and it was in the arena of human interaction that the differences in TNG would be most striking. While Kirk's crew was on a five-year mission, the new starship was to be outfitted for an assignment of ten years or longer. Because of that, officers and crew would be allowed to bring their families along, and that in turn created the need for a ship twice as long and eight times the volume of the original *Enterprise*. This new ship would have a whole community of services to support its population. More than ever before, the starship truly would be a city in space.

"Most twenty-fifth-century humans believe that 'Life should be lived, not postponed,'" the new bible stated, reiterating Starfleet's view that "people need people . . . in both family and community life, as well as other agreeable forms of human bonding." Of course, this wasn't a new concept. "The old navy sometimes took families along," Roddenberry later pointed out. "The wagon trains going west took families, of course."

Star Trek's creator also coined the term "Technology Unchained," referring to it as a concept used by twenty-fifth-century poets to describe how technical improvement in their era had moved beyond developing *things* that were smaller or faster or more powerful, in favor of concentrating on quality of life improvements.

TNG's holodeck (shown here in the episode "Code of Honor") was a concept refined from earlier Trek incarnations.

The Great Bird of the Galaxy further emphasized this point in the design of a new larger, brighter, and less "battleship-sterile" starship, with the original *Enterprise*'s dials and gauges largely replaced by flat, programmable supercomputer access panels.

One unique and dramatic use of technology to improve the quality of shipboard life was the holodeck. This had its roots, again, as far back as a never-realized concept postulated for the 1960s series—a holographic entertainment center. This idea, called the "rec room," was a major plot point in one of the animated *Star Trek* shows, "The Practical Joker," but the idea of combining transporters and replication with a hologram system was not fully developed and finally filmed until TNG was born.

Finally, the writers' guide opened with the familiar "These are the voyages" prologue, another link to the past, but it ended by promising to go "where no *one* has gone before," a far less sexist phrase than the famous "no *man*" tag line that was still being used in the Trek films of the 1980s.

Assembling the Team

With a writers' guide in hand, Roddenberry turned to filling out a production staff to further flesh out the writers' bible and get the series pilot rolling. Trek veterans Justman, Milkis, and Gerrold were soon joined by newcomer Robert Lewin as a writing producer. This new position represented the division of responsibility needed on a complex show like *Star Trek*—a division that Roddenberry had first conceived of for the 1970s series.

Lewin, the first top-level staffer on the new series not associated with original Trek or any of its film sequels, joined the staff in January after being recommended by Justman, who had worked with him on *The Man from Atlantis*. The producer of *The Paper Chase* and the writer of hundreds of episodes for series like *Gunsmoke*, *The Rifleman*, and *Rawhide* told his new boss he didn't know much about Trek or about science fiction and was told that he was wanted as a good character writer.

Dorothy "D.C." Fontana, who served for two years as story editor on the original Trek and penned the introduction of Spock's parents in the popular "Journey to Babel" episode, was hired by early December of 1986 to write the series' two-hour pilot script. She later became an associate producer at GR's invitation after he assured her the tone of this series would follow a new trail, not that taken by the movie features.

The initial design staff was also assembled from a crew of familiar names. Andrew Probert and Rick Sternbach, who were artists and fans as well as Trek movie contributors, were among the first to be signed on. Sternbach recalls pulling his car off the freeway when he heard the news of Trek's revival on the radio. He called Susan Sackett, GR's personal assistant, from the first available phone.

Probert, who was responsible for the final look of the starship *Enterprise* in the first film, had also worked on *Battlestar Galactica*, *Airwolf*, and *Streethawk*, and on the movie *Indiana Jones and the Temple of Doom*. Sternbach was assistant

art director for Carl Sagan's Emmy-winning *Cosmos* series on PBS and later worked on TV's *Greatest American Hero* and the movies *The Black Hole* and *Halloween II*.

From the field of television commercial production in his native Hawaii came scenic artist Michael Okuda. His design submissions had impressed the producers of *Star Trek IV: The Voyage Home* and led to his being added to the TNG staff later in 1986 as a scenic artist. Okuda was in charge of designing the distinctive graphic look of consoles, computer readouts, door labels, and so forth for Starfleet and for alien cultures.

What was seen as merely a bonus in the beginning—the background in science and aerospace that all three men brought to their TNG jobs—later turned out to be a great asset. Their contributions eventually went far beyond their job descriptions. They helped enliven one of Gene Roddenberry's oldest maxims by offering viewers some real science, without hitting them over the head with it.

GR tapped original Trek costume designer Bill Theiss to plan Starfleet's new look, and Milkis and Justman helped bring in art director Herman Zimmerman.

"Bob and I together work[ed] very well," Milkis recalled. "He and I totally supervised the development of the physical look of the show and hired the people. And then things would reach a point from time to time where we'd take them in to Gene and get his okay."

As the team began feverishly working on the first-draft bible, memos that had been flying since October were being updated in light of the new questions that popped up daily. Lewin had a box taped to his desk just to hold them all.

Early in the process, egged on by fan and press reaction to the thought of a new Trek without the old cast, Roddenberry decided to completely avoid such original-series aliens as Romulans, Klingons, and even Vulcans. That worry proved groundless by midway through the first year, however, as new races, both friendly and

Mike Okuda and Rick Sternbach view the Mordan city, the last landscape model built for TNG.

hostile, began appearing. By the time the first revision of the writers' guide was completed in February 4, 1987, some 907 officers and family members were said to be aboard the new *Enterprise*, now designated as the fifth one so named, NCC-1701-D. The final first-season writers' guide of March 23 later increased the number of shipboard personnel to 1,012, its final mark, and honed the time frame to seventy-eight years after Kirk and Spock.

By mid-January 1987 Fontana's first draft for the two-hour pilot telefilm "Encounter at Farpoint" was well underway. While it was the staff's chief concern, advance scripts for the early first-season schedule were already being prepared by Gerrold and John D.F. Black, another veteran of the original series.

After working in separate quarters and one-on-one for weeks, the new series production team met as a full unit for the first time on February 18, 1987, having just received Fontana's first draft for "Farpoint" only a few days earlier. Gathered around the table with Gene Roddenberry were Justman, Milkis, Lewin, Fontana, Gerrold, Theiss, Sackett, GR's attorney–business manager Leonard Maizlish, Zimmerman, Probert, Sternbach, and Okuda; Herb Wright, another writing producer like Lewin, would soon be added. The staff discussed details of the show—such as the look of the new communicators, phasers, and tricorders—and specific production problems stemming from Fontana's pilot script.

Finally a fifty-five-page first-season writers' and directors' guide was issued on March 23. This, too, was largely assembled by Gerrold and the staff and then polished by Roddenberry himself.

Of Stars and Starships

As the heart and soul of the new series continued to evolve over that winter of 1986–1987, so did its physical presence on the Paramount lot. Mindful that the budget constraints could be even more of a problem than they were in the sixties, Milkis and Justman as early as October were scrounging all they could from the existing inventory of Trek's feature films, even to the point of merely re-dressing sets and miniatures and rehashing optical effects.

Justman recalled the day the two men were allowed to view the movies' standing sets to see what use they could make of them. "Cats inhabit studios. They live on the stages," he said, laughing. "And since this stage hadn't been shot on in a long time it was *shat* on by a whole bunch of cats!"

"It was horrendous," Milkis agreed. "You couldn't even walk on the stage!"

Eventually, as Gene Roddenberry's new concept of "Technology Unchained" evolved, a new *Enterprise* became a necessity. Though many of the film sets would be refurbished, the new look and feel of the twenty-fourth century would be fully symbolized by the bridge set, historically the most-filmed area aboard the starship.

The Great Bird had originally wanted a huge forward viewscreen four times the size of its predecessors, with a conference table right on the bridge,[4] but those ideas gradually changed over the winter. A large open command area replaced the table, and the observation lounge became a separate room just "behind" the bridge.

The final layout reflected Roddenberry's belief that the *Enterprise*'s basic functions should be automated. The simple conn and Ops (for "operations") forward stations left their operators free for less mechanical tasks such as discussion and investigation. Probert had also designed a transporter just off the bridge, but GR wanted the characters to have conversations en route to the transporter room, so that idea was dropped.

In a memo dated November 9, Justman first proposed creating a captain's ready room, a space close to the bridge where the crew could have private conversations. (Similar areas are used by today's navy). Roddenberry initially agreed with Probert, who proposed placing the office so that it opened onto the upper bridge level for more dramatic impact. But it was eventually moved down to its current location to provide a shorter, more direct route to the command chair.

In addition to the center seat, Probert included some other touches that would ring true to longtime fans: a dedication plaque and ship silhouettes on the walls, and a red warning sensor flasher at the base of the viewscreen. Improvements over the old design included more than one turbolift shaft and, in response to gibes about its ancestors' comfort, a bathroom! Its entrance, labeled "Head," is tucked out of sight in the aft starboard alcove leading to the conference lounge. A private washroom was also added to the ready room.

The result was an *Enterprise* bridge set that, thanks to its nine-foot-tall viewscreen and sprawling overhead window, seems immense. In reality, however, it's only thirty-eight feet wide, the same width as the original, but it is two feet longer and has a fourteen-foot ceiling. The side ramps and various levels add to the illusion of height.

Next, Probert turned his attention to the starship itself. Having done the final reworking of the TV-to-film refit of the old *Enterprise*, he largely based its Galaxy-class cousin—as the new design came to be called—on a "what if?" painting of an all-new starship he did shortly after the first film. Here again, the lines of the final model suggest that art and technology have merged into a design of sleeker, rounder contours, with windows—lots of them, in various sizes and shapes—to keep the crew and passengers in touch with their environment. Still, the overall design is dominated by the familiar sublight-driven saucer section and the battle module with warp nacelles.

Probert built into this starship a major concept that was mentioned first for TNG in the final writers' guide, though it dates back to earlier Trek incarnations. It is the *Enterprise*'s ability to separate its two main sections in time of emergency or attack and then later reconnect. Ship separation was referred to in the original series as well—in "The Apple," when a planetbound Kirk tells Scotty to "jettison the nacelles and get out in the saucer section if you have to"—but it was never shown because of budgetary restraints.

The film *Enterprise was* built to separate, but the feature was never utilized.[5] Even TNG's "ship sep" feature was not approved by the studio until well into the pilot's development because of the extra expense in optical effects and filming models.

Twin drawings of the new 1701-D, dated December 8, 1986, eventually graced the cover and an inside page of the final writers' and directors' guide and first appeared to fans in Gerrold's July 1987 column in *Starlog* magazine. Probert later said he faced his biggest challenge in producing a starship that looked as good in two pieces as it did in one.

At the same time he urged that a battle bridge be added. In effect, the concept of the old Constitution-class starship's auxiliary bridge was relocated atop the cobra head of the battle module and given a direct emergency turbolift from the main bridge. A sketch for this concept, dated March 23, reveals how he won his case: the set of the film *Enterprise*'s bridge would be inexpensively re-dressed. This was the first of many times the old set would be revamped for TNG's use. Located on Paramount's old Stage 6, the entire set was moved during the hiatus after the first season to the rear of Stage 8, where the new main bridge and ready room had been taking shape since March.

Meanwhile, on Stage 9, most of the movie ship's other standing sets were being re-dressed and expanded. The main engineering area, with

The "new" *Enterprise* (*below*) and its bridge (*opposite, both shots*) retained the feel of their forebears, while evoking Roddenberry's "Technology Unchained": a harmony of science and quality of life.

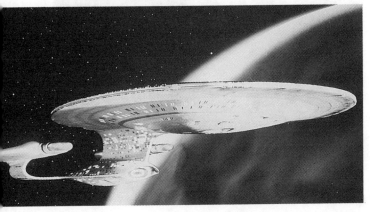

many of its components repainted and its spaces enlarged, acquired the Starfleet Command console from *Star Trek IV,* which was soon referred to as "the pool table." McCoy's movie sickbay lost two office walls. One, a bank of consoles, became the back wall of the engineer's office looking onto the main reactor. The other, the wall of stored samples, eventually turned up as the rows of access plates in the transporter room.

As another money-saver, the first-season observation lounge was a make-over of the movie sickbay. Its windows were covered with carpet for the medical scenes. (A new lounge was built for season two.) Finally all the connecting corridors were made longer and widened for TV use by removing the film sets' A-frames. The multipurpose cargo bay–shuttle bay–holodeck–gymnasium set would be erected, over time, from scratch.

Thus, with construction dating back to the first Trek film and the aborted 1977 series, the Stage 8–9 complex houses what Paramount veterans like to point to as the oldest standing sets in Hollywood!

The crew and guest cabins, carved from the movie-set captain's quarters, are built for complete versatility. Upward-sliding walls and modular wall panels can be reversed to suggest a dormlike, mirror-image floor plan.[6] All of the windows would eventually be equipped with a motorized starfield backdrop to avoid costly visual effects whenever the ship was not at warp speed.

Just as the original series had done twenty years earlier, TNG erected on nearby Stage 16 a multilevel canyon-cave set, made of reinforced concrete, to represent planet interiors and exteriors. This set came complete with an area capable of holding water for a "lake" and a gigantic white backdrop that could reflect colored lights to represent any planetary sky color. Because of the hostile environments and strange habitats represented there, the cast and crew soon began to refer to Stage 16 as "Planet Hell."

Meanwhile, Sternbach stayed busy updating Trek's famous props and equipment while Okuda began developing the "look" of TNG's graphics and its new generation of computers. Though

Note minute changes in the first-version tricorder (*above*) and its successor (*below*).

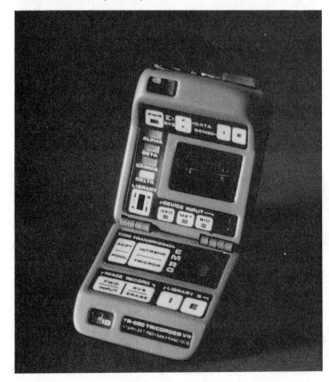

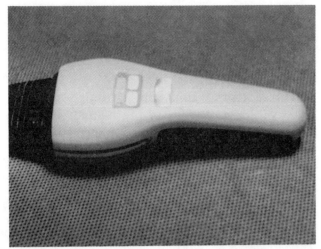

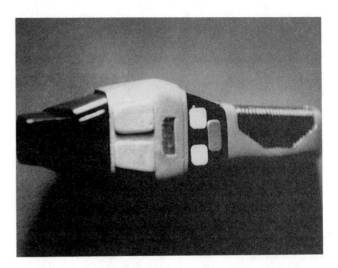

The "dustbuster" Phaser II (*above, left*) gave way to a more angular design (*right*) in Season Two, while the first phaser rifle (*below*) since the second original Trek pilot appeared in Season Four.

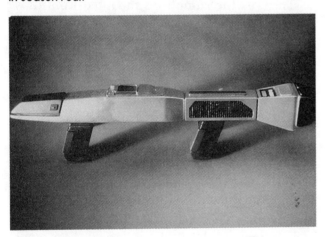

they would be modified later after filming began, the tricorder, hand phaser I, and pistol phaser II were all completed in the sketches dated February 6, which Probert prepared for construction bidders. Originally the communicator was to be a wrist device, as in the first Trek movie and outlined in the first two TNG writers' bibles, but their function was later built into a new metallic Starfleet insignia worn on the chest. A personal monitor tied in to the ship's computer, not unlike the perscan biomonitor buckles of the first film, was also made a part of the new communicator. The design of the new medical syringe was inspired by a present-day commercial inhaler.

While the full-scale environments of TNG were under construction, the miniatures also be-gan to take shape. These models and special optical effects had to be completed on time, on budget, and on the mark in order to meet the expectations of an audience grown accustomed to the optical effects of the feature films.

Early on, a new process was adopted so that TNG could compete for top quality while adhering to a television budget and schedule. All optical effects would be composited digitally on one-inch videotape so as to avoid the slower and more costly process involved in using film stock—not to mention the rapid deteriorating quality of film from one generation to the next when building composites. All live action shot on film would be transferred to tape as well for final editing.

For a time, Milkis revealed, he and Justman considered using only computer-generated effects and miniatures. One company even ran several tests using the old *Enterprise* design to demonstrate the look that could be produced by computers. "It was incredibly good," Milkis recalled, "and it took some real thinking on our part, but ultimately we decided that if something ever happened to that company and they couldn't deliver, then we'd have nothing. We were very concerned about that, and ultimately they did go out of business."[7]

Finally, he and Justman turned to Lucasfilm's legendary Industrial Light and Magic (ILM) to provide the models of the new *Enterprise*—a two-foot version and a six-foot model with modules that actually separated. They were built from Probert's specs and cost about $75,000. Work on the models got under way in March 1987 by an ILM crew of six headed by Greg Jein, a veteran maker of Trek models since the first movie, and Ease Owyeung.

Even before that work got under way, TNG's producers had looked down the road and decided they could get more FX bang for the buck by building a library of stock shots that could be reused with each other or with new footage each time a different effect was needed.

But after getting budget-busting bids back from four or five effects houses, Justman recalled that ILM, through lucky timing, gave the infant series another break. The famous shop found itself idle for about six months between major motion picture jobs with a lot of overhead to carry—a plant and lots of one-of-a kind personnel.

"What they decided was to make a bare-bones bid, enough to keep their doors open and keep everyone on that they needed," Justman said. "Oh, it was a tremendous bid. I couldn't believe it was so cheap! But it was ILM, you know? The best in the business!"

One new effect, described in a March 15 Justman memo, would come to be a signature of the new series: its own warp-speed jump. The Trek filmmakers had experimented with different types of animation, but Justman considered the results "too cartoony." So the producer got ILM and TNG's own Rob Legato—hired by new post-production superviser Peter Lauritson to super-vise TNG's in-house video effects—to design and film what came to be called the "rubber-band effect." It was a look that Doug Trumbull had actually sought for the first motion picture but

had to abandon when he ran out of time: the saucer stretches out until the rear end snaps forward to catch up with it in a huge flash of light, which then fades to reveal the starship, long disappeared.

Throughout all this, fans had only the tanta-lizing snippets of news in the mainstream and industry press to keep them posted on the evolv-ing show—along with the ever-active rumor mill via fan clubs, newsletters, and computer bulletin boards. In his *Starlog* magazine column, Gerrold sought to reassure the faithful that this new Trek would be faithful to the Great Bird's vision of the future. "Should the new *Enterprise* find itself in a military situation," he wrote, "then it will be seen as a *failure* of the ship's *diplomatic* mis-sion."[8]

Then, as the rumblings mounted from those who had condemned the show months before it had even evolved, much less aired, Justman took it upon himself to appeal to fans directly. "I'd heard that we were 'ripping off our own show,' " he recalled. "Now there's a quote!"

Although he had never been a guest at a Star Trek convention in his life, Justman spoke at the April 18 Equicon in Los Angeles. There he thanked the attendees for keeping the Trek con-cept alive for twenty years against all odds, and he asked them to "hang in there with us, please" on this new venture. "If we fail, it won't be for lack of trying," he told the crowd. "So please bear with us if the new *Star Trek* doesn't always meet your expectations. Our little show has be-come a legend, and it's hard to live up to a legend. We're trying hard. We want to succeed. We want to excel. We hope we can. We're sure going to try."

Drafting a Crew

In creating the new *Enterprise* crew, Gene Roddenberry and his team continued to distance TNG from its forebear by striving to shed the familiar and dominating duality of the Kirk-Spock relationship. This time they chose to divide the attributes of that dynamic pair among the new characters so that they could assemble an ensemble cast in the style of 1980s TV dramas like *Hill Street Blues*, *St. Elsewhere*, and *L.A. Law*.

The first casting call went out to talent agencies on December 10, 1986. That outline now serves as a sort of historical snapshot, a first official look at the characters as they were shaping up. Here it is, as published in one fanzine newsletter,[9] with the original spelling, punctuation, and capitalization intact:

TO: ALL TALENT AGENCIES
RE: PARAMOUNT "STAR TREK: THE NEXT GENERATION"
1-HR. SERIES FOR SYNDICATION
2-HR. TV MOVIE TO START END OF MARCH
24 1-HR. EPISODES TO START END OF MAY
Exec. Producer: Gene Roddenberry
Supv. Producer: Eddie Milkis
Producer: Bob Justman
Director: TBA
Casting Director: Helen Mossler
Casting Assistant: Gail Helm
WRITTEN SUBMISSIONS—ONLY—TO: HELEN MOSSLER, PARAMOUNT, BLUDHORN 128, 5555 MELROSE AVE., LOS ANGELES, CA 90038
PLEASE BE ADVISED THAT WE DO NOT HAVE A SCRIPT YET AND ARE JUST IN THE PRELIMINARY CASTING STAGES.

SEEKING THE FOLLOWING SERIES REGULARS:
CAPT. JULIEN PICARD—A caucasian man in his 50s who is very youthful and in prime physical condition. Born in Paris, his gallic accent appears when deep emotions are triggered. He is definitely a 'romantic' and believes strongly in concepts like honor and duty. Capt. Picard commands the Enterprise. He should have a mid-Atlantic accent, and a wonderfully rich speaking voice.
NUMBER ONE (A.K.A. WILLIAM RYKER)—A 30–35 year old caucasian born in Alaska. He is a pleasant looking man with sex appeal, of medium height, very agile and strong, a natural psychologist. Number One, as he is usually called, is second-in-command of the Enterprise and has a very strong, solid relationship with the Captain.
LT. COMMANDER DATA—He is an android who has the appearance of a man in his mid 30's. Data should have exotic features and can be anyone of the following racial groups: Asian, American Indian, East Indian, South American Indian or similar racial groups. He is in perfect physical condition and should appear very intelligent.
LT. MACHA HERNANDEZ—26 year old woman of unspecified Latin decent who serves as the starship's security chief. She is described as having a new quality of conditioned-body-beauty, a fire in her eyes and muscularly well developed and very female body, but keeping in mind that much of her strength comes from attitude. Macha has an almost obsessive devotion to protecting the ship and its crew and treats Capt. Picard and Number One as if they were saints.
LT. DEANNA TROI—An alien woman who is tall (5'8–6') and slender, about 30 years old and quite beautiful. She serves as the starship's Chief Psychologist, Deanna is probably foreign (anywhere from Italian, Greek, Hungarian, Russian, Icelandic, etc.) with looks and accent to match. She and Number One are romantically involved. Her alien "look" is still to be determined.
LESLIE CRUSHER—An appealing 15 year old caucasian girl (need small 18 or almost 18 year old to play 15). Her remarkable mind and photographic memory make it seem not unlikely for her to become, at 15, a Starfleet acting-ensign. Otherwise, she is a normal teenager.
BEVERLY CRUSHER—Leslie's 35 year old mother. She serves as the chief medical officer on the Enterprise. If it were not for her intelligence, personality, beauty and the fact that she has a natural walk of a striptease queen, Capt. Picard might not have agreed to her request that Leslie observe bridge activities; therefore letting her daughter's intelligence carry events further.
LT. GEORDI La FORGE—a 20–25 year old black man, blind from birth. With the help of a special prosthetic device he wears, his vision far surpasses anything the human eyes can see. Although he is young, he is quite mature and is best friends with Data. Please do not submit any 'street' types, as Geordi has perfect diction and might even have a Jamaican accent. Should also be able to do comedy well.

These initial descriptions of the characters would undergo further revisions as the new production team bandied ideas about and, later, when actors began auditioning for the roles. Not the least of these changes would be the addition of the Klingon, Worf.

"Kirk came out of an earlier time in my life when I was pretending to be part of my macho southern background, and [the character] reflects some of that," Gene Roddenberry would later tell an interviewer. "Macho feelings about women, and so on. But in twenty-five years, my feelings have changed enormously about those things and I think Picard represents that. He's more mature."[10]

The back story for Picard—given a French heritage in homage to the many Gallic explorers, including Jacques Cousteau—was set down in the very beginning and mentioned a twenty-two-year stint as mission commander of the USS *Stargazer*. His first name, as well as the spelling of Riker, would not take on their eventual form until sometime between the February 4 revision of the writers' guide and the final version dated March 23. At that point, however, the captain was given the nickname Luke.

The first-draft bible mentions the historical British navy tradition of calling the first officer "Number One." It does not acknowledge the use of that title in *Star Trek*'s own history, however: in the very first 1964 *Star Trek* pilot, "The Cage," Captain Pike's right-hand officer was a woman known only as Number One. Also, Riker and Troi's past relationship was originally described as "intimate," but it was changed to "unconsummated" in the March guide, as he was said to be torn between his feelings for her and a perceived need for detachment in his career. Along with an action-oriented command style and a healthy libido, Riker also shares with predecessor Kirk the middle initial T, although his actual middle name has now gone unrevealed through five seasons.

One of the first real character dynamics to emerge from the early memo-writing phase, after that of Picard and Riker, was the Picard-Wesley relationship—ironic in light of the disdain many fans would later express for Wesley. The latter two roles, incidentally, carried the names as early as November 8, according to a Justman memo, despite the December 15 mention of a girl named Leslie.

"Although I identify with every character," Roddenberry would say later, "I identify probably more so with Wesley because he is me at seventeen. He is the things I dreamed of being and doing."[11]

Actually, the issue of whether the teenager would be a boy or a girl was bandied about for some time. According to Justman, the character began as a male called Wesley—GR's own middle name—even though he pushed to make the teenager a girl. The female character remained through the October 26 bible and the casting call, but had been changed back to the boy, Wesley, for good by the time the February 4 revision was completed.

"I thought, Jeez, anybody and everybody has had boy teenagers; let's do a girl," Justman recalled. "Let's explore the problems that female adolescents go through, because that's never done. . . . Then Gene switched it back to Wesley because he felt there would be a wider range of stories available dealing with the character if he were a male instead of a female."

What might surprise those who later objected loud and long that Wesley was too young and inexperienced for bridge duty is the fact that their arguments had been foreseen. Despite the character's brilliance, "The question will be raised as to why he was selected for this all-important mission rather than someone older who would have the maturity and experience which he has not, as yet, attained," Justman wrote in a memo to GR way back on November 12. "Because of his youth, Wesley Crusher has not yet had to learn to go with the herd and compromise his thinking just because compromising is easier and more socially acceptable. He has the ability to grow with the job and to devise new approaches and new capabilities for whatever unforeseen events we encounter. In effect he is a one-man 'think tank' without preconditioned limitations."

Though it was dropped before the final writers' guide was issued, one new development—a landing-envelope forcefield for away teams on inhospitable planets—was suggested at one point as a Wesley creation to help explain why he holds such a unique position. Coming up with a reason for Wesley's special status that viewers would accept proved difficult for writers and producers alike.

Although it was not mentioned in the casting announcement, Justman and the staff had worked out the story of Wesley's father Jack being killed under Picard's command and the dilemmas that posed for the captain, Wesley, and his mother. In fact, Beverly Crusher at first was referred to only in relation to Wesley and didn't rate her own page of background notes until the final writers' guide edition.

Only a few other role changes were made by the time of the February 4 revision: Geordi has the rank of ensign and Troi is promoted to lieutenant commander, though she is still referred to as the chief psychologist.

The cocky yet insightful Lieutenant (j.g.) Geordi La Forge was named for a quadriplegic fan, George La Forge, who died in 1975 after having endeared himself to Gene Roddenberry and much of fandom. The character's eventual rank was established later on.

Though her alien roots are not explained in detail on the call sheet, presumably for simplicity's sake, Troi was described in the very first bible as a quarter-blood Betazoid who possessed some telepathic powers due to her "Starfleet officer grandfather having lived on Betazed with one of its humanoid females." In the final draft (most likely with the first-season script for "Haven" in progress) her heritage was changed to half-blood Betazoid, her Starfleet father having lived with her mother on Betazed.

The name of the new female security chief was changed from Macha Hernandez—inspired by the tough Hispanic space marine Vasquez in the 1986 film *Aliens*—to Tanya, for two days around March 13, and finally to Natasha "Tasha" Yar. Aside from the name and ethnic changes, her background remained consistent throughout the character's inception.

Of all the new regulars it was probably the android Data whose premise changed the least. A Starfleet graduate and the highest scorer ever on the Turing Test of Sentience, he is on an eternal quest for the impossible goal of knowing what it is to be human. Roddenberry admitted that this character sprang from Questor, a similar android seeking its creator in his well-received yet unsold 1974 TV pilot movie, *The Questor Tapes*. From the beginning, Data and Geordi are said to be close friends—a virtual "walking library" (Data) and a "walking tricorder" (Geordi).

There were a number of unrealized details in these early character bios that now seem curious:

- Data was assembled by an alien race, his name rhymes with "that-a," and he "usually" avoids the use of contractions.
- Riker "doesn't fully appreciate the female need to be needed."
- Macha-Tasha considers Wesley-Leslie "the childhood friend she never had."
- Picard has visited Tasha's homeworld, which failed due to "environmental disasters and fanatical leaders."
- Riker is privately called William by Picard and Bill by "female friends."
- Geordi's shipboard specialty is listed as "the starship school for children."

Interestingly enough, the evolution of the regular characters went hand in hand with that of the bridge layout, as Justman and Milkis wrote GR that perhaps some of the regular characters needed more efficient on-screen development time. On the eve of the February 4 revisions, Data was to occupy the command circle with Picard and "Ryker," but the two producers realized that Troi would be strengthened both in her shipboard role and as a character if she took the third central seat. From there she could also advise Picard during Riker's absence on away missions.

A second point concerned Tasha (then called Macha) and Geordi, who also were homeless as to duty station. To remedy that, Tasha was made tactical officer and given one of the two forward seats, placed similarly to those in the original series, apparently before the new bridge's tactical horseshoe console was conceived. Geordi is suggested as her partner up front, allowing him character-development exposure that might be lost if the conn and Ops positions were staffed by extras only.

Justman, with Milkis, also proposed that Data be allowed to roam from one aft console to another as an information provider. The android was later stationed at forward Ops to fulfill this function, however, and the rear bridge duty appears to have been Worf's original assignment once he was added to the cast. During the ongoing brainstorming, two ideas were suggested but not adopted: that Data remain aboard during away missions, and that Geordi serve as an ombudsman who would speak to the captain about the concerns of the thousand-plus aboard—a duty eventually and informally seen as Troi's.

Worf, the lone Klingon in Starfleet, almost suffered from Gene Roddenberry's insistence that "no old races"—that is, alien races that appeared in the original Trek—be featured at first in order to distinguish TNG from its predecessor. As noted, Justman was among those lob-

bying for a "Klingon marine," a concept the Great Bird finally agreed would show in the most obvious way the difference between this generation and the last—detente and even alliance with the Klingon Empire.

Still, Worf is absent throughout the evolving first-season bible and, though the character was written into the April 13 final draft script for "Farpoint," he is not present in the initial cast portrait that was taken on the Planet Hell set on June 1. Perhaps the first published word of his existence appeared in Gerrold's July 6 *Starlog* column only a month before the series debut.

Faces for the Names

As preliminary casting began in March 1987, one of the earliest of the inevitable staff shakedowns occurred, one that would have long-term implications for the series: producer Eddie Milkis was replaced by Rick Berman.

Having begun in the fall of 1986 as the studio's TNG liaison, Berman came aboard early in 1987 to take over for Milkis, who had decided to check out early on his one-year contract. "By that time I'd decided I had to get back to my other commitments," Milkis said. "But it was a very, very easy transition. Rick was very up-to-the-minute; he was in total sync with us."

Berman had come to Paramount from Warner Brothers in 1984 and performed a succession of studio roles: director of current programming, executive director of dramatic development, and finally vice president of "longform and special projects"—miniseries, TV movies, and then "the new Star Trek." He shared the title of supervising producer with Justman as "Encounter at Farpoint" prepared to shoot.

"I had been Paramount's 'studio guy' for the series for about two weeks when Gene Roddenberry asked me to lunch, and it was love at first sight," Berman recalled. "He went to the studio and said, 'Can I have him?' and they said yeah."

And that, he added warmly, was the beginning of a relationship with GR that was "very special," although at the time Berman had no idea he'd end up as the "new" Great Bird in a few years.

Berman's track record for quality work and a caring attitude had already been established. He had produced informational projects for TV such as HBO's *What on Earth* and the award-winning PBS special *The Primal Mind*. He was also an Emmy-winning executive producer of ABC's *The Big Blue Marble* from 1977 to 1982.

"He was just perfect," Justman recalled in an interview on March 20, 1992. "We couldn't have found someone better to do the show. He's a perfect executive producer, and a perfect hands-on producer at the same time. My only fear is that he's going to overwork himself!"

So now it was Justman and Berman who set to work casting the regulars, screening their choices with Paramount casting agents before presenting them for GR's approval and eventually a final nod from the studio.

Finally, on May 15, Paramount announced the cast of largely unknown actors who would become "The Next Generation." Most news accounts emphasized LeVar Burton in the role of

Bob Justman's choice for captain, Patrick Stewart (*above, left*), finally won the job; Jonathan Frakes (*above*) received special coaching from the Great Bird himself during auditions; while Brent Spiner (*below*) brought his extensive stage, mime, and musical experience to the role of the android Data.

Geordi La Forge, thanks to his high-profile role in the landmark miniseries *Roots*.

The news reports also mentioned a longtime member of the Royal Shakespeare Company and occasional movie actor, Patrick Stewart, as the new Captain Picard, and Jonathan Frakes, best known for his role in the two *North and South* miniseries, as Riker. The main Associated Press dispatch didn't mention the remaining cast members but did note that the show had been sold in 150 markets and would reach 90 percent of U.S. viewing households.

The story of how Stewart landed the center seat was quick to take its place in TNG lore. As Justman loves to tell it, only weeks into the show's development Justman and his wife attended a dramatic reading at UCLA in which Stewart took part. Inspired by the Englishman's performance, Justman suddenly turned to his wife and said, "I think we have just found our captain!" Later he would say, "I'd never thought of him before, but once I saw him, that was the captain in my mind. I just couldn't shake it. I've never been so sure of anything as I was with that."

Still, Gene Roddenberry had his heart set on a French actor for the role, and Justman knew that. He set up a meeting between Stewart, Milkis, and GR soon after "discovering" the actor, urging that he be included in the cast somehow. He even wrote in an October 17 memo that Stewart be considered for the part of Data! After that, the audition process went on, with Justman and others persisting in a subtle "campaign," as he called it, to choose Stewart as captain.

"We couldn't find anyone who would satisfy Gene—or ourselves, really—who was good enough," Justman went on. "And finally at the end Gene relented and said, 'Well, let's go with Patrick. He's our best choice.' See, Patrick didn't fit his concept, but once he decided that Patrick was the character, he wrote the character for Patrick!"

Stewart, known in the United States mainly for his role as Sejanus in the highly acclaimed BBC-PBS miniseries *I, Claudius* and for supporting roles in the films *Dune* and *Excalibur*, has said that his naïveté about Trek's impact allowed him to avoid any apprehension about tackling the new show—that is, until a friend floored him by asking how it felt to be playing "an American icon."

Frakes, whose TV credits also included *Bare Essence*, *Paper Dolls*, *Falcon Crest*, and *The Doctors*, survived seven auditions in six weeks to finally claim the role, and has credited GR with making him his favorite and doing a little coaching on the side. At the time he was ironically linked with another up-and-coming genre TV star. "I had just finished a stage play with Ron Perlman called *My Life in Art*," Frakes said in an interview. "I played a goat who became a man and ends up starring on Broadway; Perlman played a theater director. We both got something good out of it—I got *Star Trek* and he got *Beauty and the Beast*."

Unlike those of any of the rest of the cast, the background stories on Deanna Troi and Tasha Yar came to be inexplicably intertwined with the actors who would play the roles. Londoner Marina Sirtis had been denied meaty roles in her native land because of her good looks. She had been in America barely five months when she tried out for TNG as the security chief, while

At first, Marina Sirtis read for the role of Macha Hernandez, not the Betazoid counselor Deanna Troi.

Denise Crosby—Bing Crosby's granddaughter—was reading for the Troi role.

Berman and Justman liked both actresses in those roles, but eventually GR switched them, deciding Sirtis's appearance was better suited to the empathic alien counselor than to the Latino security chief. "Once we had an 'exotic' for Deanna Troi, it seemed logical that we should have a different physical type for the head of security," Justman recalled. "We didn't want to have another brunette." At that point Macha Hernandez became Natasha Yar, who was given a Ukrainian background to match Crosby's blond hair. The final decision came in early May—just as Sirtis was packing to return home to England to restock her nest egg.

Sirtis's prior credits included *The Wicked Lady* with Faye Dunaway and *Death Wish 3* opposite Charles Bronson and TV guest spots on *Hunter* and *The Adventures of Sherlock Holmes*. Along with numerous TV guest-star credits and a role on *Days of Our Lives*, Crosby, a Hollywood native, had film roles in *48 HRS.*, *Desert Hearts*, and *The Man Who Loved Women*, and she makes no apologies for a funky 1979 pictorial layout in *Playboy* during her "rebellious period."

Brent Spiner, who became Data, grew up in Houston, Texas. He moved up through the off-

When Denise Crosby (*above*) was cast as the *Enterprise's* security chief, the producers changed the character's name to Tasha Yar.

Thanks to his exposure in the miniseries *Roots*, LeVar Burton (*above*) was the most recognizable "name" in the new cast; Gates McFadden (*below*) had worked in dance, mime, and with Jim Henson's Muppets before being cast as Dr. Beverly Crusher.

Broadway and Broadway ranks, winning roles in such musicals as *Sunday in the Park with George*, *The Three Musketeers*, and *Big River*. He appeared in Woody Allen's *Stardust Memories* and, perhaps most memorably for sitcom fans, as a luckless hick in a recurring role on *Night Court*.

LeVar Burton auditioned largely because of the suggestion of Justman, who had once worked with him in a TV movie pilot called *Emergency Room*. Included in its cast was Gary Lockwood, star of *2001: A Space Odyssey* and the original Trek's second pilot, "Where No Man Has Gone Before." Along with his *Roots* credentials, Burton had hosted the PBS youth series *Reading Rainbow* for five years and in August 1988 would devote a segment of the PBS show to a peek behind the scenes of his famous "other job."

Gates McFadden came to the role of Dr. Beverly Crusher as a New York–based world veteran of the stage, mime, dance, and improvisation. She had also been on *Another World* and *The Edge of Night* and had served as choreographer and director of puppet movement for Jim Henson's *Labyrinth*. A student of mime and theater with Jacque LeCoq in Paris, she later served on several university faculties for theater arts.

Wil Wheaton had been best known as Gordie in *Stand by Me* before becoming young Wesley Crusher.

Michael Dorn brought so much presence to the character of Worf that the Klingon was soon made a regular.

Despite a disastrous first callback that convinced him he'd lost the part, Wil Wheaton, a veteran of film since he began appearing in commercials at age seven, was asked back for another try and wound up landing the role of Wesley Crusher. Highly acclaimed by moviegoers and critics alike as Gordie in Rob Reiner's *Stand by Me*, Wheaton had also appeared in *The Last Starfighter*, *The Buddy System*, and the telefilm *The Young Harry Houdini*. His voice was heard in *The Secret of NIMH*, and he was a guest on numerous series.

Casting delays didn't help clarify the early unsure status of Worf. Justman recalled that one trim black actor after another was auditioned—blacks being considered mainly to simplify the application of the dark Klingon makeup—before finally settling on the stage-trained Michael Dorn, who was free of any so-called street accent. The part was first conceived as a recurring role in seven of thirteen episodes for a couple of years,

according to Berman, but was expanded after filming and editing of "Farpoint" began and the producers decided that Worf had presence.

"I did not wear makeup," Dorn said of his audition, "but I took on the psychological guise of a Klingon. I walked into Paramount in character. No jokes. No laughing with the other actors. I sat by myself waiting for my interview. When my turn came, I walked in, didn't smile, did the reading, thanked them, and walked right out."[12] And eventually got the job.

A native of tiny Luling, Texas, Dorn was raised in Pasadena, California, and played in rock bands when he was in college, where he became a fan of the original Trek and drifted into acting. He was previously best known for his three years as a costar on *CHiPS*. On the big screen he played a small part as Apollo Creed's bodyguard in *Rocky*. The sash he would initially wear on the new series was the original Trek Klingon prop, explained as an heirloom.

Countdown and Launch

As work began shifting from an emphasis on the show's background to the specifics of the pilot episode, which was due to begin filming on June 1, 1987, members of the creative staff that would make this Trek fly were quickly getting their feet wet. One of the miracle workers who'd come aboard to crank out the magic under weekly TV's many limits was makeup designer Michael Westmore, the 1981 Academy Award winner for *Mask*. On the Monday after his Thursday interview Westmore hit the ground running on everything from the makeup of various aliens to such crucial details as Worf's Klingon look and Data's appearance. (Justman later recalled that the staff had to talk Roddenberry out of using "bilious bluish gray" makeup for Data at one point during the android tests.)

Applying Worf's makeup, which has been refined over the years, is a two-hour process. A headpiece fits over Dorn's hair and is attached to his skin above the nose. After twenty-four tests, Data's look eventually evolved to include the famous beige-gold contact lenses, an opalescent base, gold powder, and dyed black hair with a penciled-in hairline. An hour in application, Spiner removes the makeup with a kerosene-based cleanser.

Meanwhile, other design work still had to be nailed down. One item that caused particular difficulty was the look of Geordi's VISOR—Visual Instrument and Sight Organ Replacement—which provided a full-spectrum electronic yet painful kind of "sight." After the art staff had spent three months trying various designs that would serve well from a technical standpoint, Michael Okuda one day brought in—as many fans have guessed—a girl's plastic hair barrette. That barrette was remanufactured, with some of Sternbach's design alterations to fit LeVar Burton's face.

It was also during this time that the final look, or set dressing, of the various standing sets was refined, and the staffers in charge left no detail unexamined. The main wall of the confer-ence lounge, for instance, was designed to echo a memorial display from the rec deck of the first motion picture. The wall is decorated with half-relief sculptures of the various *Enterprise* namesakes, beginning with the Terran American naval carrier. The ready room features Probert and Sternbach's original painting of the *Enterprise* and a model of their version of the *Stargazer* design, which was not accepted by the producers until needed in filming. Actually, the miniature is not stenciled with the name of *Stargazer* or any other ship, but it does carry the designation NCC-7100, not that of Picard's former command or, supposedly, that of the class ship *Constellation* (NCC-1974).

Elsewhere on that set, the rare tropical "lion fish" in the captain's fishbowl is alive, but fake plants adorn the bottom shelf of the end tables on either side of the sofa. Other details of Picard's office include his Shakespeare tome, which can be seen in the "Hide and Q" episode, a set of logo-etched glasses, and a crystal sailing ship.

Barely nine months after the world learned of the new *Star Trek* series, the cameras were set to roll on the pilot episode. Live special effects chief Charlie Washburn wrote a good-luck memo "on our offspring" to his fellow original series old-timers still engaged in the new venture—Fontana, Justman, Theiss, set decorator John Dwyer, and of course the Great Bird—and reminded them where they were twenty years ago that day by sentimentally enclosing a call sheet from 1967, issued during shooting of the original series episode "The Changeling."

As the sweat and toil of carving out a new series went on, Paramount TV chief Mel Harris, who had first announced just ten months earlier that *Star Trek* would return, was now back for another appearance. In early August he spoke via satellite to those linked to the 170 stations that would carry the new series, to over 94 percent of the TV households in the United States.

Harris introduced a slick production featuring footage from the yet-unaired pilot and using the new sets as background. He described for this business-oriented audience the commercial tie-ins, media publicity, and promotional efforts in the works for what he called "some of the best-looking television anywhere on anybody's air this fall."

From Cheerios to Coca-Cola, from books and software to models and toys, from linens and shirts to jewelry and credit cards, America's advertisers were paying dearly for a piece of what they knew was a major event. As a sign that the earlier information vacuum was over, Harris announced the impending media coverage—major papers nationwide, *Time,* and *TV Guide.* TV's *Entertainment Tonight,* he said, would be "the official video chronicler." Harris then described the studio's "pre-launch" promo campaign, which was tied to the theme "The 24th Century is about to begin!"

And the "final secret weapon" in this "unprecedented" effort? A one-minute commercial for TNG that would be seen on some 2 million copies of the hit *Star Trek IV* videocassette, due for release just days before the debut of the new series. Harris estimated that this commercial would be seen by over a quarter of all American TV households in just the first month of release.

Who needs an old network, anyway?

The Response to "Farpoint"

After all the pressure, work, and long hours, the pilot film pleased most critics. Ed Bark of the *Dallas Morning News,* writing for the Knight-Ridder-Tribune service, thought the pilot "soared with the spirit of the original," coming off as a "fine redefining of a classic and a considerable breakthrough for non-network syndicated television." Don Merrill in *TV Guide* proclaimed that TNG "is a worthy successor" to the original and said that Gene Roddenberry had "lost none

of his ingenuity or his taste in selecting stories." On the other side, while John J. O'Connor in the *New York Times* hoped "that things would get a little livelier in coming weeks," he may have needed to do his homework: in discussing the "new" technology of the show he included the "doors that open and shut effortlessly"!

And then there was the most important judge of all—the audience. Thanks to the lure of the original series, the heavy advance promotional campaign, and maybe even the often skeptical press, "Encounter at Farpoint" beat its prime-time network competition in Los Angeles, Dallas, Seattle, Miami, and Denver. This time around, the audience ratings *would* be on Trek's side, and despite a few rough times in its early days the new series would never have to look over its shoulder again.

Notes

1. Interview by David Schonauer, New York Times News Service, March 1988.
2. Schonauer, ibid.
3. "Inside 'Star Trek: The Next Generation,'" Mark A. Altman, *Galactic Journal,* No. 23, Winter 1988, p. 42.
4. Photos of a model of this early design are in *Starlog,* No. 118, May 1987, pp. 14–15.
5. Dan Madsen, *Official Fan Club Magazine,* No. 60, February-March 1988, p. 3.
6. Built later, along with Ten-Forward and the new observation lounge before season two, were senior officers' quarters, with a window wall that could be tilted to simulate an outer location in either the upper or the lower half of the saucer.
7. A similar incident occurred with the first optical-effects house used on the original series, Milkis recalled, but at least the models that had been built could be photographed by someone else.
8. David Gerrold, *Starlog,* No. 118, May 87, p. 15.
9. *The Propagator,* March 1987, Vol. 2, Issue 30; Lisa Wahl, editor; Hawthorne, Calif.: Mark "Adam" Baum, contributor, cited copies he'd received from "friend of a friend" employee at an unnamed L.A. talent agency.
10. *OFCM,* No. 70, Oct.-Nov. 1990, p. 4.
11. Ibid.
12. Marc Shapiro, *Starlog,* No. 124, Nov. 1987, p. 50.

ENCOUNTER AT FARPOINT

Production No.: 101–102 (as two separate episodes)/721 (as two-hour TV movie pilot) ▪ Aired: Week of September 28, 1987
Stardate: 41153.7 ▪ Code: ef

Directed by **Corey Allen**
Written by **D. C. Fontana and Gene Roddenberry**
Music by **Dennis McCarthy**

GUEST CAST
Q: **John de Lancie**
Groppler Zorn: **Michael Bell**
Admiral Leonard H. McCoy, retired: **DeForest Kelley**
Conn Ensign: **Colm Meaney**
Mandarin Bailiff: **Cary-Hiroyuki**
Main Bridge Security: **Timothy Dang**
Bandi shopkeeper: **David Erskine**
Female computer ensign: **Evelyn Guerrero**
Drugged military officer: **Chuck Hicks**
Lieutenant Torres: **Jimmy Ortega**

The USS *Enterprise*, NCC 1701-D, the first new Galaxy-class starship, is launched, with veteran Jean-Luc Picard in command. The ship's first mission is a puzzling one. While picking up new crew members from Deneb IV on the rim of explored space, they must figure out how the low-technology Bandi there could have built the gleaming new Farpoint Station they now offer to the Federation for use as a base.

The new ship is almost sidetracked permanently by a being claiming to be part of an all-knowing super race known as "the Q." This Q, who considers humanity too barbarous to expand further, hijacks Picard's command crew and sentences them to death in a kangaroo court. Picard is able to save their lives only by offering to prove humanity's worth during his ship's upcoming mission to Farpoint.

Freed by Q and allowed to arrive there, the crew can find no explanation for the Bandi's mysterious new technology until a vast alien ship appears and opens fire on the old Bandi city. Q tries to goad Picard into firing on the newcomer, but the *Enterprise* away team finds that the attacker is actually a sentient life-form trying to free its mate from the Bandi's clutches.

Initially, Q (John de Lancie) tried to condemn Picard and all humanity.

Unlike original Trek, TNG's pilot depicted many of the characters' first meetings.

Farpoint Station, it turns out, was built entirely by this enslaved creature. As the freed aliens leave the planet, a disappointed Q vows he'll be back to test humanity yet again.

For the first time, a Trek pilot had been presold as a series, shifting the pressure from selling the show to introducing the characters. But that by no means simplified the work of the writers.

Fontana's more action-oriented original outline concerned a being captured by a simian race known as the Annoi. The captors built an orbiting gun platform around the alien, intending to use it to fuel their dreams of expansion, while feeding their prisoner just enough of the mineral balmine to keep it alive. The USS *Starseeker* arrives with the *Enterprise,* but is destroyed after opening fire when the Annoi demand the two crews beam down, surrender, and become balmine gatherers. As part of an away team sent to

DeForest Kelley's one-hundred-thirty-seven-year-old "Admiral McCoy" provides a surprising and poignant send-off on TNG's maiden voyage.

disable the platform, Troi makes mental contact with the captive entity and persuades it to crash-land on the planet, where her people will help it to free itself by leading a prisoners' revolt. In later drafts the people would come to be called the Annae and the starship opening would be deleted, but many of the plot points and character introductions can be seen in this earliest concept.

Gene Roddenberry added the Q subplot, partly because of indecision over the length of the pilot. "Gene wanted an hour show, but the studio wanted a two-hour movie," as originally announced, Berman recalls. "They tried to get him to agree to a ninety-minute show as a compromise, but they eventually won out." According to Justman, both the ship separation sequence and a touching scene in which an aged Admiral McCoy meets Data were a help in filling out what Fontana had intended to be a ninety-minute script.

"As I had feared, the show was woefully short when we cut it together," Justman said. He added that director Corey Allen's typically faster-than-usual scene pacing increased their difficulties. "In order to make the show two hours we had to skillfully edit it and cut it not as tight as we ordinarily would for pace. So at times that two hours drags a bit here and there.

Despite that, the final version is missing a short scene that was included in the final draft script dated April 13. In that scene Riker is introduced to Geordi and an enthusiastic ensign named Sawyer Markham. Riker overhears the ensign calling Picard "the old burrhog" when the *Enterprise* is overdue.

Other slight changes from the final draft script: Torres, the crewman frozen by Q, was initially named Graham; Troi, too, was frozen by Q after rushing to Tasha's aid; and Picard's tag line, "Let's see what's out there," was added.

The dates of the new United Nations and its demise are given as 2016 and 2049, but changed to 2036 and 2079 in the final film. The references to a "post-atomic horror" on Earth jibe with information in the original series that the planet escaped nuclear war.

The Fontana-written McCoy scene does appear in this final draft script, although the "old country doctor" is given the age of 147, not 137, and is identified merely as "Admiral" in the dialogue—presumably to keep the cameo scene a secret. A New York *Post* columnist visiting the set stumbled across DeForest Kelley and got only a "no comment" when he asked what had brought the veteran actor to the set.

"It was a late addition," Justman said later of the McCoy scene. "I think it had been on Gene's mind, and he invited De to lunch and he said, 'How would you feel about it?'—expecting De to say no—and De said, 'I'd be honored.' And not only that, but he refused to take any more than SAG scale [Screen Actors Guild base salary]. He could have held us up for a lot of money, but he didn't. And it really got to me; it was a beautiful, beautiful scene."

"I just wanted scale, to let it be my way of saying thank-you to Gene for the many good things he has done for me," Kelley said later.

One of the background actors was Colm Meaney, an unsuccessful veteran of the original casting call who won enough points with the staff to be included here in the role of the battle bridge conn ensign. Meaney would eventually return to take up one of the most popular recurring roles, that of Lieutenant Miles O'Brien. The Dublin native was a member of the Irish National Theatre and also played stage roles in London, New York, and Los Angeles. He

Though his role remained nameless for one and a half seasons, Colm Meaney's O'Brien appeared on the Battle Bridge in "Farpoint."

settled first on the East Coast, where he appeared on *One Life to Live* as a British thief, and then in Hollywood, where his screen career took off.

Already being pumped up as the new alien threat, the Ferengi, too, are mentioned, although they would not be seen until the third regular episode aired (and the fifth filmed).

One scene in "Farpoint" was shot on location in Los Angeles' famous Griffith Park: the scene at the holodeck stream where Riker and a soggy Wes meet Data.

And the cannibalizing of old Trek sets continued: part of the Klingon Bird of Prey sickbay from *Star Trek III* was turned upside down to become part of Zorn's council room wall.

Interestingly enough, the end credits were on a crawl but would be listed on cards screen by screen for the remainder of TNG's run. Also, the opening credits do not include the name of the character along with each actor's name, as they would later.

For trivia's sake: aside from Troi's onetime appearance in uniform during this voyage, in the final bridge scene Tasha became the only other regular of either sex to wear the "skant" (basically a unisex miniskirt) uniform. And, possibly indicating that the time frame of the series was still not set in stone, Data refers to himself as a member of the "Starfleet Class of '78," but his graduation date is later established as 2338 (in "Conundrum"/214*).

*Note: Numbers following episode titles are production numbers: episodes in this book will be discussed in production order.

FIRST SEASON

After its successful launch, TNG faced

the even larger task of staying on schedule while fleshing out the new mythos, meeting all expectations, and silencing its naysayers. Although the budget would be upped to $1.5 million per episode by year's end, the season would prove to be a shakedown cruise for the 129 full-time actors, producers, crew, staff, and designers aboard.

Filming began on July 6, 1987, for the very first hour-long episode, "The Naked Now," only ten days after "Farpoint" wrapped and with very few alterations in the series' infant format. One change concerned the character of Deanna Troi. Deemed too "loose" and cheerleaderlike in her skant, she was given a nonregulation uniform and a severe bun hairstyle. At the same time, Troi's telepathic abilities were softened to mere empathy with most species—a lessening blamed on her half-human genes—to avoid the emotional soliloquies even the actress cringed over in "Farpoint."

Still, the writing staff would continue to find the Troi char-

The first season "Smoky Bridge" cast shot (*opposite*)—this time with Worf.

An unused post-pilot Troi look: both the "bun" *and* the "skant."

success would take some time to catch the attention of both the industry and the public at large since the series never showed up in the weekly Nielsen Top 10 lists. For a nationwide gauge, a composite had to be compiled by weighing the demographic figures in each market against those of other series.

The studio reported that fan mail was running 95 percent in favor of the new show, while the Colorado-based *"Star Trek: The Official Fan Club"* reported a 90 percent approval rate in mail from members. So much for the worry that TNG couldn't hold its own without rehiring the original actors or recasting the 1960s roles. This was a great relief for Paramount and all concerned, considering their investment of money *and* Trek's good name.

But then reports began to surface regarding the turnover in the writing staff that had been under way since before cameras rolled on "Farpoint." After Milkis's exit, Gerrold left in May of 1987, before weekly production began, although he received a "program consultant" credit through the seventh show filmed, "Lonely Among Us" (108). At the time he said he was leaving to write and produce a four-hour CBS science-fiction miniseries called *Trackers*, but later Gerrold let it be known he was upset about "promises made and not kept." He was appar-

acter one of the hardest to write for. According to Marina Sirtis, the character was almost dropped in November after Troi went unused in four shows: "Hide and Q" (111), "Datalore" (114), "11001001" (116), and "Heart of Glory" (120).[1]

Despite those who complained of a copycat format and episodes, ratings began to rise as soon as the series hit the air. "The Naked Now," the first regular installment, would continue the pilot's success by taking its time slot in Boston, Denver, and Houston, according to A. C. Nielsen. *TV Guide* reported on December 26 that thirteen ABC affiliates and two with CBS had dumped their network programming to carry TNG in prime time, and perennial sixth-place Chicago station WPWR-TV jumped to the number two slot at 6:00 P.M. on Saturdays with TNG—an 1,100 percent ratings increase.

However, because TNG was syndicated, its

Troi's first-year "severe" look.

Data and Worf—successors to Spock's logical and alien mystiques.

ently referring to the shelving of an allegorical script he'd written about AIDS, called "Blood and Fire."

Fontana became the next in a long line of writers who grew upset with the extensive rewrites on this incarnation of Trek. She remained through October and was listed in the credits until her tenure ended completely after "The Big Goodbye" (113).

For the last top member of the old guard that had originally breathed life into TNG (aside from GR), departure was a health matter. Justman had signed on for a year, but unlike Milkis he had included a second-year pickup option in his contract. Midway through season one, though, he let it be known he wanted to reduce his work load. "I was still motivated, it was a good show, but I was just working myself into a dither; I was very tired and very cross," he said later. And he soon grew angry: he demanded and received a front-page apology from *Daily Variety*—the first in the trade paper's history—a day after it ran a story saying he'd been fired amid a "big shakeup at Star Trek."

The studio agreed to his request to cut back to handling only casting, rewrites, and editing in a consulting-producer role for the last eight

shows of the season, beginning with "Coming of Age" (119). With that, the staff was restructured. Berman received the title of co-executive producer, Maurice Hurley became the new writing producer, and David Livingston was promoted to line producer after having been hired by Justman as unit production manager for the pilot. Hurley, who had come aboard as a writer-producer at the start of weekly production with "The Naked Now" (103), left Universal to come to TNG after having worked on staff during the debut years of *Miami Vice* and *The Equalizer*.

Carrying the title of producer were writers Lewin, who stayed all season long, and Wright, who remained on staff from the pilot through "Skin of Evil" (122) in January 1988, when he left to become creative consultant on Paramount's *The War of the Worlds*.

Johnny Dawkins was credited as story editor in "The Naked Now," "Code of Honor," "Where No One Has Gone Before," and "Too Short a Season" (103, 104, 106, and 112). The title then went unused until the restructuring caused by Justman's leaving, when Richard Manning and Hans Beimler took over the chore until the end of the season (and later returned to serve in a similar capacity during the show's run). In the interim, Greg Strangis worked as creative consultant on "The Big Goodbye," "Datalore," and "Angel One" (113–115) before he, too, left to develop *The War of the Worlds*.

This revolving door for writers began to be blamed for the perceived lack of continuity on the series. Though most fans stayed patient, as reflected in the ratings, some criticized the lack of growth and interplay between the characters, as well as the thin or too crowded story lines.

After his departure a year later, Hurley talked about the story-writing system, which he had tried to change during his tenure. This system included a pattern of memo-writing among the story staff. "In the beginning there was a lot of [plot] clutter," Hurley said. "Too many ideas being thrown into one script. . . . There was a tendency to do a real quick wrap-up. Too much in the bag, trying to fill the bag too full."

"We were trying hard to put our house in order during the first season," Berman recalled.

"The writers were being rewritten by Gene, and there was a lot of tumult because people didn't know where they stood."

Why so many story problems? The most obvious reason was the sheer enormity of developing stories that were entertaining and thought-provoking while staying true to GR's unique unifying vision of Trek. The most frustrating thing for writers was his ban on interpersonal conflicts among the crew, based on his belief that such petty and ego-driven problems would be a thing of the past by the twenty-fourth century.

"Yes, there was a lot of rewriting done and it bruised some egos," Hurley would say later, chalking it up to typical first-year growing pains. "But I think it was really necessary."[2]

Even Hurley professed his disbelief in what he called GR's "wacky doodle" hope-filled future vision, but he acknowledged that viewpoint was what defined Trek. "You suspend your own feelings and your own beliefs and you get with his vision—or you get *rewritten*."[3] Ironically he would soon find himself clashing with more than one writer over just how to interpret that vision.

Actually, the original *Star Trek* had undergone exactly the same tortuous search for stability during its formative year—pages rewritten the day and even the hour before they were to shoot, and so on—but the older series spent its lifetime crying for attention while it remained largely unexamined under the microscope of fans and the Hollywood press that later magnified everything that was done—or rumored to have been done—on TNG.

Eventually, as an embryonic continuity eventually surfaced, the revolving door slowed down—or at least seemed to. Hannah Louise Shearer, teleplay writer on "When the Bough Breaks" (118), was named to the new position of executive story editor beginning with that episode. Two shows later, Tracy Tormé—a *Saturday Night Live* and *SCTV* veteran with TNG credits already on "The Big Goodbye" (113) and "Haven" (105)—was added in that same position. Shearer, whose background included producing *Emergency!*, *Knight Rider*, and *Quincy* and writing for *Cagney and Lacey* and *MacGyver*, served with Tormé through the rest of the season.

But delays due to last-minute rewrites took

Andy Probert designed the underbelly of the Ferengi "Marauder" with its own (as-yet-unseen) shuttlecraft.

up only a part of each TNG episode's production schedule. Each show requires about sixteen weeks from the commitment to develop a story idea to the time its post-production optical effects, music, and titles are added, and each in turn overlaps the others in various phases of evolution. On any one day, according to Berman, one show is being filmed live, writing or design work is in process on upcoming scripts, and segments already shot are being edited and having FX, sound, music, and titles added.

A TNG director usually has only seven days to shoot about fifty-five pages of script. That means shooting eight or nine pages a day. The design staff gets about two weeks' notice on a script prior to shooting—or, as Zimmerman put it, "ten working days to do the thinking, drawing, construction, and get it ready to shoot." For the producers during the first season, that meant days stretching from 5:00 A.M. to 9:00 or 10:00 P.M., while the actors and stage crews were at it from 6:00 A.M. until 6:00 to 10:00 P.M. or later.

Meanwhile, Legato realized that the original idea of a library of optical-effects shots wouldn't save much time and money after all. "The plan was to take the library shots from ILM and add about five per show," he explained. "That was probably a little naive. . . . Then the pilot needed two hundred and ten FX shots, the second show had seventy-five, the third eighty, and so on, so by the sixth or seventh show we found it was cheaper just to 'trick' [custom-shoot] each one out."

Eventually, dropping the library concept allowed more movement in FX scenes, because elements freshly photographed—a ship, a planet, a nebula—didn't have to be static to match one element that had been shot for an earlier show. "Since we're filming [what amounts to] a feature a week, you need specific shots—a ship thrown into orbit, a Wizard of Oz head," Legato explained. "If you want to do it right and do it effectively, you've got to shoot it and do exactly what you want done. It's really less work and more powerful visually and dramatically."

And less work would quickly become crucial, as the shorthanded visual-effects chief nearly drove himself to exhaustion by handling the stu-dio work solo through the pilot and the first nine episodes. "It got to where they'd finish live shooting at ten P.M., I'd go from there to work in the lab until five A.M., and they'd be ready to start live shooting again in another hour." Legato sighed. "We weren't just doing the work—we were learning *how* to do the work."

The last straw came when "The Last Outpost" (107) was moved up in the production schedule with 110 effects shots, right after the backbreaking visuals required for "Where No One Has Gone Before" (106).

"The effects budgets were running $100,000 over and we had a meeting to discuss why," Legato recalled. "I finally said, 'Look, this is costing $2,000 an hour just for me to sit here.' They said, 'How do you figure that?' and I told them that's how much the overtime and lab cost with me sitting there and not out working. Finally an executive said, 'Well it's obvious you need more help!' and that's how we got Dan!"

Dan Curry, mirroring Legato's role, would begin on the tenth hour-long show filmed, "Too Short a Season," (112) and alternate episodes with him to split up the work load. For the second season, each was promoted to visual effects supervisor and given his own associate. Gary Hutzel was hired to work with Legato, and Ron B. Moore became Curry's assistant.

About that time Legato also at last persuaded the producers to let him head a second-unit camera crew to film the special live-action shots needed for FX interfacing—like those before the blue screen in which live action will be mated with background paintings or visuals, and close-up inserts of computer displays and hands on controls. "If a director shoots something and doesn't understand how the visual effects tie in, you have to go back and repair that, and it costs more anyway," he noted.

Practically all the animated computer displays are matted in because the screens are usually not bright enough to be seen. Some live action is done on set, though—as when a finger traces a path shown by the display. Created by Okuda with Macintosh animation software, the sequences, like other second-unit shooting, use actors' photo doubles to save time and money.

Because of what they had to accomplish every week, TNG's visual-effects staff soon became pioneers in video special effects equipment and techniques for the entire industry. For example, Hutzel developed an inexpensive and quicker method of filming revolving planets by using slides of them projected on a dome, providing five or six finished sequences in an hour.

Regardless of how it stacks up against the original show in other areas, TNG wins hands down in series continuity. While *Star Trek* did a miraculous job for its day in keeping its back story intact, that effort simply pales next to the effort put forth by Sternbach, Okuda, and Probert (before he left at year's end to join Disney's *Imagineering* subsidiary) in matters of historical and technological consistency. They began injecting and describing what might be called preemptive backgrounding, or the anticipation of background needs, before the demand for it cropped up in a particular script. Okuda and Sternbach would later be rewarded for their efforts and officially given the added title of technical consultants with early script input.

By year's end, TNG would finish with a 10.6 rating—or about 9.4 million households watching from 210 local stations—and rank first among eighteen- to forty-nine-year-olds, the prime demographic group sought by advertisers. Beyond the United States and Canada, in eight European and Asian countries where first-run airing was initially restricted, TNG picked up a direct $2 million in videocassette sales by its first summer hiatus.

Though comparisons to the old show persisted, by season's end TNG had developed an identity all its own. *TV Guide* writer Gary D. Christenson compared the differences between the two Treks with the differences in his generation of Americans: "*Star Trek* depicted us in reckless youth, with a starship captain who tamed space as vigorously as we laid claim to the future. . . . *Star Trek: The Next Generation* reveals the child grown—a little more polished, but also more complacent. And if there's a bit of gray and a wrinkle or two, so much the better."[4]

THE NAKED NOW

Production No.: 103 ■ Aired: Week of October 5, 1987
Stardate: 41209.2 ■ Code: nn

Directed by **Paul Lynch**
Teleplay by **J. Michael Bingham**
Story by **John D.F. Black** and **J. Michael Bingham**

GUEST CAST
Chief Engineer Sarah MacDougal: **Brooke Bundy**
Assistant Engineer Jim Shimoda: **Benjamin W.S. Lum**
Transporter Chief: **Michael Rider**
Kissing crewman: **Kenny Koch**
Conn: **David Rehan**
Engineering crewman: **Skip Stellrecht**

A hauntingly familiar disease is unleashed aboard the *Enterprise* after it makes contact with the *Tsiolkovsky*, a now-dead research ship that had been investigating a nearby star's collapse. Those afflicted act intoxicated and mentally unstable.

As Dr. Crusher races to find a cure, the disease's symptoms ring a bell with Riker, who goes looking through decades of records with Data until they realize that the original *Enterprise* encountered much the same disease.

But the old cure doesn't work, and before Dr. Crusher can discover why, her afflicted son helps disable computer control, putting the ship at the mercy of the nearby collapsing star. Eventually almost the entire crew—including the doctor, Picard, Yar, and Data—come down with the virus.

Finally Data and Chief Engineer MacDougal hold off illness long enough to subdue Wesley; the android then uses his speed and dexterity to restore the computer memory in a desperate race against time to get the ship functioning in time to avoid a head-on collision from a chunk of the former star.

After a working cure is finally discovered, the crew ruefully gets on with life.

The Tsiolkovosky virus: a close call for Picard and Crusher.

CODE OF HONOR

Production No.: 104 ▪ Aired: Week of October 12, 1987
Stardate: 41235.25 ▪ Code: ch

Directed by **Russ Mayberry**
Written by **Katharyn Powers and Michael Baron**

GUEST CAST
Lutan: **Jessie Lawrence Ferguson**
Yareena: **Karole Selmon**
Hagon: **James Louis Watkins**
Transporter Chief: **Michael Rider**

A plague on Styris IV sends the *Enterprise* to the only known source for an organic vaccine, Ligon II.

Negotiations go smoothly for the vaccine until the planet's chief, Lutan, suddenly kidnaps Yar after being impressed by both her beauty and her strength. To get her back, Picard must abide by the Prime Directive and the Ligonians' strict patience and code of honor—and Yar must combat Lutan's current "First One" wife, who now feels her honor challenged, in a fight to the death.

Picard tries every diplomatic trick in the book, but he is finally left to hope that Yar can score a hit in the poison-tipped glavin combat. She does, and the fighters are beamed aboard, where Dr. Crusher concocts an antidote to the Ligonian poison.

Not only is honor served and Yar rescued, but wife Yareena's "death" satisfies tradition. Alive in reality, though, Yareena transfers her land and property rights to Lutan's lieutenant Hagon when she claims him as her new husband, in effect dethroning the chief. But Lutan takes it all in stride with Ligonian pride and calls the orderly transfer far more "civilized" than the *Enterprise* crew's society.

Amused but wiser, the crew warps out to help fight the plague.

This episode sparked the first of many waves of early criticism from fans who felt that too many TNG plots were being lifted from original-series stories. In this case, however, that was exactly what Gene Roddenberry wanted: a story, like "The Naked Time" of 1966, in which the wants and needs of new characters could be quickly revealed to a waiting audience. Black, listed here as coauthor, wrote the original; J. Michael Bingham is Fontana's pseudonym. "It was an homage, not a copy," Berman said of the episode. "We even mentioned the old *Enterprise* and its remedy, which doesn't help our crew in this new situation after all."

This era's story roots go back to the opening thirteen pages of an unfinished teleplay GR began called "Revelations." The same opening points are included, except that Geordi makes a move on Tasha, who is the next to get the *Tsiolkovsky* virus even though she brushes him off. Fontana initially turned out a teleplay with a harder edge: Data turns down Tasha's advances but becomes a "perfect little boy" so as to become human a là Pinocchio; Troi bemoans an empath's lack of mental privacy among hundreds of humans; Riker fears a lonely captain's career; and Picard worries over the families he has aboard this ship.

Brooke Bundy's one-time appearance as Chief Engineer MacDougal began a season-long parade of characters in that position. In three more episodes MacDougal would be "replaced." Rider began a three-show stint as the first regular yet unnamed transporter chief; the actor would reappear from time to time in other positions.

Beginning an Okuda tradition for most "new" ships, a dedication plaque on the bridge identifies the *Tsiolkovsky* as an Oberth-class vessel (actually a minor redress of the USS *Grissom* in *Star Trek III*), a descendant of today's Soviet Baikonur Cosmodrome, although little did anyone know then how dated the USSR reference on the plaque would be! A copy of the plaque was sent to the Kaluga Museum in the hometown of the starship's namesake, Russian space pioneer Konstantin Tsiolkovsky.

Writer Katharyn Powers, an original-series fan and a veteran of series such as *Kung Fu*, *Logan's Run*, and *Fantastic Journey*, had known D. C. Fontana for some time when she got invited to pitch

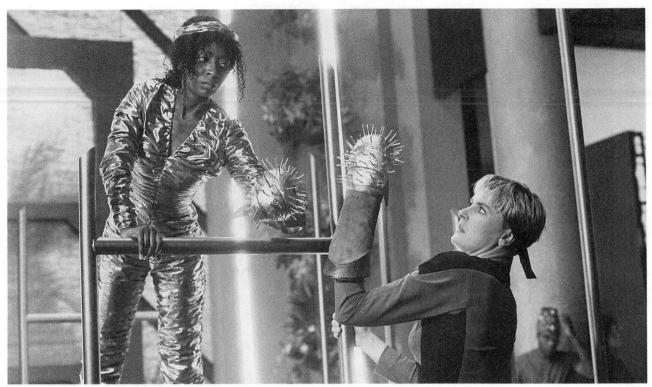

Yar fights to the "death" against Yareena (Karole Selmon).

story ideas for the new show. She and writing partner Michael Baron initially tried to base the Ligonian "honor is all" culture on that of the Japanese Samurai, using a reptilian race called the Tellisians.

Not everyone was pleased with the results, though. Tracy Tormé, an eventual writing staffer, later said he was embarrassed by the show's "1940s tribal Africa" view of blacks and by the fight's uncanny resemblance to the win-or-die battle between Kirk and Spock in "Amok Time" in 1967.

The yellow-on-black grid of the empty holodeck wall made its debut here, but a phonelike programming unit used by Tasha—a seeming redundancy with vocal commands—was never seen again. Tried here and once more—in "The Last Outpost" (107)—before being scrapped was the building of Picard's extreme pride in his Gallic heritage to the point of humorous defensiveness in his banter with Data—an echo of the original series' recurring "Russian joke" with young Chekov, who believed his motherland was the home of all discoveries and inventions.

Fred Steiner made a onetime musical contribution to TNG with this episode, the only composer from the original series to do so.

HAVEN

Production No.: 105 ■ Aired: Week of November 30, 1987
Stardate: 41294.5 ■ Code: hv

Directed by **Richard Compton**
Teleplay by **Tracy Tormé**
Story by **Tracy Tormé and Lan O'Kun**

GUEST CAST
Lwaxana Troi: **Majel Barrett**
Wyatt Miller: **Rob Knepper**
Victoria Miller: **Nan Martin**
Steven Miller: **Robert Ellenstein**
Mr. Homn: **Carel Struycken**
Valeda Innis: **Anna Katarina**
Wrenn: **Raye Birk**
Ariana: **Danitza Kingsley**
Transporter Chief: **Michael Rider**

At planet Haven, Picard and his crew meet up with Lwaxana Troi, Deanna's mother, who blusters aboard when her late husband's best friends, the Millers, insist on seeing the childhood genetic bonding vows consummated between Deanna and their son, Wyatt.

Deanna dutifully agrees and comes to find Wyatt a good companion, much to *imzadi* Riker's confusion. Wyatt is puzzled because Deanna is not the blonde he has seen in visions since childhood.

The wedding plans go on despite the mothers-in-law's comical feuding: First the pre-wedding dinner turns into a shambles; then the Millers want no part of the traditional nude Betazoid wedding.

Everyone's plans go out the window, though, when a number of plague-ridden Tarellians, long thought dead, show up at Haven. Wyatt, a doctor, finds the blond girl of his visions is a Tarellian. She had pictured him for years as well without knowing why.

Wyatt apologizes to Deanna and shocks his parents by following his perceived destiny at last: joining the Tarellians to help them and his love find a cure.

Picard is glad to get his counselor back and to see Lwaxana's flustering flirtations end.

Troi ponders the marriage her mother (Majel Barrett) helped arrange.

This episode, which barely resembles Lan O'Kun's original story called "Love Beyond Time and Space," became the ticket that won Tracy Tormé a place on the writing team. After impressing the staff without making a story sale, the son of singer Mel Tormé was contacted in a last-ditch try to save O'Kun's concept. Tormé played up the in-fighting between the families to a caustically comic intensity that was later softened and edited out, to his regret.

Majel Barrett was hardly a newcomer to the Trek universe, having portrayed Nurse Christine Chapel in the 1960s series and Dr. Chapel in the first and fourth movies—and having been Gene Roddenberry's wife for nearly twenty years. Here she began what turned into a yearly visit as the "Auntie Mame of the Galaxy" and the bane of Picard's existence as well as her daughter's.

Troi here calls Riker "Bill"—the second (after "The Naked Now") and last time any of the regulars does so in the series. This also marks the last time she would use the Betazoid word for "beloved," *imzadi*, until the end of the second season (in "Shades of Gray"/148)—a barometer for the direction their relationship would take.

In one of the loveliest coincidences of Trek trivia, Richard Compton found himself directing this episode exactly twenty years to the day after appearing in a one-line walk-on role on the old show—as Lieutenant Washburn, a member of Scotty's team trying to repair the dead *Constellation* in "The Doomsday Machine."

WHERE NO ONE HAS GONE BEFORE

Production No.: 106 ▪ Aired: Week of October 26, 1987
Stardate: 41263.1 ▪ Code: wn

Directed by **Rob Bowman**
Written by **Diane Duane and Michael Reaves**

GUEST CAST
Kosinski: **Stanley Kamel**
Traveler: **Eric Menyuk**
Maman Picard: **Herta Ware**
Lieutenant Commander Argyle: **Biff Yeager**
Crew member: **Charles Dayton**
Ballerina: **Victoria Dillard**

The brave new warp theories of a supposedly brilliant Starfleet consultant go awry when the "expert" plunges the ship first into a neighboring galaxy and then into a dimension where the physical and mental worlds converge.

The trouble turns out not to be with expert Kosinski's theories but with his mysteriously meek "assistant," whose race can travel among dimensions and times.

The strain of propelling the entire ship, though, has put the so-called Traveler gravely near death—threatening to strand the *Enterprise* forever. And in this nether-space, crew members begin seeing alternate realities that threaten their sanity as well.

Finally it is discovered that Wesley's friendship has a curative effect on the Traveler; he strengthens the alien just enough to get the ship home.

Before he does so, though, the Traveler advises Picard secretly of Wesley's prodigious abilities and urges him to not let them go undeveloped. With a proud mother standing by, Wesley is promoted to acting ensign by Picard, and his Academy training begins.

Even though producer Maurice Hurley did numerous uncredited rewrites on their script, Duane and Reaves's initial story survives as adapted from her Kirk-era novel, *The Wounded Sky*, in which an unusual alien resembling a glass spider performs warp experiments that mix physics with metaphysics and strand the original *Enterprise* far from home.

In the original teleplay, Kosinski was responsible for both the warp effects and the accident; he also had a son who felt he spent more time on his career than with him. The crew was in awe of Kosinski in the original script, and the hallucinations were even more bizarre, including the image of Jack Crusher appearing to both Picard and Beverly. The starship reappeared within a monoblock, or cosmological egg, and in exploding it to escape, the starship in effect caused the birth of a new universe. Significantly, the *Enterprise* has been missing for six days and the captain orders that the next day be observed as a day of rest!

The Traveler role was a consolation prize of sorts for Eric Menyuk, who only weeks before had come close to winning the part of Data. An original Trek fan at age six, he picked up drama in college and went from Boston-area theater to TV guest work in *Hill Street Blues*, *Matlock*, *L.A. Law*, and *Cheers*, among others.

Justman has said that hiring twenty-eight-year-old Rob Bowman to direct this segment was one of his proudest achievements on the show; Bowman was called in to replace Daniel Petrie, who dropped out to film the movie *Mystic Pizza*. It was a terrifying time for young Bowman, who wanted to make a good impression on his first assignment and overcome any doubts about his youth. Once he got his script, he worked for twenty days before filming began. He walked around the sets in off-hours, using storyboards and blocking out scenes to prepare his action lines and camera angles. Bowman went on to become one of the infant series' most prolific directors.

Wesley and the Traveler
(Eric Menyuk).

The episode's dazzling optical effects were quite literally homemade, Legato recalled. "We got the usual kind of vague explanation for the end-of-the-universe visuals in the script," he said. "But I did it simply, at home in my basement, with water. I had always noticed water reflections on the wall, so I shot multiple layers of that through dissolved Mylar bits. It was peculiar and bizarre. And I used little suspended moving Christmas tree lights for the little blinkies."

Worf's pet targ is actually a Russian wild boar named Emmy Lou, wearing a Theiss-designed original. "That pig smelled horrid," laughed Justman. "A sweet-sour, extremely pungent odor. I showered and showered, and it took me a week to get rid of it!"

Biff Yeager debuts here as the longest-running chief engineer of the first season, although Riker introduces him as "one of our chief engineers"; and Dennis Madalone, seen here as the sciences division ensign who is terrified by his self-conjured fire, is a stuntman who would receive screen credit beginning with the third season as stunt coordinator and would continuing to appear as various crew members.

THE LAST OUTPOST

Production No.: 107 ■ Aired: Week of October 19, 1987
Stardate: 41386.4 ■ Code: Io

Directed by **Richard Colla**
Teleplay by **Herbert Wright**
Story by **Richard Krzemien**

GUEST CAST
Letek: **Armin Shimerman**
Mordoc: **Jake Dengel**
Kayron: **Tracey Walter**
Portal: **Darryl Henriques**
DaiMon Tarr: **Mike Gomez**

History is overshadowed by danger as the *Enterprise* is readied for the first direct Federation meeting with the Ferengi, the supercapitalists of the galaxy. The ship is hot on the trail of a Ferengi vessel suspected of stealing an outpost's T-9 energy converter.

The chase ends when both ships find themselves immobilized over a distant planet. A stymied Picard is ready to try anything, even pretending to surrender, when he and his opponent,

The first meeting with Ferengi (Armin Shimerman, Jake Dengel, Tracey Walter).

This episode was a dramatic, if sometimes confusing, introduction of the Ferengi, but ultimately it did not live up to all the advance hype for the Federation's new alien threat. As developed by Herb Wright and Gene Roddenberry, the Ferengi first appeared in furlike wraparound outerwear and used blue energy-bolt whips, which were never seen again. According to Zimmerman, the Ferengis' poor eyesight accounts for their beady eyes and brightly lit ship interiors; their huge ears help to compensate by providing them with better hearing.[5]

Their ship, described in the script as resembling a horseshoe crab with an extendable neck, was designed by Andrew Probert; the earwiglike pincers on the forward ends were his idea. Greg Jein built four models for different uses, the largest being 2½ feet long. The rear area is cargo space; a boarding ramp and a shuttle can be seen on the underside.

Richard Krzemien's initial story concerned a planetary caretaker named Dilo, precursor to Portal, as the latter-day Rip Van Winkle who slept while his empire fell. Riker's concluding request to beam over several replicated Chinese finger puzzles to the pesky Ferengi echoes Scotty's solution at the end of "The Trouble with Tribbles"—transporting the prolific fur balls detested by Klingons to their ship. The Tkon Empire seal that appears in the revolving holographic display is also seen as the blade design on Portal's staff.

LONELY AMONG US

Production No.: 108 ■ Aired: Week of November 2, 1987
Stardate: 41249.3 ■ Code: la

Directed by **Cliff Bole**
Teleplay by **D. C. Fontana**
Story by **Michael Halperin**

GUEST CAST
Ssestar: **John Durbin**
First Security Guard: **Colm Meaney**
Assistant Chief Engineer Singh: **Kavi Raz**

The spat between two neighboring planets would be almost comical if it weren't for the *Enterprise*'s serious task of transporting their ambassadors to Parliament, a UFP diplomatic outpost.

En route there, the ship passes through a strange energy cloud, and puzzling malfunctions start to occur. Worf and Dr. Crusher then show bizarre personality shifts while attending to them.

DaiMon, realize it's the world below and not the other's ship that is the source of the mysterious power drain holding both vessels captive.

The planet is an outpost of the ancient but unknown Tkon Empire, now extinct. A cooperative landing mission to investigate is arranged, but the deceitful Ferengi double-cross Riker's team and stun them.

An automated Tkon "portal" guard then emerges from his centuries-old sleep and challenges the two sides. At first, Data tries to reason with Portal and informs him that his time and his empire are long gone.

The childish Ferengi tire him, but Riker's wisdom and the philosophies of the Federation finally impress Portal and he allows the two ships to go their way.

After an assistant engineer is murdered while inspecting the malfunctions, Data adopts the methods of Sherlock Holmes. But Troi's hypnosis of Crusher and Worf reveals that they have accidentally taken aboard a long-lonely life-force. The creature is now looking for a host body to return it to the energy cloud.

The crew is shocked when the being chooses Picard as its host. After apologizing for the damage it caused, the alien has Picard resign his command and divert the ship back to the cloud—where it beams out as pure energy.

Just as Riker is about to take over the stunned ship, Troi senses that the union did not work. Sure enough, Picard uses the transporter circuits to rematerialize in his human form.

Once back, the tired captain gives Riker the job of keeping the cannibalistic races' diplomats from eating each other.

Michael Halperin's original story contained the final basic plot, but a dilithium breakdown on the starship was the subplot. The diplomatic conference was added by Fontana, as in her 1967 original-series script, "Journey to Babel." Halperin's story ended with Picard, his ship basically powerless, bringing the energy creature home by using the slingshot time-traveling effect seen in various Trek episodes and *Star Trek IV*.

This show was the first of many TNG treks for director Cliff Bole, a veteran of *The Six Million Dollar Man, V,* the new *Mission: Impossible, Paradise,* and every other *Vega$* shot. Bole recalled that the show got mail criticizing its depiction of what amounted to cannibalism on the part of the carnivorous doglike Anticans.

Seen as a hapless security ensign chasing the ambassador was "Farpoint" actor Colm Meaney, still in an unnamed role. The

Rivan (Brenda Bakke) gives Riker a feel for life among the Edo.

The debut of TNG's dress uniform, from "Lonely Among Us."

"part" was not consistent with the pilot, where he had appeared as a command-division ensign, but at least here he wore the same mustard-color uniform he would sport in season two as Lieutenant O'Brien, the transporter chief.

TNG's dress uniform, designed to evoke memories of the deck waistcoats of the eighteenth-century British navy, made its debut here. The look would be slightly altered the following season: the gold edging would be reduced in width, and the front flap would follow the collarbone panel line instead of spiraling down from the collar. Two nice visual effects are seen in this episode: the stars warping by outside the ready room window, and their reflection on the desktop.

A few odd notes: one of the scenes in which Kavi Raz could be seen as Singh in the background had to be reshot when the actor wasn't available, so a wig on a chair was used as a stand-in! Okuda and Sternbach winced at the use of the transporter in this early story as a life-pattern restorer, so they came up with the official explanation that the system had come under the unique electromagnetic influences of the cloud-entity. A clunker of a prop that would not be reused after this episode is Beverly Crusher's surgical cap with its bizarre eyepiece.

JUSTICE

Production No.: 109 ■ Aired: Week of November 9, 1987
Stardate: 41255.6 ■ Code: ju

Directed by **James L. Conway**
Teleplay by **Worley Thorne**
Story by **Ralph Wills and Worley Thorne**

GUEST CAST
Rivan: **Brenda Bakke**
Liator: **Jay Louden**
Conn: **Josh Clark**
Mediators: **David Q. Combs, Richard Lavin**
Edo girl: **Judith Jones**
Nurse: **Brad Zerbst**
Edo boys: **Eric Matthew, David Michael Graves**

The pastoral planet of Rubicun III beckons after the *Enterprise* delivers a party of colonists to the nearby Strnad system. Rubicun's healthy people—the Edo—and their ways of love and open sensual pleasure make this planet seem like the perfect R-and-R stop.

But trouble looms in paradise after Wesley inadvertently chases a ball into one of the Edo's always shifting forbidden zones, drawing the planet's simple punishment for every crime—death. Dr. Crusher is furious, but Picard feels helpless under the Prime Directive.

As the captain pleads for Wesley's life, a machinelike being begins to orbit the planet and sends a probe to scan Data's brain. Proclaiming itself the Edo's god, the being demands that the *Enterprise* people leave its "children" alone—and take the Strnad colonists back, too.

The Edo are shocked that the once-friendly visitors protest their law; one Edo is even given the chance to see her "god," much to the machine-being's displeasure.

Finally Picard agrees to take the boy from his Edo captors by force. He confronts the Edo, who cave in but bitterly taunt the crew with their own law.

But "God" won't let the crew beam back. Picard argues that when laws are absolute there can be no real justice, and this convinces "Him" to let them go on their way.

John D.F. Black put his pseudonym, Ralph Wills, on this script, which as aired bears only slight resemblance to the story on terrorism he originally pitched. His first treatment featured the colony of Llarof where random "punishment zones," originally designed to fight anarchy, are now enforced for any offense and, it turns out, against only those not deemed immune from the law. An *Enterprise* guard, protecting two children on shore leave who happen upon a crime scene, is shot dead by an overzealous local cop, who in turn is killed on the spot by his dutifully law-abiding partner.

In Black's first draft Picard refuses to back the first of the timid rebels who want a change, but he finds a loophole just as the rebels' army wins out and reestablishes order. Black's second draft saw the rebel leader Reneg put on trial and executed for treason, with Picard musing that the people have the right to decide their own justice without interference. Later major rewrites by Worley Thorne and Gene Roddenberry would add the "Edolord" and the culture's preoccupation with sex.

"Justice" was the first episode to feature location shooting since the brief holodeck scene in "Farpoint" (102). The Edo exteriors were shot at the Tillman Water Reclamation Plant in Van Nuys, a north Los Angeles suburb (see "The First Duty"/219), and Wesley's fall was filmed at the Huntington Library in Pasadena.

Director James L. Conway, an original-series fan who had directed everything from Sunn Classics' pseudo-documentaries to Westerns to horror movies to industrial films, had just completed a *MacGyver* at Paramount when he was chosen to direct for TNG. Brad Zerbst became the first actor to play a recurring med tech or nurse in sickbay; his unnamed part lasted through two more shows, "Heart of Glory" (120) and "Skin of Evil" (122). And a character trademark, Worf's curt one-liner, began here with his observation on the friendly, mostly nude Edo: "Nice planet!"

THE BATTLE

Production No.: 110 ■ Aired: Week of November 16, 1987
Stardate: 41723.9 ■ Code: ba

Directed by **Rob Bowman**
Teleplay by **Herbert Wright**
Story by **Larry Forrester**

GUEST CAST
DaiMon Bok: **Frank Corsentino**
Kazago: **Doug Warhit**
Rata: **Robert Towers**

While waiting to meet the Ferengi, Picard is amazed when his old ship, the *Stargazer*, turns up.

But the unusual headache he's having increases when DaiMon Bok of the Ferengi welcomes him as the hero of the Battle of Maxia, the incident in which Picard had to abandon the *Stargazer* after it was mysteriously attacked.

To his own's crew's amazement, Bok presents the derelict starship to Picard as a gift—most unmercenary for a Ferengi. But there's method in his madness: at Maxia, Bok's son was the other captain, who was killed after attacking the *Stargazer*. Bok has forged log tapes on *Stargazer* showing Picard firing first.

As Riker, Data, and La Forge work to clear their captain, Wesley finds that energy waves from the old ship match Picard's brain scan. He has stumbled onto the other part of Bok's trap—a mind-control device planted among Picard's old belongings.

Aboard his old ship, Picard is reliving the Battle of Maxia, and is about to use the acclaimed "Picard maneuver"—but with the *Enterprise* cast as the enemy ship. Data devises a defense for the tactic, and Riker breaks through to Picard, who destroys the device.

Before leaving, they see Bok removed from command for insanity—demonstrated by his giving away the *Stargazer*.

The Ferengi do better in their second appearance, but their "silliness quotient," as Rick Berman put it, made them a "disappointment as a major adversary." Larry Forrester's first story outline included several scenes aboard the Ferengi ship, but the scenes were dropped and the chance to provide some insight into their culture was lost. No mention has ever been made of the nine years in Picard's life between the *Stargazer* abandonment and his taking command of the *Enterprise,* although several incidents are mentioned as having occurred in that era—in "The Measure of a Man" (135) and "The Wounded" (186)—including Jack Crusher's death "Family" (178).

In his second directorial outing Rob Bowman particularly enjoyed working with Stewart, who had the stage all to himself during filming of the ghostly *Stargazer* battle scenes. The director used a Steadicam in these sequences to evoke an unsteadiness—the first such use on TNG—and Legato shot each of the *Stargazer* bridge crew separately with fog and filters, which were video-composited in later.

The *Stargazer* bridge was a re-dress of the Trek movies' original bridge, previously seen in "Farpoint" as the battle bridge. The starship's four-foot filming miniature was built anew by Greg Jein from Probert and Sternbach's design after they persuaded the producers not to use the movie-style 1701-A's design; this model would turn up often as other ships.

A long-running joke had its roots in this episode: the gesture Stewart makes as he pulls his uniform's shirtwaist down when rising soon came to be called the "Picard maneuver." The episode also provides one of the most offbeat moments in the first and only "blooper reel" of outtakes to be leaked so far. While exploring a darkened corridor of the *Stargazer* as Data, actor Brent Spiner shines his light across that starship's dedication plaque and stammers in his best Jimmy "It's a Wonderful Life" Stewart voice: "For God's sake, Mary, they built this thing in Bedford Falls!"

Kazago (Doug Warhit) examines Data.

HIDE AND Q

Production No.: 111 ■ Aired: Week of November 23, 1987
Stardate: 41590.5 ■ Code: hq

Directed by **Cliff Bole**
Teleplay by **C. J. Holland and Gene Roddenberry**
Story by **C. J. Holland**

GUEST CAST
Q: **John de Lancie**
Disaster survivor: **Elaine Nalee**
Wes at 25: **William A. Wallace**

The meddling, troublesome Q returns just as the *Enterprise* is racing to help a disaster-struck mining colony—but this time his target is Riker.

The alien creates a bizarre test for the first officer and his away team by sending fanged humanoids in Napoleonic costumes to attack them. Then he tempts Riker with the Q's power and lets him use it to restore Worf and Wesley, who were killed in the "skirmish."

Riker is worried about the power's influence on him, and when the *Enterprise* reaches the survivors of the mining disaster he refuses to help revive a dead girl.

Guilt over that leads him to yield to the power, and when Q presses him to grant his friends' wishes, Picard does not object: sight for La Forge, adulthood for Wesley, a Klingon mate for Worf, humanity for Data. But, as Picard has predicted, they all turn down the gifts because of their origin—Q.

Riker understands the lesson, and a humiliated Q gets "called home" by his continuum for losing the bet. Riker's power and the crew's wishes all disappear.

Maurice Hurley used his pen name, of C. J. Holland, on this episode, a move he later called a "misunderstanding" over Gene Roddenberry's extensive rewrites. That issue was soon resolved, and in fact proved to be a turning point in the way scripts would be handled. Hurley's original story postulated that there were only three Qs but that a hundred thousand residents lived on their dying planet. Those residents needed assistance to escape their dying world.

Riker is on the spot during Q's (John de Lancie) second appearance.

Returning director Cliff Bole, who noted that the series was still trying to find its tone with this show, had prepared by reviewing Q's previous appearance in "Farpoint." However, once the episode began shooting, he found that de Lancie's affinity for the character and the actor's sheer talent made much of that work unnecessary.

It is during the head-to-head battle of wits between Picard and Q in the ready room that the title of the captain's prized display book can be read: *The Globe Illustrated Shakespeare.* What isn't so clearly visible is that the book, as usual, is opened to Act III, Scene 2, of *A Midsummer Night's Dream,* with two illustrations showing.

Although Q refers to the Federation "defeating" the Klingons, later events, such as those in "Heart of Glory" (120), suggest he is being typically sarcastic. As hinted at in "Justice" (109), Klingon foreplay is seen here as rough, at Michael Dorn's suggestion, with extra Faith Minton as the first Klingon "warrioress" depicted in TNG. In a later episode, "The Dauphin" (136), Worf would imply that it is the male who is submissive.

An admiral's dress uniform is briefly seen here for the first time, before the duty uniform debuted in "Too Short a Season" (112). As worn by Q, it has wider gold braid for the tunic flap and collar.

TOO SHORT A SEASON

Production No.: 112 ■ Aired: Week of February 8, 1988
Stardate: 41309.5 ■ Code: ts

Directed by **Rob Bowman**
Teleplay by **Michael Michaelian and
D. C. Fontana**
Story by **Michael Michaelian**

GUEST CAST
Admiral Mark Jameson: **Clayton Rohner**
Anne Jameson: **Marsha Hunt**
Karnas: **Michael Pataki**

A hostage situation on Mordan IV brings the *Enterprise* and Admiral Mark Jameson, who successfully negotiated a peace there forty years earlier, back for another case.

Unknown to Starfleet and Federation historians, Jameson actually appeased the planet leader Karnas with arms for his hostages then but kept the Prime Directive by supplying all his enemies, thus sparking four decades of civil war. Karnas doesn't need Jameson to negotiate on behalf of hostages now; the invitation is just a ruse to get him there so the governor can exact his revenge.

But the wheelchair-bound admiral has another surprise, which he has kept secret even from his wife, Anne. Another planet, grateful for Jameson's diplomacy, has revealed their de-aging compound to him, and he has been using it.

His youthfulness startles his wife and the crew until the overdoses start to backfire: his body can't take the strain.

Meanwhile, Picard arrives at Mordan and confronts Karnas with the truth, but the leader wants Jameson and doesn't believe the young man he sees before him is his enemy of so long ago. Only Jameson's display of their blood-cut scar convinces an amazed Karnas, but by now even vengeance is futile: the governor allows Jameson to die as his wife watches, and the admiral is buried on Mordan IV at her request.

Rapidly growing younger, Admiral Jameson (Clayton Rohner) draws Dr. Crusher's concern.

Michael Michaelian's original story used the reverse aging device to deal with the issue of male menopause. In that version Jameson helps Governor Zepec and his rival, the high priest, sit down to peace talks and does not die at the end. Instead, he regresses to the age of fourteen and loses all memory of his wife. Fontana tightened up the terrorism trap as the dramatic story's lure and had Jameson die for having tampered with nature.

Rob Bowman, the director, remembered being excited about working on weekends with actor Clayton Rohner to build up the character of Jameson, but otherwise he recalled the show as a "sit-and-tell" script that was long on dialogue. Other problems with this episode included a sub-par makeup look for the aged admiral Jameson and a malfunctioning $10,000 wheelchair.

Michael Pataki had previously played another K-role on the original Trek: that of Korax, Captain Koloth's aide who taunts Scotty and Chekov in "The Trouble with Tribbles."

This show marks the first appearance of a Starfleet admiral in TNG and of his duty uniform, which would eventually be revised for season two. Little used here is a miniature of the Mordan city, built by Okuda and Sternbach. This marked the last time miniatures were seen; from this point on, matte paintings were used. The wall behind Karnas's desk is lined with "old-style" phasers from the 1960s and the Trek movie eras. The Portal's Tkon-style staff from "The Last Outpost" (107) also hangs there.

THE BIG GOODBYE

Production No.: 113 ■ Aired: Week of January 11, 1988
Stardate: 41997.7 ■ Code: bg

Directed by **Joseph L. Scanlan**
Written by **Tracy Tormé**

GUEST CAST

Cyrus Redblock: **Lawrence Tierney**
Felix Leech: **Harvey Jason**
Lieutenant Dan Bell: **William Boyett**
Whalen: **David Selburg**
Lieutenant McNary: **Gary Armagnac**
Desk Sergeant: **Mike Genovese**
Vendor: **Dick Miller**
Jessica Bradley: **Carolyn Allport**
Secretary: **Rhonda Aldrich**
Thug: **Erik Cord**

Data and Beverly Crusher's lark on the holodeck almost turns deadly.

Protocol is all to the insectoid Jarada, who insist that they be greeted successfully in their own tongue without fail before diplomatic relations can begin. It has been twenty years since the Federation last tried to contact them, and the demise of the Starfleet vessel that failed is a tale so horrible that no one wants Data to repeat it.

To relieve the stress of his preparations, Picard tries a little role-playing in his favorite holodeck program, a 1940s hard-boiled detective named Dixon Hill. He is so excited after a short

Picard-as-Dixon Hill reads of his client's murder, while Data and Whalen (David Selburg) look on.

holodeck visit that he takes Data, Dr. Crusher, and literary historian Whalen back with him.

But a long-range Jaradan scan glitches the holodeck programming, and the game turns deadly: Whalen is shot by mobsters, and the party is trapped with no exit. Wesley and La Forge try to make repairs, but a wrong move would kill the players.

Finally the holodeck is opened, and the mobsters gleefully leave, intending to plunder the *Enterprise*, but of course they dematerialize. Hill-Picard's police friend, in a metaphysical twist, ponders about reality for holodeck inhabitants as he watches them go.

Still in his trench coat, Picard emerges from his stressful play at last and delivers the Jaradan greeting perfectly, to his bridge crew's applause.

This 1940s-style romp that ponders the question of existence became an instant hit with the fans and an award-winner as well. Tracy Tormé credits the initial idea of Picard's detective fantasy

It takes a holodeck glitch that creates the image of an ice planet to convince Cyrus Redblock and henchman Felix Leech (Lawrence Tierney and Harvey Jason, *rear right*) and Lt. McNary and the thug (Gary Armaganal and Erik Cord, *rear left*) that they are not real. Meanwhile, Beverly tends to literature historian Whalen's (David Selburg) gunshot wound.

on the holodeck to Roddenberry and the staff, but Tormé added some *film noir* references, including Redblock and Leech as echoes of the Sydney Greenstreet and Peter Lorre characters from *The Maltese Falcon.* He also included a metaphysical twist at the end, when the holodeck creations become self-aware.

Rob Bowman had been set to direct the segment, but it was given to Joe Scanlan at the last minute, when problems developed with "Datalore" and the two were switched in production order. The director joined Tormé in suggesting that the 1940s scenes be filmed in black and white, but Berman and Justman disagreed, noting that the holodeck could not change the real Picard and crew.

The episode was "jeered" by *TV Guide* as too derivative of an original-series episode, "A Piece of the Action," a comic turn that featured a planetary culture based on 1930s gangland Chicago. Tormé and most of fandom disagreed. The writer felt the comparison was based merely on the appearance of "three-piece suits." Eventually those suits were good enough to help snare an Emmy award for series costuming, and "The Big Goodbye" was chosen by the George Foster Peabody Award Board for its "best of the best" award—the first for an hour-long first-run drama.

The private eye was originally named Dixon Steele, an homage to the character in Tormé's favorite Bogart movie, but he was told to change it because of its resemblance to the title of a TV series, *Remington Steele.*

The Jarada themselves became a casualty of budget prob-lems; in the finished episode, they are only heard, not seen. Tormé had done a terrific amount of work on the aliens, creating a hive mind culture he wanted desperately to depict. Still, Marina Sirtis, as Troi, gets a chance to do some linguistics coaching in this episode, and Spiner, McFadden, and Stewart all get to display their rarely used comedic talents. One detail in this script almost equals the "Chinese rice picker" explanation of Spock's ears from the original-series "City on the Edge of Forever," and that is the explanation of Data's skin color: "he's from South America"!

Those with good VCRs can take note of the detailed but little seen period graphics Okuda created for the Dixon Hill computer file. Tormé is credited as the author of "The Big Goodbye," Hill's debut story, published in *Amazing Detective Stories* magazine in 1934, followed by the novel *The Long Dark Tunnel* in 1936. According to his business card, Hill's office address is Room 312, 350 Powell, Union Square, San Francisco, Calif., telephone PRospect 4631.

Known here only as "secretary," Dixon Hill's gal Friday gets a name, Madeline, in their next reincarnation, "Manhunt" (145). And O'Reilly, playing the scar-faced "second hoodlum," would return in a much more sinister role in "Reunion" (181) and "Redemption (Parts 1 and 2) (200/201). An appropriate music cue, "From Out of Nowhere," is heard as Picard enters the holodeck for the first time.

And for those who doubt the holodeck could ever work on a spatial basis: all the sets used for the Dixon Hill scenes were actually built within the confines of the holodeck stage!

DATALORE

Production No.: 114 ■ Aired: Week of January 18, 1988
Stardate: 41242.4 ■ Code: da

Directed by **Rob Bowman**
Teleplay by **Robert Lewin and
Gene Roddenberry**
Story by **Robert Lewin and Maurice Hurley**

GUEST CAST
Lieutenant Commander Argyle: **Biff Yeager**

Spiner as Lore (*right*) confronts his photo double as Data.

Data experiences an almost human expectancy when the *Enterprise* returns to his "home" planet in Omicron Theta to discover the secret behind the disappearance of its 411 colonists twenty-six years before.

An away team finds the lab of the reclusive Dr. Noonian Soong, a renegade Earth scientist who originally built a "twin" of Data's named Lore. Over time, the crew learns that Lore was disassembled at the demand of the colonists for being "too perfect." Data was the second model.

Lore's disassembled parts are found, rebuilt, and reanimated aboard the ship. But the reason for the android's original disassembly soon becomes clear—he turns Data off and assumes his identity. He then summons the huge life-draining crystal entity that destroyed the colony years before after being lured there by him as revenge for his disassembly.

Wesley senses the switch, but no one listens to him until it's almost too late. Finally his mother learns the truth and reactivates Data, but by then the crystalline being is almost upon the ship.

The two androids fight each other in a cargo bay until Lore is thrown into a wide-dispersal transporter beam. The crystalline being now has no contact with the *Enterprise*, and it departs.

By the end of season one, this episode was being cited by Berman as the one that changed the most from its inception. Lore was originally a female android, a non-lookalike love interest for

Data. Her job was to go out and repair dangerous situations à la Red Adair, the oil well fire fighter. It was Spiner who suggested the old "evil twin" concept.

Because of the delays caused by rewrites, Rob Bowman landed this segment instead of its predecessor, switching with Joe Scanlan when the two stories traded places in the shooting schedule. Though he regretted losing a chance to direct "The Big Goodbye," Bowman and Spiner met the challenge of "Datalore" and its troubled history head on. They produced a winner, thanks in no small part to an extra eighth day of shooting and to Spiner's virtuosity in the dual role.

The original back story of Data's creation by an alien race was tossed out. What emerged in its stead was the story of an android who originated in the laboratories of the Federation's most brilliant cybernetics expert, Dr. Noonian Soong. Data's positronic brain—an homage to the late sci-fi writer, Isaac Asimov—was foreshadowed as early as October 28, 1986, when Justman suggested in a memo that the author's "Laws of Robotics" be used and that a spoken credit be given. We discover in this episode that Data spent four years at Starfleet Academy, three years as an ensign, and ten or twelve years in the lieutenant grades. We also learn that only Beverly Crusher knows about his off switch. Two additional stories, "Brothers" (177) and "Silicon Anatar" (204), eventually stemmed from this episode. In addition, we learn that there is an "emergency close" vocal command that can shut the turbolift doors in a second, and that a phaser beam can be trapped within a transporter beam if timed just right. This episode would be the last of Yeager's two stints as Chief Engineer Argyle, though he had been mentioned in "Lonely Among Us" (108).

In a rare verbal blooper, Riker drops a digit from his away team log stardate, giving the date as 4124.5—the style used in the original Trek's stardates.

ANGEL ONE

Production No.: 115 ■ Aired: Week of January 25, 1988
Stardate: 41636.9 ■ Code: ao

Directed by **Michael Rhodes**
Written by **Patrick Barry**

GUEST CAST
Beata: **Karen Montgomery**
Ramsey: **Sam Hennings**
Ariel: **Patricia McPherson**
Trent: **Leonard John Crofoot**

Searching for survivors from a freighter that's been missing for seven years, the *Enterprise* visits the matriarchal planet Angel I and gets a frosty reception from its female leaders. Riker especially seems out of place as Yar and Troi handle the diplomacy, but he finds a more personal way to gain leader Beata's trust.

Survivors are found, but they refuse to return. They have taken wives from among outcasts on the planet who don't like the status quo: dominant women and submissive men.

Back aboard *Enterprise* crises break out as a virus from a holodeck file ravages the ship and Starfleet wants a response to a reported Romulan incursion near the Neutral Zone.

The renegade women are discovered and sentenced to death along with their Federation mates as enemies of society. Riker wants to intercede and violate the Prime Directive by beaming the outcasts aboard, but with the epidemic in full swing, Dr. Crusher forbids it.

Finally both dilemmas are resolved: the doctor finds an antidote to the virus, and Riker persuades Beata to forgo the death penalty. She allows the group instead to be exiled to a remote part of the planet, and the *Enterprise* warps out to counter the reported Romulan activity.

Heavy rewrites changed Patrick Barry's original story—a direct, action-filled allegory on apartheid using the sexes instead of the races to make its point. In the original, Riker beams down with an otherwise all-female away team and stops the leader, "Victoria," from striking him. Tasha immediately phaser-stuns Riker to prevent

Troi and Yar lead the away team on the matriarchal Angel One.

his on-the-spot execution by the natives. Data, with his machine nature, is held in higher esteem than Riker, who is thrown into jail with other slaves on the eve of a revolt led by the marooned human, Lucas Jones. Jones is killed after a verbal attack on Victoria, and his death inspires the rebels to strike at last as the *Enterprise* leaves. A recovered Picard, the only one taken ill in this version, is reassured by Number One that the members of his team were only witnesses to, and not instigators of, the uprising.

Except for a nice scene in which Troi and Tasha get to guffaw at Riker's revealing outfit, the revised teleplay is a one-note morality tale with yet another shipboard disease as the subplot. Director Michael Rhodes, a four-time Emmy winner on the series *Insights*, came to his TNG assignment as part of a deal with the series *The Bronx Zoo*, also shot at Paramount. He recalls that he gave Wil Wheaton his first starring role, in a 1981 ABC After School Special.

Two notes of interest in this episode: Troi remarks that Angel I's matriarchal oligarchy is "very much like" Betazed; and the Romulans are mentioned for the first time in TNG, as a reported threat in the Neutral Zone. And for students of stage design, Herman Zimmerman's cleverly designed Stage 16 sets, which were used as Soong's lab in the preceding episode, were re-dressed here and would be altered throughout the rest of the season to get even more mileage out of his budget.

1001001

Production No.: 116 ■ Aired: Week of February 1, 1988
Stardate: 41365.9 ■ Code: oo

Directed by **Paul Lynch**
Written by **Maurice Hurley and Robert Lewin**

GUEST CAST
Minuet: **Carolyn McCormick**
Commander Quinteros: **Gene Dynarski**
Zero One: **Katy Beyer**
One Zero: **Alexandra Johnson**
Zero Zero: **Iva Lane**
One One: **Kelli Ann McNally**
Piano Player: **Jack Sheldon**
Bass Player: **Abdul Salaam el Razzac**
Drummer: **Ron Brown**

The *Enterprise* visits Starbase 74 for an upgrade to the ship's computer facilities—a task that will be performed by the Bynars. They are a race grown so dependent upon computers that they work in pairs and communicate directly in binary language.

While the crew puts in for shore leave, Riker tries out a new holodeck program for a New Orleans jazz bar where he can play trombone. There he meets Minuet, a sultry brunette and the most realistic character a holodeck ever created.

Soon Picard joins them, and he is amazed at the difference the Bynars' upgrade has made—Minuet is almost too good. The reason why is soon discovered: the Bynars were using Minuet as a decoy, while faking a magnetic shield breakdown to empty the ship. The aliens' ruse works and they hijack the *Enterprise* to take them home.

To avoid its capture Picard and Riker program the ship to self-destruct. But when they emerge on the bridge, they find the Bynars not defiant, but dying.

The aliens feared an electromagnetic pulse from a nearby nova would ruin their world's master computer, so they wanted to "borrow" the *Enterprise*'s—the only mobile memory core large enough. But the pulse has already hit.

Now that they understand the problem, the officers use the ship's computer to help rejuvenate the Bynars. But Riker discovers his Minuet is gone and can't be re-created.

Another sign that both script quality and overall continuity were on the rise was this tale by Maurice Hurley and Robert Lewin in which we finally get some insight into Riker's character. The story even allows Jonathan Frakes to demonstrate his real-life trombone playing. His rendition of "The Nearness of You" would be repeated later ("Conundrum"/214), and Minuet would appear again in "Future Imperfect" (182). Number One's relationship with Minuet and his feelings about it showed that Frakes could do things with Riker if given the chance, and the Bynars and their troubled homeworld computer proved to be one plot frame that worked.

The four actors used for the Bynars were all women dancers whose voice track was mechanically lowered in pitch; initially, covert dialogue among them was designed to be subtitled. Gene Dynarski should be familiar to longtime Trek fans as Ben Childress in "Mudd's Women" and Krodak in "The Mark of Gideon" from the 1960s series. His character, who says he headed the team that put the *Enterprise* together, is given the first name of Orfil in the script.

This episode features several subtle optical effects. The *Enterprise* seen outside a Starbase 74 window is reflected in the wall controls, and Probert's painting of the docked *Enterprise* includes matted-in figures walking through the gangway tunnel. The shots of the planet Tarsas III, its moon, and the orbiting starbase are

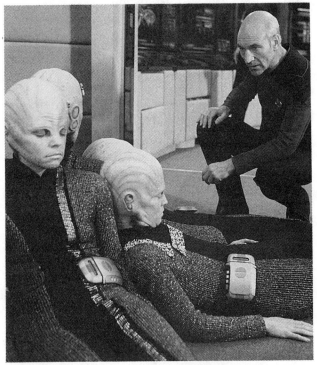

The Bynars are found near death after hijacking the *Enterprise*.

stock shots reused from *Star Trek III*. The autodestruct sequence is much more informally worded than the three-person code used in the Kirk-era's "Let That Be Your Last Battlefield" and in *Star Trek III*, and for the first time an emergency evacuation of the starship is shown. Also, a scene with a nonspeaking character named Dr. Terrence Epstein, a twenty-six-year-old research hero of Beverly's, was cut to save time, and he became only a mention.

Home Soil

Production No.: 117 ■ Aired: Week of February 22, 1988
Stardate: 41463.9 ■ Code: hs

Directed by **Corey Allen**
Teleplay by **Robert Sabaroff**
Story by **Karl Guers, Ralph Sanchez, and Robert Sabaroff**

GUEST CAST
Kurt Mandl: **Walter Gotell**
Louisa Kim: **Elizabeth Lindsey**
Bjorn Benson: **Gerard Prendergast**
Arthur Malencon: **Mario Roccuzzo**
Female Engineer: **Carolyne Barry**

The *Enterprise* is asked to check up on a remote terraforming station on Velara III that is working to transform the supposedly lifeless planet into a fertile, habitable Class M world.

But during the visit, an engineer is mysteriously killed when the laser drill in the hydraulics room goes berserk. Minutes later, Data narrowly avoids the same fate. As he and La Forge check it out, they discover what comes to be called a microbrain.

This unusual inorganic entity is a real lifeform native to the planet. As Dr. Crusher and Data investigate the aliens, the tiny being declares war on the humans. By pumping and desalinating the Velarans' narrow subsurface water ecosphere, the terraformers were killing its race.

The power it draws is strong enough to deflect the ships' transporter beam. Finally it is deduced that the microbrain is photoelectric, and a shutdown of power weakens it enough so that it can be sent home.

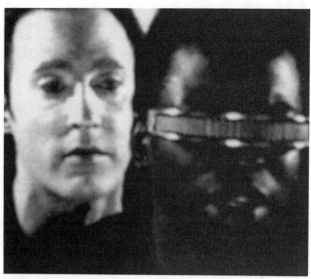

Data and La Forge discover the tiny crystalline Velara III lifeform dubbed "microbrain."

In doing so, Picard's crew promises to abide by the Velarans' request for no UFP contact for three hundred years. The planet is quarantined.

This story's theme of unintended destruction echoes that of original Trek's "Devil in the Dark," in which a silicon-based mother creature attacks the miners who are unknowingly taking her eggs. This TNG, however, was a lackluster show, which Hurley recalls as the one where just about everything that could have gone wrong did—including pages having to be rewritten the day before shooting. About the best thing this episode has going for it is an explanation of terraforming and the Velarans' name for humans: Ugly Bags of Mostly Water. Walter Gotell, who plays Mandl, will be remembered as General Gogol in the James Bond films. An unused matte painting of the Velara III station, complete with parked shuttlecraft, was prepared by Andrew Probert.

The crew finds the microbrain's growth in sickbay amazing.

WHEN THE BOUGH BREAKS

Production No.: 118 ■ Aired: Week of February 15, 1988
Stardate: 41509.1 ■ Code: wb

Directed by **Kim Manners**
Written by **Hannah Louise Shearer**

GUEST CAST
Radue: **Jerry Hardin**
Rashella: **Brenda Strong**
Katie: **Jandi Swanson**
Melian: **Paul Lambert**
Duana: **Ivy Bethune**
Dr. Bernard: **Dierk Torsek**
Leda: **Michele Marsh**
Accolan: **Dan Mason**
Harry Bernard: **Philip N. Waller**
Toya: **Connie Danese**
Alexandra: **Jessica and Vanessa Bova**

Retrieving the kidnapped children from Aldea provides a challenge for both Wesley and Picard.

The *Enterprise* stumbles across the planet Aldea, a world completely cloaked from outsiders by a powerful force-shield. But the find is no accident: the seemingly friendly Aldeans kidnap seven youngsters, including Wesley, from the ship to perpetuate their race.

Parents begin to panic as all attempts at negotiations fail. The Aldeans, convinced they are permanently sterile, stubbornly offer only to trade for the children. As a show of force, their defense system knocks the *Enterprise* three days' distance with one bolt.

But there Wesley finds holes in the Aldeans' technology: their age-old Custodian supercomputer shows wear and tear, and no one now knows how to maintain it. A secret scan by his mother shows the race is dying from radiation poisoning due to an ozone leak caused by their shield.

When Wesley organizes a hunger strike, Picard and Dr. Crusher are asked down to the planet for help. Riker and Data use the opportunity to secretly beam into a computer center, and, backed with control of the cloaking shield, the *Enterprise* crew is finally able to convince the Aldeans of the nature of their true problem.

Picard pledges UFP aid to help them regain their ecology and their health.

This was an opportunity to utilize those often ignored shipboard families that Shearer initially pitched to Fontana, and it was this story that helped win her a spot on the writing staff. A subplot involving ship separation and the saucer being held hostage was phased out to focus on the main story.

The nonspeaking young hostages included Wil Wheaton's younger siblings, Jeremy and Amy as Mason and Tara. Makeup designer Westmore's daughter McKenzie played Rose. All three youngsters' appearances were uncredited.

This was another script in which Legato would provide an impressive yet inexpensive FX solution to a story need: the Aldean computer's power room. "The script called for a 'little black box' power station, but that wasn't enough," he said. "It needed to be something that left you awestruck—but how, on a low budget?"

First Legato had a two-foot-tall model of a reactor and a cavern-shaft built with a ledge. Then he shot actors against a simple black background with a single hard white light rising on them, as if from a door opening from floor to ceiling. Next he burned their image into the black side of the model to establish the scale for a few seconds before camera picked up the live-action shooting on the set. "At three thousand dollars it was much cheaper than compositing the scene with mattes," he added.

COMING OF AGE

Production No.: 119 ▪ Aired: Week of March 14, 1988
Stardate: 41416.2 ▪ Code: ca

Directed by **Michael Vejar**
Written by **Sandy Fries**

GUEST CAST

Admiral Gregory Quinn: **Ward Costello**
Lieutenant Commander Dexter Remmick: **Robert Schenkkan**
Mordock: **John Putch**
Lieutenant Chang: **Robert Ito**
Jake Kurland: **Stephen Gregory**
T'shanik: **Tasia Valenza**
Oliana Mirren: **Estee Chandler**
Technician No. 1: **Brendan McKane**
Technician No. 2: **Wyatt Knight**
Rondon: **Daniel Riordan**

As Wesley prepares to beam down to Relva VII to take his long-awaited entrance exam to Starfleet Academy, Picard's old friend, Admiral Quinn, beams up for surprise business that he won't explain: a tough interrogation of the captain's senior officers.

Wesley learns despite losing an Academy opening to the Benzite Mordock (John Putch).

Meanwhile, Wes consoles his friend Jake, who didn't make the final cut, and begins his grueling challenge while meeting the other candidates. He's in a neck-and-neck race for the single Academy slot open, and he's nervous about the infamous psych test.

Picard, along with Riker and the crew, grow increasingly bitter over the demeanor of Remmick, Quinn's probing aide, but the admiral won't talk until he's ready. He suspects a conspiracy growing within Starfleet, and he had to test Picard's loyalty . . . before offering to make him commandant of the Academy.

Picard is flattered but wants to think it over. In the meantime, Wesley returns rejected: his success on the psych test gave him food for thought, but he came in a close second in the competition. After consoling Wesley and saving a dejected runaway Jake from a near-fatal shuttle crash, Picard decides to stay on board.

This episode provides further evidence that Wesley was already being better written as a character, thank you, and the title is indicative of TNG's emerging self-confidence as well as the story. The show marks a number of firsts for the series: the first Vulcan in a speaking role, the first retrospective look at the crew's new starship as seen through Remmick's prying eyes, the first attempt at a true continuing plotline—threads of which would be picked up in "Conspiracy" (125)—and the debut of TNG's shuttlecraft.

Filmed but cut to save time was a scene in which Wesley's friends help him celebrate his sixteenth birthday, with predictably pithy comments from Worf and Data about human birthday rituals. Also revealed here was Wesley's enjoyment of the equivalent of today's computer bulletin boards. On the trivia side, the head of Starfleet Academy carries the title "commandant," but this would later be changed to "superintendent" in "The First Duty" (219).

Original Trek fan Robert Schenkkan, whose turn as the inquisitor Remmick was so well received that he was asked to return for "Conspiracy" (125), came from the New York stage and racked up credits in the films *Sweet Liberty* and *The Manhattan Project* and in miniseries such as *George Washington*, where he played Alexander Hamilton.

The tale of this first appearance of the shuttlecraft, initially named the *Copernicus III* by Probert, is another uncanny echo of the original Trek. In both series, the building of a full-scale shuttlecraft was put off for budgetary reasons until writers made the craft an integral part of a story so that it had to be built. In the original Trek, that episode was appropriately titled "Galileo Seven." In this case, though, to save money, only a quarter of the shuttlecraft filming set was built. Added sections were made for specific story requirements during the next season, as money allowed.

Unfortunately, piecemeal construction could not match the expensive formed curves seen in Probert's miniature, and the full-scale mock-up eventually looked nothing like the small-scale model. Because of that, the majority of the live shuttlecraft filming needs would be met by the quick-and-dirty "shuttlepod" seen first in "Time Squared" (139) and later by the Magellan-class craft "Daimok" (202), though the original would turn up occasionally when a whole view wasn't needed ("The Host"/197).

HEART OF GLORY

Production No.: 120 ■ Aired: Week of March 21, 1988
Stardate: 41503.7 ■ Code: hg

Directed by **Rob Bowman**
Teleplay by **Maurice Hurley**
Story by **Herbert Wright and D. C. Fontana**

GUEST CAST
Commander Korris: **Vaughn Armstrong**
Lieutenant Konmel: **Charles H. Hyman**
Commander K'Nera: **David Froman**
Kunivas: **Robert Bauer**
Nurse: **Brad Zerbst**
Ramos: **Dennis Madalone**

Responding to signs of a battle in the Romulan Neutral Zone, the *Enterprise* finds only a battered Talarian freighter and—thanks to La Forge's new VISOR's visual feed—three Klingons, one near death. Their leader, Korris, explains that the ship was attacked by Ferengi and they were beamed away just before the ship exploded.

But after their comrade dies and Picard assigns Worf as a guide, the two survivors proclaim their hatred of the UFP-Klingon Alliance; they want to reclaim what they call the true Klingon warrior spirit. They appeal to Worf to listen to his heart and give up his life with the humans; the Starfleet Klingon is torn by their words.

Meanwhile, a Klingon Defense Force cruiser approaches and explains what really happened: the Klingons are rebels, who hijacked the Talarian freighter and destroyed a Klingon ship sent to pursue them. The two Klingons are detained, but they escape later with a homemade weapon; one is killed.

Korris, threatening to destroy the warp inter-mix chamber in Engineering, demands to be given the battle section and tries again to sway Worf, who tries to talk him out of sabotaging the ship. Korris lunges, Worf fires—and it is over.

The Klingon captain is impressed by Worf, but the lieutenant politely turns down his invitation to serve in the KDF fleet, electing to remain aboard the *Enterprise*.

At last—a Klingon show! Hurley, who spent just two days creating a teleplay based on Fontana and Wright's premise, was proud of this first-year episode, which finally shed some light on Worf's background and on the current Klingon-Federation relationship. The seeds of the Klingon saga to come are planted here with the story of Khitomer and the Romulan betrayal, and Dorn truly gets a chance to shine. This tale of personal conflict does for Worf what "The Naked Time" did for Spock back in the early days of the first series.

What may be overlooked in the later introduction of Worf's foster parents from Earth ("Family"/178) is the revelation here that he grew up with them on the farming colony of Gault and had a foster brother, still unseen, who joined him at Starfleet Academy but later left to return to the farm.

Klingon renegades Korris (Vaughn Armstrong) and Konmel (Charles H. Hyman) tempt Worf to join them.

Bowman said he lost his late-season fatigue in the excitement over this script. Again he used the Steadicam aboard the disintegrating *Batris*. He designed an elaborate sequence of vertical shots for the final battle in the multi-decked main engineering section, and he toughened up the Klingon Konmel so that three phaser hits were needed to bring him down.

Footage of the old *K't'inga*-class Klingon cruiser is lifted straight from *Star Trek: The Motion Picture*. The Klingon phrases spoken here were written without any particular pattern by Hurley, but all later Klingonese would come from Mack Okrand, the linguist who developed the alien tongue for the Trek movies and wrote *The Klingon Dictionary*. The freighter *Batris* is referred to in the episode as a Talarian craft; the Talarian race would not be mentioned again until the fourth season ("Suddenly Human"/176).

Dennis Madalone here appeared in the second of many stunt roles as various crew members; he was first seen in "Where No One Has Gone Before" (106). Outside of Trek Robert Bauer, a drummer, was in a band (The Watch) with bass guitarist Michael Dorn for a time.

THE ARSENAL OF FREEDOM

Production No.: 121 ▪ Aired: Week of April 11, 1988
Stardate: 41798.2 ▪ Code: af

Directed by **Les Landau**
Teleplay by **Richard Manning and Hans Beimler**
Story by **Maurice Hurley and Robert Lewin**

GUEST CAST
The Peddler: **Vincent Schiavelli**
Captain Paul Rice: **Marco Rodriguez**
Chief Engineer Lieutenant Logan: **Vyto Ruginis**
Ensign Lian T'Su: **Julia Nickson**
Lieutenant (j.g.) Orfil Solis: **George de la Pena**

The *Enterprise* is sent to the planet Minos to search for the missing USS *Drake*. The famed world of arms merchants hails the ship with a commercial for weapons, but surprisingly the sensors show no sentient life on the planet.

On Minos, Riker meets the *Drake*'s captain, an old friend, but quickly realizes he is dealing with a holographic projection. It transforms itself into a small flying fighter drone that encases Riker in a stasis field. The drone is destroyed, but increasingly smarter ones appear.

While fleeing them, Picard and Dr. Crusher

Yar and Data confront the Echo Papa 607's killer drones.

fall into a cavern; she's hurt and they can't get out. Above them, Data, Riker, and Yar fight off the drones, but one of them goes into orbit to attack the *Enterprise*. Left in command there, La Forge must contend with not only a green helm crew but also a pompous engineer who wants command. After separating the ship, he leaves orbit to devise a defense.

In the cavern, Picard stumbles onto the core of the mess—an automated "ultimate defense" system, which he realizes was probably responsible for killing the Minosians as well. La Forge pulls a tricky atmospheric tactic to destroy the attacking probe, just as Picard discovers the attack is an automated demonstration and ends it.

This episode was originally conceived as a Picard-Crusher love story, but Lewin recalled that Gene Roddenberry changed his mind and opted instead for this extremely ambitious action-adventure yarn/morality tale about arms merchants. Les Landau, an assistant director who became the first of many production staffers allowed to direct, suggested that it be Beverly Crusher and not Picard who is hurt in the fall into the pit, putting the captain in a "fish out of water" situation.

This fast-moving hour for once made good use of the entire ensemble, and gave Geordi his first shot at command. We also learned a little about Beverly's background, and for the last time until the fourth-season opener we saw the expensive ship-separation sequence.

The cave set was built not on Stage 16 with the aboveground exteriors but on the cargo bay set, where Stewart recalled he and McFadden had to deal with flea-infested sand. Riker also gets in a good joke, telling the image of Captain Rice that he's from the USS *Lollipop*—"it's a good ship."

SKIN OF EVIL

Production No.: 122 ■ Aired: Week of April 25, 1988
Stardate: 41601.3 ■ Code: se

Directed by **Joseph L. Scanlan**
Teleplay by **Joseph Stefano and Hannah Louise Shearer**
Story by **Joseph Stefano**

GUEST CAST
Armus: **Mart McChesney, voiced by Ron Gans**
Lieutenant Commander Leland T. Lynch: **Walker Boone**
Nurse: **Brad Zerbst**
Lieutenant Ben Prieto: **Raymond Forchion**

Tasha meets her fate against Armus (Mart McChesney, voiced by Ron Gans).

Troi and her shuttle pilot are pulled off course. They crash on Vagra II, the home of the sadistic being Armus, created from the cast-off sins of his race and then abandoned.

An away team beams down to rescue the counselor, but Armus and a forcefield of his creation are in their way. Then, acting out of sheer malice, the black oozing form of goo tortures Riker, taunts La Forge and Data—and kills Yar.

Worf, who is now acting security chief, and Wesley discover that Armus loses his power when provoked. Using that weakness, Picard is finally able to get his people out, but not before trying to reason with Armus one more time. He even has the splintered shuttle destroyed to prevent Armus from leaving the planet.

Back on board the *Enterprise*, crew members play a recorded hologram of Yar's will and her last thoughts to her friends. All of them—even Data—derive strength during their grief from their friendship with the security chief.

Long before this episode was filmed, rumors were flying about the manner of Denise Crosby's departure and the reasons for it. She was, after all, the first regular Trek character ever to be permanently killed off—the movies' resurrection of Spock notwithstanding. Thanks to media reports, it became widely known that Crosby was dissatisfied with her role's development and had asked to bow out on friendly terms so that she could pursue a film career. Shearer, who was handed the task of rewriting the original draft by *Outer Limits* veteran Joseph Stefano, said the in-house debate on the nature of her exit finally went the way Gene Roddenberry wanted, with a "senseless" but typical sudden death befitting a security chief. Originally, Tasha's demise came much earlier in the episode and the focus was more on the Armus creature than on the crew's reactions to their comrade's death.

"Gene felt we couldn't kill the creature, because it is not up to us as human beings to make a moral judgment on any creature that we encounter because we are not God," Hannah Louise Shearer has said. She added that her job was to devise a satisfactory punishment for Armus without resorting to "eye for an eye" justice.

Everyone involved in this episode knew that the look and mechanics of the alien villain Armus had to be believable if the story was to work. "You're talking about a living tar pit," recalled Legato, who felt the episode was the series' biggest special-effects flop. "It's not attractive if you do it *well*, and if it's even worse it's not even that." Director Joe Scanlan, though noting the ironic and "wonderful intellectual quality" of Armus, told the staff: "If we don't make this monster believable, we are in deep shit."[6]

A surrealistic mime-type actor modeled on the Mummenschanz group was the original concept for Armus. This was later changed to a more concrete "shroud" creature that would draw its oil slick up off the ground when arising. A plan to achieve this effect by reversing the film of a melting ten-inch figure on a hot plate had to be discarded. Finally, a grave-size pit ten feet deep was dug on the Planet Hell set and a hydraulic step was used for the rising-up effect. A mix including Metamucil was used for the black goo. Scanlan recalls that the "oil" was so heavy that actor Mart McChesney's suit began to disintegrate and new ones had to be built overnight. At one point he had to wear an open-backed costume in scenes where his back wouldn't show!

Recalling the final memorial scene, Scanlan said he filmed Tasha's "hologram tape" two ways: straight ahead, as if looking into her "holo-camera" (his preference), and the version used, in which she nods to each listener. "Don't ask me how she knew where they'd be standing," he said.[7] Still, if the sadness of the scene looked tearfully real, it was: Yar's death and Crosby's departure were sad for the actors as well as for the characters. Marina Sirtis began sobbing during reaction takes as her friend cued her from off-camera, leading Frakes and the others into one of the most moving scenes shot for the young series.

Ironically, Crosby said later that if scenes like the opening between her and Worf had been written more often, she would not have asked to leave the show. She would soon have second thoughts about departing the series, though, and would eventually find herself back in TNG through some of the most bizarre plot twists even Trek had ever come up with.

Symbiosis

Production No.: 123 ■ Aired: Week of April 18, 1988
Stardate: unknown ■ Code: sy

Directed by **Win Phelps**
Story by **Robert Lewin**
Teleplay by **Robert Lewin, Richard Manning, and Hans Beimler**

GUEST CAST
Sobi: **Judson Scott**
T'Jon: **Merritt Butrick**
Romas: **Richard Lineback**
Langor: **Kimberly Farr**

While studying drastic solar flares around De-los, the *Enterprise* picks up a confusing distress call from a disabled freighter in the system. Only four of its six passengers are beamed away in time because the crew members insist on send-ing over the cargo first.

The survivors are from two neighboring worlds, Brekka and Ornara, and the cargo is felicium, a drug grown only on Brekka, which cures a two-hundred-year-old Ornara plague. The two haggard Ornarans demand the ship-ment; the Brekkians insist the deal's off.

The desperate Ornarans convince Picard to mediate; he gets them one dose apiece. But Dr. Crusher realizes the "cure" is a narcotic. The Brekkians have kept the unknowing Ornarans addicted for profit for two centuries!

Crusher demands to let the Ornarans know, but Picard cites the Prime Directive. He does find a solution to the dilemma, however: he refuses

Merritt Butrick returned to Trek as T'Jon, one of the "addicted" Ornarans.

to repair the Ornarans' remaining freighters. Now no trade in the low-technology system will occur and the Ornarans, although they will suffer withdrawal, will conquer their addiction.

This episode will likely be remembered for three things: the teaming of two *Star Trek II* actors in guest roles, the late Merritt Butrick (his name was misspelled in the credits as "Merrit") and Judson Scott; the overbearing Nancy Reagan–era "Just Say No" anti-drug speech Tasha gives Wesley; and the *real* last scene for Denise Crosby.

Butrick, who reprised his role as Kirk's son, David Marcus, in *Star Trek III,* died after a long illness in March 1989, barely a year after filming this episode. Judson Scott, uncredited as one of Khan's followers in *Star Trek II,* played the lead in the series *The Phoenix.* In an uncredited speaking role, veteran character actor Kenneth Tigar appears as Margan, an Ornaran leader.

Because this story was filmed *after* "Skin of Evil" but would air *before* it, Crosby's real last scene as Tasha came in the cargo bay in act five. She can be seen wildly waving good-bye from behind a console just as the cargo bay doors close behind Picard and Crusher! Her name would continue to be listed in the opening screen credits for the rest of the season.

WE'LL ALWAYS HAVE PARIS

Production No.: 124 ■ Aired: Week of May 2, 1988
Stardate: 41697.9 ■ Code: wa

Directed by **Robert Becker**
Written by **Deborah Dean Davis and Hannah Louise Shearer**

GUEST CAST

Jenice Manheim: **Michelle Phillips**
Dr. Paul Manheim: **Rod Loomis**
Gabrielle: **Isabel Lorca**
Lieutenant Dean: **Dan Kern**
Edouard: **Jean-Paul Vignon**
Francine: **Kelly Ashmore**
Transporter Chief Herbert: **Lance Spellerberg**

The romance that didn't quite click: Jenice Manheim (Michelle Phillips) and Picard.

While the ship is traveling to Sarona VII for shore leave, a bizarre time loop distortion causes a literal déjà vu effect on the *Enterprise*. Soon after this, the ship receives a distress signal from Dr. Paul Manheim's science outpost on Vandor IV.

They rescue Manheim and his wife, Jenice, who turns out to be an old love of Picard's. But the nonlinear time experiments Manheim and his now-dead team were conducting not only ended in disaster on Vandor, but were responsible for the disturbance that the *Enterprise* experienced earlier. Those disturbances now threaten to spread and rip open the interdimensional fabric of space.

Manheim himself is dying, since his body can't deal with the strain of partial interdimensional existence. On top of that, Picard's unresolved feelings for Jenice—he stood her up in Paris to ship out with Starfleet twenty-two years ago—are left hanging by a therapeutic session on the holodeck. Even Dr. Crusher finds herself jealous of Jenice.

Finally, using Manheim's directions, Data beams into the Vandor lab to reseal the center of the dimensional breach with a hunk of antimatter; although he finds himself in three time continuums at once, he sorts it all out and succeeds.

Manheim is instantly cured, and he and Jenice prepare to begin his work again. And this time, thanks to the Parisian holodeck program, Picard gives Jenice a proper good-bye.

If this story doesn't quite come off as another *Casablanca* (the source for the episode's title), it's not surprising. Shearer and her friend Deborah Dean Davis, who originally pitched the idea, wrote the script on five days' notice, aiming for an "utterly romantic" story, but she says the teleplay was "toned down 75 percent."[8]

As late as the final draft, dated February 22, Jenice's name was Laura, Riker was Picard's fencing partner, Paul Manheim was much more of a loose cannon, Picard and Jenice actually spent a night together, and Troi confronted Beverly about her feelings for the captain, which she had not yet sorted out. The crew reversed the Manheim effect by first bypassing a multilevel laser-guided security system; Worf then held open a door to cool an overheated silolike power room while Riker scaled the tower to switch out a chip and Data input commands to the system below.

Completed just a week before filming began, the revised script suffered again when the Writers Guild strike of 1988 shut down production on the climactic scene—Data's repair of the ripped time stream in Manheim's lab—because the dialogue and special effects had not yet been tied down!

"We just ran out of script," Legato recalled. "It was one of those 'We'll fix it when we get there' things, and suddenly we were there, and the writer was out on the picket lines. The director had never worked with effects before; I had to do it. I ran over to Rick Berman's trailer and said, 'We're out of script!' We spent forty minutes. We got the writer on the phone and Rick would say, 'Well, you weren't on strike, the character might say this,' and she'd say yes or no. I had to make up [the direction] on the spot. I came out with handwritten notes, I figured out how to shoot the three Datas in different time-streams with a whip-pan instead of an effects shot."

Shearer and others complained that a lack of chemistry between Jenice and Jean-Luc diluted the story's romantic feel, but Michelle Phillips, who played Jenice, felt the problem lay in the story's conception; while her character wanted to see Picard again, and was quite willing to tease him, she was also fully committed to her husband and had been for a long time.

Phillips, an original-Trek fan who was one of the Mamas and the Papas, a 1960s group, began her acting career in 1970. Her roles include the miniseries *Aspen,* the film *Bloodlines,* and one season on *Knots Landing.* Rod Loomis, who acted in his first play while in the army, is best known for playing a confused Dr. Sigmund Freud in *Bill and Ted's Excellent Adventure.* Lance Spellerberg appeared a year later as the same transporter chief, Ensign Herbert, in "The Icarus Factor" (140).

The matte painting of twenty-fourth-century Paris seen in the holodeck nicely combines the old Eiffel Tower with the new antigrav craft flying by. Eduoard's Okudagraph menu included joke items such as Croissants D'ilithium, Targ Klingon à la Mode, and Tribbles dans les Blankettes.

Conspiracy

Production No.: 125 ▪ Aired: Week of May 9, 1988
Stardate: 41775.5 ▪ Code: co

Directed by **Cliff Bole**
Teleplay by **Tracy Tormé**
Story by **Robert Sabaroff**

GUEST CAST
Admiral Savar: **Henry Darrow**
Admiral Quinn: **Ward Costello**
Lieutenant Commander Dexter Remmick: **Robert Schenkkan**
Admiral Aaron: **Ray Reinhardt**
Captain Walker Keel: **Jonathan Farwell**
Captain Rixx: **Michael Berryman**
Captain Tryla Scott: **Ursaline Bryant**

Picard realizes alien invaders have also possessed Captain Scott (Ursaline Bryant).

Picard is disturbed when his old friend Walker Keel summons him to a secret meeting with two other captains on a deserted planetoid, but he warily agrees. The subject? The trio's suspicion, much like Admiral Quinn's on Relva VII, that a conspiracy is spreading within Starfleet. Picard is skeptical until Keel's ship explodes and Data finds a disturbing pattern among command orders. Picard makes a decision: the *Enterprise* will return to Starfleet Command on Earth to check the suspicions firsthand.

Three top admirals, including Quinn, greet the ship with surprise and invite Picard and Riker down for dinner to discuss their concerns. But something does not feel right.

Then all hell breaks loose: the crew discovers that Quinn, aboard the *Enterprise* for a visit, is controlled by a tiny intelligent parasite, whose presence is revealed only by a quill-like protrusion from the host's neck.

Picard walks into a trap set by the other two admirals and Remmick, Quinn's former aide,

but a fake "quill" on Riker helps him foil the ambush. Soon the admirals are dead, along with Remmick, who housed the mother creature.

Quinn is cured and Starfleet saved, but the aliens' source and purpose remain a mystery.

This, the first moody episode of the series and one of its darkest ever, almost didn't come to be. The idea began as a one-sentence idea from Gene Roddenberry called "Assassins," which Robert Sabaroff fleshed out to a thirty-page treatment. Unfortunately it was deemed too expensive to produce, and Tormé got the assignment of starting the process all over again. Tormé said some on staff thought his treatment too dark, too bizarre; the assignment was going to someone else until GR read and loved it.[9]

Planned to push the limits as a hard-edged thriller, the story was originally inspired by *Seven Days in May,* and the conspirators were not aliens but members of a faction within Starfleet—all Picard's friends—who rebel against the Prime Directive and Federation-wide complacency following the Klingon detente. Ironically, although GR ruled against painting Starfleet in such dark colors, just such a conspiracy within the service later became a major plot point in the movie *Star Trek VI: The Undiscovered Country.*

The mail brought some cries against the gory scenes of death and worm-eating, but Tormé took issue with *Variety* for labeling it TNG's "most notorious" episode so far. Remmick's "hosting" of the mother alien and his exploding head were added later in post-production; originally, Picard and Riker were to meet up with the full-grown mother creature.

Henry Darrow, the first to play a speaking Starfleet Vulcan character and deliver the legendary neck pinch in TNG, has a long résumé that includes roles in the daytime soap *Santa Barbara* and the part of Manolito on the 1960s series *High Chaparral.* Jonathan Farwell, whose character introduced Jack Crusher to Beverly, was another longtime Trek fan and veteran guest star. He appeared in *The King and I* opposite Yul Brynner and on *The Young and the Restless.*

The Probert-designed Ambassador-class starship was first mentioned here as Keel's ship, the *Horatio* already having been designated as the *Enterprise*-C's class ("Yesterday's Enterprise"/ 163). The FX shots of Earth and spacedock and the matte painting of Starfleet Command were all from the Trek movies; the banquet room's heavy doors with inset etched-glass ovals would be used on the standing set for Ten-Forward, which was built during hiatus.

Though the story left room for a sequel, the parasites have never been seen again.

THE NEUTRAL ZONE

Production No.: 126 ■ Aired: Week of May 16, 1988
Stardate: 41986.0 ■ Code: nz

Directed by **James L. Conway**
Television story and teleplay by **Maurice Hurley**
From a story by **Deborah McIntyre** and **Mona Glee**

GUEST CAST
Commander Tebok: **Marc Alaimo**
Sub-Commander Thei: **Anthony James**
L. Q. "Sonny" Clemonds: **Leon Rippy**
Clare Raymond: **Gracie Harrison**
Ralph Offenhouse: **Peter Mark Richman**

The first glimpse of Romulans in fifty-three years: Thei (Anthony James) and Tebok (Marc Alaimo).

As the *Enterprise* awaits Picard's return from a special briefing, Data can't resist investigating a three-hundred-year-old capsule that floats by. Three humans are found frozen inside the capsule. They are the only survivors of the fad of cryogenic preservation for the terminally ill.

But the last thing Picard needs is a sideshow of relics; his return brings news of disappearing outposts and the suspicion that at long last the Romulans are returning to activity along the Neutral Zone.

The revived humans have their own problems: a broker demands access to his money, a homemaker misses her kids, a bored country singer wants to party. Picard relies on Troi and Data to help solve their problems while he deals with another challenge: a cloaked Romulan ship, the UFP's first contact with its old foes in fifty-three years. A tense exchange yields the information that outposts are disappearing on the Romulan side of the Neutral Zone as well. The two sides agree to exchange information in the future, but the Romulans leave no doubt they mean to be reckoned with again.

With tensions eased somewhat, the *Enterprise* heads back, arranging a long ferry ride to Earth so its three new passengers will have enough time to get used to their new home century.

Hurley recalled putting this script together in a day and a half, a rushed and possibly unrefined casualty of the continuing Writers Guild strike. Originally, the rendezvous with the Romulans had been discussed as the first of a multi-part story that would have united the two governments against the newly discovered Borg, who were developed as a replacement for the disappointing Ferengi. The strike nixed that idea, though, and the Borg had to wait (Q Who/142). References to the pattern of their destruction, however, remained in the script. The subplot of the revived twentieth-century Americans—criticized by some as too reminiscent of the original Trek's "Space Seed"—came from a fan story by Deborah McIntyre and Mona Glee.

Peter Mark Richman once starred in the series *Cain's Hundred* and has racked up more than five hundred television guest roles, from *The Twilight Zone* and *Perry Mason* to *Bonanza* and *Mission: Impossible* and even to *Three's Company*, where he played Suzanne Somers's father. Leon Rippy appeared in both parts of *North and South* with Jonathan Frakes and in Steven Spielberg's *The Color Purple* as the storekeeper with eventual TNG cast member Whoopi Goldberg.

Sharp-eyed fans may notice a longer-than-usual shot of a skant-wearing female sciences officer departing a turbolift. That's Susan Sackett, a writer and Gene Roddenberry's personal assistant since 1974. She got the walk-on after winning a bet over losing weight. A TNG staff member until GR's death in late 1991, she would later contribute two episodes with writing partner Fred Bronson ("Ménage à Troi"/172, "The Game"/206).

In this episode Data makes history of another kind when he mentions the current Earth year as 2364—yet another sign that after more than twenty years, the many loose ends of Trek's background were being tied down once and for all. We also learn from Data here, ironically, that television had "died out" by 2040.

Finally, fans knew the Romulans' boast—"We're back!"—was no idle threat when their new vessel, eventually dubbed a Warbird, turned up here. Probert's size-comparison sketch comparing it to the 1701-D is dated March 25, 1988, and the miniature, which Greg Jein built, was released a year later by AMT as a plastic kit, along with the Ferengi and Klingon Bird of Prey vessels. The ships boast the new Romulan crest: a stylized bird of prey clutching the twin homeworlds of Romulus and Remus, one in each claw.

All the models were enhanced by Legato's first use of a moving camera on TNG for visual-effects sequences, allowing objects to move in relation to one another as the crews began getting away from the lock-off static shots needed in compositing the old stock-library elements.

Notes

1. Dave McDonnell, *Starlog*, No. 133, August 1988, p. 24.

2. Mark Dawidziak, *Cinefantastique*, March 1989, p. 26.

3. Eduard Gross, *Starlog*, No. 152, March 1990, p. 29.

4. *TV Guide*, July 23, 1988, p. 40.

5. For a visual evolution of the Ferengi through Probert's sketches, see *OFCM*, No. 60, February-March 1988, p. 7.

6. Gross, *Starlog*, No. 135, October 1988, p. 45.

7. Gross, p. 48.

8. Mark Altman, *Cinefantastique*, March 1989, p. 61.

9. Altman, p. 61.

PRODUCTION STAFF CREDITS—FIRST SEASON

(In usual roll order; numbers in parentheses refer to episode numbers.)

Main Title Theme: +**Jerry Goldsmith and** *** Alexander Courage**
Music: **Ron Jones (103, all even-numbered episodes, 106–126, except 112); Dennis McCarthy (101–102, all odd-numbered episodes, 105–125); George Romanis (112);** ***Fred Steiner (104)**
Director of Photography: **Edward R. Brown, A.S.C.**
Production Designer: **Herman Zimmerman**
Editor: **Tom Benko (101–102, 107, 110, 113, 116, 119, 122, 125); David Berlatsky (105); J. P. Farrell (103, 106, 109, 112, 115, 118, 121, 124); William Hoy (108, 111, 114, 117, 120, 123, 126); Randy Roberts (104)**
Unit Production Manager: **David Livingston (101–118); Kelly A. Manners (119); Bruce A. Simon (120); Sam Freedle (121–126)**
First Assistant Director: **Les Landau (101–102, 104, 106, 108, 110, 112, 116, 118, 124, 126);** ***Charles Washburn (103, 105, 107, 109, 114); Babu (T.R.) Subramaniam (111, 113, 115, 117, 119, 121, 122, 125); Bruce A. Simon (120, 123)**
Second Assistant Director: **Babu Subramaniam (101–110); Brenda Kalosh (109–114); Bruce A. Simon (111–118); Larry M. Davis (115–122); Bob Kinwald (119–122); Robert J. Metoyer (123–126); Adele G. Simmons (123–126)**
Costumes: ***William Ware Theiss, Executive Consultant (EMMY WINNER: "The Big Goodbye" [113])**
Art Director: **Sandy Veneziano (101–109, 120–126)**
Assistant Art Director: **Gregory Pickrell (110–118)**
Visual Effects Coordinator: **Robert Legato (101–111, 113, 116, 118, 120, 122, 124, 126); Dan Curry (112, 114, 115, 117, 119, 121, 123, 125)**
Post-Production Supervisor: **Brooke Breton**
Set Decorator: ***John Dwyer**
Makeup Supervisor: **Michael Westmore**
Makeup Artist: +**Werner Keppler (EMMY WINNER: "Conspiracy" [125])**

Hair Designer: **Richard Sabre**
Hair Stylist: **Joy Zapata (101–105); Carolyn Ferguson (106–126)**
Production Assistant: +**Susan Sackett**
Consulting Senior Illustrator: +**Andrew Probert**
Illustrator: +**Rick Sternbach**
Scenic Artist: +**Michael Okuda**
Set Designer: **Richard McKenzie (101–122); Louis Mann (123–126)**
Script Supervisor: **Cosmo Genovese**
Special Effects: *+**Dick Brownfield**
Costume Supervisor: **Janet Stout (101–106); Elaine Scheiderman (107–115); Ed Sunley (117–126)**
Key Costumer: **Phil Signorelli (114–116); Richard Butz (117, 120, 122, 124); David McGough (118, 119, 121, 123, 125, 126)**
Camera Operator: **Lowell Peterson (101–102)**
Property Master: **Joe Longo (101 and all even-numbered episodes); Alan Sims (all odd-numbered episodes except 101)**
Chief Lighting Technician: **Richard Cronn**
First Company Grip: **Brian Mills**
Sound Mixer: **Alan Bernard, C.A.S. (all except 114); Dean Gilmore (114)**
Music Editor: **John LaSalandra, S.M.E. (101–114); Gerry Sackman (115–124)**
Supervising Sound Editor: **Bill Wistrom (101–118, 120–121, 123–125)**
Sound Editor: **James Wolvington; Mace Matiosian; and Wilson Dyer (105, 112–126) EMMY WINNERS (with crew): "11001001" [116])**
Casting Executive: **Helen Mossler**
Casting Associate: **Elisa Goodman (120–126)**
Production Coordinator: **Diane Overdiek**
Construction Forepersons: **Steven Monroe and John Clayton (101–102)**
Construction Coordinator: **Al Smutko (103–126)**
Special Visual Effects: +**Industrial Light and Magic (ILM) a division of Lucasfilm Ltd.**
Video Optical Effects: **The Post Group**
Special Video Compositing: **Composite Image Systems**
Editing Facilities: **Unitel Video**
Post-Production Sound: **Modern Sound**
Casting: **Junie Lowery**

---

[*] denotes a veteran of the original Trek series; [+] indicates a veteran of one or more Star Trek films.

SECOND SEASON

Its shakedown season over, TNG was

on its way as not only a worthy successor to its namesake but also a commercial hit, ending its debut year as the number one first-run hour-long series in syndication and the number three syndicated show over all, behind game show kings *Wheel of Fortune* and *Jeopardy*.

Unfortunately, what precious momentum had finally built up during the stretch run of season one would now be lost through no fault of the staff: a strike by the Writers Guild went unsettled for six months through spring and summer, delaying the TV industry's fall 1988 schedule. Having already caused problems during the tail end of the premiere year, the strike forced the studio to cut TNG's second season back from twenty-six shows to twenty-two, and even at that the writing staff had to dig out the decade-old scripts in storage from the abortive *Star Trek II* series to see what might be usable (see "The Child"/ 127).

Many changes were made for the show's sophomore year. A

Second-season group portrait *(opposite)*. Gates McFadden (Dr. Crusher) is gone, replaced by Diana Muldaur's Dr. Pulaski.

new doctor, Diana Muldaur's Katherine "Kate" Pulaski, came aboard to replace Gates Mc-Fadden's Beverly Crusher. Also added to the cast was longtime fan Whoopi Goldberg as Guinan, hostess in the new Ten-Forward lounge; her character was named for the popular nightclub owner and hostess "Texas" Guinan. Commander Riker gained a beard when the producers liked the one Frakes came back with from vacation, and Wesley was given a new, West Point–inspired uniform. Geordi was promoted to chief engineer, ending the absence of a regular character in that position, and Worf's promotion to security chief was made permanent. Worf also acquired a new, twenty-pound "baldric" sash, and Troi received a much-welcomed wardrobe and hairstyle change, ending her affectionate cast nickname— "old bunhead."

McFadden's departure was said to be no reflection on her as an actress. "There were those who believed at the end of the first season that they didn't like the way the character was developing, vis-à-vis Gates's performance, and managed to convince Mr. Roddenberry of that," Rick Berman said years later, adding: "I was not a fan of that decision." By way of contrast, the new doctor, Kate Pulaski, was created somewhat in the image of Bones McCoy, as crusty and transporter-wary, and the second-season writers' guide even gave her three children by three different men. But while the sparks she brought were welcome, the handling of the change angered many fans and fired up the show's first real protest letter-writing campaign.

In addition to having guest-starred as two doctors on the original series—Dr. Anne Mulhall in "Return to Tomorrow" and Dr. Miranda Jones of "Is There in Truth No Beauty?"—Muldaur had most recently spent one season in a recurring role on the short-lived but highly acclaimed series *A Year in the Life*. Although she's no stranger to Broadway and film, she is perhaps best known for her TV work: regular stints on *McCloud* and *Born Free* and guest spots on series such as *Murder, She Wrote*, *Hart to Hart*, *The Master*, *Charlie's Angels*, and a Gene Roddenberry pilot, *Planet Earth*. She was also the first woman to be elected president of the Academy of Television Arts and Sciences, the organization that awards the Em-

mys. Runner-up for the part of Kate Pulaski, a choice that Berman recalled as "a very tough decision," was Christina Pickles, a regular on *St. Elsewhere*.

But while the switch in doctors got most of the fans' attention, the world at large was taking note of the new *Enterprise* bartender. The addition of Goldberg, a longtime Trek fan, to the cast was even more serendipitous. The news of Denise Crosby's departure prompted Goldberg to let the producers know—through her friend LeVar Burton—that she'd like to join the cast. Disbelieving, they ignored her until she finally called the TNG office and said, "Hey, I know I'm no blonde, but . . . !"

A 1991 Academy Award winner for *Ghost* and an Oscar nominee and Golden Globe winner for *The Color Purple*, superstar Goldberg also has an Emmy nomination and a Grammy on her résumé. She credits Nichelle Nichols, who played Uhura, original Trek's communications officer, as a childhood inspiration for her. In addition to the acting awards, she has been honored in many ways for her devotion to causes. Those honors include the 1989 Starlight Foundation Award as Humanitarian of the Year for her work in behalf of children, the homeless, human rights, and AIDS.

Both Diana Muldaur and Whoopi Goldberg received "special guest appearance" billing at the end of the opening guest credits. Muldaur declined the offer to be listed with the regular cast in the opening title.

Meanwhile, there were further changes in the writing staff as the series tried to generate some energy once the writers' strike finally ended. During the hiatus Robert Lewin had left the series because he felt it was moving away from character shows and toward action-adventure. Hannah Louise Shearer also left, though she contributed a story during each of the next two seasons: "Pen Pals" (141) and "The Price" (156).

Along with Gene Roddenberry, of course, the returning team included Rick Berman and Maurice Hurley, Peter Lauritson, David Livingston, and, also on the writing side, Tracy Tormé, who later relinquished his title of co-executive story editor for the looser status of a "creative consultant" after a clash with Hurley over the script for "The Royale" (138). Meanwhile, Burton Armus began the second season as a producer, but relinquished that role for the season's last nine segments to Robert L. McCullough after overlapping with him on "Time Squared" (139).

That episode was also the last show for staff newcomers John Mason and Mike Gray, who had served as writing coproducers for the first thirteen shows of the year. Beginning two episodes later with "Pen Pals" (141), two positions for executive script consultants were created and filled by Hans Beimler and Richard Manning, longtime Trek fans who had been story editors for the last eight shows of season one. In addition, Leonard Mlodinow and Scott Rubenstein

By Season Two a moving "star field" was added outside the windowed sets.

worked as story editors from "The Outrageous Okona" (130) onward until Melinda Snodgrass, a science fiction novelist, was added in that capacity after selling the impressive script for "The Measure of a Man" (135). After four more shows, Mlodinow and Rubenstein left, and Snodgrass, another original series fan, carried the title alone for the rest of the season.

Around the sets modifications took place as well: the bridge was fitted with new, swiveling Conn and Ops chairs that had a less severe backward slant; the captain received a more distinctive command chair that better fit Stewart's body, with armrest panels permanently mounted open instead of hinged; and, to allow the new chief engineer an occasional piece of the bridge action, the aft stations were also redesigned. From portside inward, the outer three stations were now Engineering, Environment, and Mission Ops rather than Environment, Emergency Manual Override, and Propulsion Systems. The custom-built observation lounge now included built-in viewscreens, and Sternbach contributed the painting behind the bar in the new Ten-Forward lounge: an abstract portrait of the Milky Way galaxy.

As TNG settled in and found its stride, confidence rose in all quarters, including those of hardworking art staffers Sternbach and Michael Okuda. Both enjoyed inserting in-jokes, homages, and occasionally pure double-talk into a

Whoopi Goldberg on the set with her "inspiration," Nichelle Nichols.

TNG graphic or design when they could get away with it. In particular, Sternbach turned his interest in *animé,* or Japanese animation—an adult, well-crafted genre that has its own large following of fans—into innocuous and barely visible references in graphics and props. He most often made reference to:

- Kei and Yuri, female secret agents code-named "Lovely Angel" but known as the Dirty Pair for the mess they leave their assignments in—drawn, incidentally, by animators who include similar original-Trek in-jokes in their work.
- *Space Cruiser Yamamoto,* the story of Earth's defense against aliens that was aired in America as *Star Blazers.*
- The film *No Totoro,* ("My Neighbor Totoro") which concerned a mythical, catlike nature sprite who befriended two lonely little sisters.
- The film *Nausicaa of the Valley of Wind* about a princess who grows up in a secluded valley on an Earth otherwise devastated by biological warfare, where insects are now the dominant species.

THE CHILD

Production No.: 127 ■ Aired: Week of November 21, 1988
Stardate: 42073.1 ■ Code: tc

Directed by **Rob Bowman**
Written by **Jaron Summers, Jon Povill, and Maurice Hurley**

GUEST CAST
Lieutenant Commander Hester Dealt: **Seymour Cassel**
Ian Andrew Troi: **R. J. Williams**
Transporter Chief: O'Brien: **Colm Meaney**
Miss Gladstone: **Dawn Arnemann**
Guinan: **Whoopi Goldberg**
Young Ian: **Zachary Benjamin**
Engineering Ensign: **Dore Keller**

The *Enterprise* is ferrying samples of a deadly plasma plague for study when Troi stuns the crew by announcing she's pregnant.

What she describes as a glowing white light impregnated her during sleep. According to new chief medical officer Kate Pulaski, the fetus will grow full term in just thirty-six hours. As Picard and his officers debate the security concerns raised by the "invader," Troi announces flatly she's having the baby.

The counselor has a remarkably easy birth—her son, Ian, appears completely harmless but continues his unusual growth rate, aging eight years in twenty-seven hours.

Almost oblivious to all of this is young Wes Crusher, who seeks counsel from the mysterious new Ten-Forward hostess, Guinan, about whether to join his mother, who has left to head Starfleet Medical. He finally decides to stay on board.

Meanwhile, one of the plague samples inexplicably begins to grow—threatening to break its containment and infect the crew within two hours.

It turns out that Ian—or at least, the life-force that took the form of the human child to learn more about humans—is a stimulus for the viral sample's growth. A tearful Troi watches Ian revert to his real form; the virus stops growing, and the ship's mercy mission can be finished.

During the writers' strike, "The Child" was chosen from among the old unused *Star Trek II* series scripts to be turned into a season opener, although Hurley stated his rewrites proceeded from premise, not from the original outline.[1] Instead of Troi, of course, in the original tale the "immaculate conception" happens to the first Trek movie's Deltan navigator Ilia—yet another parallel between the two female characters, who already share an empathic trait and similar onetime love interests, Decker and Riker. That original final draft story of January 9, 1978, opened with the same glowing light that was used here, but in that case the fast-growing baby was causing the ship's hull to turn to powder. Overseen by a nearby probe via an "umbilical" scanner beam, the child was being made to develop through its race's past stages of evolution prior to noncorporeality.

Meanwhile, Ron Bowman, the director, secured permission to film this season opener with extra camera work and equipment, including the impressive opening shot, and he credited Marina Sirtis with meeting the challenge of an expanded role for Troi. By making her son her father's namesake, the writers let us know that Troi's father was named Ian Andrew.

Wesley asks Guinan whether he should join his mother at Starfleet Medical.

Epsilon Indi, one of the stars seen by Guinan and Wesley in this episode, was home to the extinct pirates in "And the Children Shall Lead," an original-Trek episode, and is traditionally the home star of the Andorians, thanks to nonfiction written by fans. Among the unreadable Okudagrams are references to several TNG staffers: the four associates of the mutated plague strain's developer are Drs. Bowman, Hurley, Summers, and Povill (the latter two were the writers of the original *Trek II* story) and the plague is believed to be related to the "Legato infection" or the "Hutzel infection."

Where Silence Has Lease

Production No.: 128 ■ Aired: Week of November 28, 1988
Stardate: 42193.6 ■ Code: ws

Directed by **Winrich Kolbe**
Written by **Jack B. Sowards**

GUEST CAST
Nagilum: **Earl Boen**
Ensign Haskell: **Charles Douglass**
Transporter Chief: **Colm Meaney**

En route to the Morgana Quadrant, the *Enterprise* suddenly finds itself inside a black void without form or dimension—a void that is unending and inescapable, no matter which direction the ship turns.

A sister ship, the USS *Yamato*, appears in the void, and Riker and Worf investigate. But the ship is part of the trap, and the men find themselves in a maze of repetition that nearly drives Worf mad with its illogic.

Finally the presence behind the void appears: Nagilum, an entity who wants to study humans' reaction to death.

The superalien, who appears on screen only as vaguely humanoid facial sections separated by darkness, announces he will use from one-third to one-half of the crew for his experiments. After much soul-searching, Picard regretfully begins the autodestruct sequence with Riker, and later outwits images of Troi and Data sent by the alien to argue against the move.

With just two seconds to spare before autodestruct, the soft-voiced entity suddenly frees the ship, saying he has learned enough about human nature by watching the crew's preparation for death. In one final debate, a relieved Picard tells Nagilum that they do have one trait in common: curiosity.

Trapped in Nagilum's void, Picard's officers weigh their options.

ELEMENTARY, DEAR DATA

Production No.: 129 ■ Aired: Week of December 5, 1988
Stardate: 42286.3 ■ Code: ed

Directed by **Rob Bowman**
Written by **Brian Alan Lane**

GUEST CAST
Moriarty: **Daniel Davis**
Lestrade: **Alan Shearman**
Ruffian: **Biff Manard**
Prostitute: **Diz White**
Assistant Engineer Clancy: **Anne Elizabeth Ramsay**
Pie Man: **Richard Merson**

After the *Enterprise* arrives three days early for a scheduled rendezvous, La Forge persuades Sherlock Holmes fan Data to use the extra time playing the role of the detective on the holodeck, with the engineer as Watson.

But Holmes's original cases are no challenge to Data's memory, so Dr. Pulaski—who has yet to accept the android as anything more than a machine—challenges him to solve a new, computer-generated case. La Forge obliges by programming a case that's a challenge match for Data: a Professor Moriarty who takes on consciousness. Holmes's archenemy not only kidnaps Pulaski in a bid to become real, but also threatens to take over the *Enterprise* with a Victorian gadget that can control the ship from within the holodeck.

In top hat and tails, Picard enters the program to confront Moriarty and convinces him his plan is useless because of the construct's true nature. A mellowed Moriarty, already transcending his character's fictional bounds, relents but asks to be recalled if a process for solidifying holodeck creations into real matter is ever found—and the captain agrees.

TNG newcomer Winrich Kolbe, whose distinctive accent earned him a nickname, "the Baron," on the set, put his years of directorial experience to good use in fighting the claustrophobia of this budget-minded "bottle show." Penned by *Star Trek II* coauthor Jack Sowards, the only scenes that take place off the *Enterprise* are aboard a sister ship!

According to Hurley, this superalien's name is the reverse spelling (minus one *l*) of Mulligan. The name was chosen because actor Richard Mulligan, the star of *Soap* and *Empty Nest*, was originally sought to play the role.

This episode also introduces Worf's soon-to-be-famous holodeck combat-calisthenics program, which will be seen later in "The Emissary" (146) and "New Ground" (210). The autodestruct sequence seen in "11001001" (116) is repeated here, but with a flexible countdown time; the device has not been used since. Whether included as yet another homage to the original *Star Blazer*'s flagship or even its namesake, the World War II Japanese battleship, the starship *Yamato*'s NCC number given here was 1305-E. In a rare continuity error, the number was changed nine shows later, in "Contagion" (137) to 71807.

Data's initial fascination with Sherlock Holmes ("Lonely Among Us" /108) goes a step further here, as does the planned Pulaski-Data friction. The ending originally filmed was dropped from the version aired: the paper with Moriarty's sketch of the *Enterprise* is

Data proves his Holmesian prowess to Pulaski, while La Forge's Dr. Watson looks on.

significant not because of what he's drawn but for the fact that it exists off the holodeck. Picard is then aware that the character can somehow be saved, as opposed to the gone-awry holodeck images of "The Big Goodbye" (113), and so his explanations to Moriarty were seen as a lie by Gene Roddenberry, who didn't want Picard to stoop to deception. The climax leaves the ship's fate purely up to the captain's persuasiveness and Moriarty's newfound good sense.

To make up for having lost "The Big Goodbye" the previous season, director Rob Bowman grabbed this period piece when offered a choice of early-season shows. The wondrous Victorian London set was built on Stage 16 in just three days. Workers toiled around the clock with fiberglass and plaster to build the street, two side alleys, the warehouse, a wharfside, and the entrance to Moriarty's lair, and after two days of filming the over-budget $125,000 set all came down again.

Sadly, the popular Holmes milieu will likely not be used again on TNG for legal reasons. After this segment aired, Paramount received notice that the Arthur Conan Doyle estate still owns a percentage of the rights to the Holmes character, after nearly a century, and would require a usage fee if it was ever used again.

Anne Elizabeth Ramsay's character, Engineer Clancy, turned up again later as a command-division bridge ensign at the conn in "The Emissary" (146).

THE OUTRAGEOUS OKONA

Production No.: 130 ■ Aired: Week of December 12, 1988
Stardate: 42402.7 ■ Code: ok

Directed by **Robert Becker**
Teleplay by **Burton Armus**
Story by **Les Menchen, Lance Dickson, and David Landsberg**

GUEST CAST
Captain Thaduin Okona: **William O. Campbell**
Debin: **Douglas Rowe**
Kushell: **Albert Stratton**
Yanar: **Rosalind Ingledew**
Benzan: **Kieran Mulroney**
Lieutenant B. G. Robinson: **Teri Hatcher**
The Comic: **Joe Piscopo**
Guinan: **Whoopi Goldberg**

Near the twin Madena planets, the *Enterprise* picks up young trader Thaduin Okona while helping him repair his small craft. The roguish charmer quickly makes friends, especially among the female crew members.

Intrigued by Okona's wisecracks, Data lets Guinan talk him into a stint on the holodeck as a comic. He conjures up a twentieth-century comedy club and a stand-up of the day to coach him.

Meanwhile Picard faces a confrontation that's more of a headache than a crisis: the two hotheaded leaders of Madena's twin worlds are demanding Okona's hide. Straleb's ruler accuses him of stealing their sacred Jewel of Thesia, while Atlec's raves that Okona made his daughter pregnant.

Picard faces the exasperating prospect of the two tiny vessels actually opening fire on his ship or each other, until an inquisitive Wes Crusher persuades the trader to "fess up."

Okona baits the Straleb leader's son into admitting everything: the two fearful children used Okona as go-between for their romance and used the jewel as a nuptial vow.

With the two planets now bound for union, a Data despondent over his bad luck with humor unintentionally spouts a Gracie Allen nugget—and cracks up the bridge.

Destined to soar three years later in Disney's *Rocketeer,* William O. Campbell—no relation to the same-named actor behind the original Trek's Squire Trelane and Klingon Captain Koloth—had almost been cast as Riker when the regulars were being assembled. Rick Berman, echoing Justman's recollection, said that the studio executives, who had the final say, considered their runner-up "too soft." Funny, if a bit predictable, and helped by the misplaced arrogance of the two planet's leaders, this teleplay by producer Burton Armus features a main plot that actually has to compete for attention with the subplot of Data's holodeck comedy adventures.

Joe Piscopo, the *Saturday Night Live* veteran, does a good turn as a buck-toothed Jerry Lewis character. Lewis himself was to have played the part, but a schedule conflict with his guest spot on the show *Wiseguy* got in the way.

In-jokes include the Charnock Comedy Cabaret sign, which honors crew paint foreman Ed Charnock, Jr., and a holodeck menu of "humorists" taken from the office phone directory for the TNG staff, producers, and aides; the file chosen is actually that of visual-effects associate Ronald B. Moore. And when Data asks for the funniest performer available, those listed besides "Stano Riga"—seen only briefly—include the Great Bird himself as well as Maurice Hurley and Farouk El-Baz, a planetary geologist at Boston University who, during his NASA days, worked with Berman on a documentary and who later had a shuttlepod namesake in "Time Squared" (139).

Of the three vessels seen, Okona's *Erstwhile* is a re-dress of the Talarian *Batris* ("Heart of Glory"/120); Debin's Atlec ship is the merchant ship from *Star Trek III,* with more length; and Kushell's Straleb ship was new, a design Rick Sternbach said was simply modeled after "a big Easter egg."

Another of Greg Jein's contributions turns up here in the background: a tridimensional chess set that's a tip of the hat to its original-Trek cousin. This set, however, features among its pieces the Jupiter II spacecraft from *Lost in Space* for bishops. The kings are modeled after the robot from that same old sci-fi series.

Data experiments
with humor.

THE SCHIZOID MAN

Production No.: 131 ▪ Aired: Week of January 23, 1989
Stardate: 42437.5 ▪ Code: sm

Directed by **Les Landau**
Teleplay by **Tracy Tormé**
Story by **Richard Manning and Hans Beimler**

GUEST CAST
Dr. Ira Graves: **W. Morgan Sheppard**
Lieutenant Selar: **Suzie Plakson**
Kareen Brianon: **Barbara Alyn Woods**

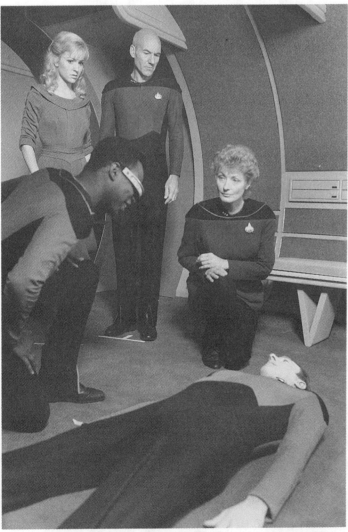

Kareen (Barbara Alyn Woods) and the crew find Data unconscious.

Dr. Noonian Soong may have been Data's "father," but the brilliant Dr. Ira Graves turns out to be Soong's mentor and Data's "grandfather."

Graves is dying of a terminal illness when the *Enterprise* answers his young female aide's call for help on their secluded research world.

Once he arrives on the planet, Data becomes close to Graves, leading the genius to reveal his last breakthrough: a device capable of transferring a human personality into a computer.

Graves dies, and his assistant, Kareen Brianon, is evacuated. But Data begins to act irrational, even accusing Picard of lusting after the beautiful Kareen. A diagnostic check of Data reveals nothing, but Troi performs a psych test that shows two competing personalities fighting to control Data: his own and Graves's.

Meanwhile Kareen is shocked when Graves-Data tells her of the transference, his love for her, and his plans to make her immortal by transferring her consciousness into another android body—which she refuses to consider.

That triggers his violent denial of the wrongness of his plans. After unintentionally crushing her hand, he hides in Engineering, rendering La Forge and an aide unconscious before Picard discovers him.

Graves knocks Picard out for arguing for the release of Data's body, but when the captain comes to, he finds the cyberneticist has reconsidered—and put himself into the *Enterprise* computer as simple data.

The tale of Ira Graves and the transfer of his intellect into Data began with Richard Manning and Hans Beimler, who wrote a concept called "Core Dump." During the rewrite process, this concept was combined with a separate but similar story that Tracy Tormé had pitched. In that tale, "Ménage," a woman comes aboard who once had a triangular love affair with two men from Omicron Theta, the now-dead colony whose memories are stored within Data ("Datalore"/114). The memories grow so strong when Data is in her presence that the two men's personalities fight for control of him.

The role of Kareen was the first that onetime Chicagoan Barbara Alyn Woods auditioned for when she arrived in Los Angeles—a departure from the "bimbos and wild girls" that, in her words, she had played in films like *Circuitry Man* and on series like *Hooperman* and *Crime Story*.

Suzie Plakson's Dr. Selar was the first female Vulcan officer ever heard in Trek, but the actress would later go on to infamy on TNG as a member of another alien race in "The Emissary" (146) and in "Reunion" (181). Tormé has since revealed that he wanted to develop a romance between Selar and Worf, but that suggestion was nixed. Suzie Plakson counted the national tour of *Stop the World, I Want to Get Off*, opposite Anthony Newley, as a highlight among her improv comedy, regional theater, Broadway, and off-Broadway credits. She later went on to guest spots on *Murphy Brown, Beauty and the Beast*, a recurring voice on *Dinosaurs*, and a role in the film *My Stepmother Is an Alien*, and then won a starring role in the fall 1992 sitcom *Love and War*.

A subplot in Tormé's script involved Data's lack of ego; trimmed along with several of the scenes featuring Data's beard was the original tag scene—already a legendary TNG story—in which he is seen trying yet again to emulate an admired and respected crew member. In this scene, to Picard's chagrin, the android is bald.

LOUD AS A WHISPER

Production No.: 132 ▪ Aired: Week of January 9, 1989
Stardate: 42477.2 ▪ Code: lw

Directed by **Larry Shaw**
Written by **Jacqueline Zambrano**

GUEST CAST
Riva: **Howie Seago**
Warrior/Adonis: **Leo Damian**
Woman: **Marnie Mosiman**
Scholar: **Thomas Oglesby**
O'Brien: **Colm Meaney**
Warrior No. 1 (Blond Solari leader): **Richard Lavin**
Warrior No. 2 (Brunette Solari leader): **Chip Heller**
Lieutenant (Traitor Solari): **John Garrett**

His Chorus dead, Riva (Howie Seago) ponders his next move.

To help settle a civil war, the *Enterprise* is sent to retrieve the great Ramatisian mediator Riva, whose résumé extends to negotiating early UFP-Klingon treaties.

The crew is surprised to learn, though, that Riva and his ruling family were born deaf and use a three-member telepathic chorus to communicate: the Woman, the Scholar, and Warrior/Adonis. The latter informs Troi that Riva is taken with her.

But an incident on strife-torn Solais V wrecks the peace mission and Riva's self-confidence as well when a terrorist opens fire, killing the chorus.

The loss sends Riva into a fit of grief and helplessness. Data learns to read his frantic signing, but Picard cannot draw Riva out. When the mediator even refuses Troi's attempts to help, she opts to try the mission herself.

Plying Riva for negotiating hints, she inspires him to use his own main strategy: "turn a disadvantage into an advantage."

Reinvigorated, Riva beams down alone, determined to start from scratch and teach both Solais factions his sign language, no matter how long it takes.

Howie Seago, who is actually deaf, met with the producers during the writers' strike to suggest a show built around a deaf actor as a guest star. This episode is the result, and in it Seago helped to change what he felt was a dangerous myth regarding deaf people: the first draft's premise had his character learning to speak overnight after the failure of a mechanical translator he used to communicate with his chorus. The day before shooting he suggested an alternative scenario, where after the killing of his chorus Riva stays on Solais V to teach the combatants sign language. To his surprise the idea was eagerly accepted; the supportive mail from both deaf and hearing people seemed to bear out the wisdom of that idea.

Marnie Mosiman kept her TNG guest role in the family: she's the wife of John "Q" de Lancie. Richard Lavin had previously appeared as the second mediator in "Justice" (109).

LeVar Burton campaigned for a time for a story line that would let Geordi's sight be restored so that he as an actor could utilize his expressive eyes, and Pulaski's claim here that she might be able to surgically restore his sight seems to be a preparation for that. It would never happen, though, as Burton grew to understand that the VISOR was an advantage for the character. He also realized that Geordi had become a role model for the blind and for other handicapped people—much as Uhura, in the original series, became an inspiration for Whoopi Goldberg and other black women and indeed for all women.

Look quick: Riva's "indigenous rock" table includes markings alluding to Kei and Yuri (more *animé!*), and one of Riva's hand signs to Data is the Vulcan spread-fingered greeting turned sideways! The mediator's youthful appearance is somewhat baffling, however. Like Sarek later (171), Riva is credited with many of the early UFP-Klingon treaties.

UNNATURAL SELECTION

Production No.: 133 ■ Aired: Week of January 30, 1989
Stardate: 42494.8 ■ Code: us

Directed by **Paul Lynch**
Written by **John Mason and Mike Gray**

GUEST CAST
Dr. Sara Kingsley: **Patricia Smith**
Transporter Chief: **Colm Meaney**
Captain Taggert: **J. Patrick McNamara**
Transporter Ensign: **Scott Trost**

Answering a distress call from the USS *Lantree*, the *Enterprise* finds by visual scans that the supply ship's entire crew has died of old age.

Mysterious "hyperaging" has also hit the ship's last stopover, the Darwin genetics lab, where the stricken staff begs to have its genetically bred "superchildren" rescued, after assuring the *Enterprise* crew the children do not carry the disease.

A skeptical Picard wants the children checked anyway; to avoid crew contamination Data pilots a shuttle so that Dr. Pulaski can examine one child in isolation.

But the youth and his "siblings" turn out to be infected, and the crew is shocked when Pulaski herself is quarantined at Darwin to help with the cure research.

Picard is not willing to accept the loss of his chief medical officer. He pushes his people to modify the transporter biofilter to screen out the virus. A hair sample finally provides the necessary pre-infection DNA, and the doctor and the lab staff are eventually cured.

Sadly, the fate of the Darwin youth cannot be so easily reversed, and because of the health threat, the "superchildren" must be isolated forever.

Dr. Pulaski shows the effects of the Darwin viral hyperaging.

The Darwin "superchildren" were originally to have appeared nude and the extras were asked to shave from the neck down. But the use of transparent furniture quickly nixed that idea, and costumes were hastily made as the extras endured stubble itch. The youth who was brought aboard the *Sakharov* was played by actor George Baxter and had a name, David, but in a budget crunch all his lines were cut to save money.

A MATTER OF HONOR

Production No.: 134 ■ Aired: Week of February 6, 1989
Stardate: 42506.5 ■ Code: mt

Directed by **Rob Bowman**
Teleplay by **Burton Armus**
Story by **Wanda M. Haight, Gregory Amos, and Burton Armus**

GUEST CAST
Ensign Mendon: **John Putch**
Captain Kargan: **Christopher Collins**
Lieutenant Klag: **Brian Thompson**
O'Brien: **Colm Meaney**
Tactics Officer: **Peter Parros**
Vekma: **Laura Drake**

In a new exchange program, Riker becomes the first Starfleet officer to serve aboard a Klingon vessel. He throws himself into the job, taking a crash course in Klingon culture and cuisine from Worf.

Meanwhile, the same program brings the young Benzite Mendon aboard the *Enterprise* but a cultural difference nearly destroys the ship when he lags in reporting the presence of hull-eating bacteria.

Aboard the Klingon cruiser *Pagh*, Riker uses Worf's lessons to gain respect from his new captain and subordinates. He enjoys a hearty meal with the *Pagh* crew and banters with its women, but the discovery of the bacteria on the Klingon ship leads its captain, Klag, to brand Riker a traitor and order an attack on the *Enterprise*.

Riker uses an emergency transponder given to him by Worf to beam Klag off the bridge when he dismisses the *Enterprise*'s warnings—making

In one last gesture, the *Enterprise* returns to the *Lantree* and solemnly atomizes the plague ship with full Starfleet ceremony.

An echo of an original-series episode, "The Deadly Years," this story almost let the proverbial "cat out of the bag" by using the transporter to reconstruct a "younger" Dr. Pulaski. To avoid a stream of endless complications (unlimited duplication of the characters, for one), specific limitations were later laid down on the use of this technology. The script is the only dual effort by John Mason and Mike Gray during their half-season stint as coproducers.

TNG's first named shuttlecraft is called the *Sakharov*, in honor of the late Soviet physicist and human rights advocate Andrei Sakharov, and a little more interior space has been added.

Riker confronts his Klingon "captain," Kargan (Christopher Collins).

Riker captain long enough to demand the "surrender" of the Starfleet ship to preserve the Klingons' honor.

A shrewd student of culture, Riker takes an uppercut from the returned Klag to let him regain his crew's respect, and Mendon makes amends by helping find a solution to the bacteria, saving both ships.

Maurice Hurley intended this story to be a reverse spin on Worf's situation aboard a human ship, and it became one of the bright spots of the second season, scoring a 12.2 rating—TNG's highest to that point—on the Nielsen Television Index used for syndicated programs. This episode gave Jonathan Frakes his meatiest role to date; he and director Rob Bowman both sank their teeth into it. "Every day it was Jonathan and I doing high-fives and trying to put forth on film all the energy and the spirit and adventure that was in that script," the director said. In one particularly nice scene

Riker trains on the firing range as he tries to become ambidextrous in his use of the phaser.

The completed episode, as often happens, ran too long and had to be cut by several minutes; the deleted scenes included the engine room of a miniature Klingon Bird of Prey.

A ladder aboard the *Pagh* in one scene is actually a bike rack Bowman picked up off the Paramount lot. And Klingons are heard here to use kilometers as a unit of measurement, even though kellicams had been used in *Star Trek III* and would later reappear in "Redemption" (200). The heart of a targ, Worf's onetime pet animal ("Where No One Has Gone Before"/106) is a delicacy in this episode, while *gagh* (pronounced "gakh") worms are said to taste best when served alive. Later, in "Family" (178), we learn that rokeg blood pie is one of Worf's favorite foods.

After seven outings, Meaney's character finally gets a last name, O'Brien; another two years would pass before viewers learned his first and middle names (178). Vekma's fellow female Klingon, a nonspeaking character, is named Zegov. And John Putch, who appeared as Ensign Mendon, made TNG trivia history by becoming the first guest star to appear twice as a member of the same alien race but in a different role (see "Coming of Age"/ 119); how convenient that some Benzites really do look alike.

THE MEASURE OF A MAN

Production No.: 135   ■   Aired: Week of February 13, 1989
Stardate: 42523.7   ■   Code: mm

Directed by **Robert Scheerer**
Written by **Melinda M. Snodgrass**

GUEST CAST
Captain Phillipa Louvois: **Amanda McBroom**
Admiral Nakamura: **Clyde Kusatsu**
Commander Bruce Maddox: **Brian Brophy**
O'Brien: **Colm Meaney**
Guinan: **Whoopi Goldberg**

Data's rights as a sentient being are questioned when Commander Bruce Maddox, a cyberneticist, wants to disassemble the android to make duplicates for Starfleet.

When Maddox seems uncertain of his ability to reassemble Data, the *Enterprise* second officer refuses to submit to his experiment and resigns from Starfleet. But that resignation is made moot when Maddox gets a ruling that the android is Starfleet property under a three-hundred-year-old law.

Picard is ready to tackle that decision in a court of law, but the insufficient legal staff at the new starbase forces Riker to serve as both prosecutor and defender. On top of that, the base's judge advocate general, Captain Phillipa Louvois, is an old flame of Picard whose zeal in handling the USS *Stargazer* inquiry years before split them up.

Riker, warned to do his best or see a summary judgment in Maddox's favor, dramatically proves that his second officer is just a machine by removing one of Data's arms and then turning him off completely.

Picard has all but conceded until Guinan helps him see that Maddox's plan for an army of androids without rights would amount to slavery.

Confident again, Picard successfully argues that all beings are created but not owned by their creator. Later he and Louvois agree to a dinner date, while Data assuages Riker's guilt for taking part in the prosecution's case.

Below: Picard argues Data's rights before Commander Maddox (Brian Brophy) and Captain Louvois (Amanda McBroom). *Opposite; top:* Captain Louvois ponders her decision. *Bottom:* Riker "proves" Data is nothing but a machine.

Writer Melinda Snodgrass drew on her own experience as an attorney to craft this timeless tale of personal rights. This episode, which marked her TV debut, was nominated for a Writers Guild award. Now an established SF novelist, Snodgrass hit the *New York Times* best-seller list with her first book, *Tears of the Singers,* also set in the Trek universe. She has coedited the Wild Cards SF book series with friend and fellow SF-fantasy author George R.R. Martin, a producer on TV's *Beauty and the Beast.*

Guest star Brian Brophy, who may be best known to genre fans as Traker from *Max Headroom,* earlier played a doctor on the "good" side of the research ethics question in the film *Paranoia.* His Maddox character, who is actually more impulsive than villainous, has since popped up occasionally. In "Data's Day" (185) he is corresponding with the forgiving android all the way from the Daystrom Technological Institute—an homage to computer genius Richard Daystrom from the 1960s episode "The Ultimate Computer."

Amanda McBroom, a longtime Trek and SF fan, had a recurring role on *Hawaii Five-O* and won the 1980 Golden Globe for co-writing "The Rose," the hit Bette Midler song from the movie of the same name. A Broadway actress, she had guested on *M★A★S★H, Hart to Hart, Remington Steele, Magnum P.I.,* and *Taxi.*

During the trial, Data is forced to reveal his on-off switch to Picard and Riker ("Datalore"/114) as well as his intimate encounter with the late Tasha Yar in "The Naked Now" (103); he keeps a small copy of the hologram she recorded for her memorial service. Here we learn that Data's Starfleet awards include decorations for valor and for gallantry; the Medal of Honor, with clusters; the Legion of Honor; the Starcross; and three others seen in a case. His computer file, as viewed by Riker, refers to the android as NFN NMI Data; the initials stand for No First Name, No Middle Initial. And, for computer buffs, Data's storage capacity is said to be 800 quadrillion bits, with a rating of 16 trillion operations per second!

The regular poker game among Picard's officers is seen here for the first time, as is the redesigned flag officer's uniform. An attempt is also made—here with a novel and later, in "Up the Long Ladder" (144), with love poetry—to reestablish an ethnic-pride joke for Worf and the Klingons, a successor to the original Trek's Russian joke for Chekov and the short-lived French joke for Picard.

THE DAUPHIN

Production No.: 136 ■ Aired: Week of February 20, 1989
Stardate: 42568.8 ■ Code: dp

Directed by **Rob Bowman**
Written by **Scott Rubenstein and Leonard Mlodinow**

GUEST CAST
Anya: **Paddi Edwards**
Salia: **Jamie Hubbard**
O'Brien: **Colm Meaney**
Crewman Aron: **Peter Neptune**
Anya as Teenage Girl: **Mädchen Amick**
Anya as Furry Animal: **Cindy Sorenson**
Ensign Gibson: **Jennifer Barlow**

A diplomatic mission provides the setting for Wesley's first romance when the ship must ferry home a princess and her overprotective guardian.

As Troi worries that the two passengers are not what they seem, Wesley seeks advice on how to handle his emotions. Meanwhile, the princess's guardian Anya grows irrational at any hint of danger to Salia.

When Anya transforms herself into a dangerously violent creature to challenge Worf, Dr. Pulaski realizes that Salia's people are allasomorphs, or shape-changers.

To avoid a fight, Picard orders Wesley to stay away from Salia, but Wesley cannot, and their meetings continue until Anya discovers them. When Salia matches Anya's transformation with one of her own, Wesley is stunned, and he deserts her.

Wes at first rebuffs Salia's apologies for having deceived him, but he finally overcomes his pride and brings her a peace offering: another bowl of the chocolate mousse they once enjoyed together.

This simple story by the early-season story editors at last gives Wesley a contemporary problem and his first romance. It was a special thrill for Wil Wheaton: not only was it the sixteen-year-old's

first screen kiss but actress Jamie Hubbard was ten years his senior! "Dauphin" (pronounced doe-fan¹), incidentally, was the title given to the eldest son of the king of France from 1349 to 1830. The original Trek had included at least two references to shapeshifters: the people of Antos IV in "Whom Gods Destroy" and the Vendorians in "The Survivor," an episode of the animated series.

Seen only briefly here, Mädchen Amick—Hubbard's runner-up for the role of Salia—would go on to much more exposure as Leo Johnson's unfortunate wife Shelly on *Twin Peaks*.

The folks at the Post Group stayed extra busy with "The Dauphin," adding a seventh twenty-hour day to their week to create the shape transformations and the world the young couple visits on the holodeck. Two of the ten shots required for the Rousseau V asteroid ring required over 110 layers each, while some twenty-five steps were needed for each of the allasomorphs' seven transformations. Still, Rob Bowman thought the monster outfits looked cheap and reduced their screen time as much as possible.

An unusual touch is seen in Wes Crusher's quarters: just as Anya resumes her shape, you can see on the shelf behind her a display cube with an old-style Kirk-era phaser and communicator.

Wesley with his first love (Jamie Hubbard).

CONTAGION

Production No.: 137 ■ Aired: Week of March 20, 1989
Stardate: 42609.1 ■ Code: cg

Directed by **Joseph L. Scanlan**
Written by **Steve Gerber and Beth Woods**

GUEST CAST
Captain Donald Varley: **Thalmus Rasulala**
Sub-Commander Taris: **Carolyn Seymour**
Tactical Ensign: **Dana Sparks**
O'Brien: **Colm Meaney**
Doctor: **Folkert Schmidt**

Crossing the Neutral Zone to answer an SOS from the USS *Yamato*, the *Enterprise* arrives in time to see widespread computer malfunctions destroy its sister ship.

When log tapes from the *Yamato* reveal that its captain had tracked the mythical planet Iconia to this location, Picard has his ship retrace the *Yamato*'s course: discovering the secrets of the extinct Iconian civilization would be worth risking an encounter with the Romulans. But after the same computer malfunctions begin to plague the *Enterprise*, La Forge realizes that an Iconian probe's energy burst infected the *Yamato* with a computer virus that rewrote that ship's control software. By downloading the *Yamato*'s logs, the *Enterprise* has now become infected as well.

A desperate Picard beams down with Worf and Data to a control tower on long-dead Iconia, where they discover a time gateway. There Data becomes infected with the Iconian virus as well.

Meanwhile, the crew is forced to raise shields and strand the away team when a Romulan ship suddenly attacks the *Enterprise*. But Riker soon learns the enemy vessel is also crippled by the virus.

Picard decides to destroy the control tower and the remaining Iconian probes, but first returns Data and Worf to the *Enterprise* through the time gateway. Once Data arrives back on

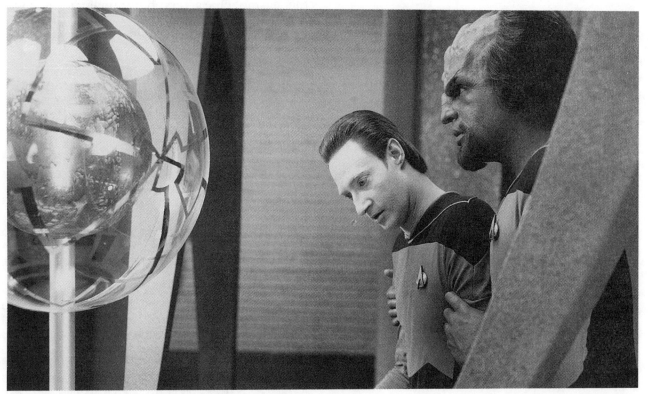

Iconia's computer virus infects Data as well as his ship.

board ship, his self-correcting function eradicates the Iconian virus in his system; that reminds La Forge that the ship's computers have the same capability.

The *Enterprise* regains transporter capability in time to rescue Picard from the planet below. The Romulans, of course, offer no thanks for the virus cure that saves them as well.

Appropriately enough, this story was conceived by a fan and computer technician (Beth Woods) who works on the Trek offices' computer systems. It also introduces another Picard interest, archaeology, which will figure prominently in two later episodes, "Captain's Holiday" (167) and "Qpid" (194). Carolyn Seymour would also turn up later as a member of a different alien race in "First Contact" (189).

This segment features Picard's first oral food-slot order for "Tea, Earl Grey—hot," and the first-ever name of a Romulan ship in twenty-three years of aired Trek: *Haakona*. A familiar character, Commander Bruce Maddox, is already being mentioned as a genius after his debut earlier in the season in "The Measure of the Man" (135).

Rick Sternbach designed the Iconian gateway with lots of Japanese inscriptions that refer to numerous *animé* titles and characters. And the names of the show's cowriters, Steve Gerber and Beth Woods, can barely be seen in the list of *Yamato*'s log entries, as the ship's first and second officers.

THE ROYALE

Production No.: 138 ■ Aired: Week of March 27, 1989
Stardate: 42625.4 ■ Code: ro

Directed by **Cliff Bole**
Written by **Keith Mills**

GUEST CAST
Texas: **Nobel Willingham**
Assistant Manager: **Sam Anderson**
Vanessa: **Jill Jacobson**
Bellboy: **Leo Garcia**
O'Brien: **Colm Meaney**
Mickey D: **Gregory Beecroft**

Puzzled by the recovery of a chunk of a twenty-first-century Earth spacecraft, Worf, Data, and Riker beam down into the middle of the lone structure they find on the nearest uninhabited planet.

After passing through a revolving door set in an otherwise black void, they cannot escape from what appears to be a resort casino named the Hotel Royale.

Bizarre scenes now unfold before them: a clichéd love triangle, gamblers who invite the Starfleet men to join them, and finally the discovery of a twenty-first-century American astronaut's remains in a hotel suite.

There Data also finds a book entitled *The Hotel Royale*, and the pieces of the mystery begin to fall into place.

By reading the astronaut's diary, the away team learns that aliens found his disabled ship and created a world in which he could live out his life. Unfortunately they used the badly written pulp mystery as their model.

As the love triangle resolves itself yet again with a mobster gunning down a bellboy, the trapped crewmen find a way to break the time-loop trap. Using the novel's ending, in which foreign investors buy the Royale, Data returns to the craps tables and breaks the bank, angering the casino characters but allowing the away team to exit for beam-up.

This story was supposed to be surreal, but if it comes across as merely unfocused, it's not surprising. The name of writer "Keith Mills" is a pseudonym of Tracy Tormé, who reportedly removed his name from the script after Maurice Hurley objected to its surrealism, comedy, and subtle satire. Hurley later said he thought it too derivative of the copycat aliens in the original-Trek episode "A Piece of the Action." The original story was good, but it was a budget-buster, according to director Cliff Bole. Later, Bole was reminded of his years directing *Vega$* when the "Royale" script took a budget cut that resulted in a casino built out of "curtains and some tricks."

The dispute led Tormé to leave active staff duty and take on a looser, nonexclusive role as a creative consultant with a commitment to just three more episodes; he would complete only one, "Manhunt" (145).

In the original final draft of "The Royale," completed on January 10—one of two scripts that had won Tormé a staff job during TNG's first season—the astronaut survivor was actually the last of his crew of seven to die. His image was then kept alive in this macabre setting, to be entertained by the captured *Enterprise* party. In the end, as with Pike and Vina in the original-Trek pilot, "The Cage," a dead away team crew woman is retained to keep the astronaut company after the unseen casino manager agrees to tell the story and release the crew.

In that early draft Dr. Pulaski at one point was supposed to say,

Data's high rolling
intrigues Vanessa
(Jill Jacobson).

"I'm a doctor, not a magician"—harking back to DeForest Kelley's Dr. McCoy, but that line was lost in the revisions.

Lending sparkle to this outing is veteran character actor Nobel Willingham, who has played many film and TV roles. He appeared on *Northern Exposure* in 1992 as Maurice Minnifield's former U.S. Marine commander.

Despite the story's unevenness, much Federation and Earth history is revealed here. As seen in Colonel Stephen Richey's uniform patch, the United States is said to have had fifty-two states in the years between 2053 and 2079, the year the "new" United Nations fell—see "Farpoint" (101). Richey's flight, launched on July 23, 2037, and overseen by NASA with its 1970s-era logo, was the third to try to push outside the solar system. Given the series' date, according to "The Neutral Zone" (126), his death 283 years earlier would have occurred in 2082.

By the way, for math fans: the missing proof for Fermat's Last Theorem, devised by the seventeenth-century inventor of differential calculus and differential geometry, would show that $x^n + y^n = z^n$ where $n>2$ and x, y, and z are whole numbers.

TIME SQUARED

Production No.: 139 ▪ Aired: Week of April 3, 1989
Stardate: 42679.2 ▪ Code: tm

Directed by **Joseph L. Scanlan**
Teleplay by **Maurice Hurley**
Story by **Kurt Michael Bensmiller**

GUEST CAST
O'Brien: **Colm Meaney**

In a bizarre turn of events, Picard is confronted by his own double from six hours into the future, out of phase and disoriented after being recovered from a shuttlecraft that has recorded the *Enterprise*'s destruction in a vast energy whirlpool.

The double Picard, dazed in a nightmare world, cannot communicate what happened, and the real-time captain begins to fear that the ship will become trapped in a time loop.

When the energy whirlpool appears on schedule and the *Enterprise* cannot escape, Picard al-

Stewart poses with his photo double/future self.

almost becomes bogged down with indecision and second-guessing.

Energy bolts attacking Picard lead Troi to suggest it is he the whirlpool wants, but when his double tries to leave the ship, Picard decides his departure "again" will only perpetuate the cycle. After stopping "himself" with a phaser stun, he orders a full-speed course directly into the vortex. After one more moment of self-doubt, the double Picard, his craft, and the whirlpool all vanish, leaving *Enterprise* alone and on course, just as before.

———

This story—originally titled "Time to the Second"—began as the first of what Maurice Hurley had planned as two consecutive but stand-alone episodes. "Time Squared" would segue into "Q Who" (142), in which the mischievous superalien is revealed as the cause of the vortex. That plan was scrapped at Gene Roddenberry's insistence, Hurley has said, and so adds confusion to the ending. "Why would going into the vortex's center save you?" Hurley asked. "It doesn't make sense. But it does if Q is pulling the strings." Still, the writer said his intent was to do a time-travel story involving just six hours, not "500 or a 1,000 years."

A cheaper alternative to the full-size shuttlecraft, the low-budget shuttlepod, debuted here. The vessel is named for one-time NASA scientist Farouk El-Baz, who had earlier received a tip of the hat in "The Outrageous Okona" (130). According to Michael Okuda, the professor sounded very surprised the morning he called in from Boston University after he and his children had seen the show for the first time!

This segment also mentions the slingshot time-travel method used in the original Trek and in *Star Trek IV*, and introduces Riker's fondness for cooking.

THE ICARUS FACTOR

Production No.: 140 ■ Aired: Week of April 24, 1989
Stardate: 42686.4 ■ Code: if

———

Directed by **Robert Iscove**
Teleplay by **David Assael and Robert L. McCullough**
Story by **David Assael**

———

GUEST CAST
O'Brien: **Colm Meaney**
Kyle Riker: **Mitchell Ryan**
Ensign Herbert: **Lance Spellerberg**

When Riker is offered command of his own ship, the *Enterprise* heads for Starbase Montgomery to meet with the civilian strategist who will brief him on the assignment. That strategist turns out to be his father, Kyle, whom Riker hasn't seen in fifteen years. Time has not softened the first officer's hostility toward the older man, and he summarily rejects his father's efforts at reconciliation.

As Dr. Pulaski—an old flame of Kyle's—and Troi ponder why Number One is so bitter, Wesley, La Forge, and Data try to diagnose the reason for Worf's increased tenseness.

Pain-dealing holodeck Klingons help Worf celebrate his
Age of Ascension.

When they discover that Worf is out of sorts because he missed a ritual marking the decade since his Age of Ascension, they surprise him by setting up a reenactment of the Klingon spiritual rite on the holodeck.

As Troi and Pulaski compare notes on "their men," Riker's continued rebuffs lead Kyle to challenge his son to an anbo-jyutsu match—a martial art the younger man never beat him at.

The two finally resolve their feelings for each other, and Number One stuns the bridge crew by revealing his intention to turn down the offered command post and remain aboard *Enterprise*.

Here's another case where a subplot—Worf's Age of Ascension ceremony on the holodeck—almost overshadows the main story line, the return of Riker's father. The segment is good in that it reveals Number One's back story and brings Pulaski closer into the fold of characters, but it's hard to compete with Klingon heritage for sheer interest.

Here Riker for the second time refuses a command post, this one on the *Aries*. We learn that his mother died when he was two and he left home at age fifteen. The almost forgotten Riker-Troi relationship gets a shot in the arm here as he confides to her his fears about advancement—and she and Pulaski compare notes about men.

The Tholians, a hot-planet race with a possible hive-mind culture who were introduced in an original-series episode called "The Tholian Web," are mentioned here in connection with a conflict a dozen years earlier—an attack that almost killed Kyle Riker and introduced him to Pulaski. The Tholians would occasionally pop up in conversation later on, in "Peak Performance" (147) and "Reunion" (181).

This show's hoopla included a visit by the *Entertainment Tonight* cameras, who were following *ET* host and unabashed Trek fan John Tesh through the two hours of makeup necessary to turn him into one of Worf's Ascension Chamber tormentors. Tesh, all six feet six of him, is the Klingon closest to the viewer on the left. Thanks to the "Klingon shortage" caused by the simultaneous shooting of *Star Trek V,* wardrobe was running low and two of the Klingons got to wear old *Planet of the Apes* boots!

Longtime character actor Mitchell Ryan who plays Kyle Riker, may be best known as the villain in *Lethal Weapon.* Lance Spellerberg appeared as Chief Herbert once before ("We'll Always Have Paris"/124). And, as with the Iconian artifact in "Contagion" (137), Sternbach filled the anbo-jyutsu mats and gymnasium set pieces with a myriad of *animé* references in Japanese.

PEN PALS

Production No.: 141 ■ Aired: Week of May 1, 1989
Stardate: 42695.3 ■ Code: pp

Directed by **Winrich Kolbe**
Written by **Melinda M. Snodgrass**
Story by **Hannah Louise Shearer**

GUEST CAST
Davies: **Nicholas Cascone**
Sarjenka: **Nikki Cox**
Hildebrandt: **Anne H. Gillespie**
O'Brien: **Colm Meaney**
Alans: **Whitney Rydbeck**

The *Enterprise* command staff decides it is time to give Wesley a real test of responsibility: oversight of a team checking into dangerous geological events in the Selcundi Drema system.

As the acting ensign seeks advice in picking and leading his team of older subordinates, a member balks at running a lengthy test Wesley feels is necessary. After soul-searching and a pep talk from Riker, Wesley gets the test run with no problem.

Meanwhile, Data interrupts Picard's holodeck horseback ride to admit he has contacted a young girl on one of the unsafe worlds, Drema IV.

Although he wanted only to reassure the girl after picking up her lonely broadcasts for help when her world became unstable, Data now fears—and Picard agrees—that his contact may violate the Prime Directive.

After a lively staff debate on the issue, Picard agrees to let Data bring the young girl, Sarjenka, aboard as Wesley's team tries to reverse the volcanic stresses that are about to wreck the planet.

Standing next to Data, Sarjenka watches from the bridge as the plan works and Wesley's team celebrates. Picard then orders Pulaski to "wipe" Sarjenka's short-term memory, and when Data takes her home she remembers nothing of her "pen pal" or of the ship that saved her.

Melinda Snodgrass, who adapted Hannah Louise Shearer's original story treatment, has called this Data's "age of innocence" story. The android had carried on a dialogue with Sarjenka for eight weeks without reporting it, much as he would later do while developing his protégé in "The Offspring" (164). In "Pen Pals," however, the writers had to limit the two characters' closeness, because Nikki Cox's orange makeup became smudged so easily on contact.

Just as she had turned to her roots in the legal profession for "The Measure of a Man" (135), Snodgrass revealed her love of horses—and Patrick Stewart's excellent horsemanship—in Picard's equestrian holodeck visit. This scene was the only location shoot of the season, filmed at a ranch near the L.A. suburb of Thousand Oaks.

A frightened Sarjenka (Nikki Cox)
won't leave her friend Data's side.

Sharp-eyed fans should spot one of the few TNG props not designed by Sternbach: the "spectral analyzer" used in the geology lab. This device was originally the "oscillation overthruster" sought by the evil red Lectroids in *The Adventures of Buckaroo Banzai Across the Eight Dimension.* Other homages to *Buckaroo Banzai* were planted throughout the series by the art staffers, most noticeably as passing references in graphics, as in "Up the Long Ladder" (144), for one.

 WHO

Production No.: 142 ■ Aired: Week of May 8, 1989
Stardate: 42761.3 ■ Code: qw

Directed by **Rob Bowman**
Written by **Maurice Hurley**

GUEST CAST
Q: **John de Lancie**
Ensign Sonya Gomez: **Lycia Naff**
O'Brien: **Colm Meaney**
Guinan: **Whoopi Goldberg**

On the edge of UFP space, the *Enterprise* encounters its old nemesis, the superbeing Q, whose anger at being refused a crew post leads him to hurl the ship into unknown space. There, they encounter a new threat—the Borg.

As the ship discovers planet after planet ravaged like those in the Neutral Zone whose destruction was first blamed on the Romulans, Guinan—an old foe of Q as well—tells Picard of the Borg's deadly attacks on her people.

Suddenly two Borg beam over from their cubelike ship to drain information from the starship's computers, ignoring the crew and quickly learning to blunt phaser attacks.

Their vessel then locks on Picard's ship and slices out a core of the saucer, killing eighteen. A brief skirmish leaves the Borg ship damaged, and Riker takes advantage of the lull to lead an away team over.

What they find is a half-humanoid, half-robotic race living as a group mind intent only on destruction and gaining technology. They also find that the Borg ship is regenerating itself.

Sure enough, the fight resumes and the *Enterprise* is soon on the brink of defeat, its shields

Data, Riker, and Worf get their first look at the Borg.

and warp drive gone. Picard admits to a gloating Q that humans can't yet handle all that the cosmos might yield—that he needs Q's help. Satisfied, the superbeing returns the *Enterprise* to its own corner of the galaxy—and vanishes.

Later a reflective Picard tells Guinan that the near-fatal Borg encounter may have been just the jolt a complacent Federation needed.

Recurring character Q takes a back seat here to Maurice Hurley's long-delayed new Federation opponents, the Borg, who were originally envisioned as a season-opening threat (see "The Neutral Zone,"/126). The new cybernetic race was meant to provide the hard-core danger the Ferengi couldn't deliver. "If somebody's interested in gold, they're not much of an adversary," Hurley said of the greedy little race. "We can make gold in our replicator."

Although the Borg began as a race of insects, a concept dropped for budgetary reasons, their relentless mentality survived. Though Guinan was not present at the time, it was the Borg who scattered and virtually killed off her people a century earlier. Perhaps her only prejudice is a hatred of them, expressed in "I, Borg" (223). This allows us to see that there is a limit to her powers. In this episode Guinan also engages in a defiant, barb-trading standoff with Q that will come back to haunt him later in "Deja Q" (161). Also, Guinan's office is seen for the first and only time in TNG's first five seasons.

Pulling the props, wardrobe, and optical effects together for the Borg's physical look was a herculean task and a learning experience, to put it mildly. The Borg armature forearm, for example, weighed about forty pounds. Some of their outfits came from the makers of the "steel suits" for *Dune* and *Batman*. Because the show went over budget by about $50,000, a planned eighth day of live shooting was dropped, and for a time, according to Rob Bowman, "we didn't know day to day if we were making a stinker or a winner."

Meanwhile, it was effects expert Dan Curry's time to shine, along with associate Ron Moore. They won an Emmy nomination for bringing the Borg ship to life. The models for the ship were built by Starlight Effects from the simple embellishments that Rick Sternbach and Richard James had created based on the description of the cubical ship given in the script.

Making his debut as a stuntman extra as the "baby Borg" was Sam Klatman, the son of Carol Eisner, David Livingston's secretary. Lycia Naff, who played a three-breasted mutant woman in *Total Recall*, showed enough comic potential in this show to be written in again in the next episode, but her character was dropped after that appearance.

SAMARITAN SNARE

Production No.: 143 ■ Aired: Week of May 15, 1989
Stardate: 42779.1 ■ Code: ss

Directed by **Les Landau**
Written by **Robert L. McCullough**

GUEST CAST
Grebnedlog: **Christopher Collins**
Reginod: **Leslie Morris**
Surgeon: **Daniel Benzali**
Ensign Sonya Gomez: **Lycia Naff**
Biomolecular Specialist: **Tzi Ma**

As Wesley prepares to take more Academy tests at Starbase 515, Picard suddenly elects to join him for the long shuttle ride after a heated argument with Pulaski.

Aboard *Enterprise*, Riker underestimates the slow-witted Pakleds, who kidnap La Forge after Number One allows Geordi to beam over to give the obese scavengers a hand with their ship.

During the shuttle ride Picard finally opens up enough to explain his reason for making the trip—surgery to replace a defective cardiac unit—and leaves Wesley spellbound with the tale of the shore leave brawl as a young officer that nearly got him killed.

Meanwhile, the Pakleds demand that *Enterprise* release all of its computer information to them. As the crew considers a show of force to rescue Geordi, Riker learns Picard is near death after surgery.

Anxious to reach their captain, the crew members trick the Pakleds with the "crimson force field"—a ruse—and rescue Geordi.

Picard awakens in post-op to learn of his close call—and to find that an amused Pulaski is the specialist who pulled him through.

Created by TNG's late-season producer McCullough, the Pakleds, with their sniffly, slow-minded ways—an allusion to fans, or to materialistic Americans?—have to be among the most humorously bizarre aliens ever created for Trek. Geordi gets a chance in the spotlight in this episode, and the "crimson force field" harks back to the corbomite trick twice used by Kirk in the 1960s.

Christopher Collins had turned up in the TNG universe once

La Forge finds the Pakleds (Leslie Morris and Christopher Collins) harmless at first.

before, as Kargan, captain of Riker's Klingon exchange ship in "A Matter of Honor" (134), while Lycia Naff here reprised her short-lived role as Sonya, as in "Q Who" (142).

Listen carefully to the tale Picard tells Wesley about his early exploits and you'll hear the alien ruffians called Nasicaans—a rare verbal *animé* reference. Also heard are references to the Jarada from "The Big Goodbye" (113), to a recreation facility named for twentieth-century astronomy artist Chesley Bonestell, and to Epsilon 9 as the site of a new pulsar cluster, though no direct connection is made to the same-named communications relay station in the first Trek movie. Picard also mentions that the Klingon-UFP alliance is only twenty or so years old.

For this episode the art staff almost got a chance to bring to life the designed but as yet unbuilt captain's yacht, but budget constraints led to the use instead of an executive shuttle for Picard and Wesley's trip.[2] A rare slipup: Wes tells the control booth that he is departing Shuttle Bay 2 in Shuttle Number 2 when he's actually in the *Sakharov* (Shuttle Number 1) in Shuttle Bay 3, as indicated on the bay floor.

Up THE LONG LADDER

Production No.: 144 ■ Aired: Week of May 22, 1989
Stardate: 42823.2 ■ Code: ul

Directed by **Winrich Kolbe**
Written by **Melinda M. Snodgrass**

GUEST CAST
Danilo O'Dell: **Barrie Ingham**
Granger: **Jon de Vries**
Brenna: **Rosalyn Landor**
O'Brien: **Colm Meaney**

Stellar flares are about to destroy the Bringloidi homeworld when the *Enterprise* rescues the colony, populated by a simple but lively people long ago forgotten except for fragmentary post-holocaust records.

The Bringloidi bring along their livestock and set up camp on a cargo bay. Riker is soon keep-

Riker and Brenna (Rosalyn Landor) take a shine to each other.

ing company with the bumbling leader's lovely but feisty daughter.

Then Picard and Data learn that the colonists' were one of two groups to settle in this solar system. The *Enterprise* heads off to warn the other of the danger.

Soon they find the Mariposans, an entire society composed of clones from the five crew members who survived the original colony ship's crash landing.

Now fearful of degeneration due to replicative fading, the Mariposans beg for fresh DNA from the *Enterprise* crew. But the idea is repugnant to the Starfleet people—just as the idea of sex is to the Mariposans—and they decline.

Desperate, the colony leaders kidnap Riker and Pulaski and collect DNA cells. But the two return to destroy the maturing bodies of the clones and bring a compromise suggestion from Picard: rejoin the Bringloidi, their original fellow colonists, and breed on a resettlement world.

———

Snodgrass's story, originally titled "Send in the Clones," began as a look at immigration and the "we don't want their kind here" prejudice, but the author admits it lost something in the push-and-shove of rewrites and budget limits. Still, she recalls the story drew some flak from two different directions. Right-to-life advocates objected to the pro-choice "I'm in charge of my body" sentiment espoused by Riker (intended) in denying the Mariposan permission to use his body for cloning, and Irish Americans protested

what they felt was a stereotypical portrayal of the Bringloidi (unintended, since Irishman Hurley conceived their look). The original title, a pun on the title of the Sondheim song "Send in the Clowns," actually survived until well after the scripts were printed.

The pregnant Bringloidi woman's condition was not faked: propman Alan Sims's wife was two weeks overdue with her baby when she appeared here. The Sims family, incidentally, bred the miniature goats that were used in the cargo bay.

Mention is made here of Earth's recovery from World War III in the early 2100s and of the European Hegemony signaling the first stirrings of world government later that century. How this war fits in with the twenty-first-century "post-atomic horror" mentioned in "Encounter at Farpoint" (101) and the Eugenics Wars of 1992–1996 from the 1967 episode "Space Seed" is not clear, although some Trek buffs explain this continuity flaw by assuming that the Eugenics Wars and the "Third World" War are one and the same, since Khan and most of his supporters were said to have come from non-Western nations.

An Okudagram seen here—Picard's search menu for Ficus sector launches—includes several humorous references. There's the SS *Buckaroo Banzai*, captained by John Whorfin with a "mission to Planet 10, Dimension 8"; and two other ships are the *animé*-related *Urusei Yatsura* and the *Tomobiki*, the setting of "Urusei." Then there are mission assignments such as "diplomatic mission to Alderan," a Star Wars homage, and the one given "Commander Gene Roddenberry" to "explore strange new worlds."

Though it can barely be glimpsed, Picard overlooks on this screen the very launch he's looking for: the sixth line is for the SS *Mariposa*. Beyond the data he reads aloud, another chart shows the ship to be a DY-500 class vessel owned by OCC, launched November 27, 2123, with U.N. registry NAR-7678 and powered by—yes—yoyodyne pulse fusion. According to the 1960s "Space Seed" episode, the DY-500 class dates back to the early twenty-first century, making it a decades-old model by the time of this launch.

Manhunt

Production No.: 145 ■ Aired: Week of June 19, 1989
Stardate: 42859.2 ■ Code: mh

Directed by **Rob Bowman**
Written by **Terry Devereaux**

GUEST CAST
Lwaxana Troi: **Majel Barrett**
Slade Bender: **Robert Costanza**
Mr. Homn: **Carel Struycken**
Rex: **Rod Arrants**
O'Brien: **Colm Meaney**
Scarface: **Robert O'Reilly**
Madeline: **Rhoda Aldrich**
Antedian Dignitary: **Mick Fleetwood**
Transport Pilot: **Wren T. Brown**

While picking up Antedian delegates on diplomatic escort duty, the *Enterprise* is graced once again by Troi's mother, Lwaxana, who checks aboard this time with full ambassadorial status as a delegate.

Her daughter is dismayed to learn that Lwaxana is not only chasing Picard again but is in the midst of the Betazoid "Phase"—a midlife female cycle that quadruples (at least) the woman's sex drive.

Picard escapes from Lwaxana's dinner-for-two trap and flees into the holodeck to hide out and play Dixon Hill, his favorite gumshoe.

Lwaxana moves on to a short-lived engagement with Riker, then tracks both men down on the holodeck, only to fall for the program's bartender.

Meanwhile, in sickbay the fishlike Antedians have remained in a trance, their race's preferred state for deep-space travel. Upon arrival at the Pacifica conference site, they awaken and prepare to beam down just ahead of Lwaxana.

The whole flight having been a waste of time for her, Troi's mother finally shows off her telepathic powers by casually pointing out that the two Antedians are assassins carrying undetectable explosives with which to bomb the conference.

With security officers sheepishly standing by, a departing Lwaxana manages to redden her old friend Picard's face one more time.

Tracy Tormé once again used a pseudonym to protest the revisions of this episode, which turned out to be his TNG swan song. He had conceived of this show as a sequel to two of his first-

Even Dixon Hill and Madeline (Rhonda Aldrich) can't shake Lwaxana Troi (Majel Barrett).

K'Ehleyr (Suzie Plakson) participates in Worf's holodeck "calisthenics."

season episodes, a chance to bring back both Lwaxana Troi and Dixon Hill. The show, designed as a Majel Barrett vehicle, was also the last for prolific director Rob Bowman until season four's "Brothers" (177). Particularly funny were Riker's reaction to the thought of Troi's sex drive quadrupling during the Phase and the scene in which the holodeck character, Rex, realizes that he doesn't know his last name.

In that fiction-within-fiction of the Dixon Hill world, we learn his drink is "scotch, neat," and that secretary Madeline's is "rye and ginger." The holodeck villains, though, come from yet another story, "The Parrot's Claw" (see "The Big Goodbye"/113). Tormé, who based this plot roughly on *Farewell, My Lovely,* had included several Chandleresque voice-overs for Picard/Hill that were removed to avoid confusion with the captain's logs. The escapism is nicely underscored by the use of three pop standards "Moonlight Serenade," "How High the Moon," and "Let's Get Away from It All."

Longtime Trek fan Mick Fleetwood of Fleetwood Mac became the second rock music figure to appear as a guest star on TNG, though as the piscean Antedian terrorist in disguise he kept a much lower profile than did Michelle Phillips in the earlier episode (124). Fleetwood, by the way, shaved off his trademark beard to accommodate the makeup, which took 2½ hours to apply.

THE EMISSARY

Production No.: 146 ■ Aired: Week of June 26, 1989
Stardate: 42901.3 ■ Code: em

Directed by **Cliff Bole**
Teleplay by **Richard Manning and Hans Beimler**
Story by **Thomas H. Calder**

GUEST CAST
K'Ehleyr: **Suzie Plakson**
K'Temoc: **Lance le Gault**
Admiral Gromek: **Georgann Johnson**
O'Brien: **Colm Meaney**
Ensign Clancy: **Anne Elizabeth Ramsey**
Tactical Crewman: **Dietrich Bader**

Sent to assist the *Enterprise* in stopping a pre-alliance Klingon sleeper ship that could awake to prey upon helpless UFP worlds is a special envoy from the Klingon Empire—a half-human, half-Klingon female named K'Ehleyr.

K'Ehleyr, whose advice to destroy the ship is rejected by Picard, turns out to be a former lover of Worf's. He resists her playful advances, finally revealing his pent-up feelings left over from their last parting.

Later K'Ehleyr tries out Worf's holodeck combat program to relieve her mounting stress. Finding her there and joining in the fight, a battle-roused Worf grabs K'Ehleyr and they consummate their passion.

The couple's newfound intimacy is shattered, though, when she storms out after refusing Worf's marriage proposal traditionally offered after making love.

K'Ehleyr's original mission finally brings the two back together. The cruiser's crew awakens before being intercepted, and Picard lets Worf and K'Ehleyr masquerade as the *Enterprise*'s commanders.

Worf doesn't blink in the ensuing standoff and pulls off the ruse, winning kudos from his captain. Seeing K'Ehleyr off privately to take command of the ship, he at last agrees with her that neither will be complete without the other.

Worf's well-ordered life is disrupted by the first in a long series of complications when Suzie Plakson's dynamic K'Ehleyr steps back into his life with this story. Credit director Cliff Bole with the Klingon's crushing hand-holding, which draws blood. The popular Plakson played a Vulcan doctor earlier in the series, in "The Schizoid Man" (131) and would return as the ill-fated K'Ehleyr again, in "Reunion" (181).

Footage of the Klingon K't'inga-class vessels is recycled from the first Trek movie, which makes sense: a seventy-five-year-old ship would still have been in use four years after the events of the *Star Trek II-III-IV* trilogy, in 2286, using TNG's years as mentioned in "The Neutral Zone" (126). K'Ehleyr arrives in a probe that was re-dressed from Spock's photon-torpedo coffin from *Star Trek II* and *III.*

The Okudagram seen here gives K'Ehleyr several other holo-deck exercise options: scuba diving, Hanauma Bay, Earth; Klingon Rite of Ascension Chamber, mentioned in "The Icarus Factor" (140); Shi-Kahr Desert survival, Vulcan, from D. C. Fontana's animated Trek episode, "Yesteryear"; carnival celebration, Rio de Janeiro, Earth; racetrack, Longchamps, France, Earth; and two Dixon Hill mysteries, "The Long Dark Tunnel" and "The Black Night."

Worf's calisthenics are seen in two other episodes, "Where Silence Has Lease" (128) and "New Ground" (210).

Anne Elizabeth Ramsey, who plays Clancy, was earlier seen as an assistant engineer in "Elementary, Dear Data" (129), although the actress's name there was "Ramsay."

PEAK PERFORMANCE

Production No.: 147 ■ Aired: Week of July 10, 1989
Stardate: 42923.4 ■ Code: pk

Directed by **Robert Scheerer**
Written by **David Kemper**

GUEST CAST
Sirna Kolrami: **Roy Brocksmith**
Bractor: **Armin Shimerman**
Ferengi Tactician: **David L. Lander**
Ensign Nagel: **Leslie Neale**
Ensign Burke: **Glenn Morshower**

To prepare for the Borg threat, Picard asks for a master Zakdorn strategist to oversee a battle simulation he will wage against Riker, who will command the revived derelict USS *Hathaway*. Strategist Sirna Kolrami, who predicts that Riker has no chance, is also a champion at the game Strategema. His shockingly easy defeat of Data leaves Pulaski and others fuming at the tactician's arrogance.

Meanwhile, Riker realizes his ship's hope in the "battle" is his own flair for off-beat tricks. With the help of a dilithium sliver from Wesley's science project, his crew stands ready.

Riker scores an early hit using the holographic image of a Romulan warbird as a distraction, but the games turn deadly when Picard mistakes an incoming Ferengi ship for another illusion. Its attack leaves his weapons fused in the harmless war games mode.

The Ferengi demand the secret weapon they surmise the *Hathaway* must be holding and threaten to destroy both vessels. But, using its jury-rigging, the older ship fakes its "shooting" in the split second as it warp-jumps, startling the materialistic Ferengi into withdrawing when they can't fathom its illogical destruction.

Kolrami (Roy Brocksmith) briefs Picard and Riker on the war games.

Meanwhile, Data gets a Strategema rematch with Kolrami. This time he coolly plays only for a draw and "wins" when the frustrated Zakdorn loses his patience.

The Ferengi return to grace here as comic foils, and they wear a more refined uniform to boot. Note the ying-yang-type collar pips signifying rank. Armin Shimerman became the second actor to play two different Ferengi after having been seen in the first encounter with that race ("The Last Outpost"/107); Zakdorn characters would also be seen again in "Ménage à Troi" (172) and "Unification," Part 2 (207).

The antimatter shards seen in this episode are actually blue candle wax, the *Hathaway*'s bridge is yet another re-dress of the film set, and the Tholians—referred to in "The Icarus Factor"/ (140)—are mentioned again here, this time as a "victim" of Riker's quick thinking during an Academy simulation. This story also includes the first known name of a Ferengi ship, the *Kreechta*. The acronym LCARS, seen prominently on *Enterprise* computer screens here and in other segments, stands for Library Computer Access-Retrieval System.

More Okudagrams with in-jokes and *animé* references: Kolrami's briefing chart calls the war games Operation Lovely Angel and lists Kei and Yuri as proper names of the three Braslota planets, along with Totoro. The *Hathaway*'s plaque, showing it was built at Copernicus Ship Yards of Luna (Earth's moon), carries two *Buckaroo* references: Yoyodyne Propulsion Systems is the builder, and the motto is the film's catch line, "No matter where you go, there you are."

SHADES OF GRAY

Production No.: 148 ■ Aired: Week of July 17, 1989
Stardate: 42976.1 ■ Code: sg

Directed by **Rob Bowman**
Written by **Maurice Hurley, Richard Manning, and Hans Beimler**
Story by **Maurice Hurley**

GUEST CAST
O'Brien: **Colm Meaney**

A painful thorn in the leg snagged during a planetary survey turns deadly for Riker when it is found to carry an organism that attacks his central nervous system.

When Riker falls into a coma and his vital signs plummet, Pulaski realizes that the invading microbe cannot be separated from the nerves it has wound itself around.

The chief medical officer is finally able to stabilize its spread, but not until it has actually reached Riker's brain. In a desperate try, she uses a tearful Troi's help in electronically stimulating his brain to help fight off the growth.

When Troi senses that Riker's romantic dreams promote the microbe's growth, she and Pulaski begin trying to stimulate the negative memories, including a recollection of Tasha Yar's death, to slow the organism. Pulaski finally decides to risk the potentially fatal all-out induction of Riker's most primitive emotions; after his body is racked with convulsions, the organism is defeated and disappears.

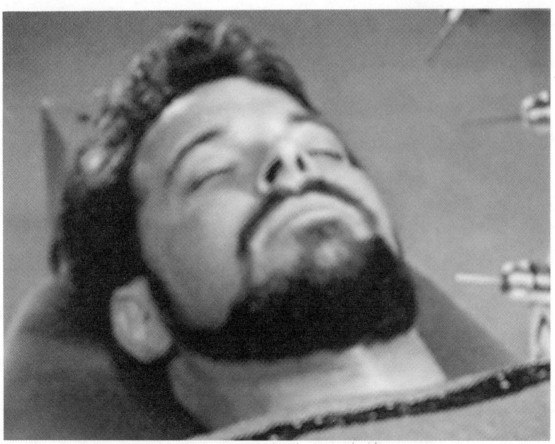

The neural stimulator proves to be Riker's only hope for surviving the Suratan microbe.

A limp "clip show" finale to the season, "Shades of Gray" is probably the weakest Trek script ever written for either generation; even writer Maurice Hurley agrees that it was "terrible, just terrible." Hurley wrote the hurried script—designed as a budget-conscious "bottle" (all-shipboard) show—on his way out the door after deciding to leave the series. Even Rob Bowman's touch as director couldn't save a show that only took three days to shoot; production assistant Eric Stillwell searched through tapes and came up with scenes representing Riker's memories to pad out the show.

For the record, those scenes included the momentary aloneness of away team command ("The Last Outpost"/107); fond first memories of Data ("Farpoint"/101); flirting with Guinan ("The Dauphin"/136); and a possible good-bye with Deanna ("The Icarus Factor"/140). More erotic memories include his times with the Edo ("Justice"/109), Minuet ("11001001"/116), Beata ("Angel One"/115), and Brenna ("Up the Long Ladder"/144). When his recollections turn increasingly negative, they cover his grief at the death of Yar ("Skin of Evil"/122) and Troi's "son" ("The Child"/127); violence at the hands of the Pagh's officer Klag ("A Matter of Honor"/134); the alien-controlled Admiral Quinn ("Conspiracy"/125); and the primal survival urge when threatened by T'Jon ("Symbiosis"/123), the Ferengi ("The Last Outpost"/107), and Armus ("Skin of Evil"/122); the possible autodestruct of the *Enterprise* ("11001001"/116), his near-death on the exploding *Batris* ("Heart of Glory"/120), and a rapid-fire mélange of many crises, including those involving Remmick ("Conspiracy"/125), the Tsiolkovsky virus ("The Naked Now"/103), the Solari traitor ("Loud As A Whisper"/132), and the infected *Lantree* ("Unnatural Selection"/133).

The drug tricordrazine—also used in "Who Watches the Watchers" (152) and in "Yesterday's Empire" (163) is a likely descendant of cordrazine, the drug that fired McCoy with enough hysterical paranoia to change history in the original-Trek episode "City on the Edge of Forever."

Notes

1. Edward Gross, *Starlog* No. 152, March 1990, p. 32.
2. Mike Okuda and Rick Sternbach, *The Star Trek: The Next Generation Technical Manual*, p. 64. Pocket Books, 1991.

PRODUCTION STAFF CREDITS—SECOND SEASON

(In usual roll order; numbers in parentheses refer to episode numbers.)

Casting: **Junie Lowery
Main Title Theme: **Jerry Goldsmith, **Alexander Courage
Music by: *Ron Jones (all even-numbered episodes, 128–146 except 136); *Dennis McCarthy (all odd-numbered episodes, 127–147 (plus 136)
Director of Photography: **Edward R. Brown, A.S.C.
Production Designer: Richard D. James (EMMY NOMINATION: "Elementary, Dear Data" [129])
Editor: *Tom Benko (127, 130, 133, 136, 139, 145, 148); Monty de Graff (142); *William Hoy (128, 131, 134, 137); Jon Koslowsky (140, 143, 146); Bob Lederman (129, 132, 135, 138, 141, 144, 147)
Unit Production Manager: *Sam Freedle
First Asst. Director: *Les Landau (127, 129); Merri D. Howard (all even-numbered episodes, 128–148); *(as 2nd AD) Robert J. Metoyer (odd-numbered episodes, 131–147)
Second Asst. Director: *Robert J. Metoyer (127–129); *Adele G. Simmons (130–148)
Costume Designer: Durinda Rice Wood (EMMY NOMINATION: "Elementary, Dear Data" [129])
Starfleet Uniforms: *William Ware Theiss
Original Set Design: *Herman Zimmerman
Visual Effects Supervisor: **Robert Legato (all odd-numbered episodes, 127–147 except 145); **Dan Curry (all even-numbered episodes, 128–148; EMMY NOMINATION, "Q Who" [142]); Coordinator: Gary Hutzel (145)
Post Production Supervisor: Wendy Neuss
Set Decorator: Jim Mees
Script Supervisor: **Cosmo Genovese
Special Effects: **Dick Brownfield
Property Master: **Joe Longo (all odd-numbered episodes, 127–147); **Alan Sims (all even-numbered episodes, 128–148)
Makeup Supervisor: **Michael Westmore (EMMY NOMINATION (with crew): "A Mother of Honor" [134])
Makeup Artists: **Gerald Quist; Sue Forrest-Chambers (127–133); Janna Phillips (134–149)
Hair Designer: **Richard Sabre (EMMY NOMINATION (with crew): "Unnatural Selection" [133])
Hair Stylist: *Carolyn Ferguson (127–132); Georgina Williams (133–148 except 136); Shirley Crawford (136)
Production Associate: **Susan Sackett
Senior Illustrator: **Rick Sternbach
Scenic Artist: **Michael Okuda
Set Designer: *Richard McKenzie
Construction Coordinator: **Al Smutko
Sound Mixer: *Alan Bernard, C.A.S. (EMMY NOMINATION, drama series: "Q Who" [142])
Chief Lighting Technician: **Richard Cronn
First Company Grip: **Brian Mills
Costume Supervisor: *Janet Stout
Key Costumer: Cha Blevins (127, 129–133); Alison Gail Bixby (128)
Costumer: Amanda Chamberlin (134, 137, 139, 148); Charmaine Nash Simmons (135, 138, 140, 142, 145); Kimberly J. Thompson (136); Cha Blevins (141, 144, 146); Carol Kunz (143, 147)
Music Editor: *Gerry Sackman
Supervising Sound Editor: **Bill Wistrom (EMMY NOMINATION (crew): "Q Who" [142])
Sound Editors: **James Wolvington; **Mace Matiosian; *Wilson Dyer
Post Production Sound: **Modern Sound
Casting Executive: **Helen Mossler
Production Coordinator: **Diane Overdiek
Casting Associate: **Elisa Goodman
Computer Monitors: Sony Corp. of America (131–148)
Special Visual Effects: **Industrial Light and Magic (ILM) a division of Lucasfilm Ltd.
Additional Motion Control Facilities: **Image "G"
Video Optical Effects: **The Post Group
Special Video Compositing: **Composite Image Systems
Editing Facilities: **Unitel Video
Research: Eric A. Stillwell (148)
Entity Animation Sequence: Stokes/Kohne Associates, Inc. (127)

[*] denotes a first-season staffer; [**] denotes the only credited or co-credited person ever in that position.

THIRD SEASON

If TNG's first season showed the birth

pangs of creation and its second creaked with growing pains, then season three was the flowering of adulthood for a series grown confident at last of its direction, its roots, and its synthesis. "The stories this year are well-written, thought-provoking and entertaining," Jerry Buck of the Associated Press wrote of the third season. The show's success could be measured in more concrete ways as well, as throughout the season the series built on its opening 10.8 viewer rating and added to its affiliation of 235 stations, already the highest among syndicated shows.

Much of the credit for the show's new-found confidence goes to the new head of the writing staff, Michael Piller. After Maurice Hurley left, Michael Wagner served briefly as coexecutive producer before recommending Piller, his *Probe* series associate, for the job.

"We did have a lot of chaos in the second season," Rick Berman recalled. "Maurice was at the helm and we had a lot of turnover among the writers. Then Michael and I took over the helm in the hiatus and things settled down."

97

The third-season cast shot (*opposite*); mother and son are reunited as Gates McFadden (Dr. Crusher) returns.

Piller recalls it wasn't quite so easy at first. "That was a panic-driven season—we were 'riding the rims,' as we called it," he said. "I can't claim full credit for [the success]; we had a lot of good writers here.

"I will claim credit for my contribution, which is that I just have an idea for what I think makes a good dramatic story, and that I can help the flow of development in the room [at writing staff meetings]."

Piller took over beginning with "The Bonding" (153)—thanks in no small part to his and Wagner's "Evolution" script (150), which made a good impression on Roddenberry and Berman, now the real chief of day-to-day operations as the Great Bird eased away from hands-on duty.

"I take great pride in trying to protect Gene's universe, which I feel after four years is mine as well," Berman said later. "Gene has come to trust me and because of that his involvement can be lessened without any conflict."[1] After getting the new series off the ground and solidly on course, GR was affectionately likened by one staffer to the queen of England: proudly surveying, and still involved with, all that he had set in motion.

Piller was a New York native who originally worked in local TV news. After arriving in Los Angeles, he began reading scripts and learning about writing while working first as a censor and then as a programmer at CBS for series ranging from *The Dukes of Hazzard* and *The Incredible Hulk* to *Cagney and Lacey*. Thinking he could do as well, he wrote and sold a script each for *C&L* and *Simon and Simon*, then left the network and joined the staff of *Simon*, where he went from writer to producer in three years, working for a time with Maurice Hurley.

Helping to ease his transition were Hans Beimler and Richard Manning, who came back for the whole season while changing their title during the hiatus from executive script consultant to coproducer. Melinda Snodgrass, promoted to their old title from story editor, was joined on the staff by Ira Steven Behr as a writing producer beginning with the year's ninth show, "The Vengeance Factor" (157). Also having a hand in scripts were Richard Danus, who helped with "Booby Trap" (154) and became

Patrick Stewart gets to act in his beloved Shakespeare as a holodeck actor with Data (from "The Defector"/158).

executive story editor from that point through "Yesterday's Enterprise" (163), and Ronald D. Moore, a talented fan whose dream came true when his spec script for "The Bonding" got him hired as story editor beginning with "Sins of the Father" (165).

On-screen, the creative staff's efforts produced a year of highlights that saw Beverly Crusher return to the *Enterprise*, her son get promoted to full ensign, the captain slug a terrorist on his bridge, Riker and Troi finally find time for a kiss, Worf get disgraced, Data find himself "with child," Geordi change his luck with women, and more and more being revealed about O'Brien—but not his first name!

The year-long letter-writing campaign to return Gates McFadden to the show was not directly mentioned when a change of heart in the great "chemistry experiment" over TNG's doctors was announced. "Diana Muldaur is a marvelous actress and it's obvious that I think so because I've used her many times," Roddenberry would say later. "But it's all just chemistry. Beverly had that little something. . . . Somehow the way the captain bounces off her works well. It works with Muldaur, too, but it just seems to work a little more with Crusher."[2] He would also say, "It was always our intention to leave the door open for her to return to the show."[3]

"It was our opinion, Gene's and mine, that the Pulaski role was not working out either," Berman said. "And rather than going and looking for a third doctor in three years, we approached Gates about coming back, and she very graciously did."

McFadden, by the way, had not been idle during her year off. She had appeared in two movies, *The Hunt for Red October* (though much of her part ended up on the cutting-room floor) and *Taking Care of Business* (with John "Q" deLancie as a subordinate), and she had starred in an off-Broadway play, *To Gillian on Her 37th Birthday*. Muldaur would go on to create a similarly crusty, though ill-fated role, that of Rosalind Shayes on *L.A. Law*.

As the writing staff began to find its rhythm at last, the production office quietly went about its business. Retaining administrative oversight of special effects, associate producer Peter Lauritson was promoted to the new title of coproducer after the fourth episode, "Who Watches the Watchers" (152). Also, beginning with "Captain's Holiday" (167), Michael Okuda and Rick Sternbach would add technical consultant to their art titles, cementing the unofficial role as science experts they had been performing for the writers ever since the pilot.

David Livingston continued his role as cost estimator and Berman's liaison to all the non-effects departments. Producing an episode from script started now with early casting concept sessions involving Piller, the writers, and casting director Junie Lowry-Johnson; she did the actual casting with Berman and the episode's director. Newly hired costume designer Bob Blackman was then involved, after which Livingston would

oversee early production meetings with the design and FX staff, the writers, Berman, and Piller. Livingston then kept tabs on all the ideas springing into action—production designer Richard James's set concepts, Westmore's makeup plans, hairstyles, Sternbach and Okuda's ideas—and made a last-minute check-in with all of them two days before principal filming began.

Blackman was among a slew of new people who came aboard for the third season, replacing his departing friend Durinda Rice Wood. One of his first tasks was to oversee the cast's long-sought end to the original uniforms. Made of spandex that had to remain taut, the hot one-piece jumpsuits actually led to fatigue and lower back pain among the actors. The new outfits cost $3,000 each and were phased in only for those above ensign rank. They were made of "breathable" wool gabardine and kept to a one-piece version for the women because of the design line.

A new main title greeted viewers beginning with the third season, featuring an incoming route from outside the Milky Way rather than a departure angle from the solar system. Also, a four-foot filming miniature of the *Enterprise* was built at mid-season, first turning up in "The Defector" (158). Though smaller, it was actually more detailed and for the first time accurately depicted the front Ten-Forward windows.

Mark "Sarek" Lenard is visited by Walter "Chekov" Koenig.

THE ENSIGNS OF COMMAND

Production No.: 149 ■ Aired: Week of October 2, 1989
Stardate: 43133.3 ■ Code: ec

Directed by **Cliff Bole**
Written by **Melinda M. Snodgrass**

GUEST CAST
Ard'rian McKenzie: **Eileen Seeley**
Haritath: **Mark L. Taylor**
Kentor: **Richard Allen**
O'Brien: **Colm Meaney**
Gosheven: **Grainger Hines**
Sheliak: **Mart McChesney**

The reclusive Sheliak Corporate breaks its 111-year silence with the Federation to demand that Tau Cygna V, ceded to it by treaty, be cleared of a human settlement within three days.

Forgotten by the UFP, a strayed colony ship deposited settlers there ninety years earlier. They have tamed the desert and now number over 15,000. News of the colony is doubly surprising, since the settlers had to adapt to the fatal hyperonic radiation that bathes the planet.

Because of that danger, Data is sent to announce the evacuation. But he runs up against a stubborn leader, Gosheven, who shrugs off the unseen Sheliak's threat and won't budge despite his people's growing qualms. Picard and Troi ask for a delay from the Sheliak, but the presumptive race is as stubborn as the Tau Cygnans.

Data gets nowhere in his mission, despite the help of a farsighted Cygnan woman, Ard'rian, until he finally shows the settlers the danger they face by launching a frightening, though restrained, show of force.

Picard congratulates Data on the creativity of his effort after achieving a victory of his own—beating the arrogant Sheliak with their own treaty to get the evacuation delayed.

A shocked Ard'rian (Eileen Seeley) watches Gosheven (Grainger Hines) threaten Data.

Though filmed first, this segment was aired after "Evolution" opened the third season. Director Cliff Bole once again came up against the budget ax as he watched his episode take a $200,000 cut at the last minute, although the impact doesn't seem as drastic as it did on "The Royale" (138). In fact, a story line with more romantic overtones between Data and Ard'rian seems to have been the main casualty, leaving the issue of Data in command of reluctant charges to be explored more forcefully later in "Redemption," II (201).

As happens occasionally, credit for a major guest player did not appear on screen. Actor Grainger Hines's dialogue all had to be dubbed in by another actor, and he asked that his name be pulled. Back under the monster suit is Mart McChesney, who played Armus in "Skin of Evil" (122). This segment is the first of several showing Data's progress in learning to play the violin; the others are "Sarek" (171) and "In Theory" (199). Music is one of several arts he studies in an attempt to uncover the secret of human creativity; O'Brien is seen playing the cello in this episode.

In another example of intergenerational continuity, the old duotronics computers that Ard'rian refers to as her guess for Data's control basis is the system installed aboard Kirk's *Enterprise*, a contemporary of her colony ship. Invented by Dr. Richard Daystrom, it was the success he was trying to surpass with multitronics at the time of the 1968 episode "The Ultimate Computer."

Data's shuttlepod is named for Ellison Onizuka, one of the seven real-life astronauts who died aboard the U.S. space shuttle *Challenger* when it exploded after launch in 1986. During filming, Tibet's exiled Dali Lam and his entourage of monks—all of them Trek fans—visited the sets and surrounded Brent Spiner as Data on one of the colony village's sets to pose for a photo.

Stubbs has come on board with a specially designed probe, set to be launched to study the once-in-a-lifetime stellar explosion of a neutron-supergiant binary. The project is threatened, though, by malfunctions of the *Enterprise*'s main computer core.

The reason for those malfunctions? Wesley's science project, in which he allowed two medical microbiotic "nanites" to interact. The creatures bred and escaped into the ship's computer core, which they are now "eating." Attempts to placate or talk to the nanites are thwarted when an obsessed, impatient Stubbs sterilizes a core element of nanites with a gamma radiation blast.

But the nanites' deadly response—they shut down the ship's life-support system—convinces even Stubbs they are intelligent, and he apologizes to them after Data volunteers himself as a face-to-face communication conduit.

Satisfied with the goodwill shown them, the high-order nanites want only to keep "exploring" and ask for an uninhabited world to colonize. They even help reconstruct the ship's computer in time to make Stubbs's project a success.

The script that brought Michael Piller into the TNG fold was designed as a "growth show" for Wesley, and on his own initiative Piller added the plot points about Beverly Crusher's reappear-

EVOLUTION

Production No.: 150 ■ Aired: Week of September 25, 1989
Stardate: 43125.8 ■ Code: ev

Directed by **Winrich Kolbe**
Teleplay by **Michael Piller**
Story by **Michael Piller and Michael Wagner**

GUEST CAST
Dr. Paul Stubbs: **Ken Jenkins**
Guinan: **Whoopi Goldberg**
Nurse: **Mary McCusker**
Crewman No. 1: **Randal Patrick**

What starts out as a science project in genetics for Wes almost dooms not only scientist Paul Stubbs's lifelong project but the ship itself.

The nanites, through Data, confront Dr. Stubbs (Ken Jenkins).

ance when it became clear this episode would actually lead off the season.

One scene cut for time's sake included a corridor conversation between Wesley and his friends, pointing up how immersed in work and cut off from social life he'd become. Scott Grimes as Eric and Amy O'Neill as the blond Annette were to be given credit until their lines were cut, but they can be seen in the crowd Beverly eyes suspiciously in Ten-Forward at show's close.

Piller delved into his own love of baseball to round out the similarities between Wesley and Stubbs (played by Ken Jenkins), whom he envisioned as a forecast of the hard-driven, often friendless youngster at age forty. The players Stubbs refers to brought about the climax of the classic 1951 National League playoff when Bobby Thomson of the New York Giants broke open the tie game with a homer off Brooklyn Dodgers pitcher Ralph Branca, bringing in runners Whitey Lockman from first and Alvin Dark from second. Wesley's interest in baseball was mentioned long ago in "Justice" (109), although we learn here that his late father taught him the game. We also discover that Guinan was married at least twice and has "a lot" of children, one of whom is several hundred years old.

Stubbs's "egg" satellite module was reworked from the viral containment unit built for last season's opener, "The Child" (127); the computer core access is built on the old movie bridge set. A nice touch is the warning sign in the shuttle bay: "Warning: Variable Gravity Area."

THE SURVIVORS

Production No.: 151 ● Aired: Week of October 9, 1989
Stardate: 43152.4 ● Code: sv

Directed by **Les Landau**
Written by **Michael Wagner**

GUEST CAST
Kevin Uxbridge: **John Anderson**
Rishon Uxbridge: **Anne Haney**

Answering a distress call from Delta Rana IV, the *Enterprise* arrives to find the planet ravaged and its 11,000 colonists dead—except for two elderly botanists, Rishon Uxbridge and her unfriendly husband, Kevin. The two say they don't know why they were spared death, but they refuse to be evacuated.

An away team finds Delta Rana IV's survivors don't want to be rescued.

Then the massive ship that leveled the planet reappears, beginning a cat-and-mouse game with the *Enterprise* that leads Picard to suspect a connection between the heavily armed mystery ship and the Uxbridges. The aliens cripple the *Enterprise* in battle, then return to blast the Uxbridges' home; in turn, the Federation starship destroys them.

Picard has the couple beamed up to the bridge against their will. There Kevin finally reveals the truth. He is actually a Douwd, an immortal superalien disguised as a human, but in all the fifty-three years they've been married, he has never revealed that fact to his wife.

His credo against killing would not let him defend the planet against the aliens, a warrior-like race known as the Husnock, and his wife is actually just an image after she too died in the fighting.

Her death enraged Kevin, who used the powers he had always denied himself and blinked out the lives of all fifty billion Husnock instantaneously, without thinking.

Stunned at Kevin's crime and sobered by his shame, Picard knows there is no court that can try Kevin and he leaves the Douwd to his own thoughts and conscience—alone.

In Michael Wagner's only solo writing effort during his short-lived tenure as a producer, veteran actor John Anderson brings great dignity and mystery to the man whose grizzled exterior masks a sad and amazing story—though the actor has since revealed he almost didn't take the role due to the death of his own wife only a year earlier.

A day of location shooting of the Uxbridges' house was done at a beach house in Malibu; the moving master shot with the beam-in effect, a first for Trek, had the house matted into the landscape painting.

The Husnock warship, built by Tony Meininger, was one of the first not designed by a member of the TNG art staff. "Usually there just isn't time to put into designing them if they're just a 'ship-of-the-week' that's going to be re-dressed later anyway," said Rick Sternbach, adding that decisions on re-use are made by the alternating TNG visual-effects teams headed by Dan Curry and Rob Legato and their model contractors.

The mention of Andorian renegades marked the first time the antennaed, blue-skinned aliens of original Trek, who debuted in 1967's "Journey to Babel," were brought into the TNG era.

WHO WATCHES THE WATCHERS?

Production No.: 152 ■ Aired: Week of October 16, 1989
Stardate: 43173.5 ■ Code: ww

Directed by **Robert Wiemer**
Written by **Richard Manning and Hans Beimler**

GUEST CAST
Nuria: **Kathryn Leigh Scott**
Liko: **Ray Wise**
Dr. Barron: **James Greene**
Oji: **Pamela Segall**
Fento: **John McLiam**
Hali: **James McIntire**
Mary Warren: **Lois Hall**

A failing reactor at a hidden cultural observers' post on Mintaka III draws the *Enterprise* to that world to render assistance. Before the starship arrives, however, the reactor explodes, injuring three scientists and causing their "duck blind" screen to fail.

An away team is sent to the planet. They successfully rescue two of the scientists but cannot find the third, a man named Palmer. But one of the natives, Liko, witnesses the landing party's beam-up, and as a result falls, critically injuring himself. Dr. Crusher beams him aboard to save his life, a Prime Directive violation that angers Picard. A memory wipe doesn't take after Liko is returned home, and he begins telling his brethren that the old god-legends they gave up ages ago were true after all—and their "Overseer" is "the Picard."

Riker and Troi beam down in native disguises to find Palmer, but when the Mintakans find the missing scientist first, even their leader, Nuria, begins to believe Liko's tales.

Riker escapes with Palmer, but Troi is trapped and kept behind as a possible sacrifice. Liko now desperately wants "the Picard" to bring his dead wife back to life.

Picard risk further contamination by bringing Nuria aboard to prove he is mortal, a tactic that almost fails until she sees he cannot save one of the scientists from dying.

Picard bids good-bye to the Mintakans (Ray Wise, Pamela Segall, and Kathryn Leigh Scott).

Meanwhile, lightning storms prompt a hysterical Liko into almost sacrificing Troi before Picard arrives. The native, disbelieving his "god's" claims of mortality, shoots Picard with an arrow, drawing blood.

Although the Mintakans are aware of the outworlders now, Picard leaves them with the knowledge that the rational path is the one they should follow—and the "duck blind" is dismantled.

If the rocky crags of Mintaka III look familiar to longtime Trek fans, it's no wonder: they're the Vasquez Rocks, a county park that was the site of location shooting for several original-series episodes: "Arena," "Friday's Child," "Shore Leave," and "Alternative Factor."

This time, shooting in 100-degree heat for two days, the hardworking cast and crew were joined by the local snakes, scorpions, and bees—meaning no attractants like deodorant or perfume could be used.

Viewing the story as a morality tale, first-time TNG director Wiemer shot his Mintakan scenes as tableaux, reminiscent of medieval morality plays. Among the guest cast, *Twin Peaks* fans remember Ray Wise as Leland, Laura Palmer's possessed father. Wise also appeared in O'Neill's *The Hairy Ape* with Frakes in New York. Kathryn Leigh Scott later portrayed Maggie Evans, the love of vampire Barnabas Collins in the short-lived *Dark Shadows* remake, while James Greene played the more than friendly elevator operator on *The Days and Nights of Molly Dodd*.

Rick Sternbach has said he based the design of the protruding scope used in the "duck blind" on the video cameras used by the TMA-1 team in *2001: A Space Odyssey*. Using Trek's own background well, Picard and Beverly refer to the memory-wipe technique that Dr. Pulaski used in "Pen Pals" (141). The disguised Troi and Riker also use subcutaneous transponders, just as Kirk and Spock did in 1968's "Patterns of Force."

THE BONDING

Production No.: 153   ■   Aired: Week of October 23, 1989
Stardate: 43198.7   ■   Code: bo

Directed by **Winrich Kolbe**
Written by **Ronald D. Moore**

GUEST CAST
Lieutenant Marla Aster: **Susan Powell**
Jeremy Aster: **Gabriel Damon**
Lieutenant O'Brien: **Colm Meaney**
Teacher: **Raymond D. Turner**

A routine mission to explore the ruins of the Koinonian civilization ends in tragedy when a bomb left over from that people's long war explodes, killing ship's archaeologist Marla Aster.

Now Picard and Troi must comfort her twelve-year-old son, Jeremy, who has already lost his father. The tragedy evokes emphatic feelings from Wesley and Worf, who led Aster's away team.

But just as the shock is beginning to wear off, the boy's mother reappears and transforms the Asters' shipboard cabin into their old home back on Earth, bringing joy but confusion back into Jeremy's life.

Jeremy Aster (Gabriel Damon) considers the alien posing as his late mother.

Aimed at showcasing the often overlooked families aboard the *Enterprise*, Ronald Moore's first script for TNG shows his flair for creating characters. Here he brings together three who lost one or both parents at an early age—Wesley, Worf, and Jeremy Aster—in such a touching fashion that the science subplot of the overly solicitous alien is almost overshadowed. With very little rewriting—though originally, Jeremy himself programmed a holodeck to re-create his mother—the final version reflects the first-draft spec script that caused an enthusiastic Michael Piller first to commission "The Defector" (158) and later to offer Moore a staff job.

Along the way, this story reveals that Worf was six years old when his parents were killed at Khitomer ("Heart of Glory"/120) and that Wesley was less than twelve when his father Jack was killed.

Booby Trap

Production No.: 154   ■   Aired: Week of October 30, 1989
Stardate: 43205.6   ■   Code: bt

Directed by **Gabrielle Beaumont**
Teleplay by **Ron Roman, Michael Piller, and Richard Danus**
Story by **Michael Wagner and Ron Roman**

GUEST CAST
Dr. Leah Brahms: **Susan Gibney**
Lieutenant O'Brien: **Colm Meaney**
Guinan: **Whoopi Goldberg**
Galek Dar: **Albert Hall**
Christy Henshaw: **Julie Warner**

Data discovers that Jeremy's "mother" is actually an energy being from the planet below. After it is trapped aboard ship by forcefields, the creature says it wants only to care for the boy, since the long-dead race it once shared the planet with was responsible for Marla Aster's death.

Picard argues that humans must endure suffering and pain along with joy, while Troi points out how Jeremy can never have a full life in the artificial environment.

The alien relents after Wesley and Worf tell their stories, and the Klingon leads the boy through the "R'usstai" bonding ceremony, making them brothers.

The crew see a seldom-revealed side of Picard as the captain gleefully leads an away team to explore an ancient Promellian battle cruiser. They find the ship intact, with all hands long dead, at the site of the battle that annihilated the Promellian race and its enemy, the Menthars.

But the mystery behind the ship's fate becomes all too clear when the *Enterprise* crew members realize they are being trapped by the same Menthar energy-draining device that snared the Promellians.

As ship reserves drain away, La Forge comes across the original plans by the Galaxy-class designers. He then re-creates one of them, Dr.

Leah Brahms, as an interactive holodeck character to help him find a way to escape the Menthars' trap.

La Forge, who has been a little unfortunate of late in his dealings with women, finds himself strangely drawn to "Leah" as they fight the clock in search of an answer.

Finally they hit on the idea of using one quick blast to free themselves; then they shut off all power.

Finally, Picard takes the helm himself and deftly slingshots his ship around a last stray asteroid, after which the *Enterprise* destroys the entire booby trap.

Originally Picard was to have become involved with Leah Brahms's holodeck simulacrum, but Michael Piller changed that to the more logical choice of Geordi, whom the writer likened to the guy who fumbles around women but is "in love with his '57 Chevy." This was the first TNG episode directed by Gabrielle Beaumont and the first episode ever directed by a woman.

Dr. Leah Brahms (Susan Gibney).

Richard Danus was invited to join the staff as executive story editor after helping out on the rewrite, which foreshadows not only Geordi's second try with Christy in "Transfigurations" (173) but the eventual appearance of the real Leah Brahms in "Galaxy's Child" (190).

This episode also provides another tiny peek into Guinan's background: she reveals she is first attracted to men's heads, especially bald ones, since a bald man helped her through a painful time—but there's no clear indication that she means Picard. The art staff originally wanted the holodeck model to be a mockup of an actual warp engine, but time worked against that idea and yielded the compromise sliding panels seen. The Promellian ship *Cleponji* is a re-dress of the Husnock ship seen in "The Survivors" (151).

THE ENEMY

Production No.: 155 ■ Aired: Week of November 6, 1989
Stardate: 43349.2 ■ Code: en

Directed by **David Carson**
Written by **David Kemper and Michael Piller**

GUEST CAST
Centurion Bochra: **John Snyder**
Commander Tomalak: **Andreas Katsulas**
Lieutenant O'Brien: **Colm Meaney**
Patahk: **Steve Rankin**

Answering a distress call from the border world Galorndon Core, an *Enterprise* away team finds a crashed Romulan craft and an injured survivor. La Forge loses contact with the rest of the away team and can't be located due to the planet's severe electrical storms.

Picard and Riker suspect the small craft was spying, since it was destroyed after crashing, but its mother ship's Commander Tomalak smilingly insists that his man—one man—was merely swept off course.

Meanwhile, efforts to rescue La Forge center on a neutrino beacon that can transmit through a break in the storms. But La Forge soons discovers what the crew above can't: there is a second Romulan, Bochra, who captures the chief engineer.

La Forge finally convinces Bochra that they must work together to survive, especially since

La Forge and Riker on the latest "Planet Hell," Galorndon Core.

neer's unique abilities, shortcomings, and sense of humor well. In an early draft he was joined on the planet's surface by Troi, who had to incapacitate the Romulan.

Another story point—that of Worf letting a Romulan die by refusing to donate blood—met resistance from the writing staff and from Dorn himself when Piller first suggested it. But allowing it to stand reveals how the series was beginning to get an alien perspective on Worf. It also shows that these "perfect" twenty-fourth-century characters could come into conflict with one another after all. And, with an audience still close to the conflicts of Kirk's earlier era, Riker's gentle reminder to Worf that Klingons once hated humans as much as they now hate Romulans is a nice way to set this Trek generation apart from the last. Beverly's shock at Worf's stand is likewise a reflection of polite human society's reaction; we also learn that she had never operated on a Romulan before.

Andreas Katsulas makes the first of three appearances on TNG as the quintessential Romulan, the snidely villainous Tomalak. He will return in "The Defector" (158) and "Future Imperfect" (182). The planet Galorndon Core will figure prominently in Romulan plans again later in "Unification," Part 2 (207).

As part of the most realistic use to date of Stage 16, the palm beacon flashlights introduced here were too strong to be run on small batteries; as a result, a cable running down each actor's sleeve to an off-camera power source can sometimes be seen.

their nervous systems are degenerating due to the planet's magnetic fields.

Tension mounts topside as Worf, the only possible blood donor, refuses to provide the injured Romulan with a necessary blood transfusion, and Picard won't order him to do so. Tomalak enters Federation space, against Picard's wishes, to pick up his man.

The Romulan dies just as his ship arrives for a fight, but the two lost below are found just in time, allowing Picard to drop shields for beam-up—and show goodwill.

War is averted and Tomalak, still feigning innocence, is curtly escorted back to the Neutral Zone.

David Carson left a declining industry in his native England and got this episode as his first directing assignment, having worked with Sirtis on one of the many Sherlock Holmes episodes he'd helmed. The second Geordi show in a row uses the chief engi-

THE PRICE

Production No.: 156 ■ Aired: Week of November 13, 1989
Stardate: 43385.6 ■ Code: pr

Directed by **Robert Scheerer**
Written by **Hannah Louise Shearer**

GUEST CAST
Devinoni Ral: **Matt McCoy**
Premier Bhavani: **Elizabeth Hoffman**
Seth Mendoza: **Castulo Guerra**
Dai Mon Goss: **Scott Thompson**
Dr. Arridor: **Dan Shor**
Leyor: **Kevin Peter Hall**
Lieutenant O'Brien: **Colm Meaney**

Troi falls for the charismatic Devinoni Ral, a soft-spoken yet determined negotiator who comes aboard the *Enterprise* to bid on an apparently stable wormhole found near Barzan II.

The wormhole allows almost instant travel to

an unexplored corner of the galaxy, and the Barzan hope that proceeds from its sale will bolster the economy of their poor planet.

Ral, a human working for another world, arouses concern when he anticipates another bidder's fears and eases him out. Then the Ferengi crash the talks and secretly make the Federation delegate too ill to finish bidding. In a pinch, Picard makes Riker take that job, hoping that the commander's poker instincts will see him through.

To check the primitive Barzan probe's report, Data and La Forge take a shuttlepod through the wormhole; the protesting Ferengi send one of their own as well. But after the Starfleet officers emerge in the wrong area, they realize the wormhole does change endpoints, and they escape just before it collapses—stranding the pooh-poohing Ferengi far from home.

Ral finally confides the secret of his success to Troi: he too is part Betazoid. She clears her conscience by revealing this to all after the Bar-zan accept his bid—and sadly discover the wormhole is no good anyway.

Ral tells Troi he needs her to be his conscience, to help him change, but they part, with her reminding him she's already got a counselor's job.

Despite the advance hype about Troi's "bed scenes"—a first in the Trek series—the finished product didn't quite live up to the rumored raciness. Other scenes, though, are wonderful: the lovers' debate on the ethics of being Betazoid among non-empaths; Beverly and Deanna's workout gossip, in which we learn that the doctor dated Jack Crusher for months ("Conspiracy"/125); and more good comic Ferengi scenes, including Goss's crashing of the wormhole negotiations.

Matt McCoy, who worked with Jonathan Frakes on *Dreamwest*, brought a slick yet sympathetic air to the role of the galactic manipulator who finally meets his match. A veteran of the Neighborhood Playhouse in New York, he later had regular roles on *We've Got It Made*, *Penn 'N' Ink*, and *Hot Hero Sandwich* and starred in the films *Deep Star Six* and *Police Academy V* and *VI*. Kevin Peter Hall, who died after this episode was filmed, stood seven feet four and had donned the alien suit for the original

Premier Bhavani (Elizabeth Hoffman) and Leyor (Kevin Peter Hall) take part in the Barzan II wormhole sale.

Predator movie and the Bigfoot costume for *Harry and the Hendersons*. In the script, Ral's traveling companion, quickly tossed aside for Troi, is named Rojay.

A re-dressed set for Troi's office turns up in this episode after it debuted in "The Icarus Factor" (140). For trivia fans, its location is given as Deck 8/3472, while her quarters are at Deck 9/0910. This story also introduces Troi's love of chocolate—a recurring theme in "Deja Q" (161) and "The Game" (206)—and she informs us that even her years with Riker were nothing like the passion she feels with Ral at first. The European Alliance, mentioned as Ral's birthplace, is likely a successor to the European Hegemony of two hundred years earlier mentioned in "Up the Long Ladder" (144).

In one background scene in Ten-Forward, a crew woman turns down a pass made by Goss, whose subtle gesture harks back to an original concept of the Ferengi: the fact that the males have large sex organs. The show also identifies the Ferengi ship as belonging to the Marauder class. Though this one turns out to be a fluke, a stable wormhole went on to become a historic find in the TNG spinoff series *Deep Space Nine*.

Mystery surrounds the talks between Brull (Joey Aresco) and Marouk (Nancy Parsons).

THE VENGEANCE FACTOR

Production No.: 157 ■ Aired: Week of November 20, 1989
Stardate: 43421.9 ■ Code: vf

Directed by **Timothy Bond**
Written by **Sam Rolfe**

GUEST CAST
Yuta: **Lisa Wilcox**
Brull: **Joey Aresco**
Marouk: **Nancy Parsons**
Chorgan: **Stephen Lee**
Volnoth: **Marc Lawrence**
Temarek: **Elkanah J. Burns**

The *Enterprise* traces an attack on a Federation science outpost back to Acamar III. There, Picard discovers responsibility for the attack lies with the Gatherers, a thieving band of renegades who split off from Acamarian society a hundred years ago. The captain decides to bring an end to the raids by healing the split between the two groups.

Marouk, Acamar's leader, agrees to offer amnesty to the renegades; Brull, the first Gatherer chief they encounter, admits a yen for peace himself.

Unknown to all, Yuta, the chef-taster to Mar-

ouk, is actually an assassin who's been cellularly altered to live for centuries. Her only purpose in life is to kill off members of the Lornack clan who massacred her own Tralesta clan.

Riker is attracted to Yuta but puzzled by her sadness over her inability to love. Thanks to Data and Dr. Crusher's research, he discovers that she murdered a Lornack among Brull's pack, and another one fifty-three years ago, among countless others.

Brull leads Picard and Marouk to his chief, Chorgan, and final talks commence, though stormily. Just in time, Riker learns that Chorgan is the last Lornack and dramatically saves him from Yuta by downing her with three phaser shots.

The talks succeed, and the two groups of Acamarians are reconciled, but peace is the last thing Riker feels.

Veteran actress Nancy Parsons welcomed the chance to play a matriarchal monarch after becoming famous to millions of moviegoers as Coach Balbricker in the *Porky's* series, while Lisa Wilcox counts among her credits a three-month stint on *General Hospital*. She also survived encounters with Freddy Krueger in parts 4 and 5 of *A Nightmare on Elm Street*. Mallon, the nonspeaking blond Gatherer whom Brull puts in charge after he leaves, was played by Sirtis's boyfriend, Michael Lamper; the two were married in June 1992.

The fusion reactor seen here is the same one used in "Who Watches the Watchers?" (152), but it's been re-dressed with more stick-on panels and labels. It is established in this episode that Data is indeed stronger than Worf.

THE DEFECTOR

Production No.: 158 ■ Aired: Week of January 1, 1990
Stardate: 43462.5 ■ Code: df

Directed by **Robert Scheerer**
Written by **Ronald D. Moore**

GUEST CAST
Sub-Lieutenant Setal (Admiral Jarok): **James Sloyan**
Commander Tomalak: **Andreas Katsulas**
Admiral Haden: **John Hancock**
John Bates: **S. A. Templeman**
Michael Williams: **Patrick Stewart**

While fleeing his own people across the Neutral Zone in a small scout, a low-level Romulan tactical clerk asks for asylum, bringing with him shocking news: the Romulans plan to retake that buffer area after almost two hundred years.

Can Picard trust the defector? A probe finds some cloaklike spatial disturbances at the Nelvana III site mentioned by Setal, the defector, but this evidence of his good faith is fragile at best—certainly not reason enough to justify crossing the Neutral Zone and risking war.

Then the lowly clerk reveals himself as the Romulan admiral Jarok, and provides Picard with defense and planning data he has seen. His defection, he says, was prompted by the blind aggression of the new Romulan command—and by concern for his daughter's future if a senseless war breaks out.

But the truth is revealed when the *Enterprise* risks a Neutral Zone encounter: no invasion is planned; the signs of activity were faked. Three warbirds decloak and demand that the *Enterprise* surrender. Jarok, already in disfavor for his protests, has been used.

All seems lost until, on a prearranged signal, three Klingon ships appear. With the odds reversed, the warbirds leave, but the Romulan admiral knows what his fate will be. He is found in his cabin, dead by suicide, leaving only a letter that Picard wistfully hopes can be delivered to his home someday—in peace.

Surprisingly enough, what writer Ronald D. Moore calls "the Cuban Missile Crisis at the Neutral Zone" at one point during rewrites became a love story between Crusher and Jarok. That angle was eventually written out except for the scene in which she treats the Romulan in sickbay. A planned Sherlock Holmes teaser with Data was cut just two days before filming began due to a lawsuit, Piller recalled, and he turned to Stewart as company scholar for help in picking out a replacement. They decided on Henry V, with a heavily made-up Stewart in the role of Michael Williams, one of the soldiers.

Adding to the tension and tragic nature of James Sloyan's performance and the story were the visual effects, which gave us for the first time in any Trek a glimpse—almost a travelogue—of Romulus. Also new for this episode were the Romulan scout vessel and the third and final version of the Starfleet admiral's uniform.

A puzzling reference into Trek's own history is the mention of renewed Romulan bitterness over their "humiliating" defeat at the Battle of Cheron, apparently fought during the original Earth-Romulan War a century before Kirk's time and first mentioned in "Balance of Terror" in 1966. Two seasons later, however, in 1969's "Let That Be Your Last Battlefield," Cheron was an unknown but long-dead world where two advanced native races had destroyed each other over racial bigotry.

More trivia: Jarok is unable to synthesize Romulan ale, referred to as illegal decades earlier in *Star Trek II*. The *Hood*, spoken of here, was Riker's prior assignment, as mentioned in "Farpoint"

The Romulan Admiral Jarok (James Sloyan)—torn between his duty, and his conscience.

(101) and an original Kirk-era starship, from 1968's "The Ultimate Computer." And in a rare verbal homage to *animé*, the alleged base site, Nelvana III, takes its name from a famous Canadian animation studio.

THE HUNTED

Production No.: 159 ■ Aired: Week of January 8, 1990
Stardate: 43489.2 ■ Code: hu

Directed by **Cliff Bole**
Written by **Robin Bernheim**

GUEST CAST
Roga Danar: **Jeff McCarthy**
Nayrok: **James Cromwell**
Lieutenant O'Brien: **Colm Meaney**
Zaynar: **J. Michael Flynn**
Wagnor: **Andrew Bicknell**

The *Enterprise* is relaying reports to back up Angosia III's application to join the Federation when it stumbles across an ugly skeleton in the planet's closet: the treatment of its war veterans.

A tenaciously cunning escapee from a lunar prison colony turns out to be Roga Danar, one of the top soldiers for the victorious planet in the Tarsian War. Now branded a murderer by the Angosians, he turns out to be a patriot who was turned into a killing machine by his government through biochemical and mind control.

Warned to shy away from this internal affair, Picard learns from Prime Minister Nayrok that the prison was constructed as a colony for those super-soldiers who could not re-adapt to peacetime civilian life.

Picard's hands are tied, and he is about to hand Danar over to the Angosians when the soldier escapes from a transporter beam, beginning a chase that ends when he commandeers a police vessel.

From there Danar attacks the prison, setting

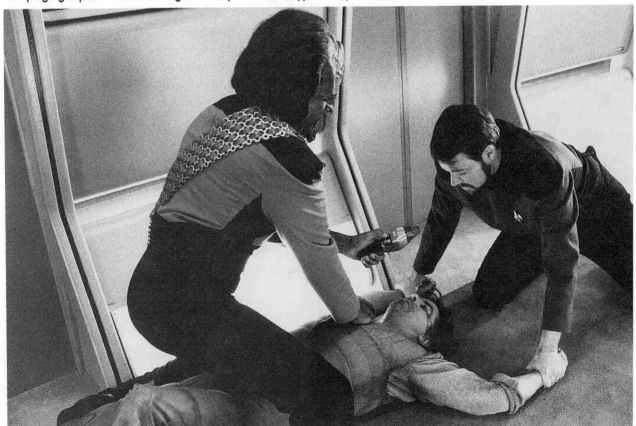

Rampaging superkiller soldier Roga Danar (Jeff McCarthy) is finally subdued.

his fellow veterans free to march on Nayrok's government and demand treatment. Held at gunpoint, the dour Nayrok now asks for help but is shocked when Picard beams up, "agreeing" that the debate is an internal matter.

If Nayrok's rule survives, Picard says, Angosia will be a welcome addition to the UFP.

This analogy to ignored Vietnam veterans was to have hit even closer to home with a planned Rambo–style eruption when the soldiers stormed the capital, but time limits and a budget crunch would again play a part in reducing an episode directed by Cliff Bole. The result is a bit anticlimactic but funny, too, as the Prime Directive for once provides both a pretext for a fast getaway and an opportunity for local action.

On the trivia side, the "Jefferies tubes" crawlways mentioned here are another homage to original Trek. That show's circuitry-access area carried the name of Matt Jefferies, art director and designer of the original *Enterprise*. The actual set for the twenty-fourth-century version, though, would have to wait another season, until "Galaxy's Child" (190). In another first for the series, the daring Danar breaks free of a transporter beam—supposedly because a chemical interferes with the signal—and powers up a transporter with a phaser's power pack. Also, the security section cell in its now familiar layout is first seen here, after debuting as a humbler set in its first and only prior appearance ("Heart of Glory"/120).

THE HIGH GROUND

Production No.: 160 ■ Aired: Week of January 29, 1990
Stardate: 43510.7 ■ Code: hi

Directed by **Gabrielle Beaumont**
Written by **Melinda M. Snodgrass**

GUEST CAST
Alexana Devos: **Kerrie Keane**
Kyril Finn: **Richard Cox**
Waiter (Katik Shaw): **Marc Buckland**
Policeman: **Fred G. Smith**
Boy (Ansata): **Christopher Pettiet**

While helping victims of a terrorist bomb blast on nonaligned Rutia IV, Dr. Crusher is taken hostage by one of the terrorists, Kyril Finn. Finn is fighting for the independence of his people, the Ansata.

Aiding the abduction and all their other terrorist acts is dimensional-shift beaming, a mostly untraceable technology whose use came with a high cost: it breaks down body chemistry and is fatal if used too often.

Finn plans to keep Crusher for her medical skills and as a bargaining chip to increase Federation pressure on the Rutians to settle the conflict with his people.

Local police chief Alexana Devos, saddened but steeled to her job, is infuriated when Riker wants to bargain for Crusher. Angered by the medical aid brought to the Rutians by the *Enterprise*, Finn leads a raid to bomb its warp chamber. His plans are foiled by a cool-headed La Forge, but the Ansatan leader manages to get away with Picard as a second hostage.

Data and Beverly tend to the wounded on Rutia IV.

After Wes develops a scan for the dimensional beaming and locates the Ansata underground base, the hostages are freed—but not until Devos kills Finn just as he's about to shoot the captain.

Devos is coldly defensive: it's better for Finn to die than to live as a prisoner. The crew leaves, thankful for their liberated officers but sobered by the unlikely prospects for peace anytime soon on the troubled planet.

Written in response to the producers' request for another action-adventure script, Snodgrass had to come up with the concept of dimensional shifting to meet Gene Roddenberry's concern that the terrorists have a logical way to defeat the *Enterprise*'s vast array of technology.

Originally conceived of as a parallel to the American Revolution, the Ansata rebels' cause was changed to resemble that of Northern Ireland, according to Snodgrass, although Finn's reference to himself as a latter-day Washington stayed in. (During the episode, Data reveals that the reunification of Ireland on Earth occurs in 2025.)

Stewart's campaign to give Picard's character more action and romance may have begun to bear fruit by this time. The normally stoic captain belts a terrorist on the bridge of the *Enterprise*, foreshadowing his encounter with the Borg later on. The story also provides this season's version of the ongoing tease of Beverly's interrupted confiding to Picard, begun in "Arsenal of Freedom" (121). We also learn that she hails from North America.

DEJA Q

Production No.: 161 ■ Aired: Week of February 5, 1990
Stardate: 43539.1 ■ Code: dq

Directed by **Les Landau**
Written by **Richard Danus**

GUEST CAST
Q: **John de Lancie**
Guinan: **Whoopi Goldberg**
Dr. Garin: **Richard Cansino**
Bre'el Scientist: **Betty Muramoto**
Q2: **Corbin Bernsen**

As if Picard didn't have enough headaches trying to keep Bre'el IV's moon from crashing into the planet, Q shows up, claiming to be powerless. The alien says he's been evicted by the Q Continuum for his past mischief.

Data is assigned to keep an eye on Q, whose story no one believes—until a gaseous Calamarain life-form catches up with Q to exact a little

Another Q? Corbin Bernsen plays the bearer of good news for Q (John de Lancie).

revenge. Realizing Q really is defenseless, Data gets a severe electrical shock trying to protect him from the Calamarain.

Q is moved by the android's sacrifice for him and steals a shuttlecraft to lure away the Calamarain so the *Enterprise* can lower its shields and get on with trying to save Bre'el IV.

But just as Picard tries to talk Q out of sacrificing himself, another Q arrives in the shuttle to say the Continuum was pleased with Q1's selfless act. The visitor restores his powers—on a probationary basis.

Overjoyed, Q celebrates by providing a mariachi band, cigars, and women for the bridge crew. Furious again, Picard orders him off the *Enterprise*—but not before Q rewards Data with a one-time belly laugh as a lesson in humanity.

As Picard is wondering whether Q is finally going to learn a lesson himself, the impish being returns with a warning: "Don't bet on it."

This story, midyear staff writer Richard Danus's only solo effort, provided some of the best comic scenes in either Trek series. After five appearances, de Lancie said his hardest TNG scenes yet to film were the bridge scenes, which went on from 7:00 A.M. to 11:00 P.M. on Thanksgiving eve. Not only did his simulated trumpet playing require several takes, but after finding no way to fake the scene in which he appears suspended in the nude, he finally just did it *au naturel*.

The script originally told the story of a looming Klingon-Federation war that was actually caused by Q, who *faked* his loss of powers and then later rushed in to become a hero. Piller said GR suggested the portrayal of a godlike creature cut down to size. Most scenes are played for laughs, especially that ending, with the mariachi band, blondes, and cigars—although Q's reunion with Guinan leaves the viewer with chills when Guinan tries to stab Q with a fork.

Best known for his well-regarded performances as divorce attorney Arnie Becker on *L.A. Law*, Corbin Bernsen has said he took the role of Q2 not so much as a fan of Trek but to be a part of its legacy and its humanistic outlook.

The Berthold rays used by the Calamarain's scanning beam were previously referred to in original Trek's 1967 segment, "This Side of Paradise." We also learn in this story that Data requires no food but occasionally "eats" semiorganic nutrient suspension in a silicone-based liquid medium to lubricate his biofunctions.

A MATTER OF PERSPECTIVE

Production No.: 162 ■ Aired: Week of February 12, 1990
Stardate: 43610.4 ■ Code: mp

Directed by **Cliff Bole**
Written by **Ed Zuckerman**

GUEST CAST
Krag: **Craig Richard Nelson**
Manua Apgar: **Gina Hecht**
Dr. Nel Apgar: **Mark Margolis**
Lieutenant O'Brien: **Colm Meaney**
Tayna: **Juli Donald**

A routine stop at a science station is anything but that when the wife of the lone researcher accuses Riker of having murdered her husband, who was killed in an explosion seconds after the first officer's departure.

Dr. Nel Apgar had been doing research for Starfleet on Krieger waves, a potential new source of energy. Apgar's wife, Manua, says Riker tried to seduce her, and his assistant backs up her claim that Riker and Dr. Apgar exchanged angry words during Number One's visit. Other evidence shows that an energy beam that struck Apgar and caused the explosion originated at Riker's beam-out point.

That is enough for Tanugan Inspector Krag to extradite Riker. Convinced of his first officer's innocence, Picard persuades Krag to use the holodeck to re-create the events prior to the explosion.

Riker is finally vindicated after La Forge, Data, and Wes look into a mysterious periodic energy burst that pulses through the ship. It turns out to be Krieger waves from the lab's ground-based generator, which is still switched on.

Actually the researcher had already made his breakthrough but was secretly trying to develop a new weapon he could sell on his own to the highest bidder. Fearing that Riker knew, Apgar aimed to disrupt Number One's beam-out with the generator—but the waves were deflected back into the lab instead, setting off the explo-

Geordi and Riker confront Tayna (Juli Donald) and Dr. Apgar (Mark Margolis).

sion. With Apgar's plot exposed, Krag drops the charges.

———

This episode's major plot device—having an officer accused of murder—recalls Scotty's dilemma in original Trek's "Wolf in the Fold," but the use of the holodeck to re-create the scene of the crime adds an interesting twist. Director Cliff Bole enjoyed what he called "our little trilogy," another conceptual device that foreshadows episodes to come, including "Cause and Effect"

(218), while filming one of the most claustrophobic bottle shows ever.

After Data's unintentionally harsh criticism of the captain's artwork in the show's teaser, Picard has never been seen painting again. And in a moment that barely keeps the Riker-Troi relationship afloat, the counselor can be seen squeezing Number One's hand when he is cleared.

The mention of duranium is a throwback to an original-series episode, "The Menagerie": here the metal is still said to be an important alloy in starship hulls and interior walls.

Yesterday's Enterprise

Production No.: 163 ▪ Aired: Week of February 19, 1990
Stardate: 43625.2 ▪ Code: ye

Directed by **David Carson**
Teleplay by **Ira Steven Behr, Richard Manning,
Hans Beimler, and Ronald D. Moore**
Story by **Trent Christopher Ganino and
Eric A. Stillwell**

GUEST CAST
Lieutenant Tasha Yar: **Denise Crosby**
Captain Rachel Garrett: **Tricia O'Neill**
Lieutenant (j.g.) Richard Castillo: **Christopher
McDonald**

A living ghost from the past, the *Enterprise*, NCC-1701-C, lost with all hands twenty-two years ago, emerges from a temporal rift. In "real" history, that ship answered a Klingon outpost's distress call, paving the way for the current union of the Federation and the Klingon Empire. By journeying through the temporal rift, the older ship has missed its appointment with

destiny and created an alternate time line; in this universe, where Tasha Yar is still alive and well, the *Enterprise*-C was not destroyed, and the Klingon-Federation detente never occurred. Instead, the two governments are engaged in a decades-old conflict that has claimed the lives of billions.

Only Guinan detects the changes in history. She tells Picard that the war, his dark and somber battleship, and time itself are "wrong" and that he must return the old *Enterprise*-C through the temporal rift to meet its intended fate.

Among the older ship's officers are Captain Rachel Garrett and helmsman Richard Castillo, who falls in love with Tasha. Picard, to the disbelief of his officers, is finally convinced of the truth of Guinan's story and prepares to send the *Enterprise*-C back through the rift. Then Garrett is killed in a Klingon attack; to take her place, Yar (who has learned of her senseless death in the "real" time line) volunteers to go back with the doomed ship; Picard reluctantly grants her permission to do so.

Attacked by three Klingon ships, the *Enterprise*-D holds out just long enough to allow its predecessor to enter the temporal rift. History immediately resumes its normal course, a change that goes unnoticed by all—except Guinan.

In spite of the multitude of writing credits, which suggest a patched-together episode, this show is continually cited as one of TNG's most popular and most powerful. Yet according to story writer Eric Stillwell, the writing staff didn't think the show would work because its teleplay was written by committee and rushed to final draft in just three days to meet a pushed-up shooting schedule. This was necessary because Whoopi Goldberg's and Denise Crosby's schedules made them unavailable during the original filming window in January.

"Most of the writers were not very happy with the script," said Stillwell (a gofer during TNG's first two seasons and a script coordinator for the next three, listed as a pre-production associate in the credits). "They thought it was going to be horrible, because they don't like having to write [something] and make it work in three days."

The tale actually began as an idea pitched by Trent Christopher Ganino a year earlier, in which the *Enterprise*-C comes forward in time and, while not changing the future, forces Picard to decide whether or not to reveal their fate to them before sending them back. Among the characters that would not survive to the final draft was Capt. *Richard* Garrett, whose last name was taken from a pizzeria in Ganino's hometown, San Jose.

Later on, Ganino and Stillwell joined forces on another alter-

nate time line story that used material from three original Star Trek episodes. A Vulcan team on an archaeological mission accidentally change history through the Guardian of Forever ("City on the Edge of Forever") when Surak, the founder of Vulcan's peaceful, logical way of life ("The Savage Curtain") is killed. His absence leads to a "new" time line in which the violent Vulcans join with their brethren, the Romulans, in a super empire, wiping out the Klingons and turning on the Federation. After being captured as a spy, Spock's father, Sarek ("Journey to Babel" and *Star Trek III, IV,* and *VI*), persuades Picard to let him takes Surak's place in the past, restoring the time line.

"We thought it would be really cool that someone from the future would replace someone in the past, and I always thought it was funny that their names were so similar, anyway," Stillwell said. But after hearing that idea, Michael Piller nixed the use of both Sarek and the Guardian—which he called a "gimmick" from the original series—but urged them to combine the story with Ganino's *Enterprise*-C tale, enlarging Tasha's part and bringing in Guinan. After eight days of brainstorming the eventual story emerged, with a female captain who dies to make room for Tasha's sacrifice and a more "honorable" death.

After another rewrite the regular staff took over and each wrote an act, with Piller sharpening Guinan's role in the incident and Ron Moore contributing the Yar-Castillo romance. Moore also stated that time constraints cut his own plans for a longer, bloodier ending for the alternate *Enterprise*-D, in which Data was electrocuted, Wesley's head blown off, and so on; of the sequence, only Riker's death was retained. Piller voluntarily took his name off the credits to meet the stringent Writers Guild credit limit of four names, and, the rest, as they say, is history.

As in original Trek's "Mirror, Mirror," little touches are used to subtly point up the differences between the real and alternate universes: the substitution of "military log" for captain's log, "combat date" for stardate, and the absence of a counselor and a friendly Klingon. On the bridge, steps replaced the side bridge ramps, the captain's chair was more thronelike, and sidearms were the norm. Other nice touches: Dr. Selar—an allusion to "The Schizoid Man" (131)—is heard being paged, as is Lieutenant Barrett, an homage to Gene Roddenberry's wife, Majel Barrett.

Among the outstanding post-production effects—the show won an Emmy for sound editing and nominations for sound mixing and dramatic score—this episode finally provided the chance for model maker Greg Jein to build a miniature from Andrew Probert's Ambassador-class design. And costume designer Bob Blackman's use of the film-era costumes (minus shirt) is a nice continuity touch, the first of many TNG appearances for the maroon jackets.

Scenes from an *Enterprise* that never was: Tasha and Picard (*opposite*) confront a mysterious intruder from the past; (*above*) Picard and Garrett confer on how to save history; (*below, left*) Castillo and Tasha steal some of what little time they have left; while Riker (*below, right*) is only one of many to die in the alternate timeline.

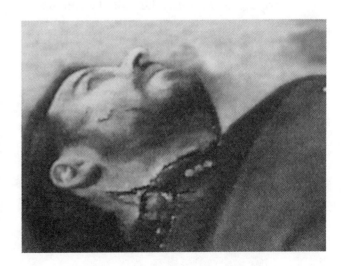

THE OFFSPRING

> Production No.: 164 ■ Aired: Week of March 12, 1990
> Stardate: 43657.0 ■ Code: of
>
> ---
>
> Directed by **Jonathan Frakes**
> Written by **Rene Echevarria**
>
> ---
>
> GUEST CAST
> Lal: **Hallie Todd**
> Admiral Haftel: **Nicolas Coster**
> Lieutenant Ballard: **Judyanne Elder**
> Ten-Forward Crew: **Diane Moser, Hayne Bayle,
> Maria Leone, and James G. Becker**
> Lal as Robot: **Leonard John Crowfoot**

Guinan introduces Data's "daughter," Lal (Hallie Todd), to the crew.

Data sparks another legal row over the status of androids when he innocently sets out to further his creator's work. He builds a "child" whom he names Lal—Hindi for "beloved."

Troi and the others are delighted when Lal chooses a human female form; her personality soon blooms, despite growing pains. But Picard is not so pleased that she was developed in secret, and has a hard time calling her Data's "child" even though the elder android duplicated his own neural nets for Lal's.

Still, the captain becomes a firm ally of the androids when Admiral Haftel of Starfleet Research insists that Lal should develop in a lab rather than aboard a ship. Despite the protests of Picard, Data, and Lal herself, Haftel perseveres—especially after he finds the new android in Ten-Forward, where Guinan and Data thought she could best study humans.

But then Lal, who shows she can go beyond Data's programming by using contractions, grows too quickly when the stress of the fight over her future leads her to develop emotions—a new trait she finds she physically can't handle.

Haftel and Data unite to repair the damage to her system, but it is too great. Data, the supposedly unemotional android, bids his dying child good-bye and then tells his grieving shipmates that Lal will always live on in their memories.

Hallie Todd, who played Joe's daughter on the Showtime series *Brothers,* is the real-life daughter of Ann Morgan Gilbert who played next-door neighbor Millie Helper on the old *Dick Van Dyke Show.* She turned in a charming and poignant performance as Lal, the spark that aided Frakes's long-sought turn in the director's chair and made viewers forget that android rights had been addressed only a year earlier in "The Measure of a Man" (135).

After producer Rick Berman told him he'd "have to go to school" before directing a show, Frakes spent over three hundred hours observing editors, watching other directors, going to the dubbing stage, attending seminars, and reading. "I think the producers were hoping I'd lose interest, but I didn't," he once said, and judging by his subsequent directing assignments ("Reunion"/181, "The Drumhead"/195, "Ethics"/216) their reaction to his initial turn in the director's chair must have been positive. This script was the first TNG sale for Echevarria, who joined the writing staff to season five.

Daytime viewers may recognize Nicolas Coster from his current role on *Santa Barbara.* Leonard John Crowfoot, in an uncredited role as the robot Lal, endured much less anonymity and special makeup during an earlier guest turn on TNG ("Angel One"/115). Once again the Daystrom Institute ("The Measure of a Man"/135) pops up; Haftel is mentioned as working at a Daystrom annex on Galor IV.

Rob Legato used a rare motion-control camera onstage for the sequence in which the robot Lal is picking holographic self-facade options. This scene includes the first appearance of an Andorian on the series.

Sins of the Father

Production No.: 165 ■ Aired: Week of March 19, 1990
Stardate: 43685.2 ■ Code: sf

Directed by **Les Landau**
Teleplay by **Ronald D. Moore and W. Reed Morgan**
Based on a teleplay by **Drew Deighan**

GUEST CAST
K'mpec: **Charles Cooper**
Commander Kurn: **Tony Todd**
Duras: **Patrick Massett**
Kahlest: **Thelma Lee**
Transporter Technician: **Teddy Davis**
Assassins: **B. J. Davis and Chris Doyle**

The *Enterprise* receives a Klingon exchange officer on board who turns out to be the younger brother Worf never knew he had. The officer, Kurn, tells Worf their family name is about to be shamed: their dead father, Mogh, has been branded the traitor behind the Romulan attack at Khitomer that killed thousands and left Worf and Kurn orphans.

With Picard's backing, Worf returns to challenge the accusations before the Klingon High Council, even though the penalty for an unsuccessful appeal is death. Shortly after their arrival, however, Kurn is attacked.

Worf had used his brother as his advocate before the council, so he asks Picard to replace him. Together they locate Worf's childhood nurse, whose tale forces the revelation of the real truth in a closed-door meeting with aging council leader K'mpec.

It was the father of Duras, Worf's accuser,

Worf and Kurn (Tony Todd) face the High Council with Picard.

and not Mogh who was the traitor. Worf and Picard are stunned when told that the truth, if exposed, would plunge the Klingon Empire into civil war.

K'mpec sadly prepares to carry out the death sentence until Worf, putting his people ahead of himself, agrees to drop the challenge and be publicly branded an outcast and coward—and to live on for another day to clear his father's name.

This landmark show gave the Trek audience its first-ever look at the Klingon homeworld, and won art direction Emmys for production designer Richard James and set decorator Jim Mees. Worf's discommendation amounted to his being branded a coward, one without honor. The withdrawal of his win-or-die Council appeal left him a nonperson in Klingon society. Worf would carry the emotional baggage of this episode through the beginning of the fifth season.

Perhaps best known as Sergeant Warren in Oliver Stone's *Platoon*, actor, playwright, and longtime Trek fan Tony Todd has played many stage, TV, and film roles. He auditioned four times for guest spots on TNG before he scored with the part of Kurn, who would return later in the series to help reclaim the family honor in "Redemption" (200) and "Redemption II" (201).

Veteran actor Charles Cooper brought pride and forbearance to the role of the elder Klingon—traits that, because of a weak script, he was unable to show off in the part of General Korrd in the movie *Star Trek V*. In uncredited roles are stuntmen B. J. Davis and Chris Doyle as Duras's assassins.

The simple Klingonese words and phrases spoken here and in future episodes were all coined by linguist Marc Okrand. They include *Qapla'!* (success), *mev yap* (That is enough!), and *cha'Dich* (literally, second—the ritual defender-supporter). When Kurn and Picard accept Worf's invitation to join him, they reply, *"jIlajnes. ghlj qet jaghmeyjaj"* (I accept with honor. May your enemies run with fear.)

Curiously, often overlooked is the actual name of Duras's father, Ja'rod—mentioned only once here and never in succeeding stories. A briefly seen computer display reveals that the *Intrepid*—another ship renamed for a Constitution-class vessel (from 1968's "Immunity Syndrome")—was commanded by Captain Drew Deighan when it reached Khitomer on SD 23859.7—perhaps a descendant of the writer of the spec script this episode sprang from.

ALLEGIANCE

Production No.: 166 ■ Aired: Week of March 26, 1990
Stardate: 43714.1 ■ Code: al

Directed by **Winrich Kolbe**
Written by **Richard Manning and Hans Beimler**

GUEST CAST
Kova Tholl: **Stephen Markel**
Esoqq: **Reiner Schöne**
Cadet Mitena Haro: **Jocelyn O'Brien**
Alien No. 1: **Jerry Rector**
Alien No. 2: **Jeff Rector**

Picard is kidnapped and replaced with a double whose actions test the loyalty of the *Enterprise* crew. Meanwhile, the real captain is trapped with three other hostages in a bizarre cell and must devote his time not only to escaping but to keeping the peace among his cell mates.

The false Picard arouses suspicion when he orders a close look at a well-known yet dangerous pulsar without telling Riker, joins in the officers' poker game, leads the crew in a drinking song, and seduces Dr. Crusher.

The mystery behind his kidnapping is revealed when one of the real Picard's cell mates, disguised as a Starfleet cadet, mentions a classified mission only Picard's crew knew about, leading him to finger her as the enemy in their midst. She transforms herself into an energy-being, and is joined by two others of her race. Their captives were being studied for their reactions to authority, like lab rats.

The captain and the aliens return to the *Enterprise* just as Riker is leading a "mutiny" against the impostor, who is then transformed into another one of the energy-beings. Picard then gives the energy-beings a taste of their own medicine by trapping them in an energy field. He releases them only after lecturing that their "research" amounts to kidnapping and is immoral.

Another turn on the old "kidnapped for alien experiments" theme (also seen in the original-series episodes "The Cage," "The Me-

Picard studies his piece of nourishment as fellow hostage Kova Tholl (Stephen Markel) looks on.

The crew needles Picard into taking a much-needed rest, but the galaxy's most reluctant vacationer soon finds himself in the middle of an adventure the likes of which he'd never get into aboard ship.

In rapid succession, he meets two Vorgons from the twenty-seventh century, traveling back in time to locate the superweapon Tox Uthat; Sovak, a Ferengi interested in buying the artifact; and Vash, a brash, striking woman whose late boss was an archaeologist also searching for the Uthat.

According to the Vorgons, Picard is destined to find the Uthat. He agrees to honor their request to return the Uthat to them and their time, but he doesn't count on falling for Vash on their overnight hike to get the artifact.

They are joined by a leering, armed Sovak, but their long dig at the presumed burial site yields nothing. Picard finally realizes that Vash found the Uthat a week ago and staged the dig to get Sovak off her trail.

She recalls how Vorgons are said to be thieves, not retrievers, and Picard has the returning *Enterprise* destroy the Uthat once and for all while beaming it up.

The Vorgons depart, while Picard and Vash muse whether they'll see each other when the alien thieves try again—in time.

nagerie," and "The Empath," among others), this segment still provides its own little gems: the false Picard's wooing and then dropping of a stunned Beverly, and his leading Ten-Forward in a drinking song and a round of ales. For the record, the song is "Hearts of Oak," first performed in 1770 with lyrics by David Garrick and music by Dr. William Boyce.

Haro's costume is our first look at a modern Academy cadet uniform and only our second look at the Bolians ("Conspiracy"/125), whom we learn are from Bolius IX. Picard visited Esoqq's anarchic world, Chalna, twelve years earlier while he was captain of the *Stargazer*—or a year before that ship was lost at Maxia. Tholl hails from the second planet of Mizar, known to astronomy buffs as Zeta Ursa Majoris, the larger of two optical binary stars in the second position inward on the Big Dipper's handle. We also see that Picard's quarters are located at Deck 9/3601.

CAPTAIN'S HOLIDAY

Production No.: 167 ■ Aired: Week of April 2, 1990
Stardate: 43745.2 ■ Code: cp

Directed by **Chip Chalmers**
Written by **Ira Steven Behr**

GUEST CAST

Vash: **Jennifer Hetrick**
Ajur: **Karen Landry**
Boratus: **Michael Champion**
Sovak: **Michael Grodenchik**
Joval: **Deirdre Imershein**

This story, the first-unit debut of assistant director Chip Chalmers, grew out of Stewart's desire for more "sex and shooting" for the captain. It also introduced the oft-mentioned Risa resort, a *Fantasy Island*-type getaway spot that apparently can meets needs even a holodeck can't satisfy.

According to Michael Piller, the first draft of the story concerned only the group's search for an ancient artifact à la *The Maltese Falcon*, but at Ron Moore's suggestion the time-travel element was added. The off-ship opening was a first for the series, but an echo of that scene planned to close the show—implying that the Vorgons were already returning to try again—was cut when it became too confusing.

Jennifer Hetrick, who began as a model and in commercials, followed in the footsteps of her onetime *L.A. Law* costar Corbin Bersen (she played Arnie Becker's wife Corinne) with her TNG guest role. She came back for more in season four in "Qpid" (194), a sequel to this episode, also written by Ira Stephen Behr. Michael Grodenchik would also return, in "The Perfect Mate" (221), though as a different Ferengi (making him the third actor to play more than one member of that race).

Other races seen in the Risian lobby are an Andorian, a Vulcan, and an Antican ("The Last Outpost"/108). The Daystrom Institute, spoken of in "The Measure of a Man" (135), is mentioned

Vash (Jennifer Hetrick) proves an attractive enigma for a vacationing Picard.

again when Vash promises to turn over the Tox Uthat. For the record, the Risian idol of sexuality is a *horgh'an,* and the state one hopes it brings is *jamaharohn.*

Notice the cave in which the treasure hunters all converge. The set is enlarged by a matte painting, but not the typical kind. As he would throughout the series on his shows, visual-effects supervisor Dan Curry created this background with pixels instead of pigment, and his computer-painted matte was then digitally blended with the live action.

Tin Man

Production No.: 168 ▪ Aired: Week of April 23, 1990
Stardate: 43779.3 ▪ Code: ti

Directed by **Robert Scheerer**
Written by **Dennis Putnam Bailey and David Bischoff**

GUEST CAST
Captain Robert DeSoto: **Michael Cavanaugh**
Romulan Commander: **Peter Vogt**
Lieutenant O'Brien: **Colm Meaney**
Tam Elbrun: **Harry Groener**

The *Enterprise* takes on board a Betazoid first-contact specialist, Tam Elbrun, to establish relations with a creature known as Tin Man—an alien life-form resembling an organic spaceship. This seems like a straightforward task—except that the Romulans also wish to contact Tin Man, and have sent two warbirds to carry out that assignment.

Elbrun is an unusually powerful telepath; on their way to rendezvous with the creature, he tells his old friend Troi about the pressure he feels as a result of being constantly bombarded by voices in his head. Troi sympathizes, but when Elbrun hints that he has already made contact with Tin Man, a suspicious Riker recalls that Elbrun's last assignment caused the death of forty-seven Starfleet officers.

Just as the *Enterprise* arrives in the star system in which Tin Man has taken up orbit around an incipient supernova, one of the Romulan ships opens fire on them and on the creature, intending to prevent the two from making contact. At Elbrun's mental suggestion, the creature destroys the Romulan warbird with a shock wave. Picard wants Elbrun to coax Tin Man into a safer sector, but the lonely alien has come to this system intending to die in the upcoming explosion. Beaming over with Data to make physical contact, Elbrun establishes an immediate rapport with the creature.

As the second warbird prepares to open fire on Tin Man, the creature emits a shock wave that sends the *Enterprise* and the warbird hurtling

Betazoid Tam Elbrun (Harry Groener) is the crew's troubled contact with "Tin Man."

through space, away from both it and the exploding star. Later it returns Data to the *Enterprise*. The android tells the crew that Elbrun has decided to remain with Tin Man, the two of them having found peace and comfort with each other.

———

Based on "Tin Woodman," a 1979 Ace book by Dennis Putnam Bailey and David Bischoff, this spin on the familiar alien encounter was the first for new composer Jay Chattaway, who late next season would take over Ron Jones's slot in alternating episodes with Dennis McCarthy. The show also gives us more background on the Betazoid race, as we learn that their mental powers, which usually blossom during adolescence, can be emotionally unsettling if they are present at birth.

Harry Groener played the insecure nerd Ralph on NBC's *Dear John* and later won a Tony for best performance by a lead actor in the Broadway musical *Crazy for You*. Here, his Tam Elbrun is the first male Betazoid depicted on TNG.

Staying true to TNG's own background story, the *Hood* here is commanded by Captain DeSoto. Riker's previous commander was mentioned by Picard way back in "Farpoint" (101–102). A script line, later deleted, revealed that the two captains had once served together as lieutenants. We also learn, in "Ménage à Troi" (172), that Troi studied psychology at the University on Betazed, where she met both Tam and Riker.

The interior sound of Tin Man—"Gomtuu" in his native tongue—was actually based on the noises in sound-effects editor James Wolvington's stomach, recorded through a stethoscope. The model was another Rick Sternbach creation built by Greg Jein. It was designed in homage to the thermal pods in *Buckaroo Banzai*. Rob Legato created the organic chair that seems to form out of Tin Man's very structure by reversing a time-lapse sequence of a melting wax chair.

Hollow Pursuits

Production No.: 169 ■ Aired: Week of April 30, 1990
Stardate: 43807.4 ■ Code: hp

Directed by **Cliff Bole**
Written by **Sally Caves**

GUEST CAST
Lieutenant (j.g.) Reginald Barclay: **Dwight Schultz**
Lieutenant Duffy: **Charley Lang**
Lieutenant O'Brien: **Colm Meaney**

Geordi experiences problems with one of his engineers, Reg Barclay, (nicknamed "Broccoli" by the crew), a nervous, shy officer who retreats to the holodeck when he can't handle real life.

After Barclay botches an antigrav repair diagnosis, Picard urges Geordi to find the man's strengths and bring him out. What the chief engineer finds is a host of holodeck fantasy programs ranging from the seduction of Deanna Troi to the casting of La Forge, Data, and Picard as Three Musketeers who are no match for Barclay's swordplay.

Meanwhile, during a routine transport of medical samples to help stop a plague, systems such as the replicator, transporter, and warp drive begin to show flaws. Suddenly the matter-antimatter injectors freeze open, catapulting the ship forward with a sudden burst of warp speed. *Enterprise* then continues to accelerate; if Geordi can't find a way to slow it down, the starship will self-destruct in minutes.

It is meek Barclay who realizes the problem stems from a little-used substance leaked from the medical-sample containers and then spread by crew members to the affected systems. That known, La Forge is able to unstick the injectors and get the ship back under control just in time.

Infused with confidence from his performance, Barclay decides to bid his holodeck fantasies good-bye once and for all, except—he smiles to himself—for program 9.

A critic-pleasing tour de force for actor Dwight Schultz—remembered by many as "Mad Dog" Murdoch, the manic pilot from *The A Team*—this story answered the questions of viewers who'd wondered if even twenty-fourth-century Starfleet officers were beyond the temptations of overdosing on holodeck fantasy, or "holodiction." Schultz had been a longtime Trek fan and, like Whoopi Goldberg, had asked to do the show if the right part came along.

While this episode provided the regular actors with some real

Only in fantasy can Barclay (Dwight Shultz) deal with his crewmates.

change-of-pace scenes—including Wesley as a pie-eating Gainesborough "Blueboy" and Troi as the sheer-robed "goddess of empathy"—those involved in this show deny they intended to make a comment aimed at that faction among Trek's most obsessive fans. Once again we see that apparently there is no privacy on the holodeck, since outsiders are free to enter someone else's program at will as also seen in "Manhunt" (145), "The Emissary" (146), and "Cost of Living" (220).

We learn more about Guinan's background here: her nonconformist slant and her mother's misfit brother, Terkim. Trivia note: the test objects made of "duranium," also mentioned in "A Matter of Perspective" (162), that O'Brien uses on the malfunctioning transporter are actually U.S. Navy sonar buoy transport cases.

THE MOST TOYS

Production No.: 170 ■ Aired: Week of May 7, 1990
Stardate: 43872.2 ■ Code: mo

Directed by **Timothy Bond**
Written by **Shari Goodhartz**

GUEST CAST
Kivas Fajo: **Saul Rubinek**
Palor Toff: **Nehemiah Persoff**
Varria: **Jane Daly**
Lieutenant O'Brien: **Colm Meaney**

Data is presumed lost by a shocked crew who watch his shuttlepod blow up while returning from dealer Kivas Fajo's ship.

Saddened, his shipmates go on to their mission, little knowing that Fajo staged the "disaster" so he could add Data to his prized galaxy-wide collection of stolen one-of-a-kind artifacts.

Fajo's comic manner hides a cunning side unhindered by ethics or conscience. Determined to break the android's resistance to being "collected," he is humiliated when Data won't "perform" for a friend and rival.

Though Fajo's assistant, Varria, seems loyal to him, Data senses she feels as trapped as he does. When Fajo finally breaks Data by threatening to kill Varria with a painful, banned disruptor beam, she finally agrees to help the android escape. But Fajo heads them off and kills Varria. Data gets control of the weapon, but Fajo taunts the android because of his directive against killing for no reason.

Kivas Fajo (Saul Rubinek) and his latest collectible—Data.

Meanwhile, the *Enterprise* officers have been researching Fajo's record and have guessed the truth regarding Data's disappearance. As they prepare to rescue him, sensors reveal a weapon being fired—a subject Data is surprisingly close-mouthed about, even after Fajo is arrested and his prize stolen collection confiscated.

An interesting story from a spec script that pushed Data to the brink of murder for a logical reason, "The Most Toys" was struck by tragedy early in the filming. Originally, the actor chosen to play Fajo was well-known little person David Rappaport, star of the series *The Wizard* and a veteran of many films and guest roles, including two memorable appearances on *L.A. Law* as a scrappy defense attorney. But Rappaport attempted suicide over the weekend after two days of filming and was hospitalized. Shortly afterward he died as a result of a second attempt. "Of course it left us very sad," Rick Berman recalled.

Left with unusable footage, the producers huddled, then hired Saul Rubinek and had him into fittings for a new costume by noon on the following Monday, although promotional photos of Rappaport in the role had already been sent out. Considering the short notice, Rubinek, a busy Canadian actor, did a remarkable job of making the quirky role his own. In the expected grief over Data's loss, Worf has a nice moment when he actually confides to Troi that his assignment at Ops is the second time he's filled in for a fallen comrade, after Tasha Yar.

This story's shuttlepod, the *Pike*, was the first on TNG actually named for a fictional person. Fans of the 1960s Trek series know that Christopher Pike was James T. Kirk's predecessor as captain of the original starship *Enterprise*. He was seen in the first pilot, "The Cage" and again later, in "The Menagerie."

The Varon-T disruptor appears to be the same prop as one of the smaller weapons Sovak used in "Captain's Holiday" (167). When Data fires it just as he is beamed out, we learn the transporter is capable not only of detecting weapons but of shutting them down as well. We also learn that Data has never killed anything. Here we see that the android has added to the mementos revealed during his human rights hearing in "The Measure of a Man" (135): a deck of poker cards and chips, his violin, and the painting he was working on in "Tin Man" (168). Fajo's lapling, a puppet, was built by makeup designer Michael Westmore.

SAREK

Production No.: 171 ■ Aired: Week of May 14, 1990	
Stardate: 43917.4 ■ Code: sa	

Directed by **Les Landau**
Written by **Peter S. Beagle**
Story by **Marc Cushman and Jake Jacobs**

GUEST CAST
Sarek: **Mark Lenard**
Perrin: **Joanna Miles**
Ki Mendrossen: **William Denis**
Sakkath: **Rocco Sisto**
Lieutenant O'Brien: **Colm Meaney**
Science Ensign: **John H. Francis**

Renowned Ambassador Sarek of Vulcan is about to oversee the completion of his career's crown-

Perrin (Joanna Miles) comforts her ill husband, Sarek (Mark Lenard).

ing achievement: the establishment of relations between the Federation and the Legaran.

But while being ferried to the meeting site aboard the *Enterprise*, Sarek weeps during a Mozart concert. The Vulcan has developed Bendii syndrome, an Alzheimer's-like disease that can erode an aged Vulcan's emotional control.

Sarek unknowingly begins projecting his lack of control onto others: Wes and La Forge fight, Dr. Crusher slaps her son, and a brawl breaks out in Ten-Forward. But Sarek's Vulcan and human aides remain in denial until Sakkath, a young Vulcan, admits he has been "propping up" Sarek's control so the Legaran mission could continue.

Confronted by that fact and Picard's insistence that he face reality, Sarek erupts in a fit of anger that even he admits proves the captain's point. The Legaran, who have been dealing with Sarek for years, will talk only to him, so as a last resort to avoid canceling the mission the captain proposes a Vulcan mind-link to share his mental control with Sarek during the negotiations.

The Vulcan agrees, and Dr. Crusher braces Picard—who always wanted to know the remarkable Vulcan better—for the onslaught of Sarek's life of repressed emotions. He is reduced to rage and sobs, but he survives the pressure as Sarek completes his mission.

After being written out of "Yesterday's Enterprise" (163), Mark Lenard here reprises the role he first played in 1967's "Journey to Babel." His appearance is the first major unifying event tying together the old and new Trek eras since McCoy's cameo in the "Farpoint" pilot (101–102).

According to Michael Piller, the original story concerned the mental problems of an ambassador other than Sarek; from there, the writing staff moved to the problems of the aging, then added the Vulcan loss of control and the telepathic "bleeding." Using Sarek was the last logical step in maximizing audience involvement and impact. "It brings home the idea that even the greatest of men is subject to illness," Piller said.

Lenard's work is complemented by the mind-meld scene in which Stewart *is* Sarek. His brilliant portrayal of pent-up emotional anguish is spiced further by the fountain of hints about the fate of Sarek's famous son, Spock. Though later seen to be very much alive in the two-part "Unification" (207–208), Spock is referred to by Picard-Sarek in the past tense. We do learn that as a lieutenant Picard attended the wedding of "Sarek's son," but Spock is not specified.

References are also made to "Journey to Babel"'s Coridan issue and to Amanda, Sarek's first wife, played by Jane Wyatt in the 1960s and in *Star Trek IV.* Given the human life span, it was

decided that Sarek would have remarried; his second wife is played here by veteran actress Joanna Miles, a new kid on the Trek block. As Riker learned in school, Sarek is given credit, among other things, for the early Klingon-Federation treaties—credit that he shares with Riva ("Loud as a Whisper"/132).

On the trivia side, note the scroll given Picard by the Mintakans ("Who Watches the Watchers?"/152) is seen draped over his chair in this episode. And for music lovers: the first selection played at the Mozart concert is the String Quartet No. 19 in C Major, also known as "The Dissonant," while—in a blooper—the second is actually by Brahms, the andante moderato movement from his Sextet No. 1 in B-flat Major.

MÉNAGE À TROI

Production No.: 172 ■ Aired: Week of May 28, 1990
Stardate: 43930.7 ■ Code: me

Directed by **Robert Legato**
Written by **Fred Bronson and Susan Sackett**

GUEST CAST
Lwaxana Troi: **Majel Barrett**
DaiMon Tog: **Frank Corsentino**
Dr. Farek: **Ethan Phillips**
Nibor: **Peter Slutsker**
Reittan Grax: **Rudolph Willrich**
Mr. Homn: **Carel Struycken**

Picard and Betazoid officials have their doubts about allowing Ferengi to take part in a biannual Betazed trade conference, but it seems to come to a smooth conclusion for all except Lwaxana Troi, Deanna's mother, who is followed by a pesky lovestruck DaiMon Tog.

Riker and Troi stay behind for a rare romantic shore leave on the planet while their ship finishes a routine assignment. But just as Lwaxana interrupts once again to nag her daughter about settling down, Tog appears and kidnaps all three, determined to use Lwaxana's telepathic skills for his own profit—and to make her his mate.

Riker and Troi outfox their guards and try to secretly signal their ship while Lwaxana keeps both Tog and her conscience at bay. Meanwhile, Wesley is due to leave to take his Starfleet Academy orals but stays behind at the last minute to

Lwaxana Troi (Majel Barrett) can't escape an obsessed Tog (Frank Corsentino).

help decode Riker's signal, which later earns him a field promotion to ensign.

Tog's doctor suspects their escape attempt almost too late, but Lwaxana, already in pain from his mind probes, asks him to let Riker and Deanna go free while she stays behind.

Then, with the young officers safely back aboard the *Enterprise*, Lwaxana signals the captain, her old would-be flame. Picard plays along by pretending to be her jilted lover. His performance is good enough to scare Tog into giving her up without an incident.

Rob Legato crossed over from his position as supervisor of visual effects to direct this episode, which included the first-ever look at the Betazed surface. Actually the Betazed scenes were filmed on location at the Huntington Library Botanical Gardens in San Marino, an L.A. suburb. Legato recalls that the show was thick with visitors, including Gene Roddenberry, since it was the first sale for his assistant, Susan Sackett, and also the yearly vehicle for GR's wife, Majel Barrett. To mark Wesley's promotion to full ensign at show's end, the Great Bird presented actor Wil Wheaton with his own ensign's bars, earned in the U.S. Navy thirty years earlier. General Colin Powell, chairman of the Joint Chiefs of Staff, was on hand for the ceremony.

Sackett recalled that the comic idea began with an O. Henry short story, "The Ransom of Red Chief"—the tale of a hostage nobody wanted. Still, aside from the moment when Riker and Troi are about to share their first on-screen kiss, the most memorable scene may be the one in which Picard mangles his beloved Shakespeare volume to get Lwaxana back.

After almost being abandoned as a Federation threat earlier, here the Ferengi are developed even further. We learn about their four-node brains which resist being sensed by empathic races like the Betazoids, and their erogenous ears that are sensitive to stroking, or *oo-mox*. Frank Corsentino became the third actor to play two different Ferengi roles ("The Battle"/110), after Armin Shimerman and Michael Grodenchik; and another *Dirty Pair anime* reference creeps in when Tog begins his access code: "Kei-ee, Yur-ee. . . ." Also, the Ferengi sidearm seen here is different from the ones used by Sovak in "Captain's Holiday" (167), suggesting that the Ferengi's may be bought off the shelf.

The USS *Bradbury*, of course, is named for the great science fiction writer Ray Bradbury, while "Cochrane distortion" pays homage to the discoverer of the space warp, Zefrem Cochran, mentioned in 1967's "Metamorphosis."

Meanwhile, Michael Westmore dug into his bag of tricks to devise the makeup for the trade conference delegates. Seen at various times in addition to the Ferengi and Betazoids are a Klingon female and uniformed male, a Vulcan woman, a Selayan, a Zakdorn male, two Bolian females, and a Mizarian male, along with the Algolian musician. And yes, body doubles were used for Barrett and Sirtis in the nude scenes.

A subtle clue is given to the background of the Troi family: Deanna's father, Ian Andrew, Sr., may not have been Lwaxana's first husband: Rheitan Grax says he and her first husband were great friends, but he's only known Deanna "since she was a child," not from birth. And Lwaxana's second husband—or next lover—was named Zon.

TRANSFIGURATIONS

Production No.: 173 ■ Aired: Week of June 4, 1990
Stardate: 43957.2 ■ Code: tf

Directed by **Tom Benko**
Written by **Rene Echevarria**

GUEST CAST
"John Doe": **Mark LaMura**
Commander Sunad: **Charles Dennis**
Christy Henshaw: **Julie Warner**
Lieutenant O'Brien: **Colm Meaney**
Nurse Temple: **Patti Tippo**

A severely injured humanoid—known as "John Doe" because of his amnesia—is found in the wreckage of an escape pod. After being linked to Geordi's nervous system to initially stabilize his body functions, the man recovers much faster than expected.

The good-natured John brings an unusually strong sense of serenity and confidence to those around him: La Forge, for one, who resumes his romance with a onetime holodeck date.

But as he recovers, John Doe is racked by fits of pain marked by a glowing energy burst within him.

The mystery man also demonstrates incredible healing powers, but increasingly severe bouts of pain frighten him into trying to steal a shuttlecraft. After he is subdued, John tells Picard he knows he is a threat to the crew and asks to leave.

The truth is revealed when a Zalkonian ship approaches and demands that the *Enterprise* turn John over to them. When the alien captain uses a paralysis beam against the *Enterprise*, John's memory finally returns. He frees the crew from the beam's effects. Then he explains that

he is among the first of his people to have taken the next step up the evolutionary ladder: transmutation into a being of pure energy. He is also the only survivor of his fearful government's attempt to exterminate this new life-form on their world so as to preserve their own power.

John now completes his transformation into an energy-being and prepares to return to his people and tell them of their own coming rebirth.

Longtime TNG film editor Tom Benko, brought onto the series by Corey Allen when he directed the pilot, got his own chance to break into directing with this simple piece, Rene Echevarria's second. The episode was originally designed as a love story for Beverly Crusher, but that plot would have to wait another year for "The Host" (197). Benko had previously sold scripts to *Magnum P.I.* and *The Fall Guy* and directed the second unit for *The Rockford Files*, *Kojak*, and *Battlestar Galactica*.

While Geordi was gaining new confidence with women, Julie Warner's character, Christy, gained a last name here—Henshaw—in an encore appearance following her series debut in "Booby Trap" (154). Also returning is the shuttlepod *El-Baz*, first seen in "Time Squared" (139), while the motor-assist bands were used again later during Worf's therapy, in "Ethics" (216). A new medical tricorder was designed and built for this show; watch closely and you'll notice that Dr. Crusher almost always has one in her hand.

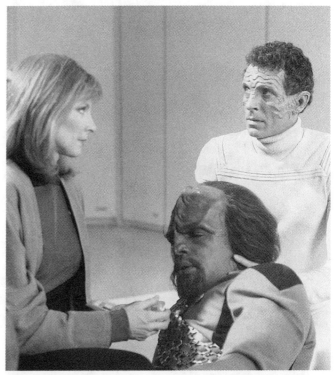

The evolving "John Doe" (Mark LaMura) brings Worf back to life.

THE BEST OF BOTH WORLDS

Production No.: 174 ■ Aired: Week of June 18, 1990
Stardate: 43989.1 ■ Code: bb

Directed by **Cliff Bole**
Written by **Michael Piller**

GUEST CAST
Lieutenant Commander Shelby: **Elizabeth Dennehy**
Admiral J. P. Hanson: **George Murdock**
Lieutenant O'Brien: **Colm Meaney**

The Borg are suspected of having caused a Starfleet colony's utter destruction, and Starfleet sends its best tactician to deal with the threat.

Riker and Borg expert Lt. Commander Shelby (Elizabeth Dennehy) investigate the destruction of Jouret IV.

Lieutenant Commander Shelby, who proves to be as smart and ambitious as she is beautiful, lets Riker know she wants his job. Riker refuses the latest command offered him, setting the stage for mounting friction, which heats up when Shelby tells him he's gone soft and lost his edge.

Meanwhile, the Borg finally appear and demand that Picard personally surrender to them. Thanks to Shelby's quick-witted strategy, the *Enterprise* breaks away and hides out in a sensor-blinding nebula to buy time for repairs and strategy.

La Forge and his team devise a weapon using the main deflector, but the ship will have to drop out of warp to use that power supply. The weapon is only part finished when the Borg find the ship, beam over, and kidnap Picard. The aliens then set course directly for Earth.

Shelby leads an away team to find Picard, who is already being assimilated by the Borg. As Locutus, he will serve as the cyborg race's speaker with humans.

Shelby's team does enough damage to force the Borg to drop out of warp, but they cannot retrieve Picard. Returning to the *Enterprise*, they find Geordi's jury-rigged weapon ready at last. The engineer insists they must fire on the Borg immediately or lose their only chance to destroy the invaders.

This spectacular movie-quality offering, the first true two-parter in this series, is still perhaps TNG's proudest achievement. Michael Piller, who says he didn't know how the saga would end when he first sat down to write it, began with the need for a cliff-hanger and came up with the Borg plot to kidnap Picard—after having tried all season long to work up a new story about the cyborg race.

Needing a so-called Queen Bee among the Borg collective for dramatic storytelling needs, Piller came up with the idea of Picard's abduction. Originally, he intended for Data and Picard to be "Borgified" into one unit. The later addition of Riker's career-advancement quandary gave Jonathan Frakes a chance to do some of his best work as Riker. For Piller personally, the subject matter was timely, coming as it did at his own contract-renewal time.

"When [Riker] talked to Troi about 'Why am I still here?' and she's telling him, 'because you're happy,' that was a conversation I had with myself several times during the course of writing that show," Piller confided. He elected to stay on in the seat he still occupies as the series enters its sixth season.

The exceptional guest cast includes Elizabeth Dennehy, the daughter of actor Brian Dennehy, and George Murdock, a vet-

concede that TNG had finally arrived. Over that summer of 1990, fan debates raged, computer bulletin board lines hummed, and fanzine letter-writers argued, fueled by rumors that Stewart's contract talks with Paramount had stalled: Would Shelby die while saving Picard? Would Picard die heroically? Would Riker be promoted to captain? Would Shelby become his first officer? Paramount's publicity department ran its first-ever promotional campaign for a single TNG episode since "Fairpoint"; ads and radio spots were specially prepared for the season opener.

Now only one question remained: could anybody write an ending that would live up to all the hype?

Kidnapped from his own bridge by the Borg (*above*), Picard has no idea of the fate that awaits him (*right*).

eran of years of character roles. Trek fans may recognize Murdock as the "godhead" from *Star Trek V: The Final Frontier;* he was also the doctor on *Battlestar Galactica.*

The freighter USS *Lalo* was first heard from in TNG's first season when it reported the time loop Manheim effect ("We'll Always Have Paris"/124); the *Melbourne,* which became the third command Riker has turned down, was one of the ships unable to give chase after the Byinars ("11001001"/116). A nice continuity touch that would be repeated later is the addition of Riker's trombone to his cabin, but a continuity gaffe has Riker and Shelby leave the main bridge for the battle bridge by way of the normal forward turbolift instead of the direct connection to starboard. We also learn here that Picard recruited Riker to be his first officer and promoted him from lieutenant commander.

All in all, so great was the impact of "The Best of Both Worlds" that even the hardest of the hard-core original-Trek fans had to

Notes

1. Marc Altman, *Cinefantastique,* Oct. 1991, p. 18.

2. *Star Trek: The Official Fan Club Magazine,* Oct./Nov. 1989, p. 4.

3. *Star Trek: The Official Fan Club Magazine,* Aug./Sept. 1989, p. 9.

PRODUCTION STAFF CREDITS— THIRD SEASON

(In usual roll order; numbers in parentheses refer to episode numbers.)

___

Casting: **(*) Junie Lowery**
Main Title Theme: **(*) Jerry Goldsmith, (*) Alexander Courage**
Music: **(*) Ron Jones (all even-numbered episodes, 150–174 except 168); (*) Dennis McCarthy (all odd-numbered episodes, 149–173; EMMY NOMINEE: dramatic underscore, series: "Yesterday's Enterprise" [163]); Jay Chattaway (168)**
Director of Photography: **Marvin Rush**
Production Designer: ****Richard D. James (EMMY CO-WINNER: art direction, series: "Sins of the Father" [165])**
Editor: **Daryl S. Baskin (171); (*) Tom Benko (151, 154, 157, 160, 163; adds ACE: 166, 169); Howard S. Deane, ACE (172); (*) J. P. Farrell (150, 153, 156, 159, 162, 165, 168, 174); **Bob Lederman (149, 152, 155, 158, 161, 164, 167, 170, 173; EMMY NOMINEE: single camera production editing, series: "Deja Q" [161])**
Unit Production Manager: **Merri D. Howard (+)**
First Asst. Director: **Chip Chalmers (all even-numbered episodes, 150–174 except 164, 168); Brad Yacobian (all odd-numbered episodes, 149–173); Bruce Alan Solow (166, 168); Adele G. Simmons (+) (162)**
Second Asst. Director: ***Adele G. Simmons (all but 162); Jeff Cline (162)**
Costume Designer: **Bob Blackman**
Original Starfleet Uniforms: **(*) William Ware Theiss**
Visual Effects Supervisor: **(*) Robert Legato (all even-numbered episodes, 150–174 except 170) (EMMY CO-NOMINEE: special visual FX "Tin Man" [168]); (*) Dan Curry (all odd-numbered episodes, 149–173 except 169) (EMMY CO-NOMINEE: special visual FX: "Deja Q" [161]); *Gary Hutzel (+) (170); Ron Moore (+) (169)**
Post Production Supervisor: ***Wendy Neuss**

Original Set Design: **(*) Herman Zimmerman**
Makeup Supervisor: **(*) Michael Westmore (EMMY CO-NOMINEE: makeup, series: "Allegiance" [166])**
Set Decorator: **Tom Pedigo (149–155); **Jim Mees (156–174) (EMMY CO-WINNER: art direction, series: "Sins of the Father" [165])**
Senior Illustrator: **(*) Rick Sternbach (added Technical Consultant, 165–67)**
Scenic Artist Supervisor: **(*) Michael Okuda (added 167; EMMY CO-NOMINEE: special visual effects: "Tin Man" [168])**
Set Designer: **Gary Speckman**
Script Supervisor: **(*) Cosmo Genovese**
Special Effects: **(*) Dick Brownfield**
Property Master: **(*) Joe Longo (all odd-numbered episodes, 149–173); (*) Alan Sims (all even-numbered episodes, 150–174)**
Construction Coordinator: **(*) Al Smutko**
Hair Designer: **Vivian McAteer (EMMY CO-NOMINEE: hairstyling, series: "Hollow Pursuits" [169])**
Hair Stylist: **Barbara Lampson (149–158, 160, 162, 164–174), Rita Bordonaro (163) (both, EMMY CO-NOMINEE: hairstyling, series: "Hollow Pursuits" [169]); Tim Jones (159, 161)**
Makeup Artists: ****Gerald Quist (all but 174), June Abston-Haymore (both, EMMY CO-NOMINEES: makeup, series: "Allegiance" [166]); Hank Edds, S.M.A. (174)**
Visual Effects Coordinator: **Ron Moore (all odd-numbered episodes, 149–173 except 169; EMMY CO-NOMINEE: special visual effects: "Deja Q" [161]); Gary Hutzel (all even-numbered episodes, 150–174 except 170; EMMY CO-NOMINEE: special visual effects: "Tin Man" [168]); NONE on 169–170**
Sound Mixer: ***Alan Bernard, C.A.S. (EMMY CO-NOMINEE: sound mixing, drama series: "Yesterday's Enterprise" [163] with re-recording mixer crew)**
Chief Lighting Technician: **Buddy Bowles**
First Company Grip: **Bob Sordal**
Costumers: ****Amanda Chamberlin (all odd-numbered episodes, 149–171); **Kimberly Thompson (150, 153, 156, 159, 162, 165, 168, 171, 174); David Velasquez (150, 152, 154, 156, 158,**

160–173); Camille Argus (149, 152, 154, 157, 160, 163, 166, 169, 172); Kris Jorgensen (151, 155, 158, 161, 164, 167, 170, 173); David Page (162, 164, 166, 168, 170, 172); Norma Johnson (174)
Music Editor: *Gerry Sackman (EMMY CO-WINNER: sound editing, series: "Yesterday's Enterprise" [163])
Supervising Sound Editor: (*) Bill Wistrom (EMMY CO-WINNER: sound editing, series: "Yesterday's Enterprise" [163])
Sound Editors: (*) James Wolvington; (*) Mace Matiosian; *Wilson Dyer (EMMY CO-WINNER: sound editing, series: "Yesterday's Enterprise" [163])
Post Production Sound: (*) Modern Sound
Production Associate: (*) Susan Sackett
Production Coordinator: (*) Diane Overdiek
Post Production Associate: Terry Martinez (151–174); Heidi Julian (+) (161–174); Wendy Rosenfeld (161–174)

Pre-Production Associate: ( ) Eric Stillwell (+)
Casting Executive: (*) Helen Mossler
Assistant Scenic Artist: Cari Thomas
Stunt Coordinator: Dennis Madalone (all but 156, 158, 168, 172)
Research Consultant: Richard Arnold (uncredited first two seasons)
Computer Monitors: (**) Sony Corp. of America
Lenses and Panaflex Cameras: (**) Panavision
Special Visual Effects: (*) Industrial Light and Magic (ILM) a division of Lucasfilm Ltd.
Additional Motion Control Facilities: (*) Image "G"
Video Optical Effects: (*) The Post Group
Special Video Compositing: (*) Composite Image Systems
Editing Facilities: (*) Unitel Video

The number of * denotes the company or staffer's prior initial season of screen credit in that position; ( ) denotes an original credited or co-credited person in that position; a (+) following indicates prior TNG work in another position.

FOURTH SEASON

By the time of its much-heralded fourth-season opening, TNG had come so far from its splashy yet wobbly origins that even the original era's movie series had a hard time keeping up. Where once the "new show," fearful of suffering in comparison, avoided using original Trek's established aliens, now Romulans, Klingons, Cardassians, and Borg were being woven into a backdrop whose scope could only have been dreamed of by fans during the rerun and movie years of the seventies and early eighties.

After resolving "The Best of Both Worlds" cliff-hanger, season four quickly became known as the sequel season: returning guests ranged from the Traveler, K'Ehleyr and Duras to Leah Brahms, Lore, Vash, and Reg Barclay. Jack Crusher, Minuet, and Noonian Soong also reappeared, as did Q and Lwaxana Troi, with Tasha Yar's sister Ishara and mystery daughter, Sela, thrown in for good measure. In all, nine of the season's first eleven episodes concerned family.

TNG made history within the Trek mythos when its widely

135

publicized eightieth episode, appropriately ti- tled "Legacy," was filmed, breaking the seventy- nine-show record of the original series. The sea- son-ending cliff-hanger, "Redemption," would be TNG's one hundredth completed hour.

Records of a more significant type were being broken as well. During the February 1991 sweeps month, "Devil's Due" (187) drew the series' high- est-ever Nielsen rating of 14.4, breaking the rec- ord of 14.0 set in November 1987 during season one. And in January, members of Viewers for Quality Television quickly voted TNG the first non-network series to make the group's list of fully endorsed television series—after VQT lead- ers had been persuaded by members to put the show on their ballot despite its syndicated distri- bution.

But there was still a long way to go before the industry's old prejudices against science fiction in general and TNG in particular completely melted away. The series again won only two Emmys from among its many technical nomi- nations and none on the so-called creative side despite such excellent actors as Patrick Stewart and Brent Spiner.

"Because our show doesn't air on one of the traditional networks, we continually face the frustration of being an anomaly," Rick Berman said in accepting the VQT award. "We hope other organizations will follow . . . in acknowledging our show, which an increasing number of view- ers have obviously been enjoying for four seasons regardless of where they watch it."

Amid the grand epics and "comeback" shows, the 1701-D family found time to continue its own evolution: the fourth season showed us an Acad- emy-bound Wesley, Data's first romance, Picard reconciling with his brother, Troi losing her em- pathic powers, Riker confronting fatherhood, Beverly falling in love (at last!), Geordi's VISOR turning against him, more shocks and sorrows for Worf and his loved ones, and O'Brien getting not only a name but a wife as well.

Credit some of that to the calmest hiatus yet for the series, thanks to the return of most of the staff—led again by Michael Piller, now settling into his second year, and Rick Berman, whose name joined Gene Roddenberry's in the closing credits as a fellow executive producer.

On his second directorial stint, Frakes shares a laugh with Dorn and Suzie Plakson ("Reunion"/181).

While many third-season staff writers left to work on other projects, Ronald D. Moore re- turned and added "executive" to his story editor title, sharing the position with newcomer Joe Menosky. They—along with supervising pro- ducer Jeri Taylor, who came on board after she helped rewrite "Suddenly Human" (176)— turned in their share of rewrites in tandem with writers who were new to the show. Among those new writers were David Bennett Carren and J. Larry Carroll, who wrote "Future Imperfect" (182) and joined the staff as story editors on the next episode, "Final Mission" (183). "Future Im- perfect" marked the last show for producer Lee Sheldon, who wrote "Remember Me" (179); he was the latest in a long line to decide that writ- ing for TNG was not for him.

"There are people who could be Emmy Award–winning writers on a lawyer show or a police drama," Rick Berman once said, "who just can't grasp what it is to write for a some- what stylized twenty-fourth-century world where the conflict between characters is very, very subtle. There are a lot of writers who just don't get it, or who have a lot of difficulty at it. It's nothing to do with how smart they are, or how good they are, but how they fit into writing *Star Trek*."

Piller described how a process called "break- ing the story" is applied to a premise or outline once it goes to development. "I don't like to get stuck in details," he explained. "I encourage the writer, after the sale, to 'hug' the whole concept—get your 'arms around it,' get it into five or six double-spaced pages with a beginning, middle, and end, what you want to accomplish, and your major character arc (the path of an individual's changes due to that story's new experiences). If you can tell that and have a real solid foundation—*then* we start talking about details."

From there, Piller said, the staff and any outsiders involved sit down and begin the show's most collaborative process. Using a marker board, they go through each writer's proposed story, seeing if it holds up to group scrutiny by diagramming and defining four to five "beats," or major plot moments, in each act. From there the story is sent back to the assigned writer to be turned into a first-draft teleplay. Even for those scripts that survive this process, however, the route to final draft might take months or even years.

"I always tell the writers what they leave with from here is just a road map for the story," Piller added. "I really believe first of all in listening to the characters—they may not want to follow that map. You may get to a point where they want to 'turn left' when you thought they were going to turn right!" While the writers were busy honing their act in the Hart Building, just across the studio street in the Cooper Building first-season veterans David Livingston and Wendy Neuss were being promoted: he by dropping the "line" from "line producer," and she by joining the senior ranks in moving up from postproduction supervisor to associate producer. They and the rest of the staff would work hard to keep production values as high as possible, especially given the spate of money-saving bottle shows that marked the second half of season four—the result of a studio effort to improve Paramount's finances in early 1991—while saving up the budget for the fourth-season cliffhanger, "Redemption" (200).

"Mom" and "son" embrace at Wil Wheaton's good-bye party.

THE BEST OF BOTH WORLDS, PART 2

Production No.: 175 ■ Aired: Week of September 24, 1990
Stardate: 44001.4 ■ Code: b2

Directed by **Cliff Bole**
Written by **Michael Piller**

GUEST CAST
Lieutenant Commander Shelby: **Elizabeth Dennehy**
Admiral Hanson: **George Murdock**
Lieutenant O'Brien: **Colm Meaney**
Guinan: **Whoopi Goldberg**
Lieutenant Gleason: **Todd Merrill**

Hopes are dashed when the *Enterprise*'s jury-rigged deflector-dish weapon fails to stop the Borg, who go on to obliterate a Starfleet armada on its way to Earth.

At the same time, Borg have tapped into Picard's knowledge of Starfleet defenses and human nature. A single tear is his only reaction to the DNA rewrites and bio-implants that have transformed his body.

Now captain of the *Enterprise*, Riker at first can't shake off the feeling of doom pervading the ship. But, inspired by Guinan's advice to turn the tables on the Borg by using their own hostage, he and Shelby, now serving as his first officer, design a daring plan. They kidnap Picard so that Data can try to tap into the Borg collective consciousness.

The going is slow, but just as Riker is prepared to give up hope and ram the Borg ship directly, Picard fights through to give Data one simple Borg network command: "Sleep."

Now dormant, the Borg experience a power feedback that destroys their ship. A shaky Picard begins his rehabilitation, thankful for his escape but deeply troubled by his experiences.

Though the logic of the Borg's demise in Data's lab is irrefutable, writer Michael Piller and director Cliff Bole both felt that this sequel did not live up to its setup. Piller has said he waited until he

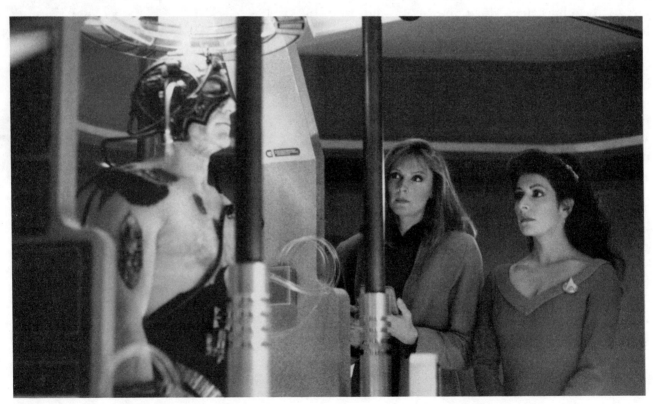

Crusher and Troi look for signs of Picard in Locutus.

returned to the lot in late July to sit down to wrap up the story—and the idea of using the Borg's interdependency as a weakness hit him just two days before filming was to start.

Despite the rumors over the summer, the talk about making the strong-willed Shelby a regular in the wake of Wesley's upcoming exit eventually evaporated. A succession of female conn officers would follow until the semi-regular Ensign Ro came aboard in the fifth season in an episode named for her (203). Meanwhile, amid all the swashbuckling, hand it to the women of this crew for saving humanity: it is Beverly who discovers the Borg's fatal flaw, and it's Troi who realizes that Picard is fighting through his programming.

Though her background remains murky, Guinan delivers an intriguing line when she tells Riker that her relationship with Picard goes "beyond friendship and beyond family." And Todd Merrill would be back to play Gleason later in "Future Imperfect" (182), though with a change in rank and duty assignment.

In another bow to series continuity, Piller's teleplay proposes using nanites as a weapon against the Borg ("Evolution,"/150) and in throwaway references, mentions Barclay's name ("Hollow Pursuits"/169, and "Nth Degree"/193). After its breakthrough use here, the main deflector dish would be utilized again in other episodes, albeit with more mixed results ("The Loss"/184, "Night Terrors"/191, "Nth Degree"/193, "A Matter of Time"/209). Data's cybernetics lab where Picard is brought, yet another re-dress of the old movie bridge, was the site where Lal was born and died ("The Offspring"/164). And we learn that a shuttle can carry its own small transporter system.

Though less favored by Rob Legato and Dan Curry and largely unused since the appearance of its four-foot cousin in season three, the original six-foot *Enterprise* model had to be hauled out of storage for the ship-separation sequence in the Borg battle, since it was the only version built in two sections. The various battle effects and Borg visuals are motion-picture quality, but again TNG struck out with the Emmys for special effects. Part 2 was nominated, but it won no awards in that category. The episode did snag Emmys for sound editing and for sound mixing, as well as a nomination for art direction.

Almost lost amid the saga and special effects in Part 2 are the slew of new starship designs—admittedly not seen here in good shape—that were crew-designed and built by "kit-bashing"—combining parts from available kits to assemble an all-new model. Among the new ships were the Cheyenne-class *Ahwahnne,* the Challenger-class *Buran,* the Springfield-class *Chekhov,* the Freedom-class *Firebrand,* the Niagara-class *Princeton,* and, as mentioned by Shelby, the New Orleans–class *Kyushu,* the Nebula-class *Melbourne* (later seen in "Future Imperfect"/182 and "The Wounded"/186), and the Rigel-calss *Tolstoy,* for the author of *War and Peace* but renamed the *Chekhov* in the final draft. Some of the dead hulks can even be seen with their hulls' lifeboat hatches open—a Greg Jein touch. Rick Sternback also revealed that the Mars Defense Perimeter ships—basically unmanned bombs—were based on the submarine model used in *The Hunt for Red October,* and quickly dubbed the "Blue-gray October."

In a later episode, "The Drumhead" (195), Admiral Satie would put Starfleet's loss at 39 ships and nearly 11,000 lives; Shelby says it should take less than a year to "get the fleet back up," though the loss definitely leaves Starfleet shorthanded, as we see in "The Wounded" (186).

Although wrecked starships won't be found there, the site of the armada's massacre is an actual star: Wolf 359 is the third-closest system to Sol, after Alpha Centauri and Barnard's Star—just 7.6 light-years from our solar system or, in Trek terms, a journey of about thirty-six hours at warp nine.

SUDDENLY HUMAN

Production No.: 176 ■ Aired: Week of October 15, 1990
Stardate: 44143.7 ■ Code: sh

Directed by **Gabrielle Beaumont**
Teleplay by **John Whelpley and Jeri Taylor**
Story by **Ralph Phillips**

GUEST CAST
Captain Endar: **Sherman Howard**
Jono: **Chad Allen**
Admiral Connaught Rossa: **Barbara Townsend**

The *Enterprise* discovers a failed Talarian craft adrift with five unconscious teenage boys, one of them human.

Raised a Talarian and known as Jono, the human checks out as Jeremiah Rossa, kidnapped a decade earlier when his parents were killed and his colony attacked by Talarians.

But Jono is the adopted son of Talarian Captain Endar, who by custom raised him after his own son was killed. He threatens war when the boy's human grandmother, a Starfleet admiral, asks that he be brought back home.

The boy also shows signs of having been abused, but Endar says the scars are only reminders of a rough-and-tumble Talarian boyhood. With Jono at the age of decision, Endar and Picard finally agree to let him decide his own fate. Photos help him recall his parents and the attack. But Jono is so agonized by the choice before him that he tries to avoid it by killing Picard so that he will be put to death.

Seeing that, Picard realizes Jono should remain with his adopted people and returns him to a grateful Endar.

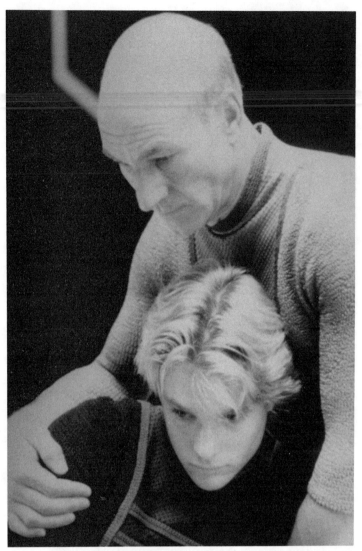

Picard tries to help Jono (Chad Allen) choose between his native and adopted cultures.

A budget-saving bottle show sandwiched in among this season's ambitious early stories, "Suddenly Human" stirred rumors throughout Trek fandom that it would address the issue of child abuse. Instead, it deals with the emotions and decisions faced by broken families and by cultures in collision.

Viewers may remember young Chad Allen as the autistic son of the doctor played by Ed Flanders on *St. Elsewhere*. He shares some fine moments with Picard who once again must confront his discomfort with children ("Farpoint"/101, "Disaster"/205). Under Troi's gentle probing, the captain wonders if the feeling stems from his lack of friends as a duty-driven child who early on wanted to be in Starfleet. His brother later speaks of Jean-Luc's childhood in "Family" (178).

"To us, it was the issue of the foster parent, having raised and nurtured the child, having as much right to custody as the natural parent," said writer Jeri Taylor. Taylor, who had been recommended by short-time producer Lee Sheldon before his exit, won an ever-expanding staff job as a result of this script. She came from a line producer's background on series such as *Quincy*, *Magnum P.I.*, *In the Heat of the Night*, and *Jake and the Fat Man*, but knew nothing about Trek until she took a crash course by watching all prior TNG and original-series episodes as well as the motion pictures.

Originally, Taylor named these aliens Phrygians, but after Okuda suggested that a once-mentioned race be used instead, the staff chose the otherwise undescribed builders of the Batris ("Heart of Glory"/120). The look of Endar's warship, *Q'Maire*, is based on the big galactic patrol vessels of E. E. "Doc" Smith's Lensman series, Sternbach revealed. The training ship, with its two great power panel "sails," harks back to the early wind-powered Coast Guard trainers. Although neither was based on the often-re-dressed Probert-designed freighter, their armament—like that of the *Batris*—includes "merculite rockets."

Judging by the art department's galactic "map," Talarian space lies adjacent to that of the Federation, opposite Klingon and Romulan territory. A historical note: the evidence given here indicates that Starfleet's uniform style changed sometime between Wesley's birth ("Family"/178) and the tape of Jono's parents, thirteen to eighteen years prior to this episode.

BROTHERS

Production No.: 177   ■   Aired: Week of October 8, 1990
Stardate: 44085.7   ■   Code: br

Directed by **Rob Bowman**
Written by **Rick Berman**

GUEST CAST
Jake Potts: **Cory Danziger**
Lieutenant O'Brien: **Colm Meaney**
Willie (Potts): **Adam Ryen**
Ensign Kopf: **James Lashly**
Lore/Dr. Noonian Soong: **Brent Spiner**

A boy's practical joke backfires, leaving his younger brother dangerously ill. But as the ship rushes toward a nearby starbase with the medical facilities the boy needs to survive, Data inexplicably malfunctions. The android isolates himself on the bridge and changes course. It turns out that Data has been automatically and unknowingly "called home" to the lab world of his reclusive creator, Dr. Noonian Soong.

Soong has at last perfected an "emotions" chip for Data, but the android and his creator are both surprised when Lore, Data's "older

Data at last meets his creator, Dr. Soong (Brent Spiner).

back Lore ("Database"/114) for this story of Data finally meeting his creator, but then, at Piller's suggestion, he changed his mind, providing Spiner with the rare opportunity to play three roles. For a time, however, veteran actor Keye Luke—an original-Trek guest in "Whom Gods Destroy"—was considered for the role of Soong, Berman revealed.

Rob Bowman, who had directed Lore's first story and was once TNG's most active director, returned to the show after a year away working for series like *Alien Nation, Baywatch,* and *In the Heat of the Night.* Piller recalled that Bowman, Legato, and Spiner worked on the elaborate Stage 16 lab set for three days before shooting began, taping off the floor and blocking out the action for camera moves, as if they were preparing a stage play or a multi-camera TV show. This is rarely done on TNG, but it was needed here to avoid costly downtime with a whole crew standing by.

During the filming in Soong's lab, Legato recalled, Spiner would shoot one day as Lore-Data and the next as the elderly scientist. Some shots, as when Soong grasped his creation's cheeks, were done inexpensively "in the camera" without post-production compositing by placing the Soong's bent elbow below the frame line. On "Soong" day, after four hours of makeup, Spiner was shot with his arm going down; on his "Data" day, the film was reshot with a photo double's hand coming up to grasp his face.

"It was difficult," Spiner recalls, "because I had to hear dialogue that I hadn't read yet coming out of somebody else's mouth before I would get to it. [I had] to remember where I was when I was Data, and so on."' To help him, the set was closed during the two and a half days when Spiner soloed.

True to Lore's story of having been picked up by Pakleds, he wears one of their outfits (143). Among other continuity threads picked up here: Data whistles the same halting version of "Pop Goes the Weasel" he tried in the pilot, "Encounter at Farpoint" (101–102), and "Often Wrong" Soong mentions the Crystalline Entity ("Datalore"/114, "Silicon Avatar"/204), whom he refers to as the "giant snowflake." At his creator's death Data finally calls the old man Father.

brother," who was left to drift in space some years earlier, responds to the same signal.

Lore disables Data and tricks Soong into installing the chip in him, then goes on a rampage, fatally injuring the doctor. Help arrives, but Soong insists on being left behind after Lore escapes.

The young boy is rushed to the starbase to receive medical care, leaving Data to ponder the emotions he could have had, his late "father," and the strange bond between him and his "brother."

Making his debut as a TNG writer, Rick Berman, in the relatively calm hiatus after the third season, finally had the chance he'd always wanted. Initially, he had rejected the idea of bringing

FAMILY

Production No.: 178 ▪ Aired: Week of October 1, 1990
Stardate: 44012.3 ▪ Code: fa

Directed by **Les Landau**
Written by **Ronald D. Moore**
Based in part on a premise by **Susanne Lambdin
and Bryan Stewart**

GUEST CAST
Robert Picard: **Jeremy Kemp**
Marie Picard: **Samantha Eggar**
Sergey Rozhenko: **Theodore Bikel**
Helena Rozhenko: **Georgia Brown**
Louis: **Dennis Creaghan**
Lieutenant O'Brien: **Colm Meaney**
Guinan: **Whoopi Goldberg**
Jack R. Crusher: **Doug Wert**
René Picard: **David Tristin Birkin**

With the *Enterprise* in dry dock for repairs after the Borg attack, Picard, full of doubts about himself and his abilities, beams down to Earth to visit his family's French vineyards. He has not been home in nearly twenty years, since a falling-out with his brother.

Meanwhile, Worf's visiting foster parents are saddened at his coldness, but they are comforted by Guinan's reassurances. They let their gruff but grateful son know they support him, as they always have, and they know he did not deserve his recent discommendation by the Klingons.

Dr. Crusher shares the literal ghost of her late husband, Jack, with the son he barely knew, by letting Wes view a stored holotape Jack made just after Wesley's birth.

Picard is made welcome by Robert's family and meets his nephew, a youngster whose dream of being in Starfleet echoes Picard's own wishes at that age. To his surprise, the captain finds himself tempted to leave Starfleet to head up a planned continent-raising project on Earth, but his brother, after a fight, reminds Picard that

Picard and his family—nephew Rene (David Tristin Birkin); sister-in-law Marie (Samantha Eggar); and brother Robert (Jeremy Kemp).

Sergey (Theodore Bikel) and Helena Rozhenko (Georgia Brown) visit foster son Worf.

wherever he stays, he must come to terms with the self-doubt and guilt caused by the Borg incident.

The captain beams back aboard *Enterprise*, which then leaves orbit, having been far more healed than the ship itself.

A daring departure for the series, "Family" is the only installment in Trek's twenty-five-year history with no scenes on the bridge. Airing right after the season-opening cliff-hanger resolution as an epilogue to the Borg two-parter, Ronald D. Moore's introspective character story was controversial even among the writing staff. Unfortunately it was the lowest-rated show of the season, even though it gave a deeper insight into more of the show's characters than virtually any other segment.

Michael Piller suggested a third segment in a proposed Borg trilogy. When that was rejected, Piller lobbied for a follow-up that would at least let Picard heal his emotional wounds on-camera after his virtual rape by the Borg. At first Berman agreed to it but insisted that a science subplot be used to round out the show. After weeks of trying various story lines that just didn't work—including a child stowaway, and a paranoid's nightmare of disappearing crew members, a story line that was used on its own in "Remember Me" (179)—Berman relented and allowed the other family-theme subplots to fill out the hour.

The lush Emmy-nominated photography in this episode was enhanced by a distinguished guest cast and two days of location shooting. The Picard family home in Labarre, France—where the hard-driven young Jean-Luc was class valedictorian, school president, and a star athlete—was actually a private residence in Encino. The vineyard scenes were shot at a private dryland operation near Lancaster in the extreme heat southwest of Edwards Air Force Base. Dan Curry digitally manipulated a matte painting background to match the windblown vineyards in the live foreground shots.

And what a cast, all with years of stage and film experience!

Samantha Eggar and Jeremy Kemp would pack enough star power into any episode. Theodore Bikel, an internationally known folksinger as well as an actor, and Georgia Brown are two of the biggest stars of Yiddish theater. Their presence initially caused some studio concern that Worf's parents might become comically "Jewish," but as Piller says the finished product "treads the line" of universal humor—and it led to a return visit by Brown in "New Ground" (210). Still, no mention is made of the Rozhenkos' own son, described by Worf in "Heart of Glory" (120), or of their years on the farming planet Gault.

Some sequences with Wesley's father, taken from Susanne Lambdin's premise after dozens of Jack Crusher spec scripts had been received through the years, were cut to save time. Piller remembers that the holotaped speech really hit home for him, arriving soon as it did after the birth of his own daughter.

In an unused sequence from the final-draft script Jack says he's about to report to the *Stargazer* and that Wesley "R." Crusher—a name later seen in Beverly's personnel file in "Conundrum" (214)—was named for Jack's grandfather, Richard Wesley Crusher, who gave Jack his first flying lesson. We also learn that a great-grandfather had a painting on exhibit in the Prado Museum in Madrid, Spain. Other Trek continuity touches in the scene included mentions of a Crusher who was a horse thief on Nimbus III (the planet in *Star Trek V*), another who served as a Confederate soldier at Bull Run, and a third who died at Station Salem One, referred to in "The Defector" (158) as the site of an enemy surprise attack à la Pearl Harbor during an unmentioned war.

Jack Crusher wears the old-style uniform of a lieutenant (j.g.) in the holotape, but his locker with his last effects is labeled with the rank of lieutenant commander and the middle initial *R*. Beverly recalls that he proposed to her when she was in medical school. As a dream image, Doug Wert would appear as Jack Crusher again in "Violations" (212).

After two seasons the full name of Colm Meaney's character is finally revealed: Miles Edward O'Brien, the name of a little boy Rick Berman knew. Curiously, Worf's foster father, a Starfleet veteran, mistakes O'Brien for a noncommissioned crew member, even though he clearly wears the two solid pins of a lieutenant, just as Sergey's own son does. The "chief" in O'Brien's title refers not to a rank, like chief petty officer, but to his duty position as transporter chief.

Trivia notes: the captain's ditty bag is stenciled simply with his name and title, Jean-Luc Picard, Captain; the bottle of family wine given to him by Robert is later seen stored and then shared in upcoming shows ("Legacy"/180, "First Contact"/189); the *Intrepid*, Sergey's old ship, had already been mentioned as the one that found Worf at Khitomer some twenty years earlier ("Sins of the Father"/165); Riker once enjoyed Worf's favorite food, rokeg blood pie ("A Matter of Honor"/134); Guinan's "prune juice" remark refers back to her gift to Worf ("Yesterday's Enterprise"/163); and Picard tells his friend Louis of the starship's efforts to stabilize the tectonics of Drema IV ("Pen Pals"/141).

REMEMBER ME

Production No.: 179 ■ Aired: Week of October 22, 1990
Stardate: 44161.2 ■ Code: rm

Directed by **Cliff Bole**
Written by **Lee Sheldon**

GUEST CAST
The Traveler: **Eric Menyuk**
Commander Dalen Quaice, M.D.: **Bill Erwin**
Lieutenant O'Brien: **Colm Meaney**

After welcoming her mentor, Dr. Quaice, an elderly man sadly reflecting on the loss of his wife and friends, Dr. Crusher visits her son in the engineering department. Wesley is working on a warp-field experiment. As Beverly watches, the project aborts in a brief flash of light. The moment is forgotten until, one by one, Quaice, her staff, and even the senior bridge officers begin to disappear. Those who remain, even Data, know nothing about the vanished.

But it is actually Dr. Crusher who has disappeared—into an alternate universe. Aboard the "real" *Enterprise*, the Traveler reappears to let Wesley know that the experiment is to blame. He, La Forge, and Data try to retrieve Dr. Crusher, but their efforts appear to her as a vortex that she resists being sucked into.

After even Picard vanishes and the universe begins eroding away, Dr. Crusher figures out what has happened. This "world" is ruled by the thought in her mind at the time of the failed experiment: the loss of friends and loved ones.

Realizing the way back to the real world is the site of the flash, she dashes back and falls into Wesley's arms just as her "new world" collapses.

Marked by the return of Eric Menyuk as the Traveler, this budget-minded bottle show actually served as a delightful showcase for the talents of Gates McFadden as Dr. Crusher soloed in her own decaying universe during about 40 percent of the script. The actress absolutely shines as she deals with increasing double-talk from Data and Picard, her own fear of insanity, and the prospect of being left with the humorless computer as her only companion.

We also learn more about Beverly's background, including the fact that she interned with Dr. Quaice only fifteen years ago—in other words, after Wesley was born. She repeats her recurring opening line to Picard when they are both alone on the bridge ("Arsenal of Freedom"/121, "The High Ground"/160).

McFadden performed all her own stunts for the swirling-vortex effects sequences, including the most outlandish maneuver—when she appears to be sucked out horizontally by the vortex while clutching the back of a chair. Rob Legato had a chair mounted on the wall, and McFadden hung down out of the chair. Legato used compressed-air machines and other devices to animate the scene; the footage was then matted in at a 90-degree angle. Only days after that strenuous shoot, McFadden learned she was pregnant—see "The Host" (197).

This story, Lee Sheldon's only contribution to the series during his short tenure as producer, began as a subplot for "Family" (178) in which crew members begin to disappear because of a wormhole. But, according to Piller, the staff felt there was not enough room for both story lines in that script, and the "Remember Me" material was cut loose to be developed on its own.

The "cochrane," by the way, is used here as a unit of measure of subspace field stress. The term was coined by Rick Sternbach and Michael Okuda as yet another homage to Zefren Cochran, the discoverer of space-warp physics—see "Ménage à Troi" (172). Mention is made here of Kosinski, the Traveler's original companion ("Where No One Has Gone Before"/106) and Dr. Selar ("The Schizoid Man"/131); we also learn that the *Enterprise* was carrying 1,014 people, including Dr. Quaice, when it docked at the starbase.

The Traveller (Eric Menyuk) returns to help Wesley retrieve his mother.

Legacy

Production No.: 180 ■ Aired: Week of October 29, 1990
Stardate: 44215.2 ■ Code: le

Directed by **Robert Scheerer**
Written by **Joe Menosky**

GUEST CAST
Ishara Yar: **Beth Toussaint**
Hayne: **Don Mirault**
Lieutenant O'Brien: **Colm Meaney**
Tan Tsu: **Vladimir Velasco**
Coalition lieutenant: **Christopher Michael**

Déjà vu sets in when the *Enterprise* attempts to rescue two Federation engineers lost on the late Tasha Yar's planet, Turkana IV. There they are surprised to discover her sister, Ishara, involved with one of two warring factions.

One faction, the Alliance, has taken the ship's engineers hostage: their rival, the Coalition, offers to help retrieve the engineers and volunteers the services of Ishara as a guide.

Ishara beams aboard the *Enterprise*, where Picard tries to reverse Ishara's view of her sister as a runaway and a quitter, and Data finds his memories of Tasha rekindled by Ishara, who shows some interest in joining Starfleet.

What Riker and Picard don't know is that the plan Ishara helps them devise is also meant to defeat the proximity detectors both Turkana factions agreed to years ago, so Ishara can disable the Alliance's power plants and cripple their defense.

Ishara leads the rescue effort but is stopped by Data at the reactor, where he dares her to shoot him. She is about to do so when Riker stuns her, then tells Data he's just learned about betrayal.

An allegory on gang warfare with added complications provided by Tasha's previously unknown sister, Joe Menosky's first script for the series will forever live in the annals of TNG trivia as the eightieth episode—the one that broke the record of the seventy-nine-episode run of the original series. To help mark the milestone, the cast and staff wrapped the filming with a party, reported by *Entertainment Tonight,* and a cake adorned by the art staff's special congratulatory logo.

Tasha Yar was given even more background history in this outing. We learn that her parents were killed in cadre crossfire just after Ishara was born, about four and a half years after Tasha. Also, Picard says he asked Tasha's former captain to transfer her to his command when the new *Enterprise* was about to be launched.

The starship *Potemkin,* the last to have contact with Turkana IV, was a former assignment of Lieutenant Riker's mentioned in "Peak Performance" (147), and a namesake of a Kirk-era starship seen in "The Ultimate Computer."

As his predecessor had done in season one, production designer Richard James made the precious budget for sets go farther by ingeniously re-dressing the Borg ship interiors, left standing on Stage 16's Planet Hell, for use as the Turkana underground tunnel complex. He would also make good use of them in several episodes to come, as would happen with the hostages' escape pod off the *Arcos,* a Sternbach design that would be re-dressed often ("Family"/183, "A Matter of Time"/209).

Data learns about betrayal from Yar's troubled younger sister Ishara (Beth Toussaint).

Reunion

Production No.: 181   ■   Aired: Week of November 5, 1990
Stardate: 44246.3   ■   Code: re

Directed by **Jonathan Frakes**
Teleplay by **Thomas Perry, Jo Perry, Ronald D. Moore, and Brannon Braga**
Story by **Drew Deighan, Thomas Perry, and Jo Perry**

GUEST CAST
K'Ehleyr: **Suzie Plakson**
Gowron: **Robert O'Reilly**
Duras: **Patrick Massett**
K'mpec: **Charles Cooper**
Alexander: **Jon Steuer**
Security Guard: **Michael Rider**
Transporter Chief Hubbell: **April Grace**
Klingon Guard #1 (Duras aide): **Basil Wallace**
Klingon (Vorn) Guard #2: **Mirron E. Willis**

Ambassador K'Ehleyr, Worf's half-human former love, beams aboard the *Enterprise* with two pieces of shocking news: Klingon leader K'mpec has been poisoned, and the young boy with her is her son—and Worf's.

K'mpec wants Picard to help him perform the ritual selecting a new leader. After revealing his suspicion that one of the contenders poisoned him, he tells Picard that no one on the Klingon Council can be trusted. One contender for the throne is Duras, who hid his own father's guilt by accusing Worf's father of being the Romulan collaborator in the Khitomer massacre.

Picard stalls for time as Duras and his rival, Gowron, beam aboard the *Enterprise* for the succession ceremony. Worf opts not to acknowledge his son so as to save him from the family's dishonor. K'Ehleyr's efforts to research the truth lead to her murder by Duras; he in turn is killed by a vengeful Worf.

Gowron is named leader of the Klingon Empire as a somber Worf sends Alexander off to be raised by his own foster parents on Earth.

The ill-fated K'Ehleyr (Suzie Plakson) presses Worf about their son.

In directing this chapter in Trek's ongoing Klingon saga, Jonathan Frakes again drew a no-lose episode for his second directorial outing, with actors like Patrick Massett, Suzie Plakson, and Charles Cooper at his disposal. Despite the multiple writing credits, the story shines. It also takes a lot of chances, including the deaths of both K'Ehleyr and Duras. Michael Piller and Ronald D. Moore defended the decision to kill off Worf's popular mate, who in an earlier draft had a relationship with Duras. We "wanted to get to a place where Worf was going to take Duras apart, and there's no good reason for him to do it unless she dies," Piller said.

And what a time for Worf! In one fell swoop he learns he has a son, his mate is killed, and he in turn kills her murderer and his family's accuser; he then sends his newfound son off to live with his own foster parents.

This episode is not exactly a vacation for Picard, either. It's a tribute to both actors and to the writers that what would always have been thought inconceivable is completely believable here: a human from the Federation choosing the next leader of the Klingon Empire!

For summer intern Brannon Braga, sitting down with Ron Moore to hash out the teleplay as his first TNG writing credit was an "illuminating, exhilarating" experience. Braga, who arrived with a strong production background from Kent State and the University of California at Santa Cruz, had produced music videos but got his first writing job as a member of the TNG staff for season five.

Dan Curry, nominally the visual-effects supervisor on alternating shows, drew on his martial arts background to design Worf's *bat'telh* weapon and helped Michael Dorn develop the unique movements used in wielding it.

Like his Klingon counterparts Plakson, Massett, and Cooper, Robert O'Reilly was also a TNG veteran, although he was first seen not as a Klingon but as Scarface, one of the hoodlums in "Manhunt" (145). Michael Rider, who plays an unnamed security guard in this show, was seen as a transporter chief in the several early pre-O'Brien shows (103–105).

During K'Ehleyr's briefing, we learn that the territories of the Ferengi and the Tholians border those of the Klingons and the Federation. And the *sonchi* pain sticks are ceremonial versions of those used for Worf's Rite of Ascension as seen in "The Icarus

Factor" (140). However, K'mpec—who is revealed to have led the Klingon Empire longer than anyone else in history—says his people and the Romulans have been "blood enemies" for seventy-five years, even through Worf once said that the two were still allies at the time of the infamous Khitomer massacre.

To this point budget constraints had forced the staff to use the two Klingon vessels from the films, but TNG finally got its own Klingon ship, the *Vor'cha*-class attack cruiser that debuted here. Roughly three-quarters the length of a Galaxy-class starship, the three-foot model—designed by Rick Sternbach and built by Greg Jein—reflects the post-alliance era with warp nacelles that have a Starfleet look. Even its color is new, midway between the old Klingon dark green and the bluish white of Starfleet. Within a year the model was released as an AMT kit.

FUTURE IMPERFECT

Production No.: 182 ▪ Aired: Week of November 12, 1990
Stardate: 44286.5 ▪ Code: fi

Directed by **Les Landau**
Written by **J. Larry Carroll and David Bennett Carren**

GUEST CAST
"Ambassador" Tomalak: **Andreas Katsulas**
Jean-Luc/Ethan: **Chris Demetral**
Minuet: **Carolyn McCormick**
Nurse Ogawa: **Patti Yasutake**
Ensign Gleason: **Todd Merrill**
Transporter Chief Hubbell: **April Grace**
Transporter Chief: **George O'Hanlon, Jr.**
Barash: **Dana Tjowander**

"Admiral" Picard and his aide Troi (*above*) come aboard the *Enterprise* to sign a peace treaty with "Captain" Riker and the Romulan "Ambassador" Tomalak (Andreas Katsulas) (*below*).

After having passed out during a mission to Apha Onias III, Riker awakens to an unbelievable scene: sixteen years have passed; he's now captain of the *Enterprise* and a widower with a teenage son!

Dr. Crusher explains that during his mission to Alpha Onias III he contracted a virus that only recently became active; the virus wiped out his memory of the years since then. Riker also discovers that a peace treaty with the Romulans is about to be signed and that his onetime nemesis

Tomalak, now an ambassador, is on board the *Enterprise,* as is "Admiral" Picard.

But Riker senses something is wrong when the ship's computer takes an unusually long time to respond to his queries about his missing years. He then discovers that his late wife was Minuet, an ideal woman created for him by the Bynars.

When he confronts Tomalak with this knowledge, the scene dissolves into a Romulan holodeck, with only Tomalak remaining. Riker is then thrown into a dungeon with his "son," who turns out to be a boy who was captured by the Romulans.

The boy then helps him escape, but makes another reference to "Ambassador" Tomalak. Finally, the boy reveals the truth: he is an alien named Barash who captured Riker and devised the elaborate memory-loss scenario to have company during his exile. Riker then invites the youngster to return with him to the *Enterprise*.

Albeit in illusory form, "Future Imperfect" continued the family theme that marked the season's first nine shows. The episode also gave Frakes a chance to show he could invest Riker's character scenes with the same level of intensity Stewart had brought to Picard's in "Family" (178). The script gained perhaps its most poignant scene at the last minute, when for once the pace of filming was going too fast. Writers Larry Carroll and David Bennett Carren had to meet after hours with Rick Berman and Michael Piller to thrash out a new scene the night before it was to be shot. What evolved was the turbo-lift scene between Riker and his "son" in which Number One admits his fear of repeating his own father's mistakes as a parent—a satisfying echo of "The Icarus Factor" (140).

Their efforts won Carroll and Carren a spot on the writing staff that would last all season. Carren had written previously for *Starsky and Hutch*, the 1980s *Twilight Zone*, and the 1970s *Buck Rogers*. Carroll had been a film editor on the original *Texas Chainsaw Massacre* and had written low-budget films for independents and for Empire, including *Ghost Warrior*, which he also directed.

Back again, though only briefly, is Carolyn McCormick as Riker's onetime holodeck soul mate, Minuet ("11001001"/116). Another nice long-term continuity touch is Andreas Katsulas's third appearance as a Romulan villain ("The Enemy"/155, "The Defector"/158). Patti Yasutake began her continuing role as a nurse here. She would go on to acquire not only a name but even a personality by season five. And, though she was seen once before, and will appear in many shows to come, it is only in this episode that April Grace's character, a transporter chief, is given a last name: Hubbell.

The transporter chief of Barash's illusion is played by an actor whose background includes both space and fantasy, sort of: George O'Hanlon, Jr., is the son of talented voice actor George O'Hanlon, perhaps best known as Hanna-Barbera cartoon star George Jetson. Todd Merrill's character, Gleason, returns but seems to have been demoted since the Borg battle; here he is a services-division ensign rather than a command-division lieutenant (j.g.), as he was in the season opener, "The Best of Both Worlds," Part 2 (175). And under the Barash alien costume is an uncredited extra, Dana Tjowander.

Barash managed to conjure up a whole new look for the Federation in his future fantasy, including new Starfleet communicators (which were quickly put on sale by Trek merchandisers), a female Klingon ensign, and a Ferengi at the conn; a scar for Worf, a cranberry uniform for First Officer Data, a replacement for Geordi's VISOR, and a gray-streaked, married Troi as "Admiral" Picard's aide.

Some things weren't changed, though: Riker still had his trombone handy, kids still got hurt playing Parrises Squares, and Number One clearly managed to pass on his love of fishing to his son.

Tomalak's fantasy Romulan warbird, *Decius*, carries the name of the fatally injured aide to Mark Lenard's unnamed commander in original Trek's "Balance of Terror," and we also learn that the original eight outposts along the Neutral Zone, seen in that 1960s episode, have grown to at least twenty-three. Once again, the original Borg interiors seen in "The Best of Both Worlds," Part 2 (175), came back to life, this time refigured by Richard James as the underground Romulan base. Next to an old twentieth-century Apollo lunar module, the other model in Riker's "future" ready room is the Nebula-class USS *Melbourne*, designed by Ed Miarecki.

FINAL MISSION

Production No.: 183 ■ Aired: Week of November 19, 1990
Stardate: 44307.3 ■ Code: fm

Directed by **Corey Allen**
Teleplay by **Kacey Arnold-Ince and Jeri Taylor**
Story by **Kacey Arnold-Ince**

GUEST CAST
Dirgo: **Nick Tate**
Chairman Songi: **Kim Hamilton**
Ensign Tess Allenby: **Mary Kohnert**

Wesley has finally been accepted into Starfleet Academy, but before he leaves, he is to accompany Captain Picard on one last mission.

They've been sent to mediate a miners' dispute, but the rattletrap of a shuttle sent for them malfunctions, and they crash-land on a desert moon. Their pilot, Dirgo, overconfident of his own planning and leadership abilities, didn't stock water, so the trio is forced to set out for some distant caves. Meanwhile, the *Enterprise* is summoned to remove an old garbage scow that is leaking radiation into a planet's atmosphere.

The crash-landing survivors finally find a fountain, but it is guarded by an energy sentry. An impatient Dirgo causes a rockslide that wounds Picard, then bullies Wesley into an attack on the sentry that results in Dirgo's death.

Riker and the crew struggle to finish their job and then go hunt for the missing shipmates. Meanwhile, Wesley works to keep Picard alive while figuring out a way to defeat the sentry. After forging new bonds with his nearly comatose captain, he does both—keeping himself and Picard alive until rescue finally comes.

An Academy-bound Wesley faces his biggest challenge yet in saving Picard's life.

Wil Wheaton bows out as a TNG regular in this story, giving what was probably his best performance of the series to date. He had asked to be let go so he could pursue the many film offers coming his way, but the door was left open for future appearances by finally shipping Wesley off to the Academy, as Gene Roddenberry had suggested. And in this last appearance, Wheaton didn't "save the ship," only his captain. "He directly saved the ship only one and a half times and had a hand in contributing to the solution of the problem two times! That's it!"[2] Wheaton once asserted, long accustomed to defending his character against some fans' scorn.

Corey Allen returns for his first directorial outing since the pilot and season one's "Home Soil" (117), just in time for two days of location shooting on the El Mirage Dry Lake Bed in San Bernadino County, east of Los Angeles. Jeri Taylor said the story, originally set on an ice planet where only Picard and Wesley crash-land, was changed to a desert locale because it was feared a Planet Hell ice-world set would be too hokey.

Nick Tate, who played Dirgo, is known best to genre audiences from his regular role on *Space: 1999*. Mary Kohnert would be the first of many (mostly female) replacements for Wesley at the conn, though her role would last only another episode.

The decrepid *Nenebek* shuttle, re-dressed from the SS *Arcos* escape pod in "Legacy" (180), features "archaic" labels and controls lifted from the present-day space shuttle by Michael Okuda. The episode's only headache was caused by the spring fountain, built indoors on Stage 16. Both live and optical effects for its shield at first failed to deliver. Finally, on two days' notice, Legato succeeded in devising what he called "an acrylic log" that rotated with reflective bits.

Trek continuity touches included Dirgo's use of "old-model" pistol phasers from *Star Trek III*; mention of the shuttle's duranium hull ("A Matter of Perspective"/162, "Hollow Pursuits"/169); and the use of hyronalin, first described in 1968's "The Deadly Years" as a treatment for radiation sickness. And Picard contributes a look forward and backward: while semiconscious he hums *"Auprès de Ma Blonde,"* the French song that he and his brother sang while drunk after their tussle in the mud in "Family" (178), and he tells Wesley about Boothby, the Academy's gardener, who would be seen a year later in "The First Duty" (219).

THE LOSS

Production No.: 184 ■ Aired: Week of December 31, 1990
Stardate: 44356.9 ■ Code: ls

Directed by **Chip Chalmers**
Teleplay by **Hilary J. Bader, Alan J. Adler, and
Vanessa Greene**
Story by **Hilary J. Bader**

GUEST CAST
Ensign Janet Brooks: **Kim Braden**
Ensign Tess Allenby: **Mary Kohnert**
Guinan: **Whoopi Goldberg**

The *Enterprise* finds it cannot resume course after stopping to check out what appeared to be images in its path. At the same moment, Troi discovers her empathic powers have completely disappeared.

The roadblock is found to be a unique cluster of two-dimensional life-forms that have caught the starship up in their wake.

Meanwhile, Troi suffers denial, panic, and even anger at friends. Despite the protests of Guinan, Picard, and Riker that she still has her professional training to lean on, she resigns as ship's counselor. Then Data and Riker realize the creatures are heading for a cosmic string that would doom the starship, and a desperate Picard turns to Troi for help.

After trying to warn the creatures of the danger, she realizes they want to seek out the cosmic string. When Data creates a "dummy" string to the ship's rear, the creatures are confused and stop long enough for the *Enterprise* to break free.

Troi's powers come rushing back to her as she realizes that the strength of the two-dimensional creatures' feelings overwhelmed her powers. She resumes her job with renewed confidence in her abilities.

"The Loss" demonstrates that the TNG writers have finally learned to create conflict in Gene Roddenberry's perfect world by using outside stimuli. This episode gave Marina Sirtis a rare chance to stretch and shine as Troi—and made those weeks of almost being written out of the series in season one seem very far away indeed. Riker here calls Troi a "blue-blooded Betazoid" who's always had a unique means of control to fall back on, giving her character a subtext that was sadly lacking in the early years. Their relationship, long shunned or even denied by the writers, revealed here how well it could survive if it was shown and not just talked about. In this show we hear the Betazoid endearment, *imzadi*, for the first time in nearly two years since "Shades of Gray" (148).

Another landmark is Troi's conversation with Guinan. One of the few criticisms of the addition of Whoopi Goldberg's character is that Guinan seems to duplicate Troi's shipboard function, but in this case that "competition" is turned on its ear and used to great effect.

Writing intern Hilary Bader added the science subplot of the cosmic string, and Michael Piller revealed that for a time the staff even toyed with the daring idea of not giving Troi back her lost empathic sense. Sirtis has remarked that many fans with disabilities reacted warmly to her performance in this episode. Ironically, the episode that almost cost her her empathy is the one that begins by finally showing her counseling an adult crew member.

We also discover here that Betazoids' empathic abilities lie within the cerebellum and the cerebral cortex. We're also told that the Breen and other races, as well as the Ferengi, cannot be sensed empathically. As a throwaway, Picard's equestrian interest ("Pen Pals"/141) is recalled during a Kabul River Himalayan ride on the holodeck.

A major concept in warp-drive design is introduced here by Michael Okuda and Rick Sternbach in a passing reference to the ship's structural integrity field, a force that keeps the ship intact under various inertial forces and stresses when the simple vacuum and null gravity of space aren't enough.

Guinan (Whoopi Goldberg) must counsel the counselor when Troi loses her empathic sense.

DATA'S DAY

Production No.: 185   ▪   Aired: Week of January 7, 1991
Stardate: 44390.1   ▪   Code: dd

Directed by **Robert Wiemer**
Teleplay by **Harold Apter and Ronald D. Moore**
Story by **Harold Apter**

GUEST CAST
Keiko Ishikawa: **Rosalind Chao**
Lieutenant O'Brien: **Colm Meaney**
Ambassador T'Pel (Sub-Commander Selok): **Sierra Pecheur**
Admiral Mendak: **Alan Scarfe**
Transporter Chief Hubbell: **April Grace**
V'Sal: **Shelly Desai**

The wedding party watches Miles (Colm Meaney) and Keiko O'Brien (Rosalind Chao).

Data's understanding of human behavior is put to the test when his friend Keiko Ishikawa gets cold feet on the eve of her wedding to Lieutenant O'Brien and calls off the ceremony.

Logically, the android reasons, if calling off the wedding makes her happy it will make O'Brien happy, too. Of course, when Data delivers the news to the transporter chief he quickly discovers otherwise. Geordi, however, assures him the ceremony will take place, so the android purchases a gift with Worf's assistance and takes dancing lessons from Dr. Crusher.

Meanwhile, the whole crew—except for Data—is made edgy by the presence of Ambassador T'Pel, a cooler-than-usual Vulcan en route to historic treaty negotiations with the Romulans in the Neutral Zone. But shortly after Data refuses to grant the ambassador access to security information for which she has not been cleared, she is killed in a mysterious transporter accident.

With her death, the treaty negotiations are called off, and the Romulans prepare to depart. But a probe, led by Data in his Sherlock Holmes persona, turns up signs that her death was faked. Confronted with this information, Romulan Commander Mendak reveals the truth: T'Pel was actually a deep-cover spy for his Empire.

The danger passed, the mood turns more joyful. Data walks his friend Keiko down the aisle, and she and O'Brien are married in a ceremony performed by Picard.

A marvelous and ambitious show relished by trivia fans, this day-in-the-life plot was the first attempted in any of Trek's various incarnations. Harold Apter first pitched the story during the third season, and various viewpoints including Picard's and that of the ship itself were considered for the narrative. Ronald D. Moore recalled that Data was the final choice because "he's the only one who's up twenty-four hours a day." Michael Piller then agreed with Rick Berman that at least one plot arc should run through the story, and the Romulan-Vulcan spy intrigue was added.

Director Robert Wiemer revealed that Brent Spiner and Gates McFadden worked up their own dialogue as well as their dance routine during after-hours rehearsals, and the lines they created were later accepted by the scriptwriters. The director, though, took credit for Data's "pasted-on" smile at the end of the dancing scene. Spiner—who, Wiener said, did "99 percent" of his own tap routine—was as good as his double but was modest enough to let the double perform to ensure the routine's quality.

The writing staff had toyed with the idea of a shipboard marriage for some time. Piller at one point even quietly inquired about marrying Picard off to provide some new story dynamics. Pairing O'Brien with the female conn officer slated to replace Wesley was also considered. Finally a wedding was proposed for the day-in-the-life story and Keiko was conceived. The part is played by Rosalind Chao, a close friend of Elizabeth "Shelby" Dennehy and an earlier candidate for a recurring role on the show. Chao is probably best remembered as Corporal Klinger's war bride on *M*A*S*H* and *After M*A*S*H*. Loads of *Enterprise* trivia can be found in this story. On SD 44390, for example, the 1,550th day since the starship's commissioning (SD 40759.5—or October 4, 2363, according to Okuda and Sternbach's technical manual. Data is still writing to Commander Bruce Maddox at the Daystrom Institute. For the first time, we see the android's cat, an idea Spiner proposed; the cat would get a name later, in "In Theory" (199). Data records that the starship's day included four birthdays, two transfers, four promotions, two chess tournaments, a secondary school play, a celebration of the Hindu Festival of Lights, various accidents, the birth of the Juarezes' baby, and the O'Brien-Ishikawa wedding.

Meanwhile, fans of the original series will notice that Picard's wedding remarks are almost the same, word for word, as those with which Kirk began in 1966's "Balance of Terror." Also, the Murasaki Quasar mentioned here may be the same as Murasaki 312, which appeared in 1967's "The Galileo Seven." The Andorians are mentioned for the first time since "The Offspring" (164) a year earlier in a reference to their bizarre wedding ritual; likewise, the Bolians reappear ("Conspiracy"/125; "Allegiance"/166) with Shelly Desai playing the first in a string of Bolian barbers ("The Host"/197, "Ensign Ro"/203). And the USS *Zhukov*, which ferries the Romulan spy, was earlier referred to as Barclay's last assignment ("Hollow Pursuits"/169).

The ship's arboretum, mentioned on several other occasions as a socializing site, makes its debut here—but as a work site for Keiko, a biologist. Another first is this show's glimpse of people "shopping" at the ship's replication center, where we discover Worf's appreciation of fine glass bird sculpture.

THE WOUNDED

Production No.: 186 ■ Aired: Week of January 28, 1991
Stardate: 44429.6 ■ Code: wo

Directed by **Chip Chalmers**
Teleplay by **Jeri Taylor**
Story by **Stuart Charno, Sara Charno, and Cy Chermak**

GUEST CAST
Captain Benjamin Maxwell: **Bob Gunton**
Keiko Ishikawa O'Brien: **Rosalind Chao**
Gul Macet: **Marc Alaimo**
Lieutenant O'Brien: **Colm Meaney**
Glinn Telle: **Marco Rodriguez**
Glinn Daro: **Time Winters**
Admiral Haden: **John Hancock**

Picard is shocked to learn a renegade Federation starship under the command of Captain Benjamin Maxwell is destroying Cardassian ships, threatening the fragile peace that the Federation and the Cardassian Empire have achieved after years of skirmishes.

He invites the Cardassian, Gul Macet, aboard to witness the pursuit of the ship, the USS *Phoenix*. Both watch in horror on long-range scan as two more Cardassian ships are destroyed.

O'Brien, Maxwell's former tactical officer, says he finds the decorated captain's acts hard to believe. Maxwell, he says, must have a reason for the attacks. Intercepted at last, Maxwell gladly comes aboard to tell Picard that he has proof the Cardassians are rearming for war.

But Picard has seen enough and relays his orders to bring the captain back for an inquiry. Maxwell agrees, but once aboard his ship he breaks off to pursue a Cardassian freighter, daring Picard to board it to prove his case.

Picard refuses and orders Maxwell to surrender, but the *Phoenix* powers up its weapons. To break the standoff, O'Brien beams over and quietly persuades his old captain to give up. A broken Maxwell agrees.

Macet expresses his thanks, but Picard sternly warns him that even though Maxwell's actions were wrong, the facts show that his information was right. He says the *Enterprise* will be back to lead the fight against the Cardassians if necessary.

A wonderful show that not only offered a strong and tragic figure in Bob Gunton's Captain Maxwell but also added some long-overdue depth to O'Brien's character. Even the scientific *deus ex machina*—transporting through one-fiftieth of a second break in recycling shields—was well done. Other nice touches included references to the depleted post-Borg fleet and the shield-dropping prefix code, a concept dating back to *Star Trek II*.

While the philosophical conflict was between the two captains, it was O'Brien who butted heads with his counterpart Cardassian and sang an Irish song with his former commander—a gem of a scene suggested by Michael Piller (which Rick Berman picked)—helping to diffuse a tense situation and returning Maxwell to a sane but broken state. (The song, "The Minstrel Boy" by Thomas Moore, figured prominently in the movie *The Man Who Would Be King*.) We also learned that young Miles Edward O'Brien was a peaceful, nature-loving boy who never killed until a Cardassian patrol forced him to. Mentioning his stint as tactics officer on the *Rutledge* provided a nice setup for future bridge duty ("Redemption II"/201, "Disaster"/205).

Only Mark "Sarek" Lenard had played three different aliens in the Trek universe until Marc Alaimo did it here as one of the Cardassians after appearing as an Antican and a Romulan ("Lonely Among Us"/108, "The Neutral Zone"/126); in his next go-round he would play a human ("Time's Arrow"/226). Also back was John Hancock as the admiral who seems to get only Picard's touchiest security problems ("The Defector"/158). And Bob Gunton, seen on Broadway in *Sweeney Todd*, did perhaps the best job of any actor since William "Decker" Windom, in 1967's "The

O'Brien (Colm Meaney) and Cardassian Daro (Time Winters) confront old prejudices.

chine," of conveying a once-strong Starfleet commander gone awry.

Greg Jein was the model maker responsible for bringing Ed Miarecki's Nebula-class starship to life as the NCC-65420, USS *Phoenix,* already seen briefly in an earlier show, ("Future Imperfect"/182); its dedication plaque hangs in Maxwell's ready room instead of on the bridge. The Cardassian warship *Trager* was designed by Rick Sternbach and built by Miarecki and Tom Hudson. As a "major" race's vessel it began as a simple ship with pods, evolved into a scorpionlike design, then lost its appendages and took its final form, which Sternbach based on an Egyptian *ankh.*

Like that of the Talarians ("Suddenly Human"/176), Cardassian space is on the "west" side of the Federation, opposite the Klingon and Romulan territories, judging from their sector numbers and the art staff's galactic plane-view "map." Continuing the tradition of giving each alien culture a signature color for its energy devices, Cardassian phasers are pink.

An emergency transmission from a Federation science station sends the *Enterprise* to Ventax II, where Picard and crew discover a peaceful but meek people about to hand over their world to a woman who claims she is the planet's devil, Ardra.

It seems the pollution-plagued, war-torn Ventaxians generations ago made a pact with Ardra: a thousand years of peace and health in return for their eternal slavery. The Ventaxians had long thought the tale a legend until the shape-changing Ardra showed up.

Picard draws Ardra's wrath when he refuses her sexual advances, and she makes the starship "disappear." As La Forge races to discover a power source behind her "special effects," Ardra agrees to a legal contest on the real-enough contracts and her identity, with Data as magistrate.

Picard tries to convince the Ventaxian leader, Jared, that his people are responsible for their own prosperity, but when Ardra runs through her illusions again, Jared agrees to submit to her judgment.

Finally, La Forge locates her cloaked orbiting ship and enables Picard to tap into its power systems, revealing Ardra as just another con artist.

DEVIL'S DUE

Production No.: 187 ■ Aired: Week of February 4, 1991
Stardate: 44474.5 ■ Code: dv

Directed by **Tom Benko**
Teleplay by **Philip Lazebnick**
Story by **Philip Lazebnick and William Douglas Lansford**

GUEST CAST
Ardra: **Marta Dubois**
Dr. Clarke: **Paul Lambert**
Jared: **Marcello Tubert**
Devil Monster: **Thad Lamey**
Klingon Monster: **Tom Magee**
Marley: **William Glover**

Picard must outwit Ventax II's "devil," Ardra (Marta Dubois).

Like "The Child" (127), this story predates TNG—to at least August 16, 1977, when the Lansford story turned up in a status memo for the 1970s *Star Trek II* TV series. Its "Devil and Daniel Webster" plot, originally unearthed during TNG's third-season story pinch, eventually bore the mark of a score of TNG staff writers. In the end, it was Trek fan and *Wings* staff writer Philip Lazebnick's comic touches that survived, along with Piller's idea of making the "devil" a female.

The 1977 outline reads like a 1960s Trek episode. In it a demonstrative Captain Kirk fast-talks planet Neuterr out of falling for an impostor's scam, exposing the "devil" as merely the mental energy of a surviving planetary elder and his original fellow council members.

Although familiar actresses like Stella Stevens and Adrienne Barbeau were considered, the role of Ardra went to Marta DuBois, *Magnum's* estranged wife on *Magnum P.I.*, after her several earlier TNG auditions were well received but did not fit the character at hand.

Though some may regard it as the Klingon devil, Fek'lhr as seen here is carefully described as the guardian of Gre'thor, the hereafter where the Klingon dishonored go after they die. This is consistent with the fact that Klingons have no devil—a detail that was revealed in 1969's "Day of the Dove."

CLUES

Production No.: 188 ■ Aired: Week of February 11, 1991
Stardate: 44502.7 ■ Code: cl

Directed by **Les Landau**
Teleplay by **Bruce D. Arthurs and Joe Menosky**
Story by **Bruce D. Arthurs**

GUEST CAST
Lieutenant O'Brien: **Colm Meaney**
Ensign McKnight: **Pamela Winslow**
Madeline: **Rhonda Aldrich**
Guinan: **Whoopi Goldberg**
Nurse Alyssa Ogawa: **Patti Yasutake**
Gunman: **Thomas Knickerbocker**

As the *Enterprise* is on its way to investigate a mysterious planet, a wormhole suddenly appears in the ship's path, knocking the crew unconscious. As they begin to come to, Data, who is immune to the wormhole's effects, tells them only thirty seconds have passed since their encounter with the phenomenon.

But soon evidence mounts that the crew was out for much longer—an entire day, in fact. A twinge of pain in Worf's wrist reveals a recent fracture, a botany experiment records a full twenty-four hours' growth, and the ship's chronometer has been tampered with.

A check of Data's systems shows nothing wrong, but an analysis of the probe he sent shows it was rigged to send false information.

Picard finally orders the crew to proceed to the mystery planet, over Data's objections. The android refuses to say why, but he does tell Picard the captain himself ordered him to lie.

Suddenly a being called a Paxan inhabits Troi's body. Data then explains the truth: the horribly isolationist Paxans stun intruders and send their ships on their way, but Data's presence foiled their plan. The *Enterprise* did go to the planet, but the Paxans demanded the starship be destroyed. Picard, though, won agreement to a short-term memory wipe for all the crew, with Data ordered to keep the secret.

During the second visit Picard assures the Paxans that the bugs in his plan can be worked out so that their existence will remain a secret.

Story creator Bruce D. Arthurs proved it can be done: the fan and Phoenix, Arizona, mail carrier had his spec script for TNG bought and turned into an episode, helped along by a rewrite that won Joe Menosky a staff job. Michael Piller called this bottle-show mystery, which includes the first appearance of Dixon Hill since "Manhunt" (145) in season two, one of his favorites for the season.

Guinan (Whoopi Goldberg) doesn't share Picard's thrill at playing detective.

Notice director Les Landau's use of longer and more fluid camera takes for the flashbacks, in contrast with a choppier style with more cuts back and forth for real time.

In addition to bringing back Rhonda Aldrich as Madeline, Dixon Hill's secretary, this segment includes the only mention of Nurse Ogawa's first name—Alyssa. There's also a fleeting glimpse of a t'ai chi class led by Worf, with Riker, Troi, and Geordi among the participants. We also learn the transporter trace records can be used to determine elapsed time judging by cellular cycle, and that a ship's clock exists apart from the chronometer—which only La Forge and Data can reset—used by the computer system. Wormholes have previously been seen in *Star Trek: The Motion Picture,* and Data mentions having encountered them twice in his own career: during the Barzan affair in "The Price" (156) and during his service aboard the *Trieste,* mentioned already as a previous assignment ("11001001"/116).

First Contact

Production No.: 189 ■ Airdate: February 18, 1991
Stardate: Unknown ■ Code: fc

Directed by **Cliff Bole**
Teleplay by **Dennis Russell Bailey, David Bischoff, Joe Menosky, and Ronald D. Moore**
Story by **Marc Scott Zicree**

GUEST CAST
Chancellor Avill Durken: **George Coe**
Mirasta: **Carolyn Seymour**
Berel: **George Hearn**
Krola: **Michael Ensign**
Nilrem: **Steven Anderson**
Dr. Tava: **Sachi Parker**
Lanel: **Bebe Neuwirth**

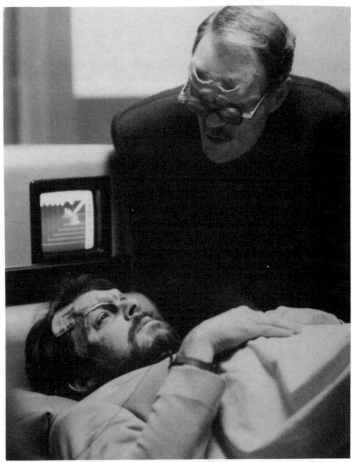

Krola (Michael Ensign) is not about to let "aliens" on his world.

A reconnaissance mission on the planet Malcoria III goes disastrously wrong when Commander Riker (in native disguise) is injured and taken to a native hospital. There, Malcorian doctors soon uncover his true identity.

To prevent worldwide panic, Picard and Troi beam down to meet with the astonished planet's leader. But though Chancellor Durken and his science minister Mirasta (in charge of Malcor's fledgeling space program) are both convinced by the *Enterprise* crew's message of peace and friendship, Durken's security officer Krola remains suspicious. After Riker unsuccessssfully attempts to escape from the hospital, Krola steps in to interrogate him, using potentially lethal drugs.

When his questioning proves fruitless, Krola stages his own death and makes Riker appear to be the executioner, hoping both to prevent the aliens from gaining a foothold on his world, and to quash Mirasta's dreams of space exploration. Dr. Crusher beams in, however, bringing both Riker and Krola back up to sickbay, where she convinces Durken of what really happened.

Though the Chancellor is satisfied of the Federation's good intentions, he realizes his people aren't ready to accept the idea that they aren't alone in the universe yet. Durken quietly puts his world's nascent space program on hold—while granting Mirasta's wish to leave with the starship.

Michael Piller had to persuade Rick Berman to let him bend the rules and tell this story—for the first time in Trek's twenty-five years, the teaser of 1967's "Tomorrow Is Yesterday" notwithstanding—from an alien culture's point of view. The gamble worked to perfection in this homage to the classic 1951 science fiction movie *The Day the Earth Stood Still*, which gave us a look at what must be an ongoing process within the Federation. We also learn that a bungled first-contact mission was the reason behind decades of Klingon-Federation conflict.

The multiple teleplay credits include versions by "Tin Man" (168) scriptwriters Dennis Putnam Bailey and David Bischoff and another by Ronald D. Moore and Joe Menosky that tried to use the point of view of the *Enterprise* crew after Marc Scott Zicree—author of *The Twilight Zone Companion*—first pitched this basic story idea during season three.

Throughout its evolution, the idea took many twists and turns. It was considered for the season-end cliff-hanger and, in a version called "Graduation," as Wesley's swan song in which he was to stay planetside permanently after a cultural-contact mission. One rejected concept, according to Zicree, had the new space travelers finding out about the Federation by taking in Picard & Co.'s crippled shuttlecraft. In another, the members of the contact team become celebrities.

The excellent cast includes George Coe, perhaps better known in genre circles for his old *Max Headroom* role as Network 23 president Ben DeVore; Carolyn Seymour, who played Romulan Sub-Commander Taris in "Contagion" (137); and Bebe Neuwirth, a longtime fan who plays Dr. Lilith Crane on *Cheers*. Here she's a Malcorian nurse in a late-draft cameo, written with her in mind; she offers to help Riker escape if he'll fulfill her greatest fantasy: to make love to an alien. Did Riker—or didn't he? Well, he escapes somehow!

Clever use is made here of Malcorian medical and anatomical terms that sound almost authentic: "cardial organ" for heart, "costal struts" for ribs, "terminus" for foot, and "renal organ" for kidney.

GALAXY'S CHILD

Production No.: 190 ■ Aired: Week of March 11, 1991
Stardate: 44614.6 ■ Code: gc

Directed by **Winrich Kolbe**
Teleplay by **Maurice Hurley**
Story by **Thomas Kartozian**

GUEST CAST
Dr. Leah Brahms: **Susan Gibney**
Ensign Rager: **Lanei Chapman**
Ensign Pavlik: **Jana Marie Hupp**
Guinan: **Whoopi Goldberg**
Transporter Chief Hubbell: **April Grace**

La Forge's joy at finally meeting Dr. Leah Brahms, the Galaxy-class engine designer whose holodeck image he once fell in love with, turns to ashes when she finally comes aboard the *Enterprise*. The real Dr. Brahms is cold and highly critical of the field changes Geordi has made in her original designs.

Meanwhile, the discovery of a new alien lifeform ends in tragedy when the creature is accidentally killed. When the saddened crew members realize the entity was pregnant, Worf and Dr. Crusher free its baby with a phaser-fired "cesarean section." The newborn attaches itself to the starship and drains energy from what it believes is its mother.

La Forge and Dr. Brahms set to work to "wean" the baby, Geordi having only recently discovered that his dream woman is in fact mar-

La Forge and Dr. Brahms (Susan Gibney) find neither is what the other expected.

ried. Their fresh start as friends is derailed, however, when she finds his old holodeck program and is infuriated to learn that he used her as a fantasy object.

As other alien adults approach from their native asteroid field, the energy drain on the ship grows critical. Finally the two engineers rise above their friction to devise a sour harmonic frequency, which breaks the link between the *Enterprise* and the baby just in time. The crisis past, Geordi and Leah find they can laugh about their feelings now—as friends.

The use of computer animation produced a very believable alien baby and adults in this story, written from Thomas Kartozian's outline by former producer Maurice Hurley, with uncredited assist from Jeri Taylor on the Geordi–Leah Brahms reunion and Ron Moore on the tale of "Junior." The chemistry between LeVar Burton and Susan Gibney was strong enough to lead many fans to hope for a return by the engineer if she ever becomes unattached.

Jana Marie Hupp, seen here as Ensign Pavlik, would fare much worse in a fifth-season episode, "Disaster" (205). The Jefferies tubes, named for original-series art director Matt Jefferies, are finally seen here, after having been mentioned during the third season in "The Hunted" (159).

In a rare blooper, "Junior" is seen attached over the starboard shuttle bay, which is spoken of as Shuttle Bay 2 even though it has always been identified in drawings as Shuttle Bay 3.

NIGHT TERRORS

Production No.: 191 ■ Aired: Week of March 18, 1991
Stardate: 44631.2 ■ Code: nt

Directed by **Les Landau**
Teleplay by **Pamela Douglas/Jeri Taylor**
Story by **Shari Goodhartz**

GUEST CAST
Keiko O'Brien: **Rosalind Chao**
Andrus Hagan: **John Vickery**
Ensign Gillespie: **Duke Moosekian**
Ensign Peeples: **Craig Hurley**
Ensign Kenny Lin: **Brian Tochi**
Ensign Rager: **Lanei Chapman**
Lieutenant O'Brien: **Colm Meaney**
Guinan: **Whoopi Goldberg**
Captain Chantal R. Zaheva: **Deborah Taylor**

The *Enterprise* finds the starship *Brattain*, missing for several weeks, adrift in space. The entire crew save the ship's Betazoid counselor, is dead.

While the crew is investigating the incident, odd events begin to occur. Troi is tormented by nightmares, and La Forge can't restart the *Brattain*'s engines. Dr. Crusher suggests that the irritability among the crew might indicate a repetition of whatever happened to the now-dead science vessel. Picard decides to leave the area only to discover the *Enterprise*'s engines don't work either.

Data, unaffected, theorizes the ships are caught in a Tyken's Rift, a spatial rupture that is draining their energy. La Forge fails in an attempt to dislodge them. Dr. Crusher finds that the crew's depression and shakiness stem from dream deprivation, and Troi realizes that her colleague's nightmares mirror her own; she wonders if they could be an attempt at communication.

While brainstorming with Data, Troi guesses that her nightmare images come from a ship trapped on the other side of the rift. The other ship is asking for their aid in freeing both vessels with a release of hydrogen; the *Brattain* crew died before they could figure it out.

Troi tries to reach the other ship in a dream while Data vents all the ship's stored hydrogen. Just as their attempts seem to have failed, there is a giant explosion and the ship is thrown free.

Troi ponders the Tyken's Rift trap with a tormented Betazoid (John Vickery).

Though it's regarded as the clinker of the fourth season by many fans and by those involved, this script—from a story by Shari Goodhartz, who penned "The Most Toys" (170) during season three—does let Troi save the ship for once. The story suffered from time problems, among other things. Michael Piller recalled that the energy and pace were so slow that the episode ran nine minutes over and had to be severely cut.

After "flying" in a suspended harness during the filming of this episode, Marina Sirtis joked that her plea for more action scenes for Troi had backfired—she is deathly afraid of heights. The scenes, shot throughout an entire day of second-unit production, "seemed like a great idea in the meetings," but were a "terrible" production mistake, Jeri Taylor said. Rob Legato was more blunt: "Horrible!"

Longtime Trek fans should recall Brian Tochi as young Ray Tsingtao in the original-series episode "And the Children Shall Lead." More recently he was the voice of Leonardo in the *Teenage Mutant Ninja Turtles* movies and has appeared in everything from *Santa Barbara* to the last two *Police Academy* movies.

Michael Okuda's plaque for the *Brattain*—inexplicably labeled "Brittain" on the re-dressed *Reliant* miniature from *Star Trek II*—identifies the ship as NCC-21166 of the Miranda class, built at the Yoyodyne Division (another *Buckaroo Banzai* reference) over 40 Eridani-A (Vulcan's sun, according to Franz Joseph's 1974 *Starfleet Technical Manual*).

More in-jokes: TNG staffers' names can be seen in the explosives manifest that Data and Troi examine. Entries include Mooride Polyronite 4 (Ron Moore, visual-effects coordinator), Takemurium Lite (David Takemura, visual-effects associate), Neussite 283 (Wendy Neuss, associate producer), Bio-Genovesium (Cosmo Genovese, script supervisor), and Hutzelite (Gary Hutzel, visual-effects coordinator).

IDENTITY CRISIS

Production No.: 192 ■ Aired: Week of March 25, 1991
Stardate: 44664.5 ■ Code: ic

Directed by **Winrich Kolbe**
Teleplay by **Brannon Braga**
Story by **Timothy de Haas**

GUEST CAST
Lieutenant Commander Susanna Leitjen:
Maryann Plunkett
Nurse Alyssa Ogawa: **Patti Yasutake**
Lieutenant Hickman: **Amick Byram**
Transporter Technician Hedrick: **Dennis Madalone**
Ensign Graham: **Mona Grudt**

La Forge is disturbed to hear from former shipmate Susanna Leitjen that they are the only two members remaining from an away team sent to Tarchannen III five years ago.

The others are disappearing and apparently headed for the planet, initially investigated after a small colony disappeared there without a trace. On the surface, three shuttles but no life signs are found.

Leitjen tells La Forge she senses the others nonetheless. She then becomes unstable and has to be beamed to sickbay. Finding that Leitjen's blood chemistry has been altered, Dr. Crusher guesses the others have undergone the same process and have somehow been transformed

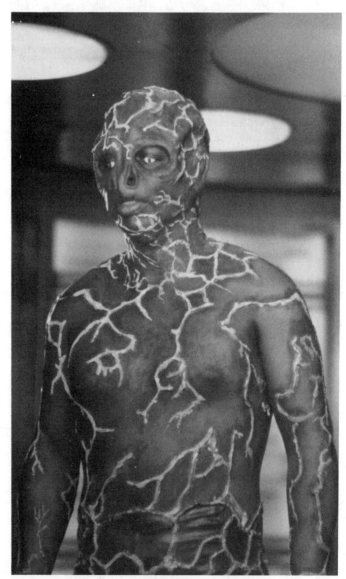

La Forge, almost entirely transformed into one of the ultraviolet light-beings of Tarchannen III.

into another species. Leitjen worries that the same thing will happen to her and La Forge. After she makes a dash to get off the ship, Geordi finds her skin broken out in blotches and her middle fingers fused together.

La Forge, working harder than ever, finds a shadow not noticed before on the team's original log tapes, indicating another entity nearby. Then he too falls ill and leaves the ship, evolving faster than any of the others.

Meantime, Dr. Crusher finds and removes a parasite from Leitjen that had been rewriting her DNA. They beam down to the planet's surface, where La Forge has been almost completely transformed; he is invisible except by ultraviolet light. Only his old friend's coaxing brings him back in time to remove the parasite.

Rescued from the slush pile of spec scripts, this story by fan writer Timothy de Haas originally concerned two non-regular crew members. The glowing transformed aliens gave Westmore, Blackman, and a company called Wildfire a chance to pioneer a remarkable optical effect using ultraviolet light. "MTV is using that a lot now," David Livingston said of the ultraviolet effect. "We didn't do it just to be glitzy—we did it because it tied in dramatically with the story."

Originally, Brannon Braga recalled, the script linked Geordi and Susanna romantically, but the word came down to give the engineer a break with his "failed love" record, which began in "Booby Trap" (154) and continued in "Galaxy's Child" (190). Braga said his first draft was more "horrific" with many more aliens on the surface, but Geordi wasn't transformed; keying the mood more to terror, of a type he described as "restrained and psychoanalytical," and involving Geordi in the emotional trauma of the change made the show click.

A nice continuity touch here is the use of the older-style uniforms, phasers, and tricorders for the visual log from the Victory's away team five years earlier—note the opening stardate, 40164.7—with Geordi as a command-division lieutenant (j.g.) when he came from the Victory ("Elementary, Dear Data"/129). The shuttlepod Cousteau from the Aries carries its ship's number, NCC-45167; it was the first ship command offered to Riker, in "The Icarus Factor" (140).

After debuting in the sciences division ("Where No One Has Gone Before"/106) and dying in the guise of security noncom Ramos ("Heart of Glory"/120), stunt coordinator Dennis Madalone here became Transporter Chief Hedrick; he's listed as a transporter technician, but he wears an ensign's pip. Likewise, Yasutake's recurring character finally gained a last name, Ogawa, here after Beverly had already called her by her first name, Alyssa in "Clues" (188).

Extra Randy Pflug models the humanoid shape that Geordi creates from the cast shadow, while among those wearing the ultraviolet suits were Mark and Brian, two L.A. disc jockeys who had become NBC variety show hosts.

Nth Degree

Production No.: 193 ■ Aired: Week of April 1, 1991
Stardate: 44704.2 ■ Code: nd

Directed by **Robert Legato**
Written by **Joe Menosky**

GUEST CAST
"Einstein": **Jim Morton**
Cytherian: **Kay E. Kuter**
Lieutenant Linda Larson: **Saxon Trainor**
Ensign April Anaya: **Page Leong**
Leiutenant (j.g.) Reginald Barclay: **Dwight Schultz**
Ensign Brower: **David Coburn**

Sent to repair the malfunctioning Argus Array telescope, the *Enterprise* discovers an alien probe near the installation. An energy surge from the probe knocks out La Forge and Lieutenant Barclay, who have been sent to study it from a shuttle.

When they come to, both officers seem to be fine, but Barclay soon begins making leaps of insight and showing abilities he never had before. He describes how to destroy the probe when it grows dangerous and then how to fix the telescope in a fraction of the time he would normally need.

A scan of the lieutenant's brain tissue reveals an underlying physiological reason for his new abilities: he is rapidly evolving into the most advanced human ever seen. The crew is edgy about his new powers, but Barclay seems innocent enough.

Then the telescope's reactors begin to fail rapidly, and even Barclay is stymied. Just as the installation is about to explode, the computer blinks out and then comes back on line—speaking with Barclay's voice.

The transformed crewman saves the installation and then propels the ship to a point thirty thousand light-years away. Picard now fears Barclay's intentions but is reluctant to sever the lieutenant's link to the computer, fearing it might kill him.

Suddenly the image of a smiling alien appears. His race, the Cytherians, studies other

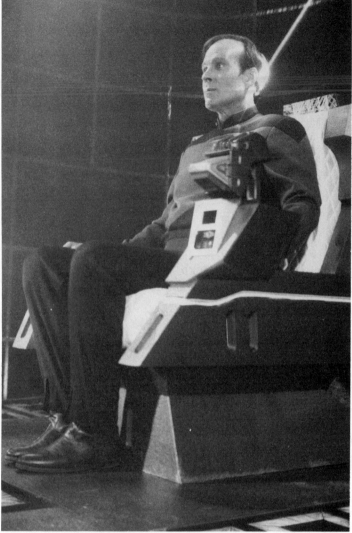

Supermind or superthreat? Barclay (Dwight Schultz) interfaces with the computer.

plot. He was proud of a camera shot on the bridge in which he rejected a series of close-ups in favor of a long continuous roll from one speaker to another.

This segment demonstrates how Gates McFadden's pleas to round out Beverly's character with "comedy and hobbies" were finally being met. We see her interest in the theater here on top of past glimpses of dance, in "Data's Day" (185), and biology in "Clues" (188). Michael Piller credited Rick Berman with suggesting the *Cyrano de Bergerac* scene between Barclay and his teacher, the "drama doctor."

Geordi and Barclay's shuttlecraft here is the *Feynman,* named for 1965 Nobel laureate physicist Richard P. Feynman. The "ODN bypass" mentioned concerns the optical data network, the starship's multiplex data transmission system. And the graviton concept, used by the Cyterians to bring their subjects home for study, was first used by the two-dimensional creatures in "The Loss" (184).

QPID

Production No.: 194 ■ Aired: Week of April 22, 1991
Stardate: 44741.9 ■ Code: qp

Directed by **Cliff Bole**
Teleplay by **Ira Steven Behr**
Story by **Randee Russell and Ira Steven Behr**

GUEST CAST
Vash: **Jennifer Hetrick**
Sir Guy: **Clive Revill**
Q: **John de Lancie**
Servant: **Joi Staton**

civilizations by transforming them using the probe, and then bringing them to their home system. Barclay is restored to normal as Picard agrees to be scanned in exchange for information about the Cytherians.

Looking for a vehicle to bring back popular guest star Dwight Schultz and his milquetoast character, the staff decided on Joe Menosky's idea of an episode focusing on superintelligence. Rob Legato made good use of his effects background here in his second outing as a director, using live lasers to "connect" Barclay to the ship's computer on the bare holodeck.

Legato recalled how the pages for the final scene arrived the day of shooting on this ever-changing script, making the alien a floating head whose purpose was much more benevolent than in earlier drafts—an attempt to get away from the standard hostage

Picard is nervous enough while preparing his keynote speech for the Federation Archaeology Council. Then in quick order he's visited by Vash, a mischievous female archaeologist he met on vacation on Risa and then by the pesky superbeing Q.

A spat erupts when Picard finds out that Vash is setting off for an illegal dig and she discovers he never mentioned her to his friends. Q, a secret witness, decides to return the favor Picard did him a year ago by getting the stubborn lovers to admit their feelings for each other—in a special simulation of Sherwood Forest, that he creates.

With the couple cast as Robin Hood and Maid Marian and Picard's senior officers as Merry Men, Q becomes the sheriff of Nottingham. He

Picard as Robin Hood, and Vash (Jennifer Hetrick) as Maid Marian.

Ira Steven Behr, a third-season producer, helped bring back both Q and Vash and jumped on the Robin Hood bandwagon. This outing provided lots of nice comic moments, including the Worf line of the season: "I am *not* a merry man!" This season having settled the real status of Riker and Troi's relationship, we now begin to get hints about how Beverly and the captain see each other, following the intoxication of "The Naked Now" (103) and the tease of "Allegiance" (166).

Director Cliff Bole revealed that the castle set was really a big "cheat"—lots of little foreground set pieces were shot through a long lens. The Sherwood Forest scenes were filmed during one day of location shooting in the Descanso Gardens, just northeast of the northeastern L.A. suburb of Glendale. The medieval fighting was not without its problems: Frakes suffered a cut eye when his quarter-staff broke under a broadsword blow just as he turned into it.

Throughout the series, Picard has been shown as Jeffersonian in his interests, which include history, science, and literature as well as archaeology. He is clearly pleased as well as apprehensive about being asked to address the archaeological symposium. Among the delegates can be seen an Algolian, a Bolian, and a Vulcan.

Q (John de Lancie) becomes the Sheriff of Nottingham to repay his "debt" to Picard.

challenges the captain to risk his crew's lives for the woman he loves. Picard sets out to rescue Vash, claiming he'd do the same for anyone else.

But "Marian" rejects his rescue, turning him in and agreeing to marry her captor, Sir Guy. Q is delighted until he sees her send a note to the crew for help; he then turns her in as well.

Heads are about to roll when the Merry Men come to the rescue; Picard, a skilled fencer, skewers Sir Guy. The game is over.

Back on the ship, Vash announces she plans to travel through the galaxy with Q. An uneasy Picard admits the two do have much in common—just before he kisses Vash good-bye and they promise to meet again.

THE DRUMHEAD

Production No.: 195 ■ Aired: Week of April 29, 1991
Stardate: 44769.2 ■ Code: dr

Directed by **Jonathan Frakes**
Written by **Jeri Taylor**

GUEST CAST
Sabin Genestra: **Bruce French**
Simon Tarses: **Spencer Garrett**
Lieutenant J'Ddan: **Henry Woronicz**
Admiral Thomas Henry: **Earl Billings**
Admiral Norah Satie: **Jean Simmons**
Nellen Tore: **Ann Shea**

An explosion in the *Enterprise*'s dilithium chamber begins a trail of intrigue that leads Worf to suspect a Klingon exchange officer. Noted investigator Admiral Norah Satie comes out of retirement to help conduct a probe of the incident.

The Klingon, J'Ddan, admits to smuggling plans to the Romulans but denies any role in the explosion. Satie's Betazoid aide, Sabin, senses he's telling the truth; the Admiral begins to hunt for co-conspirators.

During the investigation Sabin senses that med tech Simon Tarses is lying about some part of his testimony. Even after the explosion is found to have been an accident, Satie bullies Tarses into admitting a forebear was Romulan, not Vulcan as he had once sworn.

Picard, uncomfortable with Satie's tactics,

Sabin (Bruce French) and Norah Satie (Jean Simmons) lead a latter-day Inquisition.

meets with Tarses to confirm the man's innocence, and then the captain openly challenges Satie. She vows to bring him down before visiting Starfleet admiral Henry.

Picard's reluctance to participate any further in Satie's hearings leads her to question him as a possible traitor. When Picard uses her famous father's words to rebut her charges, she begins a groundless tirade, accusing him of violating the Prime Directive. Her rage shocks everyone in the room, disgusts Admiral Henry, and breaks up the witch-hunt at last.

What was to have been a money-saving "clip show"—(like the second-season finale "Shades of Gray") turned into one of the season's most chilling episodes. Determined to mount a meaningful story on a slim budget with no visual effects, Berman and Piller turned to this tale, which rings with echoes of the McCarthy hearings and the Salem witch-hunts.

Jeri Taylor's script, the one she is most proud of, was inspired by a Ronald D. Moore idea called "It Can't Happen Here," and echoes the groundless investigation of Picard from season one "Coming of Age" (119) and weaves in references to his abduction by the Borg in "The Best of Both Worlds" (174–175), the alien parasitic invaders "Conspiracy" (125), the T'Pel-Selok spy scandal in "Data's Day" (185), and the developing Klingon-Romulan intrigue. And it still came in $250,000 under budget!

In his second directorial outing, Jonathan Frakes recalls he had a good time and wasn't too intimidated by the presence of Oscar nominee Jean Simmons, with whom he had worked on *North and South*. The acclaimed actress, a longtime unabashed Trekker, also played the matriarch of the Collins family in the short-lived revival of *Dark Shadows*.

After twenty-five years of Trek, we finally learn that the Federation's governing document is called a Constitution, and its various Bill of Rights is composed of Guarantees, the seventh roughly corresponding to the U.S. Fifth Amendment's ban on self-incrimination. Also, Tarses's birthplace on the Mars Colony was noted in the original Trek as the home of the Fundamental Declaration of the Martian Colonies, mentioned in 1967's "Courtmartial" as a landmark in interstellar law.

Satie's ferrying starship, the *Cochrane*, is of the Oberth class (a modified *Grissom* from *Star Trek III*), like the *Tsiolkovsky* from "The Naked Now" (103) and another namesake of the warp-drive discoverer "Ménage à Troi" (172). And Picard isn't the only one with a reputation as an advocate: Riker seen previously in a lawyer's role in "Angel One" (115) and "The Measure of a Man" (135) is chosen to defend first Tarses and then Picard.

On the tech side, we learn here that an individual communicator provides a traceable ID on computer and other system use and that the dilithium "cradle" ("Skin of Evil"/122) is called the "articulation frame"—a defective one was installed during the post-Borg refit in "The Best of Both Worlds," Part 2 (175).

And for pure trivia fans: Picard says he took command of the *Enterprise* on Stardate 41124; that was after the ship was commis-

sioned on SD 40759.5, inscribed on the bridge plaque, and before the first aired captain's log entry of SD 41153.7, in "Encounter at Farpoint" (101).

HALF A LIFE

Production No.: 196　■　Aired: Week of May 6, 1991
Stardate 44805.3　■　Code: hl

Directed by **Les Landau**
Teleplay by **Peter Allan Fields**
Story by **Ted Roberts and Peter Allan Fields**

GUEST CAST
Lwaxana Troi: **Majel Barrett**
Dara: **Michelle Forbes**
B'Tardat: **Terrence E. McNally**
Lieutenant O'Brien: **Colm Meaney**
Mr. Homn: **Caryl Struyken**
Dr. Timicin: **David Ogden Stiers**

Picard is nervous when Troi's mother returns for a visit, but this time the ebullient Lwaxana has set her sights on Dr. Timicin, a quiet scientist who's abroad to test stellar ignition theories that may enable him to save his world's dying star.

Timicin, who invested his life's work in the plan, is crushed when it eventually fails. Lwaxana can't understand why he's so despondent until he tells her he is nearly sixty, the age of the

Lwaxana (Majel Barret) questions Timicin (David Odgen Stiers) about his world's custom of ritual suicide.

resolution: a ritual suicide to save children the burden of their parent's aging.

Enraged, Lwaxana demands that Picard intervene. He can't, of course, so she turns on Timicin herself: why doom his entire world by committing suicide when his research is so close to success? At first he resists, but eventually he agrees with her and seeks asylum.

His decision causes an uproar among his people, and armed ships are sent to retrieve him. Timicin stands firm, though, until his daughter beams up to plead with him to stand by the heritage he taught her. Touched, he agrees, and tells a tearful Lwaxana that the revolutionary will have to be someone else.

Later, Timicin is surprised when Lwaxana shows up as he prepares to beam down. If she is one of his loved ones, she tells him, she wants to be there with all the others when he says good-bye.

Fans had looked forward to the guest appearance of M*A*S*H regular David Ogden Stiers in this outing, but it was Majel Barrett who surprised them by pulling off a well-done first look at the non-comic side of Lwaxana Troi; the segment features the two guest stars as perhaps no other TNG hour ever has. Its theme, the worth of older citizens and the problems of the aged, was handled in a thought-provoking way by Peter Allan Fields, who was hired as a staff writer the following season, and his partner Ted Roberts.

Though she had only one small scene, actress Michelle Forbes more than stepped out of the shadow of the two guest leads with her performance as Timicin's loving yet embittered daughter, Dara—so much so that she would land a new recurring TNG role in the coming season. A student at the Performing Arts High School in Houston, she moved to New York at sixteen to audition for a movie and wound up staying. She worked on The Guiding Light for almost three years and moved on to TV guest roles.

The mention of oskoid leaves dates back to Lwaxana's visit last year in "Ménage à Troi" (172) while her nickname for the security chief—"Mr. Woof"—first appears here. And Rigel IV, where Lwaxana says she once persuaded a young astronomer to name a star after her, was the home of Argelian administrator Hengist, who was possessed by the Redjac evil spirit in 1967's "Wolf in the Fold."

THE HOST

Production No. 197 ■ Aired: Week of May 13, 1991
Stardate: 44821.3 ■ Code: ho

Directed by **Marvin V. Rush**
Written by **Michel Horvat**

GUEST CAST
Governor Leka Trion: **Barbara Tarbuck**
Kareel: **Nicole Orth-Pallavicini**
Kalin Trose: **William Newman**
Nurse Ogawa: **Patti Yasutake**
Odan (Trill host): **Franc Luz**

Dr. Crusher falls in love with Odan, a Trillian mediator en route to settle a bitter dispute between Peliar's Alpha and Beta moons.

But while shuttling down to the surface he is mortally wounded by a marauding ship; in surgery his "Dr. Beverly" is shocked to find a parasite living inside him. Her surprise is compounded when she learns that Odan himself is the parasite occupying the host body in a joint symbiotic arrangement the Trill have used for generations.

As the dispute grows more intense, Riker volunteers to be Odan's host while a replacement is sent. Although Riker's human body adjusts to its new "co-tenant" Dr. Crusher cannot accept the first officer as her lover. Odan agrees to stay away.

The moons' delegates are just as uneasy about the situation, but Odan convinces them he can be trusted. Finally Dr. Crusher decides she can accept Odan, even in Riker's body, and they spend one more night together. Odan then settles the political dispute in a marathon session that greatly weakens Riker's body.

Dr. Crusher removes Odan to save Riker's body; both recover well. Then the expected Trill host body replacement arrives only to turn out to be female.

Crestfallen, Beverly admits she can't take Odan's constant changes. The two do, however, exchange vows of love before he leaves.

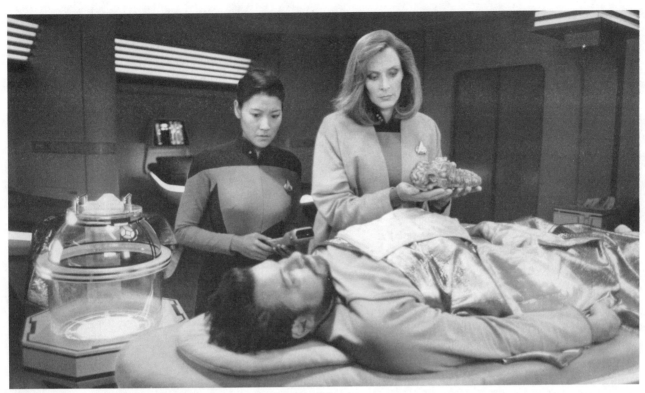

Crusher and Ogawa (Patti Yasutake) prepare a new host for Odan.

Another tale that could only be told in science fiction, Horvat's script gives Gates McFadden a rare chance to show Beverly as a woman of passion, and even dallies with homosexuality (more precisely, asexuality) until the doctor admits she is unable to accept Odan in a female form.

Marvin Rush, director of photography since season three, became the first of three in-house staffers in a row to get a turn in the director's chair. Rush started out on the original *WKRP in Cincinnati* as a camera operator before moving on to low-budget films and sitcoms such as *Dear John* and *Frank's Place*, where he caught the eye of the TNG staff. He recalls that much of his effort went into helping Franc Luz and Jonathan Frakes establish a continuity for Odan—and into disguising McFadden's seven-month pregnancy. James Cleveland McFadden-Talbot, her first son, would be born over the hiatus on June 10 in Los Angeles—a well-timed delivery.

In a nice echo of the workout scene from "The Price" (156), we now see Beverly talk to Deanna about her new lover. The scene is played out in the ship's barbershop, where we meet another Bolian barber, as in "Data's Day" (185) and "Ensign Ro" (203). An uncredited Robert Harper played the speaking role of Lathal Bine, representative from Peliar Zel's Beta moon.

The large shuttle seen here—named the *Hawking* for American physicist Stephen F. Hawking—is not new; it is the original full-scale set, little seen due to its piecemeal construction history ("Coming of Age"/(119).

THE MIND'S EYE

Production No: 198 ▪ Aired: Week of May 27, 1991
Stardate: 44885.5 ▪ Code: mi

Directed by **David Livingston**
Teleplay by **Rene Echevarria**
Story by **Ken Schafer and Rene Echevarria**

GUEST CAST
Ambassador Kell: **Larry Dobkin**
Taibak: **John Fleck**
Lieutenant O'Brien: **Colm Meaney**
Governor Vagh: **Edward Wiley**
Computer Voice: **Majel Barrett**

En route to a vacation and seminar on Risa, La Forge is kidnapped by Romulans as part of a complex plot to split the Federation-Klingon alliance.

Picard disarms the mind-controlled La Forge and the Romulan assassination plot.

While he is gone, Klingon Ambassador Kell comes aboard the *Enterprise* to investigate a Klingon governor's charge that Starfleet is aiding rebels fighting for independence on his colony. La Forge, who returns with false memory implants of his Risa trip, and Data work to show that phaser rifles seized by Governor Vagh are really Romulan replications. Their work does little to change Vagh's mind, though, especially when a shipment of arms is detected being beamed from the ship.

The cargo was beamed over by La Forge, who is being mind-controlled by the Romulans. The engineer's next task: assassinate Vagh and split the Federation-Klingon alliance.

Kell, ostensibly the cool-headed mediator, turns out to be the Romulan sympathizer manipulating La Forge. Data, meanwhile, has been tracking strange E-band emissions and finally discovers what is going on, and warns Picard, who knocks La Forge's phaser fire astray just in time. Vagh is furious, but even more so when Data explains the story.

Kell's quick asylum request is refused by Picard and he uneasily departs in Governor Vagh's custody, while Troi sits down to the painful task of helping La Forge regain his memory.

Line producer David Livingston had come from ABC way back in February 1987 to be production manager for the "Farpoint" pilot (101–102). He got a powerful story for his first shot at directing: a retelling of *The Manchurian Candidate* that foreshadowed the mounting Klingon civil war that would reach its climax at season's end. It features a chilling depiction of Geordi's reprogramming

aboard a warbird and the first use of his VISOR as the camera's point of view since season one's "Heart of Glory" (120).

Livingston, an unabashed fan of *The Manchurian Candidate*, tried unsuccessfully to get someone from the movie to appear in this episode as an extra. There's even an homage camera shot in which the possessed O'Brien is shot in Ten-Forward.

Geordi's preference for guitar music on his lonely ride is an echo from his dinner date with Leah Brahms in "Galaxy's Child" (190). His Shuttlepod 7 is the *Onizuka* from "The Ensigns of Command" (149), formerly Shuttle 5, which was seen earlier as the *El-Baz* in "Time Squared" (139).

For some time Rick Sternbach had played with various designs for a phaser rifle, and when it was at last needed for this show Livingston made the final choice. And the first TNG look at the Klingon and Romulan transporter beams occurs here. The Klingon beam is a quick solid red wipe from top to bottom with a few residual gold sparkles; the Romulans use a green beam that dissolves rapidly with little shimmer.

The reality of the new Klingon Empire is artfully brought home when Vagh longs for the old days when an insurrection could be violently put down. Curiously, Krios may be a Klingon colony fighting for independence, but somehow it is also involved in a centuries-old civil war with Valt Minor, as seen in "The Perfect Mate" (221).

IN THEORY

Production No: 199 ■ Aired: Week of June 3, 1991
Stardate: 44932.3 ■ Code: it

Directed by **Patrick Stewart**
Written by **Joe Menosky and Ronald D. Moore**

GUEST CAST
Ensign Jenna D'Sora: **Michele Scarabelli**
Keiko O'Brien: **Rosalind Chao**
Lieutenant O'Brien: **Colm Meaney**
Ensign McKnight: **Pamela Winslow**
Guinan: **Whoopi Goldberg**

Data takes one more step on the road to understanding humanity when a shipmate, Jenna D'Sora, begins to view him as more than a friend.

The two had grown close while studying a dark-matter nebula, the *Enterprise*'s latest assignment. After getting mixed advice from his friends when she comes on to him, Data decides to pursue the relationship and creates a special program to provide a guide to love. He and Jenna have their ups and downs, and eventually his true nature gets through to her: his seemingly artificial behavior is, of course, artificial.

Meanwhile, a Class M planet in the nebula suddenly winks out and then reappears. Data theorizes that the nebula causes pockets of deformed matter that phase out anything they contact, and with his ship's vital areas endangered, Picard orders the *Enterprise* out of the nebula.

But the starship is too large to sense and dodge the pockets, so the captain pilots a scout shuttlepod himself to relay back course directions. His craft is nearly lost, but the ship breaks clear at last.

That crisis over, Jenna tells Data she now realizes she went from one unemotional boyfriend to another who was even more so and now she wants to break the pattern. He agrees and erases his special program without a second thought.

Following up on Jonathan Frakes's lead, Patrick Stewart became the second cast member to direct an episode. The story chosen for Stewart's debut was a no-fail Data show by Ronald D. Moore and Joe Menosky that confronted questions about the android and love that TNG had backed away from in "The Ensigns of Command" (149).

Television SF watchers will recognize Michele Scarabelli as Sam Francisco's wife Susan on *Alien Nation*. A name for Pamela Winslow's character had been mentioned during the Paxan affair in "Clues" (188). Among the uncredited extras were Ritt Henn as the alien bassoonist, Phil Mallory as the French horn player, Gary Baxley as engineer Ensign Thorne, and Georgina Shore as the ill-fated Lieutenant (j.g.) Van Mayter.

Introduced earlier in "Data's Day" (185), the android's cat finally gets a name here—Spot. And the O'Briens turn out to be a musical family: Keiko plays the clarinet, and Miles is a cellist, as we learned in "The Ensigns of Command" (149). Meanwhile, Data is seen to have learned to play the oboe and the flute as well as the violin (149, 171). Longer-term Trek references include a mention of Saurian brandy, often referred to in original-Trek stories like "The Enemy Within." Also mentioned is milk from a targ, the Klingon boar that can be either a pet (106) or a food source (134). Transparent aluminum, the subject of some necessary historical meddling by Scotty and McCoy in *Star Trek IV*, is spoken of here, too.

Jenna D'Sora (Michelle Scarabelli) decides Data is the man for her.

REDEMPTION

Production No.: 200 ■ Aired: Week of June 17, 1991
Stardate: 44995.3 ■ Code: rd

Directed by **Cliff Bole**

Written by **Ronald D. Moore**

GUEST CAST
Gowron: **Robert O'Reilly**
Captain Kurn: **Tony Todd**
Lursa: **Barbara March**
B'Etor: **Gwynyth Walsh**
K'tal: **Ben Slack**
General Movar: **Nicholas Kepros**
Toral: **J. D. Cullum**
Guinan: **Whoopi Goldberg**
Klingon First Officer: **Tom Ormeny**
Computer Voice: **Majel Barrett**
Commander Sela: **Denise Crosby**

In his role as Arbiter of Succession, Picard returns to the Klingon homeworld to oversee Gowron's installation as emperor. The captain also urges Worf to confront Gowron over his family's discommendation.

En route, the starship is intercepted by a Klingon vessel bearing Gowron, who informs Picard that a faction of the Empire, led by the family of the dead Duras is mounting a rebellion against his throne. Picard refuses to get involved, though: he won't risk dragging the Federation into a Klingon civil war.

In turn, Gowron refuses to restore Lieutenant Worf's family honor, citing the need to shore up his own power. Worf's younger brother, Kurn, wants to join the rebellion against Gowron, but the lieutenant persuades him not to do so—the family will back Gowron, for now.

Then Duras's bastard son, Toral, makes a surprise claim to the throne, backed by his powerful family, including Duras's sisters. But Picard, knowing full well their Romulan ties, rejects their claim to the throne.

As Worf again presses Gowron to restore his

Worf gets a moving farewell when he resigns to fight in the Klingon civil war.

Klingon traitors: B'Etor (Gwynyth Walsh), Toral (J. D. Cullum), and Lursa (Barbara March).

family name, Duras's forces ambush them; only Kurn's timely appearance saves them from defeat.

Gowron is installed as leader, and restores Worf's honor. Feeling the tug of his heritage, the lieutenant resigns his Starfleet commission.

Meanwhile, members of the Duras family meet with their Romulan backers, who include a woman who looks amazingly like Tasha Yar. . . .

Opening the final chapter of the Klingon trilogy that began with "Sins of the Father" (165) and "Reunion" (181), Ronald D. Moore's epic provided this season's cliff-hanger: Worf's departure from Starfleet to fight alongside his brother and Gowron to preserve the Klingon Empire. The return of Denise Crosby to the series, already hinted at in "The Mind's Eye" (198), occurs here but will not be explained until the concluding segment that will launch the fifth season.

Also returning are actors Robert O'Reilly from "Reunion" (181) and Tony Todd, who appeared in "Sins of the Father" (165). Meanwhile, befitting his rise in stature, Gowron has left behind his Bird of Prey, *Buruk,* in favor of the *Bortas,* a Vor'cha-class attack cruiser.

Guinan continues to be full of surprises, as she again proves to be no slouch with a weapon, a skill we first saw in "Night Terrors" (191); she actually tops Worf's score on the phaser range.

We learn that the UFP-Klingon alliance treaty includes a pledge of mutual defense. And we are told that Worf's son, Alexander, who first appeared in "Reunion" (181), is already having a hard time on Earth, foreshadowing his return next season in "New Ground" (210). Gowron's father is M'Rel—though once again, Duras's name is used for his family in place of Ja'rod, as in "Sins of the Father" (165). A script description that was not included in the show's dialogue reveals that K'tal is the longest-serving member of the Klingon High Council, which here is given eight members besides him.

Bob Blackman's costume designs include a revealing bustline for the Duras sisters' standard Klingon outfit that quickly came to be known among fans as "Klingon kleavage"—but those on the show attest that, like Ricardo Montalban in *Star Trek II,* neither actress used chest padding.

And for the truly trivial: note the use of "kellicams" as the Klingonese unit of distance (established in ST III) is renewed here (see "A Matter of Honor"/134), and Movar's title, "general"—the first ever non-naval rank used for a Romulan.

Notes

1. *Star Trek: The Official Fan Club Magazine,* Oct./Nov. 1991, p. 4.

2. *Star Trek: The Official Fan Club Magazine,* Dec. 1990/ Jan. 1991, p. 3.

PRODUCTION STAFF CREDITS— FOURTH SEASON

(In usual roll order; numbers in parentheses refer to episode numbers.)

Casting:(*) Junie Lowery-Johnson, C.S.A.; Ron Surma

Main Title Theme: (*)Jerry Goldsmith, (*)Alexander Courage

Music: *** Jay Chattaway (179, 197, 199); (*)Ron Jones (all odd-numbered episodes, 175–195 except 179); (*)Dennis McCarthy (all even-numbered episodes, 176–200)

Director of Photography: ***Marvin Rush (EMMY NOMINEE: cinematography, series: "Family" [178]

Production Designer: **Richard D. James (EMMY NOMINEE with art staff: art direction, series: "The Best of Both Worlds" Pt. 2 [175]

Editor: *Tom Benko, ACE (177, 180, 183, 189, 192, 195, 198); ***J. P. Farrell (175, 178, 181, 184, 187, 190, 193, 196, 199); *William Hoy (186); **Bob Lederman (176 with Stephen Tucker, 179, 182, 185, 188, 191, 197, 200); Stephen Tucker (176 with Bob Lederman, 194)

Unit Production Manager: ***Merri D. Howard (+)

1st Asst. Director: ***Chip Chalmers (176); ***Brad Yacobian (all odd-numbered episodes, 175–199); Doug Dean (all even-numbered episodes, 178–200)

Second Asst. Director: *Adele G. Simmons

Costume Designer: ***Robert Blackman (EMMY NOMINEE: costume design, series: "Devil's Due" [187]

Set Decorator: **Jim Mees

Visual Effects Supervisor: (**)Robert Legato (+) (all odd-numbered episodes, 175–199 except 189) (EMMY CO-NOMINEE with FX crews: special visual FX: "The Best of Both Worlds" Pt. 2 [175]); (**)Dan Curry)(+)(all even-numbered episodes, 176–200 except 192); *Gary Hutzel (+) (189); ***Ron Moore (+) (192)

Senior Illustrator/Technical Consultant: (*)Rick Sternbach

Scenic Artist Supervisor/Technical Consultant: (*)Michael Okuda

Make-up Designed and Supervised: (*)Michael Westmore (TWO-TIME EMMY NOMINEE (with crew): makeup, series: "Brothers" [177], "Identity Crisis [192]

Visual Effects Coordinator: ***Ron Moore (all even-numbered episodes, 176–200 except 192); ***Gary Hutzel (all odd-numbered episodes, 175–199 except 189)

Set Designer: ***Gary Speckman

Assistant Art Director: Andy Neskoromny

Original Set Design: (*)Herman Zimmerman

Original Starfleet Uniforms: (*)William Ware Theiss

Script Supervisor: (*)Cosmo Genovese

Special Effects: (*)Dick Brownfield

Property Master: (*)Joe Longo (all odd-numbered episodes, 175–199); (*)Alan Sims (all even-numbered episodes, 176–200)

Construction Coordinator: (*)Al Smutko

Assistant Scenic Artist: (***)Cari Thomas (dropped Assistant beginning 190)

Hair Designer: Yolanda Toussieng

Hair Stylist: ***Rita Bordonaro [Bellissimo after 191] (175–196); Bill Howard (175); Kim Santantonio (176–98); NONE on (200)

Makeup Artists: **Gerald Quist, ***June Abston-Haymore

Sound Mixer: *Alan Bernard, C.A.S. (EMMY WINNER: sound mixing, series: "The Best of Both Worlds" Pt. 2 [175]

Chief Lighting Technician: ***Buddy Bowles

First Company Grip: ***Bob Sordal

Costumers: **Mandy Chamberlin (all even-numbered episodes, 176–200); **Kimberly Thompson (all odd-numbered episodes, 175–199); Charles Evan Drayman (all odd-numbered episodes, 175–197); David Roesler (199); ***David Page (174, 178); Carol Kunz (182, 200); Maurice Palanski (even-numbered from 184–198, except 182)

Visual Effects Associate: David Takemura (175–200 except 180, 191)

Music Editor: ***Gerry Sackman**
Supervising Sound Editor: **(*) Bill Wistrom (EMMY CO-WINNER: sound editing, series: "The Best of Both Worlds" Pt. 2 [175]**
Sound Editors: ***James Wolvington; *Mace Matiosian; *Wilson Dyer (EMMY CO-WINNERS: sound editing, series: "The Best of Both Worlds" Pt. 2 [175]**
Post Production Sound: **(*)Modern Sound**
Production Associate: **(*)Susan Sackett**
Production Coordinator: **(*)Diane Overdiek**
Post Production Associate: *****Terry Martinez, ***Heidi Julian (+), ***Wendy Rosenfeld**
Pre-Production Associate: **(***)Eric Stillwell (+)**
Casting Executive: **(*)Helen Mossler**
Stunt Coordinator: **(***)Dennis Madalone (+) (all except 176, 182, 184–187, 190–191, 195–196, 198)**

Research Consultant: **(***)Richard Arnold (uncredited first two seasons)**
Lenses and Panaflex Cameras: **(**)Panavision**
Special Visual Effects: ***(*)Industrial Light and Magic (ILM) a division of Lucasfilm Ltd.**
Additional Motion Control Facilities: **(*)Image "G"**
Video Optical Effects: **(*)The Post Group**
Special Video Compositing: **(*)Composite Image Systems**
Editing Facilities: **(*)Unitel Video**
Prosthetic Electronics: **Michael Westmore II (177, 180)**
Choreographer: **Gates McFadden (+) (185)**
Lasers Provided by: **Laser Media Rentals (193)**

The number of * denotes a returning company or staffer's initial season of credit in that position; ( ) denotes they are an original credited or co-credited person in that position; a (+) following indicates prior TNG work in another position.

FIFTH SEASON

The fifth year of TNG would provide

more than its share of high points—and yet prove to be the show's saddest as well. The series enjoyed its share of the hoopla as *Star Trek*'s year-long twenty-fifth anniversary celebration climaxed in September, but that joy was overshadowed by the death of the Great Bird of the Galaxy on October 26, 1991, after a series of strokes.

Even though the debate will undoubtedly rage forever as to which Trek generation was better, both in its time and afterward, one thing is certain: buoyed by the two-part Spock episode "Unification" (207–208) and the anniversary celebrations during the November 1991 sweeps period, TNG's Nielsen ratings hit an all-time Trek high. In the key demographic group of men age eighteen to forty-nine the show received a rating of 14.6 against prime-time competition, with the composite for both sexes not far behind. Astoundingly, that rating left other major TV series in the dust. TNG beat *60 Minutes* (10.7), *Coach* (11.6), *Roseanne* (12.7), *Cheers* (12.8), and even *Monday Night Football* (13.9).

Fifth-season cast portrait (*opposite*); the departed
Wil Wheaton would guest-star twice.

In other words, as Matt Timothy of Paramount's research department put it, "If we were a network show we'd be showing up in the Nielsens' Top Ten every week."

TNG's ever-increasing popularity showed up in other ways as well. Echoing what happened on the old *Batman* TV series, more and more Hollywood stars began to seek guest spots on the show. Following in the footsteps of Corbin Bernsen, Bebe Neuwirth, Jean Simmons, and Mick Fleetwood in past seasons, distinguished guests in year five included Kelsey Grammer of *Cheers* and Paul Winfield, with Robin Williams, Elliott Gould, John Goodman, Christopher Lloyd, and others waiting in line. The fifth season, though, would be the first in which Q would not appear. "We had a couple of stories in development, but they just didn't work out," Rick Berman said.

One of the major reasons for the show's continuing success was stability in the ranks. For the first time, TNG's upper echelon stayed relatively unchanged all season long. Berman, Michael Piller, and Jeri Taylor retained their titles while Ronald Moore and Joe Menosky were promoted to coproducer. For a time they were joined by Herbert J. Wright, a veteran of the very first season who was coaxed back aboard for six episodes (213–218) before leaving again. His replacement was Peter Allan Fields, a veteran of *Columbo* and, with Piller, the short-lived *Helligan's Law*. Fields was invited to join the staff as an executive script consultant after writing the fourth-season Lwaxana Troi episode, "Half a Life" (196). On the production side, Peter Lauritson, David Livingston, and Wendy Neuss all returned, with unit production manager Merri D. Howard filling in on one show, "Power Play" (215), and receiving credit as a line producer.

Such was the closeness of the fifth year's writing staff that when mid-season burnout set in during the fall and neither staff nor freelancers seemed to have a new story idea, Piller offered his house in Mexico as the site of a weekend retreat to recharge their creative batteries. That weekend's brainstorming sessions provided the basis for a string of six episodes that closed out the season, from "The Outcast" (217) through "I, Borg" (223), with only one exception: "Imaginary Friend" (222).

The weekly episodes were being turned out for basically what they cost in 1987 dollars, according to Berman. "Aside from the salaries going up and the cost of living raises, we're still doing the show with the same budget—no more for sets or special effects. But," he added, "after five years we are spending it much more efficiently than we did in 1987."

For Season Five, a new "captain's jacket" was designed for Patrick Stewart.

Redemption II

Production No.: 201 ▪ Aired: Week of September 23, 1991
Stardate: 45020.4 ▪ Code: r2

Directed by **David Carson**
Written by **Ronald D. Moore**

GUEST CAST

Commander Sela: **Denise Crosby**
Commander Kurn: **Tony Todd**
Lursa: **Barbara March**
B'Etor: **Gwynyth Walsh**
Toral: **J. D. Cullum**
Gowron: **Robert O'Reilly**
Captain Larg: **Michael G. Hagerty**
Admiral Shanthi: **Fran Bennett**
General Movar: **Nicholas Kepros**
Lieutenant O'Brien: **Colm Meaney**
Lieutenant Commander Christopher Hobson:
Timothy Carhart
Guinan: **Whoopi Goldberg**
Kulge: **Jordan Lund**
Hegh'ta Helmsman: **Stephen James Carver**
Ensign Craig: **Clifton Jones**

Having made good on his decision to leave Starfleet and fight at Gowron's side in the Klingon civil war, Worf begins to suspect Romulan involvement in the conflict when Duras's faction remains strong despite the loss of most of its weaponry to raids.

Picard finally decides to cast aside his non-interventionist stance. He advocates exposing Romulan support of the rebellious clan because a Duras victory would pose a threat to the UFP-Klingon alliance.

After winning approval for a nonaggressive blockade, Picard deploys a fleet along the Neutral Zone. His crew spreads out to lead the task force as the starships are joined by an active tachyon web, which will enable them to detect even cloaked warbirds. While Worf is kidnapped and tortured, Data faces his own test of command before a skeptical crew. He finally wins them over when his apparent disobedience to Picard helps plug a hole in the Federation's defenses the Romulans were about to exploit.

Exposed, the Romulans withdraw, leaving the Duras sisters helpless. They flee, leaving Toral behind as Gowron at last assumes leadership of his empire.

Worf, realizing he belongs to two different cultures, decides his place is aboard the *Enterprise*. Picard and crew are left to wonder how the late Tasha Yar could have borne Sela, the half-human Romulan commander—said to be Tasha's daughter—who led the operation.

Michael Piller said he initially thought of using the saga of the Klingon Empire and Worf as third season's cliff-hanger, but the Borg epic began to take shape at that time and he shelved the Klingon idea for a year. He praised Ronald Moore's treatment of the Klingons—here and in "Sins of the Father" (165) and "Reunion" (181)—calling them probably the most-explored alien culture in Trek.

"I've come to think of Part One as Shakespearean-style royal drama, *I, Claudius*-type intrigue at the highest levels," Piller said. "Here we add[ed] Data's command dilemma and the subplot of Sela that Denise Crosby came to us with." Data's leadership skills had already been tested on a smaller scale, of course, when he evacuated Tau Cygne V in "The Ensigns of Command" (149).

"In all of our two-parters, we always end up writing the conclusion after we return from hiatus," Berman recalled, and then deadpanned: "It's something we kind of look forward to over the summer!"

It was fitting that David Carson was chosen to direct this episode in which Sela is revealed to be Tasha's daughter; he, after all, had directed "Yesterday's Enterprise" (163), in which Tasha was sent back in time in the first place. Guinan's interest in Tasha Yar here was set up by that earlier episode's final sequence, where she asked Geordi about the late security chief. We learn

Sela (Denise Crosby) confirms the unbelievable: she's Tasha's daughter.

here that Sela is twenty-three, born a year after the 1701-C was retrieved twenty-four years ago—which figures to out to 2344, as reckoned according to "The Neutral Zone" (126)—and that Tasha was killed in an escape attempt after four-year-old Sela turned her in.

A clue is also given to the duration of the UFP-Klingon alliance when Picard says the Romulans have been undermining it for "over twenty years," a statement that jibes with the Romulan-Federation peace of over fifty-three years, mentioned in the season one show "The Neutral Zone" (126).

Practically all of the staff's stockpiled ship designs make an appearance here in the Starfleet armada, including the Nebula-class *Sutherland,* Data's command, NCC-72015 (previously seen as the *Phoenix* in "The Wounded" (186). Riker's command, the *Excalibur,* is of the Ambassador class, like the 1701-C, and the USS *Tiananmen* commemorates the central Beijing square that was the scene of a bloody Chinese populist uprising in 1989.

DARMOK

Production No.: 202 ▪ Aired: Week of September 30, 1991
Stardate: 45047.2 ▪ Code: dm

Directed by **Winrich Kolbe**
Teleplay by **Joe Menosky**
Story by **Philip Lazebnik and Joe Menosky**

GUEST CAST
Tamarian First Officer: **Richard James**
Lieutenant O'Brien: **Colm Meaney**
Captain Dathon: **Paul Winfield**
Ensign Robin Lefler: **Ashley Judd**

The *Enterprise* tries for the eighth time in a century to contact the Children of Tama, a peaceful, well-intentioned advanced race whose language is indecipherable. Their words translate as descriptive phrases of people and places.

When the two races fail again in their attempt to understand each other, the Tamarians beam Picard and their own captain Dathon to a rugged planet nearby. The Tamarian ship blocks all attempts by the *Enterprise* crew to beam up Captain Picard.

A wary Picard, realizing Dathon means him no harm, accepts help to survive the night. He's still trying to fathom the Tamarian's purpose when the two are forced to combine their efforts to fight a predatory electromagnetic creature.

Above, Riker and the Tamarians dicker over their captains' safety and almost go to war when the starship makes a concerted effort to rescue Picard.

That attempt ends in failure, but not before Picard's momentary dematerialization allows the magnetic creature to critically injure Dathon. Finally Picard catches on: the Tamarians speak in abstract narrative images based in folklore. "Darmok and Jalad at Tenagra" learned to understand each other by facing a common foe—just like "Picard and Dathon at El-Adrel."

A second rescue attempt by the *Enterprise* succeeds in saving Picard from the creature, but the Tamarians are ready to open fire until the *Enterprise* captain speaks to them, praising their late leader. Contact having been successfully established, Picard is left to wonder if he would knowingly sacrifice his life for the sake of making contact with another race.

Picard and the ill-fated Dathon (Paul Winfield) learn to communicate against a common enemy.

Joe Menosky, who would leave the staff at season's end for a sabbatical in Italy, drew high praise from Michael Piller for the work he did bringing to life this episode, which Piller said had the longest gestation period of any episode during his tenure. The inability to communicate had been the central theme of a story by Philip Lazebnik, but it was Menosky who worked out the Tamarians' language of allusion and metaphor. He also changed the story's focus from a complex and confusing "ant farm" visit to an exploration of the two strong commanders, Picard and Dathon.

Ashley Judd, the youngest sister of Wynnona of the singing Judd family, makes her debut here as Ensign·Lefler. She will pick up a first name and a love interest in "The Game" (206). We also learn that Data has met some 1,754 different races in his twenty-six years with Starfleet.

Outdoor scenes were shot over two days near the Bronson Caves, an area off the canyon below the famous Hollywood sign. Legato said the glowing creature, portrayed by stunt extra Rex Pierson, was realized with a less expensive version of the *Terminator 2*–type melting effects. Going from tape to film and back again, the creature was shot against a blue screen on fast video and developed on film 10 stops over the exposure.

Though its name is unseen, the *Magellan* shuttlecraft debuted here, giving the series a long-sought larger shuttle whose miniature matched its full-scale set. And in one of the series' rare effects bloopers, phaser fire is seen erupting from the forward photon torpedo launcher.

ENSIGN RO

Production No.: 203 ■ Aired: Week of October 7, 1991
Stardate: 45076.3 ■ Code: er

Directed by **Les Landau**
Teleplay by **T. Michael Piller**
Story by **Rick Berman and Michael Piller**

GUEST CAST
Ensign Ro Laren: **Michelle Forbes**
Keeve Falor: **Scott Marlowe**
Gul Dolak: **Frank Collison**
Orta: **Jeffrey Hayenga**
Transporter Officer: **Harley Venton**
Barber Mot: **Ken Thorley**
Admiral Kennelly: **Cliff Potts**
Guinan: **Whoopi Goldberg**
Computer Voice: **Majel Barrett**

After Bajoran extremists attack a Federation colony, Ensign Ro, a troubled young Starfleet officer, comes on board the *Enterprise*. The crew resents her presence: Ro was court-martialed after disobeying orders on an away team mission that led to eight deaths.

Starfleet Admiral Kennelly has pardoned Ro, who is also Bajoran, hoping she can help persuade the militant Bajoran leader Orta to call off the raids and agree to resettlement. The Bajorans were displaced from their home world by the Cardassians some forty years ago.

Already uneasy at Ro's presence, Picard angrily confines the ensign to quarters after she gets his away team taken hostage while tracking Orta. But Picard soon learns the Bajorans were not responsible for the raid on the Federation colony. Guinan then befriends Ro and persuades the ensign to reveal Kennelly's secret reason for sending her on the mission to Picard: in return for her freedom, Ro is secretly to offer Orta arms and ships, then allow his vessel to be destroyed by a Cardassian ship once he comes out of hiding. Kennelly will order the *Enterprise* not to interfere, in order to protect the peace treaty with the Cardassians.

Picard allows the plan to proceed, but with a twist: the Cardassians destroy an empty ship. At first furious, Kennelly is shocked to find the Cardassians staged the raid on the Federation themselves to enlist aid in destroying the Bajorans.

Afterward, Picard offers Ro a chance to remain in Starfleet—aboard his ship. She accepts.

This episode's roots were simple, according to Rick Berman: the show was specifically designed to introduce a sharp-edged character, an idea that had been floating around as far back as Wesley's departure from the conn seat a year earlier. "The other characters in the cast are relatively homogenous; some might even say bland," Berman explained. "So we wanted a character with the strength and dignity of a Starfleet officer but with a troubled past, an edge." The introduction of a strong woman often embroiled in conflict and her acceptance by the fans and writers was "one of our greatest achievements of the season," Michael Piller added. Michelle Forbes was asked back to play the new recurring character after making a strong impression as Timicin's daughter Dara in "Half a Life" (196).

Actor Harley Venton's character, a transporter officer, gets no on-screen name in either appearance, but he is named Collins in the script for this show and Hutchinson eight shows later, in "Hero Worship" (211).

The troubled Ro (Michelle Forbes) finds a friend in Guinan (Whoopi Goldberg).

Though it was not known at the time it was written, this episode would lay much of the groundwork used for the new *Star Trek: Deep Space Nine* series, set aboard an abandoned Cardassian space station in the Bajoran system. This episode establishes that Bajor was occupied forty years ago; that Ro served on the *Wellington*, one of the ships the Bynars upgraded in "11001001" (116); that she is not the only Bajoran in Starfleet, as we'll see in "The First Duty" (219); and that her father was tortured to death before her eyes when she was only seven.

The Bajorans, Berman added, were not modeled on any one real-life ethnic group: "The Kurds, the Palestinians, the Jews in the 1940s, the boat people from Haiti—unfortunately, the homeless and terrorism are problems [in every age]."

Scenes of the Bajoran encampment were shot in one day in Bronson Canyon near the area used in the preceding episode. Michael Westmore's subtle Bajoran makeup makes use of a nose-bridge piece reminiscent of those worn by actors who play Ornarans and Brekkians in "Symbiosis" (123).

SILICON AVATAR

Production No.: 204 ■ Aired: Week of October 14, 1991
Stardate: 45122.3 ■ Code: Si

Directed by **Cliff Bole**
Teleplay by **Jeri Taylor**
Story by **Lawrence V. Conley**

GUEST CAST
Dr. Kila Marr: **Ellen Geer**
Carmen Davila: **Susan Diol**

Riker and an away team are helping a group of colonists survey their new home when they are suddenly attacked by an old nemesis: the Crystalline Entity. All but two of the colonists and the away team are eventually rescued by the *Enterprise.*

Dr. Kila Marr, on the trail of the destructive alien ever since her son Renny was killed on Omicron Theta, now joins the starship in a hunt for the entity. Blaming Data for her son's death because his "brother" Lore lured the entity to Omicron Theta, Marr is ice-cold to the android until she learns he has the stored thoughts of the colonists—including her son. Through Data—who can even mimic his voice—she is able to relive her son's last few months of life.

Meanwhile, she and Picard clash over how to treat the Entity once it is contacted: the captain wants to try talking to it first, arguing the creature may not know it is killing. Marr simply wants revenge.

They lure the Entity with graviton pulse emissions, and the moment of truth arrives. The starship and the entity appear to be communicating—until Marr coolly and quietly raises the frequency of the pulse. The emissions shatter the entity.

Outraged, Picard can barely contain himself, but back in her quarters, Marr is strangely calm. She asks Data to talk like her son again, repeating that she "did it for him." As dispassionate as ever, Data tells her that Renny would be sad that his mother had ruined her career for his sake.

Just when the writers had decided on no more sequels and no more "cannibalizing," as Jeri Taylor put it, along came this premise by free-lancer Lawrence V. Conley, who took a bus down from Oregon to pitch the idea. "And of all the characters to bring back, who'd have thought the Crystalline Entity?" Taylor said. "But the *Moby-Dick* premise of this obsessed woman whose son's consciousness was stored in Data was too good to pass up."

It didn't hurt that the staff loved the title, Taylor adds, even though "no one ever knew exactly what it meant." One meaning of "avatar" is "the appearance on earth of a god in bodily form," but Taylor prefers another meaning: "a repository of knowledge," referring to Data.

The pastoral opening scenes of the Melona IV colony before its destruction were shot in a day at the Golden Oaks Ranch, also known as the Disney Ranch, in the Santa Clarita Valley north of Los Angeles.

The Entity's destruction, though, was accomplished by adding eighteen-inch miniature trees to the foreground after the live filming of the fleeing colonists. The light beam was animated on computer later, Rob Legato said, but the "sand trap" was actually a four-foot-wide tarp spread along the ground with air shot up from under it through the mesh. As with its first appearance, the Entity itself was generated entirely by computer.

Disaster

Production No.: 205 ▪ Aired: Week of October 21, 1991
Stardate: 45156.1 ▪ Code: di

Directed by **Gabrielle Beaumont**
Teleplay by **Ronald D. Moore**
Story by **Ron Jarvis and Philip A. Scorza**

GUEST CAST
Keiko O'Brien: **Rosalind Chao**
Lieutenant Miles O'Brien: **Colm Meaney**
Ensign Ro Laren: **Michelle Forbes**
Marissa: **Erika Flores**
Jay Gordon: **John Christopher Graas**
Patterson: **Max Supera**
Ensign Mandel: **Cameron Arnett**
Lieutenant (j.g.) Monroe: **Jana Marie Hupp**

Riker and Data seal off survivors from the Crystalline Entity.

As Captain Picard is playing host to three young winners of a shipboard science contest, a catastrophe strikes the ship, causing violent power failures, total disruption of communications, and an almost complete shutdown of its systems.

On the bridge, Troi is shocked to find herself in command and facing a momentous decision; the disaster has weakened the magnetic containment field surrounding the ship's antimatter pods. An explosion could occur at any moment. Ensign Ro argues she must separate the saucer section immediately, while O'Brien points out that they have no way of knowing if anyone is still alive in Engineering.

On a ship in crisis, Worf delivers Keiko's baby.

A pitchman might best describe this plot as "Star Trek Meets *The Poseidon Adventure*," but Ronald D. Moore's teleplay as usual didn't miss many chances to let all of the regular characters grow by placing them in a fish-out-of-water predicament—especially Picard, who's trapped in a turbolift with three children, and Troi, who is forced to make life-and-death command decisions. Michael Piller remarked that his only hindsight regret was in seeing Ro "lose a rough edge" in her infant character development by apologizing so easily to Troi.

As often is the case in Hollywood, twins portrayed the newborn O'Brien baby during Worf's hilarious display of Klingon bedside manner; the same pair would later make a repeat appearance as Molly O'Brien in "Power Play" (215). Beverly's coaching of Geordi for *The Pirates of Penzance* harks back to her love of performing, as seen in "Data's Day" (185) and "Nth Degree" (193) and we learn that O'Brien's dad with the roving eye, spoken of in "Family" (178) is named Michael, while Keiko's father is Hiro.

In Ten-Forward, Riker, Data, Worf, and Keiko O'Brien, who is pregnant, treat the injured while Geordi and Dr. Crusher find themselves trapped in a cargo bay and threatened by a radioactive fire. And Captain Picard, his leg broken, is trapped in a damaged turbolift with three very frightened children.

While Troi struggles to come to a decision regarding saucer separation, Riker and Data decide to leave Ten-Forward for Engineering, where they will attempt to restore power. After being trapped in an access tube by an electrical current, Data is forced to sacrifice his body—but not his head—to allow them to continue. Meanwhile, Keiko shocks Worf by going into labor.

Picard and the three children attempt to reach safety as Dr. Crusher and La Forge decide their only hope of extinguishing the fire is to blow the airlock.

Riker reaches Engineering and uses Data's head to tap into the ship's control circuits, where he notes the failing pod field in the nick of time. Troi, seconds away from jettisoning the drive section, is overjoyed when power is restored. Picard and the children are rescued, La Forge and Crusher escape the cargo bay, and Keiko, with Worf's assistance, gives birth to a baby girl.

THE GAME

Production No.: 206   ▪   Aired: Week of October 28, 1991
Stardate: 45208.2   ▪   Code: gm

Directed by **Corey Allen**
Teleplay by **Brannon Braga**
Story by **Susan Sackett, Fred Bronson, and Brannon Braga**

GUEST CAST
Ensign Robin Lefler: **Ashley Judd**
Etana Jol: **Katherine Moffat**
Lieutenant Miles O'Brien: **Colm Meaney**
Nurse Alyssa Ogawa: **Patti Yasutake**
Cadet Wesley Crusher: **Wil Wheaton**
Ensign: **Diane M. Hurley**

During his first visit back aboard since entering the Academy, Wesley Crusher falls for a young engineering ensign, Robin Lefler, while the rest of the crew seem to fall for a new interactive video game that is worn over the eyes like antique eyeglasses and rewards the player with a pleasurable sensation.

Riker has brought the game back from his latest trip to Risa, and it proves so popular that Wesley and Robin begin to get the creeps. It seems as if the others are playing it all the time.

First step to mental addiction: Etana (Katherine Moffat) shows Riker her "game."

Indeed they are. Sensor scans show that the game induces a chemical release in the brain that leads to psychological addiction and interrupts higher reasoning processes. All of the crew members are affected except Data, who was mysteriously "injured" shortly after Riker brought the game on board. Wesley and Robin find the android, but cannot reactivate him. They decide to fake addiction to avoid suspicion. Shortly thereafter, Etana Jol, Riker's "date" on Risa, appears. She had passed on the game as part of a plan to conquer the Federation one starship at a time. She now orders an all too compliant crew to begin distributing the game to other vessels.

The crew soon catches on to Wesley and Robin's deception; they capture and convert Robin, who tells them where to find Wesley. As they're about to force him to play the game, Data emerges carrying a neuro-optic burst device. Its flash reverses the game's effects, robbing Etana of her would-be foot soldiers just in time.

Braga's first assignment on staff was to polish this comment on game addiction, which Susan Sackett and Fred Bronson, who wrote "Ménage à Troi" (172), had pitched the year before. "Wesley's come home and his family's out to get him" is how Braga summarized his more sinister treatment. He made a conscious effort to make Wesley "a little hipper," showing him as a ladies' man and a cadet capable of pulling a practical joke or two. Michael Piller, pleased with the treatment, said it also marked the birth of a good writer. "If you can get away with having Troi describe how to eat chocolate for thirty-five seconds so that it doesn't slow down the story, then you're doing something."

Pleased with Ashley Judd in her first outing as Lefler, in "Darmok" (202), the staff had been looking for a vehicle in which to bring her back, and this story seemed perfect; a hoped-for third appearance in "The First Duty" (219) later in the season, though, couldn't be arranged.

Though dressed in his Academy cadet's uniform, Wesley did not yet wear the rank pips that would be established in "The First Duty" (219).

UNIFICATION I

Production No: 208 ■ Aired: Week of November 4, 1991
Stardate: 45236.4 ■ Code: u1

Directed by **Les Landau**
Teleplay by **Jeri Taylor**
Story by **Rick Berman** and **Michael Piller**

GUEST CAST
Spock: **Leonard Nimoy**
Perrin: **Joanna Miles**
Capt. K'Vada: **Stephen D. Root**
Klim Dokachin: **Graham Jarvis**
Senator Pardek: **Malachi Throne**
Proconsul Neral: **Norman Large**
Romulan No. 1: **Daniel Roebuck**
B'ljik: **Erick Avari**
Admiral Brackett: **Karen Hensel**
Sarek: **Mark Lenard**
Soup Woman: **Mimi Cozzens**
Computer Voice: **Majel Barrett**

Picard is shocked to learn that the legendary Vulcan scientist and ambassador, Spock, appears to have defected to the Romulan Empire.

While traveling to Vulcan, where Spock's equally legendary father, Sarek, lies near death, the captain learns that Spock may be working toward rejoining the Vulcan and Romulan peoples, who split aeons ago when the Vulcans adopted logic as the cornerstone of their civilization. Sarek's human wife, Perrin, reveals her bitterness at Spock's continued estrangement from his father, especially in her husband's last days. Picard is soon saddened to hear that Sarek has died.

After securing a cloaked Klingon ship and disguising themselves as Romulans, Picard and Data venture on to Romulus in the hope of meeting Spock's contact, Pardek, an aging peace advocate now back in favor. Neral, also an apparent reformer, has been elected proconsul.

Meanwhile, Riker and the crew track a Vulcan deflector stolen by the Ferengi. The search leads them to a ship junkyard, whose manager is surprised when several Vulcan vessels turn up

missing. Encountering an unidentified ship at one of the vanished ship berths, the *Enterprise* fires a warning shot at the mystery vessel—which promptly self-destructs.

On Romulus, Picard and Data are discovered and taken hostage, but their captors turn out to be members of Pardek's Romulan underground who help them, finally, to meet Spock.

If any doubts remained that TNG had become a worthy sequel to its namesake after five years, even the most skeptical diehard had to admit that Leonard Nimoy's presence as Spock quashed them. There had always been rumors that more of the original cast would turn up following De Forest Kelley's appearance in the pilot, and scripts had actually floated around to that effect. Tracy Tormé, for example, had been signed to do a second-season opener called "Return to Forever," bringing the movie-era Spock together with the Spock of the twenty-fourth century through the Guardian of Forever time portal from 1966's "City on the Edge of Forever." But, during the Writers Guild strike that summer, talks with Nimoy fell apart just as the outline was being finished, and the project never went any further.[1]

But things had changed in the intervening three years. Nimoy, an even hotter property than before, thanks to his success as a director of *Star Trek III* and *IV* and *Three Men and a Baby*, could not afford to ask much less than a salary that by itself would have soaked up most of the episode's budget. As *Star Trek VI: The Undiscovered Country* went into planning, Rick Berman said, the key turned out to be an idea of Paramount president Frank Mancuso's—"to somehow find a way to lock the two together" during Trek's silver anniversary.

On his deathbed, Sarek (Mark Lenard) tells Picard of his love for Spock.

Berman recalled that he and Nimoy talked about story ideas. After that "we structured a deal with him: he got very little, a little more than scale [union salary minimum]. But with Leonard as executive producer of *Star Trek VI*, what you had in essence was a cross-promotion. It made everybody happy."

Star Trek VI director Nick Meyer was brought in to discover ways to bridge references between the generations in his movie script and in "Unification," since the motion picture filmed long before the episode did. "Nimoy loved the idea of making slight references in the future" to the Kirk era, Berman recalled. The recent filming of the movie helped in other ways, too: the movie's Klingon Bird of Prey bridge and other sets on Paramount's Stage 5 were used for Picard and Data's cloaked ship in both segments.

Michael Piller was to have written the teleplay for both parts, but the time squeeze and the shift in production order proved too demanding and he offered Part I to Jeri Taylor. At first disappointed to do only the story setup, she had no idea how much a part of her life "Unification" would become. When Pocket Books called to suggest a novelization of the historic meeting of the Trek eras, Taylor—who wanted to break into books—asked for the job.

"The hitch was that I had thirty days to do it!" she said. "Yes, September 1991 was a month I'll never forget. I was writing Part One, I was writing the novel—it was like an endless finals week. You live on coffee, you're wired, you shut yourself off from family and friends: I had no other life but 'Unification'!"

After a month like that, and writing around the on-set changes made to Part 2, which was filmed before Part 1, Taylor finally got the manuscript off on time, only to receive another surprise: a "stunning" party thrown by the staff, complete with a full-size framed and autographed print of the book cover by Pocket's cover artist Keith Birdsong. The deal provided her with yet another first when she attended her first convention, the giant TNG fifth-anniversary celebration in March 1992 in L.A., for a book signing.

Picard assumes Romulan disguise for his mission to retrieve Spock.

UNIFICATION II

Production No. 207 ▪ Aired: Week of November 11, 1991
Stardate: 45245.8 ▪ Code u2

Directed by **Cliff Bole**
Teleplay by **Michael Piller**
Story by **Rick Berman and Michael Piller**

GUEST CAST

Spock: **Leonard Nimoy**
Captain K'Vada: **Stephen D. Root**
Senator Pardek: **Malachi Throne**
Proconsul Neral: **Norman Large**
Romulan No. 1: **Daniel Roebuck**
Omag: **William Bastiani**
Romulan No. 2: **Susan Fallender**
Commander Sela: **Denise Crosby**
D'Tan: **Vidal Peterson**
Amarie: **Harriet Leider**

Having found Spock on Romulus, Picard must perform the uncomfortable task of telling the ambassador his father has died. The news, combined with Picard's attempt to fulfill his friend Sarek's requst by telling Spock of his father's love, breaks the tension between the two. Spock then reveals he is indeed undertaking an unauthorized mission to pursue the reunification of the Vulcan and Romulan peoples. While Data begins working to crack the Romulans' computer net, Picard confides to the ambassador that he mistrusts the Romulans.

Meanwhile, the trail of the missing Vulcan ships leads Riker to a Ferengi smuggler, who finally admits that Romulans are involved. Number One contacts Picard, who has met Proconsul Neral in person and still does not trust the Romulan's intentions.

Soon they find Spock has indeed been double-crossed: a proposed peace envoy of Vulcan ships is just a ploy staged by Commander Sela, Picard's Romulan nemesis in the Klingon civil war. She and Neral plan to send the stolen ves-

Leonard Nimoy's appearance as Spock joined the *Star Trek* generations at last.

sels filled with Romulan troops as a "Trojan horse"—a sneak attack to conquer Vulcan.

Sela captures Spock and the two disguised *Enterprise* crew members, but can't force the Vulcan to publicly endorse the phony peace mission. She then reveals a holotape in which the ambassador does just that. Left unguarded in her office, Spock and Data send a coded signal to Riker and use a holotape of their own to escape Sela and her guards.

When Riker intercepts the "peace envoy," the Vulcan ships are destroyed by their cloaked escorts to remove any trace of the mission. Spock decides to stay on Romulus and work with the underground for real peace. At the last he bids his father good-bye by sharing Sarek's previous mind-meld with Picard.

Pardek (Malachi Throne) and Commander Sela (Denise Crosby) mastermind a plot to destroy Vulcan.

P art 2's production number precedes that of the opening segment because it was filmed first to accommodate Leonard Nimoy's schedule. During his five days of work, the set was closed to visitors, although Rick Berman recalled that the week was like most others on the series. Nimoy has said that his TNG experience was a sentimental yet hectic reminder of his days of weekly television, a stark contrast to the more leisurely pace of motion picture production.

Michael Piller used the unification of Germany as his basic thematic metaphor but was disappointed that his teleplay couldn't provide more chemistry in the Picard-Spock scenes. "We got some good moments, and Leonard was splendid," he said, "but I thought a lot of it was flat, talky, and dull." The historic meeting of Data and Spock was one of his favorite scenes, though, and he took issue with fans who ridiculed the idea of a Romulan invasion force of only three ships bound for Vulcan. "That's the only way you *could* do it, with a Trojan horse," he said. "You couldn't launch an all-out attack."

With two episodes to spread the cost over, the size and scope of the Romulan street-office complex built on Stage 16 rivaled the Victorian London holodeck set in "Elementary, Dear Data" (129). Production designer Richard James also re-dressed the cargo bay—last seen as the control room of the attack cruiser *Bortas'* in "Redemption" (200)—to the Quaylor II piano bar seen here.

"One of the show's major strengths," observed Rick Sternbach,

"is how they can put these Tinkertoy set pieces together again and again in different ways and repaint them and come up with completely different looks."

The Vulcan ships were originals, built by Greg Jein from an original design by Sternbach, with a *Reliant*-like feel featuring long, pointed engine pods and a bridge-over-hull look. Urged to go for a more alien non-Starfleet look, Sternbach said he based the design on a central core surrounded by a wraparound circular generator.

Notable among the nonspeaking actors in the Qualor II bar scene—which includes Riker's Trek play on words, "Andorian Blues"—were Jerry Crowl as yet another background Antican, Shana O'Brien and Heather Long as Omag's women, Leonard Jones as the Zakdorn waiter, and April Rossi as an extra known as Space Hooker.

The title of this most unusual of all TNG episodes carries more than the usual layers of meaning. The hoped-for reunion between Romulans and Vulcans is only the first of many "unifications." Symbolically carried out through Picard's mind-meld with Spock, it extends not only to a posthumous reconciliation between Sarek and his estranged son but indeed to both incarnations of Gene Roddenberry's vision, *Star Trek* and *Star Trek: The Next Generation*. When this episode is viewed in tandem with *Star Trek VI*, it's clear the torch has been passed, and any breach that may have existed between productions and between fans has been closed.

A MATTER OF TIME

Production No.: 209 ■ Aired: Week of November 18, 1991
Stardate: 45349.1 ■ Code: ma

Directed by **Paul Lynch**
Written by **Rick Berman**

GUEST CAST
Dr. Hal Mosely: **Stefan Gierasch**
Berlingoff Rasmussen: **Matt Frewer**
Ensign Felton: **Sheila Franklin**
Female Scientist: **Shay Garner**

While trying to reverse the nuclear winter–type effects caused by a crashed asteroid on Penthara IV, the *Enterprise* is visited by a time-traveling historian from twenty-sixth-century Earth, Berlingoff Rasmussen.

The officers' initial suspicions give way to impatience when Rasmussen asks repeatedly to see their "artifacts" and to have questionnaires filled out. Troi is convinced he is hiding something, but most crew members go along with his teasing and his annoying cheeriness.

The ship's first try at helping Penthara IV only makes matters worse; then La Forge comes up with an alternative plan that will either clear the atmosphere or burn it off entirely, killing every living thing on the planet. Desperate for help, Picard turns to Rasmussen, but the time traveler says he can't divulge the future. When the Pentharans agree to Geordi's plan so does Picard. Luckily, it works.

Rasmussen quickly moves to leave after the planet is saved, but Picard first demands he be allowed to search the time pod for items reported missing by his crew. The time traveler agrees to let Data enter because he can be ordered not to divulge any secrets of the future, but once the two are inside the pod, Rasmussen pulls a phaser and reveals he is really from the twenty-second century. He appropriated the real twenty-sixth-century time traveler's craft and came forward in time to gather trinkets—which now include Data—that he could claim to have invented.

But a suspicious Picard had Rasmussen's phaser deactivated. Helpless, Rasmussen is stranded in the twenty-fourth century when the pod's timed return mechanism whisks it away without him.

Supposed "time traveler" Rasmussen (Matt Frewer) doesn't impress everyone aboard.

Rick Berman said he'd always been interested in the idea of someone traveling through time to steal Data, and he got the chance to do it in this, his second turn at storytelling and his only solo writing credit during the first five seasons. "It's like imagining what Newton could have done if he'd had a calculator," Berman said. "What would someone of the nineteenth, twentieth, or twenty-first century do with Data? He'd be a very powerful individual!"

The effort to replace Wesley with a female conn officer had of course ended with the addition of Ro, but beginning here and for five shows this season, Sheila Franklin's Ensign Felton filled in as well. Though never spoken aloud, the name Felton appeared in all of the scripts she turned up in "New Ground," "Hero Worship," "The Masterpiece Society" and "Imaginary Friend" (210, 211, 213, and 222).

Among the tidbits of Trek information provided here: a phaser on maximum stun is required to stun Data; the Federation was founded after the Romulan War "The Outcast" (217); and phasers, medical forcefields, and the warp coil were all invented after the twenty-second century.

NEW GROUND

Production No.: 210 ■ Aired: Week of January 6, 1992
Stardate: 45376.3 ■ Code: ng

Directed by **Robert Scheerer**
Teleplay by **Grant Rosenberg**
Story by **Sara Charno and Stuart Charno**

GUEST CAST
Helena Rozhenko: **Georgia Brown**
Alexander: **Brian Bonsall**
Dr. Ja'Dar: **Richard McGonagle**
Kyle: **Jennifer Edwards**
Ensign Felton: **Sheila Franklin**
Computer Voice: **Majel Barrett**

Worf and Troi find newfound common ground over raising Alexander.

On the eve of testing the Soliton Wave, a historic new drive system, Worf receives an unexpected visit from his foster mother, Helena Rozhenko, and his son, Alexander. To Worf's surprise, Helena tells him that he must take custody of his son for the boy's own good.

The lieutenant soon discovers what his mother is talking about: he finds Alexander has been lying and acting up in class. After Worf threatens to send him to a rigorous Klingon school, Troi points out Alexander may be feeling neglected after his mother's death and his father's virtual abandonment of him.

When the Soliton Wave experiment goes awry and reaches power levels that could wipe out a colony in its path, the *Enterprise* must start a "backfire" effect, using its photon torpedoes. As they prepare to break up the wave, Alexander is visiting his favorite animals, unaware that the biolab is unprotected by shields. He is trapped there when the wave is penetrated; a fire breaks out in the lab, forcing Worf and Riker to rescue him.

Worf then realizes how much he would miss his son if he were sent away; Alexander agrees to remain aboard the *Enterprise*.

For the only time this season, the writing credits carried no staff names; still Michael Piller credited Ronald D. Moore with lending "a big hand" in the polishing of Grant Rosenberg's teleplay, taken from a story by TNG veterans Sarah and Stuart Charno, who wrote "The Wounded" (186).

After child actor Jon Steurer originated the role of Alexander in last season's "Reunion" (181), the slightly older Brian Bonsall—who'll best be remembered as Andy, the youngest Keaton in the later seasons of *Family Ties*—was brought in; he had the series track record desired for what was now to be a recurring role. Alexander's age became a topic of some discussion and not a little confusion when he first appeared in "Reunion" so soon after his apparent conception in "The Emissary" (146), but some clues are provided here. His birthday, the twenty-third day of Maktag, is a nice bit of trivia, but his stardate birth, 43205, falls during the time of season three's "Booby Trap" (154), only 304 stardate units after K'Ehleyr's first *Enterprise* visit and 1,041 units before the boy turns up with his mother later—although 1,000 units are generally considered to be a year. Of course K'Ehleyr's half-human makeup may have altered Alexander's maturation process from the Klingon norm.

A nice bit of continuity was provided by the Klingon legend of the fighting brothers Kahless and Morath, whose statue Worf refers to in his quarters. Kahless the Unforgettable was one of the evil images in an original-Trek episode, "The Savage Curtain," in 1969. The statue was a stock piece, but the figures "grew" Klingon ridges thanks to Michael Westmore's deft touch.

The experimental Soliton Wave glider is a re-dress of the Mars defense ships that were easily picked off by the Borg in "The Best of Both Worlds," Part 2 (175).

Hero Worship

Production No.: 211 ■ Aired: Week of January 27, 1992
Stardate: 45397.3 ■ Code: hw

Directed by **Patrick Stewart**
Teleplay by **Joe Menosky**
Story by **Hilary J. Bader**

GUEST CAST
Timothy: **Joshua Harris**
Transporter Chief: **Harley Venton**
Ensign Felton: **Sheila Franklin**
Teacher: **Steven Einspahr**

The *Enterprise* is sent to check on the missing USS *Vico*, a research ship sent to explore the interior of a Black Cluster—the remains of hundreds of protostars. The cluster generates gravitational tidal waves that are capable of buffeting a starship but pose no real danger.

Data finds a lone survivor among the wreckage of the *Vico*, a boy named Timothy, who tells his rescuer an alien vessel destroyed the ship. The evidence soon indicates otherwise, however, and Troi urges Data to foster his friendship with the boy to get the real story. Timothy, meanwhile, is so impressed by Data that he takes to mimicking the android.

Picard orders his ship into the Cluster to further investigate the *Vico*'s demise, whereupon the shock waves surprisingly grow more intense.

The captain urges Timothy to recall what he can of his ship's destruction, but the boy steadfastly refuses to change his story of alien invaders, until Data tells him androids do not lie. Timothy then breaks down and says he destroyed the *Vico* by accidentally touching a console.

Incredulous, Picard, Troi, and Data convince him that cannot be, that his action was just a coincidence. Timothy has trouble believing them, however, especially when he hears more and more power being ordered to shields; he tells Data his ship did the same thing. As a huge wave approaches the *Enterprise*, Data finally realizes that all shields should actually be lowered: they're magnifying the waves' effect. Timothy decides to drop his android act, but he and Data vow to stay friends anyway.

This big Data–little Data episode provided a charming turn not only for the android but for ship's counselor Troi as well, expanding on the depiction of her duties. "Jeri Taylor and I say that since we've been here the counseling scenes have become much more numerous and realistic," Michael Piller said. "But that expertise doesn't come from practicing—it comes from being a patron!"

We also get a rare bit of Geordi background in this story, learning of a traumatic fire he suffered through at age five before receiving his first VISOR. The scenario was originally one of the memory scenes not used in "Violations" (212).

This time around, Harley Venton's transporter officer who also appeared in "Ensign Ro" (203), is named Hutchinson in the script, although the name remains unspoken. The USS *Vico* is a new model of *Star Trek III's Grissom*, built and detailed as a wreck by Greg Jein. The Breen, one of the races suspected of having destroyed the *Vico*, were mentioned in "The Loss" (184) as a race that could not be sensed telepathically.

Data and Timothy (Joshua Harris) study the art of painting.

VIOLATIONS

Production No.: 212 ■ Aired: Week of February 3, 1992
Stardate: 45429.3 ■ Code: vi

Directed by **Robert Wiemer**
Teleplay by **Pamela Gray and Jeri Taylor**
Story by **Shari Goodhartz, T. Michael Gray and
Pamela Gray**

GUEST CAST
Keiko O'Brien: **Rosalind Chao**
Jev: **Ben Lemon**
Tarmin: **David Sage**
Dr. Martin: **Rick Fitts**
Inad: **Eve Brenner**
Lieutenant Commander Jack Crusher: **Doug Wert**
Crewman Davis: **Craig Benton**
Computer Voice: **Majel Barrett**

A forced memory: Beverly Crusher views her husband's corpse with Picard.

The *Enterprise* takes aboard three Ullians, members of a race of telepathic historians who do their research by probing their subjects' long-forgotten memories. Their leader, Tarmin, is surprised by the crew's reluctance to be probed, while his son Jev is embarrassed by his father's continued attempts to gain the crew's permission. That evening Troi has a flashback to a romantic encounter with Riker—but Jev replaces Riker in her memories. As she struggles against him, she lapses into a coma.

The same thing happens to Riker, who remembers a shipboard disaster that cost a crew member's life, and then to Beverly, who is forced to recall the time years ago when Picard took her to see her late husband's body.

Picard is increasingly suspicious of the Ullians, but they protest their innocence. Troi finally comes to and readily agrees to be mind-probed by Jev about the night she slipped into a coma. This time it is Tarmin who takes Riker's place in her dreams.

The elder Ullian is taken into custody, but when Jev visits Troi, the flashback returns and she realizes he's the real mental rapist. The timely appearance by Worf and Data saves her. Researching a history of similar comas on other worlds, they had discovered Jev was the only

Ullian present when all the incidents took place.

Tarmin apologizes for his son, saying he'd thought his once-violent race had put memory rape behind it.

This story began as the second outline TNG bought from Shari Goodhartz; the first was "Night Terrors" (191). This script evolved through numerous drafts, each of which approached the rape metaphor differently. Jeri Taylor and Pamela Gray, an intern, came up with the atypical science fiction angle of mental rather than physical assault.

"We had been doing so many political shows that the success of this one reminded us that maybe we could do more with the mental side of SF, exploring the bizarre possibilities of psychological dramas," Taylor said.

Lots of memory flashbacks were generated for every major character before those of Troi, Riker, and Beverly were chosen. One alluded to Ro's yet-unexplained trouble on Garon II, mentioned in "Ensign Ro" (203), while another involving Geordi's childhood brush with fire was so popular that Joe Menosky picked it up to use in the previous episode, "Hero Worship" (211). Goodhartz's first treatment had featured Miles O'Brien as victim.

Director Robert Wiemer sought and received permission from Rick Berman to use a number of different camera tricks to set apart the bizarre memory scenes implanted by Jev, then used conservative camera work in the "reality" scenes to heighten the contrast between the two. The tricks included the use of wide-angle lenses during Beverly's flashback; at one point both Gates McFadden and Patrick Stewart are sitting on the moving dolly (rolling camera crane), generating an eerie floating effect.

After several mentions and one false start ("Where No One Has Gone Before"/106), the time of Jack Crusher's death is finally established here, albeit vaguely. Actor Doug Wert makes a brief reappearance here in a casket, after having been seen earlier in "Family" (178).

The Riker-Troi flashbacks caused a stir of their own, Jeri Taylor remembered, from fans who were disappointed that later episodes did not continue the rekindled intimacy between the two (105, 148, 184). The fans had obviously missed the point that these scenes were flashbacks. In this sequence, though, we do learn that it was Troi who decided to cool their relationship for the sake of professionalism when they learned that they had both been assigned to the *Enterprise.*

Other trivia: Keiko's grandmother was named Obachan, and Geordi got his first pet—the Circassian cat mentioned in "Galaxy's Child" (190)—at age eight.

THE MASTERPIECE SOCIETY

Production No.: 213 ■ Aired: Week of February 10, 1992
Stardate: 45470.1 ■ Code: ms

Directed by **Winrich Kolbe**
Teleplay by **Adam Belanoff and Michael Piller**
Story by **James Kahn and Adam Belanoff**

G U E S T C A S T
Aaron Conor: **John Snyder**
Hannah Bates: **Dey Young**
Martin Benbeck: **Ron Canada**
Ensign Felton: **Sheila Franklin**

While monitoring the progress of a neutron star's core fragment, the *Enterprise* crew is shocked to learn of an unknown human colony

Aaron (John Snyder) and Martin (Ron Canada) describe their fragile society to Troi and Riker.

on Moab IV, now threatened by the fragment— and even more surprised when the residents refuse to relocate.

Their leader, Aaron Conor, explains that the colony has been genetically planned and engineered to be the perfect society. Any contact with outsiders is bound to be corrupting. Conor reluctantly agrees to let *Enterprise* officers beam down to discuss the danger posed by the fragment.

The colony's chief scientist Hannah Bates begins working with La Forge to develop a tractor beam that will be powerful enough to deflect the core fragment. When Bates must beam aboard the *Enterprise* with Geordi to continue her research, Troi stays behind, fascinated by the soft-spoken Conor. After spending the night with him, she berates herself for allowing the brief affair, knowing her Betazoid DNA would not be welcome in the genetically closed colony.

Ironically it is the VISOR of an "imperfect" blind man that inspires the needed tractor beam enhancement; but to install the equipment necessary to deflect the fragment, fifty more people from the *Enterprise* will have to beam down.

Conor reluctantly agrees to their presence. The engineers' plan works, and the fragment is diverted. But the colony's problems are far from over. Hannah, after a taste of the outside world, decides to leave. She fakes an alarm to force evacuation, but Geordi sees through her ruse. Yet despite pleas from Conor and other colonists, Bates and twenty-three others decide to leave. Conor decides he can't stop them, despite the irreparable damage their departure will cause.

Picard is left to wonder which ultimately posed the greater threat to the colony, the core fragment or his ship's "help."

In the most reasoned and focused Trek position on selective human breeding since 1967's "Space Seed," Picard echoes the classic Roddenberry-inspired argument against eugenics as dehumanizing and a detriment to free choice. Michael Piller himself took over this script after it had passed through five other writers' hands over a season and a half. He struggled mainly with the question, "What exactly *is* a genetically engineered society?"

Hannah's laboratory, once again, was built over the frame of the old two-level movie bridge set with the "science lab" set pieces in place; her computers use black-on-white, almost Macintosh-like computer visuals.

Conundrum

Production No.: 214 ■ Aired: Week of February 17, 1992
Stardate: 45494.2 ■ Code: cn

Directed by **Les Landau**
Teleplay by **Barry M. Schkolnick**
Story by **Paul Schiffer**

GUEST CAST
Commander Keiran MacDuff: **Erich Anderson**
Ensign Ro Laren: **Michelle Forbes**
Kristin: **Liz Vassey**
Crewman: **Erick Weiss**

After being scanned by an unknown alien ship, *Enterprise* crew members discover both their own and their computer's memories have been selectively wiped out.

Though they can't remember their names or their functions, they've all retained the knowledge necessary to operate the ship. They grope their way to some kind of structure: Worf assumes command; Data decides he's the bartender in Ten-Forward; and Ro feels attracted to Riker, Troi even more so. Finally the ship's computer is able to provide them with name, rank, and serial number; among the bridge crew is Commander Kieran MacDuff, listed as first officer.

The computer also reveals their mission: the *Enterprise* is part of a fleet fighting a decades-old war with the Lysians. Their current assignment, to be conducted under radio silence, is to destroy the aliens' Central Command.

Picard grows concerned, though, when the Lysian vessels they meet prove no match for his ship. His conscience finally forces him to call off the attack. Angered, MacDuff tries to assume control of the ship. Worf stuns him, and the phaser blast reveals that MacDuff is actually an alien.

Dr. Crusher soon restores the crew's memories, whereupon they identify MacDuff as a Sartaaran, a race that's been at war with the Lysians for decades. Despite their skill with computers and memory suppression, his race's weak weapons technology forced their thwarted hijacking of the *Enterprise*.

One of several amnesia stories from season four, this episode was put on hold for a year and then developed into this script, which Michael Piller felt didn't quite do justice to the original and fascinating tale of drafting soldiers by rewriting their memories. Staff and fans alike, though, loved the Riker-Troi-Ro triangle that emerged here, especially the fact that all three retained the memory of their past "interactions."

In his cabin, Riker plays few notes of "The Nearness of You," the song he played for Minuet on the holodeck in "11001001" (116), and looks over his *horgah'n* from Risa, first seen in "Captain's Holiday" (167).

Curiously, while the ships of the two warring sides were not new staff designs, the Lysian command center miniature dates all the way back to season one, when it was hazily photographed as the *Edolord* over Rubicum III in "Justice" (109).

His memory erased, Picard doesn't suspect the true nature of his "Number One," Commander Kieran MacDuff (Erich Anderson).

POWER PLAY

Production No.: 215 ■ Aired: Week of February 24, 1992
Stardate: 45571.2 ■ Code: pw

Directed by **David Livingston**
Teleplay by **Rene Balcer, Herbert J. Wright,** and
Brannon Braga
Story by **Paul Ruben and Maurice Hurley**

GUEST CAST
Keiko O'Brien: **Rosalind Chao**
Lieutenant Miles O'Brien: **Colm Meaney**
Ensign Ro Laren: **Michelle Forbes**
Transporter Technician: **Ryan Reid**
Computer Voice: **Majel Barrett**

After receiving an old-style distress call from a moon of Mab-Bu VI, previously thought to be uninhabited, and after learning also that magnetic storms prevent the use of the transporter, Riker, Troi, and Data take a shuttlecraft down to the moon's surface to investigate.

Stranded after the shuttle crash-lands, they are relieved when O'Brien risks his life to beam down to them. He brings along transport enhancers to enable them to beam back to the ship. As they depart, a strange cloud envelops all but the injured Riker.

Troi, Data, and O'Brien have been possessed by alien entities, who soon secure themselves in Ten-Forward with hostages—including a bewildered Keiko and little Molly—until Picard agrees to their chief demand: move the ship to the area over the moon's south pole.

The entities claim to be from the USS *Essex* and say they want only to be buried in peace. Troi, possessed by the spirit of Captain Bryce Shumar, says they were disembodied when their ship broke up over the moon two hundred years ago.

But their violence belies this story, and Picard eventually learns the truth: the entities were actually prisoners condemned to the penal colony Mab-Bu VI. They tried to possess the *Essex*'s crew and use that ship to escape—as they plan to do now with the *Enterprise* and its crew.

Taken hostage by the three, Picard accompanies them to a cargo bay where the rest of the entities are beamed up. The captain then turns the tables, saying he will open the outer cargo bay doors and kill all of them, including himself, rather than allow the entities to take his crew. The entities relent, abandon their host bodies, and return to their prison.

Bearing a slight conceptual resemblance to an original-series episode, "Return to Tomorrow," another tale of alien possession, this story went through several script treatments by free-lancers before being assigned to Braga. Herb Wright brought in the ghost angle when the two teamed up for the version eventually used.

"It was supposed to be the ultimate bottle show, a tense psychological drama between Picard and the possessed Troi, crammed into one room, but it became one of the costliest of the year with the shuttle crash and the phaser fight," Braga said. "It has no socially redeeming value, but it sure is action-packed!"

"It was wonderfully directed," Michael Piller agreed, praising David Livingston for his second outing behind the camera. "That's why it was successful." Marina Sirtis finally got into some rough stuff, and Brent Spiner found an edge different from Lore's for his character as well. They and Colm Meaney invented nicknames for their "possessed" personae: Slugger, Buzz, and Slash.

Once again Planet Hell lived up to its nickname: filming spilled over an extra half-day on Stage 16, where Livingston recalled worrying about Spiner's contact lenses and where Sirtis got so dirty from the blowing sand she had to take a midday shower and get made up again.

Possessed by an alien entity, Troi terrorizes the *Enterprise*.

The crashed shuttlepod was the *Campbell,* named for pioneering science fiction author Joseph W. Campbell. Inspired by the movie *Cape Fear,* a 360-degree rotating camera was used to film the craft's interior crash scenes.

A bit of early Federation history is revealed here with the mention of the NCC-173 *Essex* and its ill-fated crew of 229. The end of service for the ship's Daedelus class is established as 172 years earlier, or 2196, and its specific loss over two hundred years prior to this episode means the Daedalus prototype was likely designed and commissioned well before the UFP's founding in 2161, as established in "The Outcast" (217). At the time of its loss, though, Starbase 12 is referred to as already in operation.

Finally, another bit of Klingon culture—their notion of spiritual possession, *Jat'yln*—is revealed here as well.

ETHICS

Production No.: 216 ■ Aired: Week of March 2, 1992
Stardate: 45587.3 ■ Code: et

Directed by **Chip Chalmers**
Teleplay by **Ronald D. Moore**
Story by **Sara Charno and Stuart Charno**

GUEST CAST
Dr. Toby Russell: **Caroline Kava**
Alexander: **Brian Bonsall**
Nurse Alyssa Ogawa: **Patti Yasutake**

Neurospecialist Dr. Toby Russell comes aboard to help treat Worf after an accident leaves the Klingon paralyzed from the waist down, but she and Dr. Crusher clash over Russell's proposal to use genetonic replication to replace his spine. Beverly considers the life-threatening procedure an unnecessary risk to her patient, who is in no danger of dying.

Worf feels that he is dead already; his shame at being helpless is so great he won't let Alexander see him. He even asks Riker to help him commit ritual suicide to avoid being pitied. Riker is torn, weighing his values against Worf's, until he learns that Klingon custom requires the son to assist in the ceremony anyway.

After Worf refuses to consider the partial mobility offered by neural implants, Beverly is shocked when Dr. Russell tempts him with her untried genetonic process. It has only a fair test

success rate and has never been tried with humanoids—and failure would mean death.

Meanwhile, during a rescue attempt, another of Russell's experimental techniques costs a patient's life. Angered, Crusher relieves her of all medical duty. But when Worf can't bring himself to ask Alexander to complete the suicide ceremony, both he and Beverly relent, and agree to try Dr. Russell's procedure.

The Klingon dies in surgery, but mourning turns to joy when a redundant Klingon body system kicks in. Worf again asks his son for help—but this time with his therapy.

This examination of medical ethics once again shows how conflict can be drawn out of the regulars using a guest star as catalyst. The story faced off not only the two doctors but Riker and Worf as well—seen here battling over Klingon ritual suicide. Picard's willingness to respect Worf's Klingon beliefs echoes his decision in "The Enemy" (155) not to force Worf to donate blood to a Romulan, but here the captain almost seems to be taking the easy way out, even given Trek's multicultural philosophy, in light of Riker's aggressive condemnation of suicide.

Seen again are the red surgical outfits used during Picard's heart surgery in "Samaritan Snare" (143). For much of the surgery sequence, Michael Dorn's photo double, Al Foster, stood in as the Klingon exo-backbone was glimpsed for the first time. We also learn about the redundancies of Klingon anatomy, discovering that Worf has twenty-three ribs, two livers, an eight-chambered heart, a double-lined neural pia matter, and of course a backup synaptic system.

Continuity with earlier Starfleet medical references was maintained with the use here of "motor assist bands" and the drugs inoprovaline in "Transfigurations" (173) and cordrazine in "Shades of Gray" (148). Other echoes of the past include Russell's ferrying

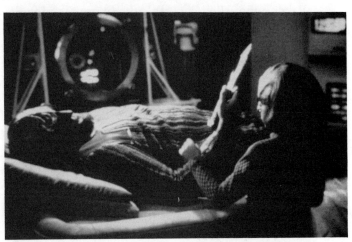

Alexander (Brian Bonsall) helps his paralyzed father choose life rather than ritual suicide.

ship, the *Potemkin,* mentioned in "Peak Performance" (147) as one of Riker's prior assignments and, in "Legacy" (180), as the last ship to visit Turkana IV. A gravitic mine, the Cardassian War leftover that does in the USS *Denver,* was referred to earlier in the Kobiyashi Maru scene in *Star Trek II.*

La Forge is seen briefly in the teaser sporting a beard—a test that the producers allowed LeVar Burton to try, once.

THE OUTCAST

> Production No.: 217 ● Aired: Week of March 16, 1992
> Stardate: 45614.6 ● Code: oc
>
> ---
>
> Directed by **Robert Scheerer**
> Written by **Jeri Taylor**
>
> ---
>
> **GUEST CAST**
> Soren: **Melinda Culea**
> Krite: **Callan White**
> Noor: **Megan Cole**

The J'naii, an androgynous race, ask the *Enterprise* for help in locating a missing shuttlecraft. An abnormality called "null space" proves to be the cause of its disappearance. Riker works to recover it with a J'naii shuttle pilot named Soren. The two become fast friends, even to the point of comparing their cultures' mating habits. Soren tells Riker that sexual preference is banned on J'naii and that all nonconformists are treated to a brainwashing "cure." Soren insists on coming along on the rescue mission with Riker, where "she" reveals the female tendencies she has always been too scared to admit.

Soren is injured on the flight, delaying their search, but now grows bolder and admits her feelings for Riker. He finds himself falling too, but they present a professional front while rescuing the shuttle and its near-dead survivors.

But after the two share a kiss at that night's celebration party, the J'naii Krite detects what's going on and takes Soren into custody with no warning. Enraged, Riker crashes Soren's "trial" and tries to defend her, but she admits her feelings in an impassioned plea for acceptance that falls on deaf ears.

Despite Picard's warnings that a rash act could ruin him, Riker tries to free her with Worf's help, but it is too late: the "therapy" has already taken hold, and Soren renounces her feelings for him.

A bitter Riker returns to the ship and assures Picard his business on J'naii is finished.

For over twenty-five years Trek's two television series had pioneered the intelligent and fair-minded depiction of various sexes, races, and ethnic groups, including aliens. One notable and controversial exception, though, was homosexuals. With the relative freedom of expression granted TNG, various letter-writing campaigns over the years grew more and more insistent that one or more gay crew members be seen.

Jeri Taylor jumped at the chance to take on this teleplay, the first of the late-season run that emerged from the writers' Mexican weekend, and she brought to the script a real empathy for the feelings of the powerless and disenfranchised.

After the show aired, Taylor received mail from viewers who ranged all the way from fundamentalists on the religious right who thought the episode "'should have been balanced with the other side,' whatever that means," to gays who thought the ending might be misinterpreted as "sanctioning" Soren's brainwashing therapy.

"I did get lots of thank-yous from both gay and straight people who appreciated the story as a science fiction treatment of the intolerance of choice and need as a tragedy," she said. "It really woke up the audience," Michael Piller agreed. "We didn't want to just blow off the issue by showing a same-sex couple holding hands in the corner." Added Rick Berman: "We thought we had made a very positive statement about sexual prejudice in a distinctively *Star Trek* way, but we still got letters from those who thought it was just our way of 'washing our hands' of the homosexual situation." TNG's executive producer added that he considered the letter-writing fan on any issue very rare—about one-tenth of a percent of TNG's total audience. And the massive write-in campaigns "where you receive three hundred letters with the same sentences" didn't carry as much weight as the simple individual letters.

Aside from the question of sexual preference, this story shows a maturity of another kind in dealing with Riker. He was the first regular to be out of control over an emotional attachment, other than Worf, whose actions were always explained away by his Klingon nature.

Riker brings out the forbidden "female" feelings of Soren (Melinda Culea).

A minor story throwaway line but a major point for trivia fans is the revelation that the UFP was founded in 2161. Michael Okuda, who calculated the in-house chronology of Trek events taken from series facts throughout the years, assumed the Federation was founded after the Romulan War, a century before Kirk's time, based on the statement in 1966's "Balance of Terror" that "Earth," not the Federation, fought the alien empire.

We also received a better view of the starship's *Magellan* shuttlecraft, first seen in "Darmok" (202). The J'naii shuttle *Taris Murn*, briefly seen, is the same craft used as the *Nenebek* in "Final Mission" (183) and as Rasmussen's time pod in "A Matter of Time" (209).

The weekly poker game: Dr. Crusher's first clue to the Typhon Expanse's time loop.

Cause and Effect

Production No. 218 ▪ Aired: Week of March 23, 1992
Stardate: 45652.1 ▪ Code: ce

Directed by **Jonathan Frakes**
Written by **Brannon Braga**

GUEST CAST
Ensign Ro Laren: **Michelle Forbes**
Nurse Alyssa Ogawa: **Patti Yasutake**
Captain Morgan Bateman: **Kelsey Grammer**

The crew's regular poker game suddenly feels too familiar to Dr. Crusher, who experiences feelings of déjà vu that are at first puzzling and then maddening. Those feelings intensify when she is called away to treat La Forge for a minor but baffling dizziness. Preparing for bed, she hears strange voices in her cabin.

Meanwhile, the *Enterprise* is continuing to chart the Typhon Expanse when the ship's propulsion systems fail, hurling it onto a collision course with another starship that appears out of the void. Picard follows Data's advice to use the tractor beam to alter the other ship's trajectory, but the tactic fails. The ships collide, and both are destroyed. . . .

The regular poker game resumes, and this time Beverly is not alone in her feelings of déjà vu. After experiencing another cycle of destruction, she records the voices she hears in her room, which Data discovers are the echoes of their own conversations from past time loops.

As another cycle climaxes, Data plants a clue for himself in the next time loop—recurring instances of the number 3. Realizing at the last second that the three refers to the pips on Riker's uniform and his plan to decompress the main shuttle bay to alter course, Data follows the first officer's suggestion rather than his own—and the loop is broken.

They find the *Enterprise* has been trapped for seventeen days, but Picard wonders how he will explain to the crew of the other starship, the *Bozeman*, that they have been caught for ninety years.

Braga, who said he'd always wanted to do a time-travel story without the cliché of the "screwed-up time lines," called this solo story the smoothest he had yet worked on, though it provided a challenge in drawing out the subtleties of the varying time loops. Beginning with what he called "the ultimate teaser," he was proud for once to be able to tie the poker game scene into the plot as a major point.

Kelsey Grammer became the third *Cheers* actor to enter the Trek universe—after Bebe Neuwirth in "First Contact" (189) and Kirstie Alley in *Star Trek II*—but his viewscreen scenes were all shot separately from the rest of the cast, again using the old movie bridge set re-dressed. The staff had wanted the first officer to the right of Bateman to be Kirstie Alley as Lieutenant Saavik, but the scheduling couldn't be worked out.

The USS *Bozeman* was a "new" Soyuz-class ship: the *Reliant* miniature from *Star Trek II* minus the roll bar and with new sensor turrets, docking port, and bridge. Originally the plan was to make the ship a 1960s-era, pre-movie Constitution-class starship, but budget demands put an end to that when the costs of creating and filming ship, props, and costumes were added up.

The enormous main shuttle bay was depicted for the first time in any form. It was actually a tabletop model built by Michael Okuda on which the two shuttlecraft were named—in lettering too small to be legible—the *Berman* and the *Piller*!

THE FIRST DUTY

Production No.: 219 ■ Aired: Week of March 30, 1992
Stardate: 45703.9 ■ Code: fd

Directed by **Paul Lynch**
Written by **Ronald D. Moore** and **Naren Shankar**

GUEST CAST

Boothby: **Ray Walston**
Cadet First Class Nicholas Locarno: **Robert Duncan McNeill**
Lieutenant Commander Albert: **Ed Lauter**
Captain Satelk: **Richard Fancy**
Superintendant Admiral Brand: **Jacqueline Brookes**
Cadet Third Class Wesley Crusher: **Wil Wheaton**
Cadet Second Class Jean Hajar: **Walker Brandt**
Cadet Second Class Sito: **Shannon Fill**
Cadet: **Richard Rothenberg**

En route to deliver the commencement address at Starfleet Academy, Picard learns that a horrifying accident has occurred. While rehearsing for the graduating ceremonies, a member of Wesley Crusher's five-person flight squadron has been killed.

A routine inquiry into the accident finds discrepancies between the cadets' filed flight plan and their testimony. Nova Squadron leader Locarno reluctantly reveals that the dead squadron member, Joshua Albert, panicked and caused the mishap. This news comes as a painful blow to his already grieving father.

But in a squadron meeting later, Wesley is angry. Locarno lied, he says. Joshua Albert

Picard (*below*) consults his old Academy mentor Boothby the gardener (Ray Walston) after the tragedy that threatens Wesley's young career. *Opposite, bottom:* The charismatic Locarno (Robert Duncan McNeill) tries to lead Wesley and Sito (Shannon Fill) astray by encouraging them to cover up their flight accident. *Top:* Picard helps Wesley choose the truth.

wasn't to blame. But the squadron leader makes an impassioned plea for the four remaining team members to stick together, pointing out that their careers will be over if they reveal the whole truth.

The next day, Wesley's testimony is countered by surprise evidence from a satellite. But to the surprise of both Picard and Beverly, he refuses to expain the discrepancy. Returning to the *Enterprise* after a talk with his old mentor, Boothby, Picard realizes that the accident occurred because Nova Squadron was practicing the Kolvoord Starburst, a spectacular exhibition of stunt flying banned for over a century, that would have made Locarno a living legend.

Picard confronts Wesley with the truth and says he will reveal it if Wesley doesn't. Despite a last-minute entreaty by Locarno to stand by his team, an anguished Wesley agrees that his first duty is to the truth. Locarno is expelled, while Wesley and his mates must repeat the past year and face the difficult time ahead.

For over twenty-five years, Starfleet Academy had been talked about but never seen—until this story, developed during the writers' Mexican retreat by Ron Moore, who wound up in a philosophical argument with Michael Piller over Wesley's ultimate decision. "I thought he should choose the truth, and Ron thought he couldn't go back on his friends," Piller recalled. "Ultimately I gave the order to go with the truth—that's what I'd want my kids to do—but I think it shows how much we can get into these characters when we find ourselves debating the points they're arguing."

Boothby, of course, had twice before been mentioned by the captain—in "Final Mission" (183) and in "The Game" (206)—but was seen here for the first time. Ray Walston, immortalized forever in TV reruns as the title alien in the 1960s sitcom *My Favorite Martian*, commented that throughout his days of shooting, the cast and crew approached him with the old character's schtick of head antenna and finger-wiggling "levitation."

Satelk is the first Vulcan captain seen in TNG, while the presence of Cadet Sito proves that Ensign Ro is not the only Bajoran in Starfleet. While the exact date of Betazed's first participation in Federation affairs has yet to be pinned down, we do know that a Betazoid headed the Academy at least as early as Riker's years, set at 2353–2357 in the Okudagram bio files that Michael Okuda prepared for "Conundrum" (214); Picard's graduation with the "class of '27" is also included there. Earlier, the head of the academy was called "commandant" when the position was offered to Picard in "Coming of Age" (119).

The exterior views of Starfleet Academy, matted into the twenty-fourth-century Starfleet environs, were location scenes filmed one day at the Tillman Water Reclamation Plant in Van Nuys, the same site that provided the exteriors for Rubicun III in "Justice" (109). Notice the Academy flag flying half mast. Dan Curry added that to the exterior matte painting.

That little touch and the Academy seal on the flag itself were just two of many the staff threw in. The seal's equilateral triangle form, adapted by Michael Okuda from a design by Joe Senna, features the sun behind the Golden Gate Bridge in the logo's center; an animated version with the sun rising into place was considered but ultimately not used. The name "Starfleet Academy" adorns the left leg of the triangle while the bottom reads "San Francisco/MMCLXI," the Roman numerals for its founding date of 2161, the same as that of the Federation, as established in "The Outcast" (217). The right leg of the triangle bears the Academy's Latin motto, *Ex astra, scientia,* or "From the stars, knowledge"—quite a pacifist notion for what some might mistakenly regard as a military school. Okuda reports the motto is taken from that of the ill-fated Apollo 13, *"Ex luna, scientia."*

The various sensor log tapes used in the inquiry were all computer-generated by Curry's team, including the brief tape of the cadets' ships in flight. Wesley's dorm room contains models of both an Apollo command-service module on display in the background and Kirk's original Constitution-class *Enterprise.*

The cadets' collar pips, descending among Nova Squadron from Locarno's four to Wesley's two, appear to be the same as the longer pins adorning the movie-era uniforms' white sleeve cuff. The inquiry's hearing bell was also used in the original series' official proceedings as seen in "Space Seed" and "Courtmartial." And the "Yeager Loop" maneuver pays tribute to an even earlier ancestor of TNG—Chuck Yeager, the pilot who first broke the sound barrier in 1947.

COST OF LIVING

Production No.: 220 ▪ Aired: Week of April 20, 1992
Stardate: 45733.6 ▪ Code: cs

Directed by **Winrich Kolbe**
Written by **Peter Allan Fields**

GUEST CAST
Lwaxana Troi: **Majel Barrett**
Alexander: **Brian Bonsall**
Campio: **Tony Jay**
Mr. Homn: **Carel Struyken**
Young Man: **David Oliver**
Juggler: **Albie Selznick**
Erko: **Patrick Cronin**
Young Woman: **Tracey D'Arcy**
Poet: **George Edie**
First Learner: **Christopher Halste**

After the *Enterprise* helps destroy a rogue aster-oid, Troi's mother Lwaxana beams aboard and makes a surprise announcement: she is getting married—to a man she has never met!

As if worrying about her mother wasn't enough, Troi must also help Worf deal with his increasingly rebellious young son, Alexander. Matters worsen when Lwaxana persuades the young Klingon to join her in a holodeck mud bath amid a colony of artists and freethinkers, frustrating both Worf and Deanna.

Lwaxana reveals she will forgo the tradi-tional nude Betazoid wedding at the request of her fiancé, Campio—whom she is shocked to find is stuffy and old.

Meanwhile, an increasing number of ship's systems are beginning to fail. The problem is eventually traced to metallic parasites the ship picked up after destroying the asteroid they were feeding on. In a race against time, Data barely gets the ship back to the creatures' home field and beams them away before life support breaks down, leaving him the only crew member con-scious.

Disaster is soon averted, and Lwaxana is free to proceed with her wedding plans. But to her fiancé's surprise, and her daughter's delight, Lwaxana turns up at the ceremony wearing basic Betazoid—that is, in the buff—sending Campio running for home. Deanna then coaxes Worf to join her mother and Alexander for one last visit to the mud bath.

After coming on staff to fill the slot that Herb Wright's departure opened up, Peter Allan Fields created his second Lwaxana Troi tale in two years—one that truly revealed the character's "Auntie Mame" roots by pairing her up with a "corruptible" Alexander, confounding Worf and Troi alike. In fact, Michael Piller revealed that for a time the staff had toyed with the idea of a Troi-Worf relationship and had been building little moments into scripts to support that if it happened: their mutual concern with Alexander, for one, and Worf making Deanna the boy's guardian if he died during surgery in "Ethics" (216).

Tony Jay's role here as the elderly and distant Campio was not nearly as powerful as Paracelsus, the tunnel-dwelling villian he played in *Beauty and the Beast*. And only in a show like TNG could Majel Barrett as Lwaxana Troi talk to Majel Barrett as the voice of the *Enterprise* computer; that moment happens outside the holodeck before her first visit with the "little warrior."

The Wind Dancer balloon effect was simple to create, Legato explained. After filming a bowling ball without holes as if it were bouncing around, the face of a made-up clown was shot on a camera following in sync with the ball's white highlight spot, and the two images were mated.

Campio (Tony Jay) and Erko (Patrick Cronin) are shocked at Lwaxana Troi's decision to appear "au naturel," as per Betazoid wedding custom.

THE PERFECT MATE

Production No.: 221 ■ Aired: Week of April 27, 1992
Stardate: 45761.3 ■ Code: pm

Directed by **Cliff Bole**
Teleplay by **Gary Percante and Michael Piller**
Story by **Rene Echevarria and Gary Percante**

GUEST CAST
Kamala: **Famke Janssen**
Briam: **Tim O'Connor**
Par Lenor: **Max Grodenchik**
Alrik: **Mickey Cottrell**
Qol: **Michael Snyder**
Miner No. 1: **David Paul Needles**
Miner No. 2: **Roger Rignack**
Transporter Chief Hubbell: **April Grace**
Miner No. 3: **Charles Gunning**
Computer Voice: **Majel Barrett**

Kriosian Ambassador Briam arrives aboard the *Enterprise* with a peace offering from his people for the ruler of Valt Minor. The gift, Briam declares, is priceless, and is intended to end years of war between Krios and Valt Minor. Picard immediately orders the object, being delivered in a stasis field, off-limits to his crew.

En route to Valt Minor the *Enterprise* rescues two Ferengi from a shuttle in distress—an act of mercy that soon backfires when the Ferengi are caught attempting to steal the Kriosian gift. In the process, the stasis field protecting the item is shattered, revealing a beautiful and exotic woman, Kamala.

She is an empathic mesomorph, a genetic rarity among her people—such creatures are born only once every seven generations. Kamala can be what any man wants her to be. Educated to fulfill her role as peacemaker, she has been prepared from birth to bond with Valt's ruler, Alric. The Ferengi's interference has caused her to be released prematurely, and the ambassador insists she be confined to her room until Alrik arrives.

Knowing she's bonded to him for life, Picard must escort empathic mesomorph "peace bride" Kamala (Famke Janssen) "down the aisle" to marry another.

That move sets off Dr. Crusher, who complains to Picard that the entire affair smacks of prostitution. The captain gamely cites the Prime Directive, but understands the ambassador's request after seeing the effect Kamala has on his crew. When Briam is accidentally injured by the Ferengi, Picard is forced to turn to Kamala for help in performing his ambassadorial duties—and soon finds even his legendary resistance weakening. Kamala is drawn to him as well; she tells Picard he is the first man who has suggested she has value in and of herself.

Alric finally arrives and confides to Picard he cares more about treaties and trade than he does for his "peace bride." Just before the reconciliation ceremony, a sad Kamala tells Picard she has chosen to bond with him, rather than become the woman Alric expects her to be. She assures a visibly shaken Picard she'll carry out her duties nonetheless—as he will carry out his.

What could have been just another romance became a much more significant story, as this episode again used a science fiction premise to turn conventional wisdom on its ear.

"We have Beverly argue the point that Kamala's mission amounts to prostitution," Michael Piller noted. "And we have Picard taking the other tack: that whether or not we approve, we can't change or interfere with the way these people are. And if you accept Roddenberry's vision, which we are built on, you have to respect that."

The only writing pseudonym requested during Piller's tenure turned up here: "Percante" was actually his friend Reuben Leder, who disliked the rewrite done on his draft. The script included an unused optional fantasy scene in which Picard, just before the actual ceremony, daydreamed that he spoke out at the wedding to claim Kamala as his own.

For once we actually got to see the Picard-Crusher morning tea ritual referred to in "Qpid" (194), which, in its own way, shows how the two officers' relationship has matured over the years. We also learn that the young Jean-Luc spoken of in "Family" (178) hated piano lessons but briefly took them to please his mother.

The best line in the script almost went to Qol, upon his discovery in the cargo bay: "I must have lost my way—I was looking for the barbershop." But ultimately that honor belongs to a painfully aroused Riker, who wipes the sweat off his mustache after barely escaping Kamala and says, "If you need me, I'll be in holodeck four!"

IMAGINARY FRIEND

Production No.: 222 ■ Aired: Week of May 4, 1992
Stardate: 45832.1 ■ Code: im

Directed by **Gabrielle Beaumont**
Teleplay by **Edithe Swenson and Brannon Braga**
Story by **Ronald Wilderson, Jean Matthias, and Richard Fliegel**

GUEST CAST
Clara Sutter: **Noley Thornton**
Isabella: **Shay Astar**
Ensign Daniel Sutter: **Jeff Allin**
Alexander: **Brian Bonsall**
Nurse Alyssa Ogawa: **Patti Yasutake**
Ensign Felton: **Sheila Franklin**
Guinan: **Whoopi Goldberg**

Troi tries to assure an officer that the "imaginary friend" created by his little daughter, Clara, is a normal reaction to a childhood of constant change. But as the *Enterprise* prepares to explore the FGC-47 nebula, Clara's friend Isabella materializes. Soon she is getting Clara into all sorts of trouble, leading her into areas of the ship that are off limits to children, like Main Engineering and Ten-Forward.

Meanwhile, the *Enterprise* has become surrounded by strands of an inexplicable nature that are draining the ship's power. At the same time, Clara and Worf's son Alexander are becoming fast friends—until Isabella sabotages their relationship. Clara's playmate now turns even more frightening, telling the little girl that she and all of the others aboard are about to die.

Summoned by Clara's father to help, Troi tries to prove to Clara that her imaginary playmate can't hurt her—and is promptly stunned by Isabella. Picard realizes there is a connection between the energy drain his ship is experiencing and Clara's playmate, a fact soon confirmed by Isabella. She says her kind will feed off the ship's energy, rejecting Picard's offer of alternative sources. She says the ship deserves to be destroyed because of the way her friend Clara is

Picard finally learns why "imaginary" Isabella (Shay Astar) has disturbed Clara (Noley Thornton) and his ship.

treated. But ultimately she relents in the face of Clara's pleas.

As reflected in the credits, this was another script turned out after several tries by free-lancers. Braga chose to develop it in place of one of the year's abortive Q stories, and by the time it was finished, his original "negative attitude" toward the tale had turned around as much as the concept of the alien. Curious and benign in earlier drafts, Isabella took on more menacing *Bad Seed*-style traits in the finished script.

Guinan was not intended to be part of this show, but Whoopi Goldberg became available and was written in just days before filming. Originally her cloud-watching scene with Data was written for Beverly and Deanna and, later, for Guinan and Deanna. The Samarian coral fish she spies is likely from the same planet as the Samarian Sunset drink that Data prepared for Troi in "Conundrum" (214) after losing a bet. Guinan also talks of her own imaginary friend, a Tarcassian razor beast.

For the first time we hear about Geordi's parents. Both were Starfleet officers; his father was an exobiologist, and his mother a command officer, apparently once assigned to a Neutral Zone outpost.

I, BORG

Production No: 223 ■ Aired: Week of May 11, 1992
Stardate: 45854.2 ■ Code: ib

Directed by **Robert Lederman**
Written by **Rene Echevarria**

GUEST CAST
"Hugh" Borg: **Jonathan Del Arco**
Guinan: **Whoopi Goldberg**

While surveying a cluster of systems for colonization, the *Enterprise* traces a distress signal to a small world, where they find crash debris and one survivor—a young Borg.

Fighting his impulse to let it die, Picard accedes to Dr. Crusher's humanitarian desire to care for the Borg. The rest of the crew are skeptical, especially Guinan, who points out that others of his kind will follow and learn of their presence if they take the young Borg aboard.

But cut off from his race's collective consciousness and influenced by the crew who help him survive and heal, the Borg known as "Third

La Forge fears for "Hugh" Borg's (Jonathan Del Arco) future.

meanor when others of his race arrive, but the glance he shoots Geordi at beam-up is telling: he'll remember.

The clamor for "another Borg show" had swelled ever since the third-season cliff-hanger "The Best of Both Worlds" (175–176), but the dilemma facing the production and writing team was obvious: when your all-out foe is so dangerous that you barely escape him once, what can you do for an encore? And how can you afford to film it?

Rene Echeverria's tale—Michael Piller's favorite of the season and the one he called "everything I want *Star Trek* to be,"—found answers to both questions by serving up a young Borg story that still packed a lot of emotional wallop. Robert Lederman, one of TNG's three rotating film editors since the second season, became the only new director to get a shot this year after last season's flood of rookies behind the camera.

Jeri Taylor, who provided uncredited help in polishing the script, commented that the story meant "we can never treat the Borg the same way again." Guinan may never be the same again, either; aside from Q, the Borg were about the only thing that could shatter her aloofness and calm detachment. But one by one we saw her and all the regulars, including Picard, examine their own prejudices. "Just when you think it's safe to hate the Borg," Piller says, "we make you look him in the eye and ask if you could still kill him."

THE NEXT PHASE

Production No.: 224 ▪ Aired: Week of May 18, 1992
Stardate: 45092.4 ▪ Code: np

Directed by **David Carson**
Written by **Ronald D. Moore**

GUEST CAST
Ensign Ro Laren: **Michelle Forbes**
Mirok: **Thomas Kopache**
Varel: **Susanna Thompson**
Transporter Chief Brossmer: **Shelby Leverington**
Parem: **Brian Cousins**
Ensign McDowell: **Kenneth Messerole**

Picard offers aid to a wrecked Romulan science ship, but the rescue mission ends in tragedy when Ro and La Forge apparently die in a transporter accident.

The two rematerialize on board the *Enterprise*

of Five" becomes more and more of an individual. He eventually acquires a name—Hugh—and starts to refer to himself as "I" instead of "we."

His evolution affects the others, who had always viewed the Borg as an intractable, unrelenting foe. When even Guinan is thrown into doubt, Picard decides to visit Hugh himself. Assuming the role of Locutus, the captain is shocked to hear Hugh plead with him not to assimilate his "friends," like Geordi.

The captain calls off a plan to plant a virus in Hugh to disable his race, figuring that the concept of the individual could be just as effective. Hugh himself opts to return to the crash site, and his newfound friend La Forge goes with him. Will Hugh's new memory and sense of self remain intact? Hugh returns to his stoic Borg debut somehow remain unseen. Ro thinks she is dead when she discovers that she can pass through walls and that others can walk through her.

She locates La Forge, who wants to find a reason other than death for their state, and they learn their presence causes chroniton particles, a harmless by-product of cloaking devices. They soon deduce the truth: thanks to an ill-fated test by the Romulans, they are cloaked!

As the *Enterprise* delivers an energy beam to the Romulan vessel to help it power up, Data attempts to clear the ship of a series of puzzling chroniton fields using an anyon beam. The android is puzzled, however, when new fields keep popping up all over the ship. Ro and La Forge are trying to get Data's attention by leaving lots of "tracks" so they can warn him of the Romulans' plan to cause a residual feedback in the energy beam and blow up the starship once it goes into warp. Their task is made considerably more difficult, though, when they encounter a Romulan who is also cloaked. Finally La Forge and Ro discover a way to leave enough chronitons to force Data into using a maximum-level spray of anyon, causing them to reappear—right in the middle of their own memorial service, and in the nick of time to save the ship.

This was supposed to be a money-saving bottle show, but like "Power Play" (215), it turned into one of the year's most expensive—with characters actually running through the walls! Actually, the walk-through effect of the cloaked characters was straightforward but time-consuming, Rob Legato reported. The actors and set pieces were filmed in second-unit shooting before a blue screen backdrop and then carefully animated into the live action.

Lots of background bits adorn this story, including the fact that Picard first met Geordi during an unspecified inspection tour and that Geordi has known Riker longer than anyone aboard. We also learn about the two-hour Bajoran death chant, and we are given their word for spirits and souls, *borhyas*. At the same time it is revealed that Worf's people view an honorable death as joyful. Riker also gets another chance to play his trombone, and Picard delivers a rare reference blooper in the script, saying Ro's troublesome incident occurred at Garon IV instead of Garon II, as in "Ensign Ro" (203) and "Conundrum" (214).

The *Goddard* is the shuttle's name here, for American rocket pioneer Robert H. Goddard, while the Romulan science vessel miniature is a re-dress of Jarok's scout ship from "The Defector" (158). The Romulan ship ejects its off-line reactor core through the top instead of the bottom, as the Galaxy-class starship does. And for the truly trivial: for the first time since "The Defector" (158) two Romulan terms of measurement are given: *melakols*, a unit of pressure, and *kolems*, a unit of engine flow or frequency. And though no captain's log is heard establishing a stardate, the one listed on Ro's death certificate is 45092.4.

Rendered invisible and immaterial, Ro and La Forge confront Worf at their own "funeral."

THE INNER LIGHT

Production No.: 225 ■ Aired: Week of June 1, 1992
Stardate: 45944.1 ■ Code: il

Directed by **Peter Lauritson**
Teleplay by **Morgan Gendel and
Peter Allan Fields**
Story by **Morgan Gendel**

GUEST CAST
Eline: **Margot Rose**
Batai: **Richard Riehle**
Administrator: **Scott Jaeck**
Meribor: **Jennifer Nash**
Nurse Alyssa Ogawa: **Patti Yasutake**
Young Batai: **Daniel Stewart**

Like father, like son: Kamin and Batai (Patrick and Daniel Stewart).

While traveling between missions, the *Enterprise* encounters an unassuming-looking probe. It begins transmitting a nucleonic beam that manages to penetrate the shields and then lock directly onto Picard. The captain collapses to the deck, unconscious.

As Dr. Crusher works over him, the captain awakens to what seems to him a dream: he is on the drought-stricken planet Kataan, where he is an iron weaver named Kamin married to a young woman named Eline.

The days pass into years for him, and Picard finally accepts his new life as reality. Eline bears two children by him, the drought continues to get worse, and despite the support of his friend Batai, people laugh at his high-tech plans to provide relief.

Back on the *Enterprise* bridge, though, only a few minutes have passed, though Picard still lies unconscious. Growing more concerned for his captain's safety, Riker orders Data to break the beam. Its disruption nearly kills Picard, and it must be restored as the crew waits in frustration.

Meanwhile, the aging "Kamin" watches his children grow, his wife and friend die, and his planet dry up. Finally the truth is revealed: the Kataan sun is going nova, but without the means to evacuate, the planetary leaders have decided to gain immortality by launching records of their world in a probe and thus revealing their

story to some future historian. The probe, Picard realizes, is the very same one the *Enterprise* encountered what now seems to him like years ago. And he is the historian the Kataan were looking for.

To his bridge crew's relief, Picard awakes to the staggering realization that he has lived over thirty years in less than half an hour.

Combining the warmth of "Family" (170) with a science fiction plot twist worthy of "Yesterday's Enterprise" (163), this story proved to be one of the simplest and at the same time most mind-boggling episodes TNG would ever attempt. Here Picard experiences all the things Starfleet could never give him: a wife and children, stability, and a home.

The warm cinematography, designed to subtly imply the oncoming supernova of the Kataan sun, almost rivals that of "Family." What's amazing here, though, is that the exterior scenes of the Ressick community were all filmed on Stage 16 *indoors;* Marvin Rush's lighting can be credited for the beautiful illusion. There is one brief moment of location shooting, however, a pickup scene filmed after principal photography had closed: Picard's hiking scene, augmented by a matte-painting vista, was shot in nearby Bronson Canyon, also seen in "Darmok" (202) and in "Ensign Ro" (203).

Some appropriate casting was employed in this episode: Stewart's own son, Daniel, played the young Batai, Picard's Kataanian son, after several auditions for the show. Another piece of trivia: Margot Rose's résumé includes her role as one of two prostitutes in the film *48 HRS.*: her partner was Denise Crosby.

TIME'S ARROW

Production No.: 226 ■ Aired: Week of June 15, 1992
Stardate: 45959.1 ■ Code: ta

Directed by **Les Landau**
Teleplay by **Joe Menosky and Michael Piller**
Story by **Joe Menosky**

GUEST CAST
Samuel Clemens: **Jerry Hardin**
Bellboy: **Michael Aron**
Doorman: **Barry Kivel**
Seaman: **Ken Thorley**
Joe Falling Hawk: **Sheldon Peters Wolfchild**
Beggar: **John M. Murdock**
Gambler/Frederick La Rouque: **Marc Alaimo**
Scientist: **Milt Tarver**
Guinan: **Whoopi Goldberg**
Roughneck: **Michael Hungerford**

Called to the scene of excavations under San Francisco to investigate evidence of alien visitors in Earth's past, the *Enterprise* crew is amazed to find Data's head among artifacts dating back to the late 1800s. Triolic wave traces in the cavern point to Devidia II as the source of the relics. After journeying there, Picard sends an away team to investigate. The team discovers a time rift and traces of life-forms that are invisible to them.

Deliberately left off the team in an attempt by Picard to cheat fate, Data must now beam down to deal with what he theorizes is a slight time shift in the life-forms on the planet below—a shift that renders them invisible. Using a mobile forcefield that he sets to match the aliens' time shift, Data begins reporting back to the ship on what he sees. Then another time vortex opens up and sends the android to nineteenth-century San Francisco.

Thanks to poker winnings and a friendly bellboy, he quickly adapts and begins building a device with which to contact the *Enterprise.* Surprised to see Guinan in a local newspaper, he arranges to run into her, only to find that she has no recollection of him. She is not surprised, how-

ever, to learn that the two of them serve together in the future. Unfortunately, she is overheard by one of her guests—Samuel Clemens.

To uncover the suspected aliens' threat to history, the crew rig a large phaseable forcefield, just as Data had done. Then Picard, unnerved by cryptic words from "his" Guinan, leads the team into the vortex. . . .

Originally, TNG's "top two"—Rick Berman and Michael Piller—had decided not to end season five with a cliff-hanger, but the planned Trek spinoff series, *Deep Space Nine,* changed all that. "Because of all the attention *Deep Space Nine* was getting and the rumors that *Next Generation* would be shutting down, we wanted to send a message that this show was alive and well and continuing to grow," Piller said.

Surprisingly, "Time's Arrow" marked the first real time-trekking for this crew, holodeck and Q-fantasies aside. At first Piller said he wanted to bring the crew to the 1990s, but he discarded that idea because it had been done in *Star Trek IV.* The staff discussed the 1960s and the 1930s before deciding on the turn of the century. Piller said that before Joe Menosky went on sabbatical, he left notes on the concluding segment that would open TNG's sixth season come fall.

Three TNG veterans were among the guest cast: Ken Thorley had played the talkative Bolian barber Mot in "Ensign Ro" (203); Jerry Hardin, *sans* the Mark Twain makeup, had led the sterile child-stealers of Aldea as Radue in "When the Bough Breaks" (118); and Marc Alaimo, who finally plays a human here, was the first TNG actor to play a leader of the Anticans in "Lonely Among Us" (108), the Romulans in "The Neutral Zone" (126), and the Cardassians in "The Wounded" (186).

Trapped in the 1890s, Data hopes Guinan (Whoopi Goldberg) will be the key that gets him home again.

The San Francisco exteriors were shot on location at historic Pico House and along Olvera Street, the restored area near the first mission in old Los Angeles. Data's hotel room and gambling table were shot on a re-dress of a Stage 9 area and in the Planet Hell caves and caverns on Stage 16.

Troi's quote from Data regarding friendship is straight from his good-bye speech to Tasha's sister Ishara Yar in "Legacy" (180), and the marker beacons used to erect the large forcefield were seen before in "Power Play" (215).

As in the past two season-enders, few clues were provided for what a conclusion might bring. But a role seems assured for Hardin's Clemens character, who appears to be the owner of the pocket watch found among the artifacts, engraved "To S.L.C. with love, 30 November 1889."

Notes

1. *Starlog* No. 143, June 1989, p. 30.

PRODUCTION STAFF CREDITS— FIFTH SEASON

(In usual roll order; numbers in parentheses refer to episode numbers. Emmy nominees and winners not known at presstime.)

Casting: (*)Junie Lowery-Johnson, C.S.A.; ****Ron Surma

Main Title Theme: (*) Jerry Goldsmith (*), Alexander Courage

Music: ***Jay Chattaway (202, 204, 206 and all odd-numbered episodes 209–225) (*); Dennis McCarthy (201, 203, 205, 207 and all even-numbered episodes, 208–226)

Director of Photography: ***Marvin Rush

Production Designer: **Richard D. James

Editor: *Tom Benko, A.C.E. (202, 205, 208, 211, 214, 217, 220, 223, 226); ***J. P. Farrell (203, 206, 209, 212, 215, 218, 221, 224); **Robert Lederman (201, 204, 207, 210, 213, 216, 219, 225); ****Steve Tucker (222)

Unit Production Manager: ***Merri D. Howard (+)

First Asst. Director: ***Brad Yacobian (all odd-numbered episodes, 201–225); ****Doug Dean (all even-numbered episodes, 202–226)

Second Asst. Director: *Adele G. Simmons

Costume Designer: ***Robert Blackman

Set Decorator: **Jim Mees

Visual Effects Supervisor: (**) Robert Legato (+) (all even-numbered episodes, 202–226) (**); Dan Curry (+) (all odd-numbered episodes, 201–225)

Senior Illustrator/Technical Consultant: (*) Rick Sternbach

Scenic Artist Supervisor/Technical Consultant: (*) Michael Okuda

Makeup Designed and Supervised: (*) Michael Westmore

Visual Effects Coordinator: ***Ron Moore (all odd-numbered episodes, 201–225); ***Gary Hutzel (all even-numbered episodes, 202–226)

Set Designer: ***Gary Speckman

Assistant Art Director: (****) Andy Neskoromny

Original Set Design: (*) Herman Zimmerman

Original Starfleet Uniforms: (*) William Ware Theiss

Script Supervisor: (*) Cosmo Genovese

Special Effects: (*) Dick Brownfield

Property Master: (*) Joe Longo (201–205, 207, 209, all odd-numbered episodes from 217–225); (*) Alan Sims (206, 208, 210–215, all even-numbered episodes from 216–226)

Construction Coordinator: (*) Al Smutko

Scenic Artist: (***) Cari Thomas (+)

Hair Designer: Susan Carol-Schwary (201–216); *Joy Zapata (217–226)

Makeup Artists: **Gerald Quist, ***June Abston-Haymore

Hair Stylist: Gus le Pre (201–209); Patty Miller (210–226)

Wardrobe Supervisor: ****Carol Kunz (+)

Sound Mixer: *Alan Bernard, C.A.S. (201–213, 217–226); Bill Gocke (214–216)

Camera Operator: Joe Chess, S.O.C. (214–226)

Chief Lighting Technician: ***Buddy Bowles

1st Company Grip: ***Bob Sordal

Key Costumers: **Amanda Chamberlin (all odd-numbered episodes from 201–223); **Kimberly Thompson (202, 204, 206 plus all odd-numbered episodes from 209–225);

****Maurice Palinski (207 plus all even-numbered episodes from 208–226); Jerry Bono (all even-numbered episodes, 202–224, except 214); Mary Ellen Boché (203, 205, 225); ***David Velasquez (201); ****David Roesler (214); Phil Maldonado (226)
Music Editor: *Gerry Sackman
Supervising Sound Editor: (*) Bill Wistrom
Sound Editors: *James Wolvington; *Wilson Dyer; Dan Yale
Post Production Sound: (*) Modern Sound
Production Associate: (*) Susan Sackett (201–212)
Production Coordinator: (*) Diane Overdiek
Post Production Coordinator: (***) Wendy Rosenfeld (+)
Visual Effects Associate: (****) David Takemura
Production Associate: ***Terry Martinez (+), ***Heidi Julian (+)
Pre-Production Associate: (***) Eric Stillwell (+)
Casting Executive: (*) Helen Mossler

Stunt Coordinator: (***) Dennis Madalone (+) (201, 205, 207, 210–212, 214–217, 221–224)
Research Consultant: (*** Richard Arnold (201–214); (uncredited first two seasons)
Lenses and Panaflex Cameras: (**) Panavision
Monitors: (**) Sony Corp. of America (201, 202, 205, 206, 209–211, 214, 216, 219, 222)
Special Visual Effects: (*) Industrial Light and Magic (ILM) a division of Lucasfilm Ltd.
Motion Control Photography: (*) Image "G"
Video Optical Effects: (*) The Post Group
Special Video Compositing: (*) Composite Image Systems
Editing Facilities: (*) Unitel Video
Prosthetic Electronics: Michael Westmore II (218)
"Soliton Wave" Animation: Stokes/Kohne Assoc., Inc. (210)

The number of * denotes a returning company or staffer's initial season of credit in that position; ( ) denotes they are an original credited or co-credited person in that position; a (+) following indicates prior TNG work in another position

Beyond the Future

And what would the coming years bring for TNG? Even looking past the conclusion to "Time's Arrow," by the end of the fifth season Rick Berman was already talking of a possible *seventh* year of shows, going beyond the six for which the regular cast was originally optioned.

The biggest impact on the series' immediate future was the mid-season announcement of a spinoff series, *Star Trek: Deep Space Nine*, set to debut in January 1993. While exact details of that show's format were being developed throughout summer 1992, one thing was certain: Rick Berman and Michael Piller, the duo to whom Gene Roddenberry had entrusted his pride and joy, would be firmly in charge and enjoy the same freedom and support from the studio that the Great Bird had received.

Planning for the new show was at a fever pitch over the normally quiet hiatus. "I would call it filling," said Piller in something of an understatement, speaking of the pace he and Berman were keeping. Though Piller had shared the title of executive producer on TNG, he had reported to Berman, but the two were working as virtual equals on the new series, as its creators and executive producers.

Although they planned to oversee both Star Trek series, the sheer time and energy involved in getting *Deep Space Nine* off the ground led to changes in TNG's writing staff for the coming sixth season. Jeri Taylor, on board since Season Four as supervising producer, won a promotion to co-executive producer, and Frank Abatemarco was hired on at her old title as her right-hand man. Abatemarco had scripts for *Equal Justice*, the remake of *Mission: Impossible*, and *Cagney and Lacey* (where he had worked with Piller) to his credit.

Joe Menosky, the two-year veteran who had worked up to co-producer status, was offered a producer's job on *ST:DS9* but elected instead to take an extended sabbatical overseas to "recharge his batteries," as Piller put it. Ron Moore returned for Season Six, as did veteran staff writers Rene Echevarria and Brannon Braga, who both won promotions to the title of story editor. Executive script consultant Peter Allan Fields went on to become a co-producer on *DS9*, while Ira Steven Behr, who had been so much of the Next Generation writing staff during the third season, returned to the Trek family to become supervising producer on *DS9*.

On the production side, David Livingston won the job as supervising producer on both series, while Peter Lauritson was named producer on *TNG*, unit production manager Merri D. Howard was promoted to line producer, and associate producer Wendy Neuss was named co-producer. Additionally, FX supervisor Dan Curry took on the title of visual-effects producer and would now oversee two alternating effects teams on *TNG*, while Rob Legato gained the same title and working arrangement on *DS9*.

The new show would affect *TNG* in ways more obvious to viewers as well. By mid-summer, after actors Colm Meaney and Rosalind Chao agreed to the move *and* the weekly commitment, plans called for Miles, Keiko, and little Molly O'Brien to transfer aboard *DS9*. Both characters would continue to serve aboard the *Enterprise* until mid-season, though, when a two-hour pilot—à la *TNG*'s own "Encounter at Farpoint"—would

launch the new series. Among other crew members, Captain Picard was slated to guest-star in *DS9*'s pilot episode as well.

The new series had already gone through one major format change before the cameras even began rolling. Michell Forbes, whose Ensign Ro character had been slated for promotion and a transfer to *DS9* as its first officer, opted instead to shoot a motion picture. Piller said she would continue as a recurring character aboard the *Enterprise*.

With *DS9* on hand to quench Trek fans' never-ending appetite for more TV adventures, the *TNG* cast seemed assured of a future in theatrical movies. Piller, Berman, and even Roddenberry had long been peppered with questions as to Picard and Company's future on the silver screen—though they'd always noted that no feature would follow until the TV series had run its course, following in the footsteps of the cast that had blazed the trail a generation before them.

With hard-core original Trek fans seemingly won over to the new show at last (thanks to its superior writing and production values, as well as generation-bridging events like "Unification"), and continued commercial success on over 245 commercial stations (with over 70 percent of the U.S. signed up already for *DS9*), it seemed certain that Gene Roddenberry's mythos, already an integral part of one generation's imagination, could look forward to an even brighter future.

ST: TNG Episode Index

Epis.	Air No.	Title	Code	Stardate	Aired Week of:	Page
145	44	Manhunt	mh	42859.2	6/19/89	89
146	45	The Emissary	em	42901.3	6/26/89	90
147	46	Peak Performance	pk	42923.4	7/10/89	91
148	47	Shades of Gray	sg	42976.1	7/17/89	93
149	49	The Ensigns of Command	ec	43133.3	10/02/89	100
150	48	Evolution	ev	43125.8	9/25/89	101
151	50	The Survivors	sv	43152.4	10/09/89	102
152	51	Who Watches the Watchers?	ww	43173.5	10/16/89	103
153	52	The Bonding	bo	43198.7	10/23/89	104
154	53	Booby Trap	bt	43205.6	10/30/89	105
155	54	The Enemy	en	43349.2	11/6/89	106
156	55	The Price	pr	43385.6	11/13/89	107
157	56	The Vengeance Factor	vf	43421.9	11/20/89	109
158	57	The Defector	df	43462.5	1/1/90	110
159	58	The Hunted	hu	43489.2	1/8/90	111
160	59	The High Ground	hi	43510.7	1/29/90	112
161	60	Deja Q	dq	43539.1	2/5/90	113
162	61	A Matter of Perspective	mp	43610.4	2/12/90	114
163	62	Yesterday's Enterprise	ye	43625.2	2/19/90	116
164	63	The Offspring	of	43657.0	3/12/90	118
165	64	Sins of the Father	sf	43685.2	3/19/90	119
166	65	Allegiance	al	43714.1	3/26/90	120
167	66	Captain's Holiday	cp	43745.2	4/02/90	121
168	67	Tin Man	ti	43779.3	4/23/90	122
169	68	Hollow Pursuits	hp	43807.4	4/30/90	124
170	69	The Most Toys	mo	43872.2	5/7/90	125
171	70	Sarek	sa	43917.4	5/14/90	126
172	71	Ménage à Troi	me	43930.7	5/28/90	127
173	72	Transfigurations	tf	43957.2	6/4/90	129
174	73	The Best of Both Worlds	bb	43989.1	6/18/90	130
175	74	The Best of Both Worlds, Pt. 2	b2	44001.4	9/24/90	138
176	77	Suddenly Human	sh	44143.7	10/15/90	139
177	76	Brothers	br	44085.7	10/8/90	140
178	75	Family	fa	44012.3	10/1/90	142
179	78	Remember Me	rm	44161.2	10/22/90	144
180	79	Legacy	le	44215.2	10/29/90	145
181	80	Reunion	re	44246.3	11/05/90	146
182	81	Future Imperfect	fi	44286.5	11/12/90	147
183	82	Final Mission	fm	44307.3	11/19/90	148
184	83	The Loss	ls	44356.9	12/31/90	150
185	84	Data's Day	dd	44390.1	1/7/91	151
186	85	The Wounded	wo	44429.6	1/28/91	152
187	86	Devil's Due	dv	44474.5	2/4/91	153
188	87	Clues	cl	44502.7	2/11/91	154
189	88	First Contact	fc	unknown	2/18/91	155
190	89	Galaxy's Child	gc	44614.6	3/11/91	156
191	90	Night Terrors	nt	44631.2	3/18/91	157
192	91	Identity Crisis	ic	44664.5	3/25/91	158
193	92	Nth Degree	nd	44704.2	4/1/91	159

*The stardate for "The Next Phase" [224] was derived from an on-screen graphic.

Writers
(SEASONS 1–5)

KEY (per episode):
Roman: Story or premise credit
Bold: Writer or teleplay credit
Italic: Both writing and story/premise credit
(*) Asterisk: Solo credit for entire show

Adler, Alan J.: *ls/183*

Amos, Gregory: mt/134

Apter, Harold: *dd/185*

Armus, Burton: ok/130; **mt/134**

Arnold-Ince, Kacey: *fm/178*

Arthurs, Bruce D.: *cl/188*

Assael, David: *if/140*

Bader, Hilary J.: *ls/183;* hw/211

Bailey, Dennis Putnam: ti/168

Bailey, Dennis Russell: fc/189

Balcer, Rene: pw/215

Baron, Michael: ch/104

Barry, Patrick: *ao/115

Beagle, Peter S.: sa/171

Behr, Ira Steven: ye/163; *cp/167; qp/194

Beimler, Hans: af/121; sy/123; sm/131; *em/146;* **sg/148; ww/152;**
    ye/163; al/166

Belanoff, Adam: *ms/213*

Bensmiller, Kurt Michael: tm/139

Berman, Rick: *br/177; er/203; u2/207; u1/208; *ma/209

Bernheim, Robin: *hu/159

Bingham, J. Michael (pseudonym of D. C. Fontana): nn/103

Bischoff, David: ti/168; fc/189

Black, John D. F.: nn/103; *see also* pseudonym "Wills, Ralph"

Braga, Brannon: re/181; ic/192; *gm/206;* **pw/215; *ce/218;** im/
    222

Bronson, Fred: me/172; gm/206

Calder, Thomas H.: em/146

Carren, David Bennett: fi/182

Carroll, J. Larry: fi/182

Caves, Sally: *hp/169

Charno, Sara: wo/186; ng/210; et/216

Charno, Stuart: wo/186; ng/210; et/216

Chermak, Cy: wo/186

Clee, Mona: nz/126

Conley, Lawrence V.: si/204

Cushman, Marc: sa/171

Danus, Richard: bt/154; *dq/161

Davis, Deborah Dean: wa/124

de Haas, Timothy: ic/192

Deighan, Drew: sf/165; re/181

Devereaux, Terry (pseudonym of Tracy Tormé): *mh/145

Dickson, Lance: ok/130

Douglas, Pamela: nt/191

Duane, Diane: wn/106

Echeverria, Rene: *of/164; *tf/173; *mi/198;* pm/221; *ib/223

Fields, Peter Allan: hl/196; cs/220; **il/225**

Fliegal, Richard: im/222

Fontana, D. C.: ef/101–102 (721); la/108; ts/112; hg/120; *see also*
    pseudonym "Bingham, J. Michael"

Forrester, Larry: ba/110

Fries, Sandy: *ca/119

Ganino, Trent Christopher: ye/163

Gendel, Morgan: *il/225*

Gerber, Steve: cg/137

Goodharz, Shari: *mo/170; nt/191; vi/212

Gray, Mike: us/133

Gray, Pamela: *vi/212*

Gray, T. Michael: vi/212

Greene, Vanessa: ls/183

Guerts, Karl: hs/117

Haight, Wanda M.: mt/134

Halperin, Michael: la/108

Holland, C. J. (pseudonym of Maurice Hurley): *hq/111*

Horvat, Michel: *ho/197

Hurley, Maurice: da/114; **oo/116;** hg/120; af/121; nz/126; **tc/127;**
    tm/139; *qw/142; **sg/148; gc/190;** pw/215; *see also*
    pseudonym "Holland, C. J."

Jacobs, Jake: sa/171

Jarvis, Ron: di/205

Kahn, James: ms/213

Kartozian, Thomas: gc/190

Kemper, David: *pk/147; en/155

Krzemien, Richard: lo/107

Lambdin, Susanne: fa/178

Lane, Brian Alan: *ed/129

Lansberg, David: ok/130

Lansford, William Douglas: dv/187

Lazebnik, Philip: *dv/187;* dm/202

Leder, Reuben: *See* pseudonym "Percanté, Gary"

Lewin, Robert: *da/114;* af/121; sy/123

Directors

About the Author

LARRY NEMECEK is a former reporter and now entertainment editor of *The Norman Transcript*, a daily newspaper in the Oklahoma university town and area where he was "Sooner born and Sooner bred." A Trek fan since the syndication era of the mid-'70s, his long-time interest in Gene Roddenberry's universe and its continuity led to contributions to the fan-produced *U.S.S. Enterprise Officer's Manual* by Geoffrey Mandel and the *Star Trek Maps* from Bantam Books, both in 1980. As a prelude to writing the *ST:TNG Companion*, he has compiled each season a "concordance" or encyclopedia called *TNG*, detailing the people, places, and things mentioned and seen on "The Next Generation"—a reference used by the series' own creative staff.

On the volunteer level, Larry founded and chaired the first two ThunderCons, Oklahoma City's charity ST conventions, and he is the "Library Computer" trivia chief for the Star Trek Welcommittee, an organization founded in 1974 to answer fans' questions and publish a directory of Trek conventions, clubs, fanzines and dealers.

Larry also "has a life" beyond Star Trek, including two degrees in theatre/directing: a B.A. from East Central Oklahoma State University in Ada, and an M.A. from the University of Kansas in Lawrence. Other interests include travel, current events, Will Rogers, history and Americana, football, music, and playing keyboards. Somehow he also finds time for his family, being new to this father/husband thing and all.